Keeping Promise Rock

Amy Lane

Dreamspinner Press

Published by
Dreamspinner Press
4760 Preston Road
Suite 244-149
Frisco, TX 75034
http://www.dreamspinnerpress.com/

Keeping Promise Rock

Cover Art by Paul Richmond http://www.paulrichmondstudio.com

ISBN: 978-1-61581-346-9

Printed in the United States of America
First Edition
January, 2010

eBook edition available
eBook ISBN: 978-1-61581-347-6

This one is dedicated to all of those people who chose family first and dreams second, because they know that making a dream come true isn't nearly as much fun without someone to share it with.

Acknowledgments

MY FRIEND Wendy has been running a horse ranch mostly by herself for the last twelve years. She has killed seventeen rattlesnakes with a shotgun, can break a horse and show it and win medals, and has never, ever let anyone tell her that a woman can't do this alone. This book's for my friend Wendy.

My friend Julie has followed her husband around as a Navy wife for over twenty years. She has worked her way back from a hand injury in a motorcycle crash via knitting, takes shit from absolutely no one, and has read more than any human being I know of. This book's for my friend Julie.

My friend Barb has lost every adult she's loved with her whole heart in the space of a year, and she's still raising her children and fighting for her home. This book's for my friend Barb.

My friend Bonnie will answer her e-mail at three-thirty in the morning because she knows that sometimes a time difference makes no difference in how much she's needed. She's spent a year and a half telling me that the people who are mean to me about my writing are fuckers and clueless bastards, and really? I can't hear that enough. This book's for my friend Bonnie.

My friend Roxie has lived a full, fierce life with enough empathy and self-assessment to look upon the screw-ups of others with compassion and understanding—she is creative, amazing, and reserves judgment except in the case of blatant meanness or bigotry, and then she has no mercy. This book's for my friend Roxie.

My friend Saren sends me *Supernatural* videos constantly, even if I don't have time to look up others to send back to her, and she has a husband who offers me virtual brisket with my real Top Ramen. Without her happy indulgence of my weird aging-cougar obsession with young and tasty veal, this book would never have been written. This book's for my friend Saren.

My friend Matt has a really flaky wife who would rather write than do housework and who keeps pinning the family's hopes on what should probably have stayed a hobby with mystique as opposed to an obsession for success. He is kind, empathetic, and never yells at me for traffic tickets even if they send us to the verge of bankruptcy, and he still loves me after twenty years. This book is especially for my friend Matt.

Amy Lane
January, 2010

Prologue

Present Day: Farah, Iraq

CARRICK JAMES FRANCIS grew up in Levee Oaks, California. While not exactly Death Valley, it was pretty hot in the summer—the temperature reached the hundreds fairly regularly between June and September, and a hot wind blew through the valley when the delta breezes were too fucking lazy to move.

After two years in Iraq, he was starting to wish it had been Death Valley. If he'd grown up in Death Valley, he figured driving an ambulance in Kuwait wouldn't feel like the seventh sphincter of the armpit demon living in hell's tenth colon.

"Two years and I still can't believe this place makes my hometown look good!" Crick had to shake his head in disgust. His whole life, he'd hated Levee Oaks. He'd almost gotten expelled from school for painting "White Trash Capital of California" on the water tower. If Deacon hadn't painted it over before the whole town had seen it, he would have been.

Just one more thing he owed Deacon Winters for. One more giant favor he'd returned with complete dumb-assery.

"Yeah, well," Private Lisa Arnold was saying, "you won't be here much longer, Punky, so you need to quit your bitching!" Crick's partner shook her head next to him, as cute and blonde and perky in full gear, flak jacket, and helmet in the front of the ambulance as she would have been wearing bottle-cap shorts and a halter-top at a family reunion. She'd always been a little burst of sweet 'n cool in the middle of the desert, and Carrick had grown to love her like a sister. An older sister, of course. He'd had enough of cleaning, diapering, and feeding his little half-sisters to last a lifetime.

Carrick blew out a breath and looked at the armored transport trucks in front of them—a whole lot of soldiers getting to go home. But first, they had to look down the long road of sand and sand and nothing but fucking sand from Farah to Baghdad, where their flight would take off.

"How long again?" They drove an ambulance with full a/c, mostly because half of what they treated was heat exhaustion. There had been wounds—and that had been bad enough, food for nightmares—but three-quarters of their job had been handing out fluids and ice packs, keeping the combat units from poaching their brains like eggs in the roasting pan that was the Middle East. The a/c was more of a suggestion than a rule, really—a pleasant suggestion, most times, but nothing like the good ozone-eating a/c of a department store in California.

Lisa looked at him sideways. "Five days. Here to Baghdad, BD to Turkey, Turkey to Germany, Germany to LA, LA to Sac. Badda bing, badda boom—you're home, boy, and this gig, it ain't nothing but a bad memory!"

Crick smiled and looked at her softly. "Gonna miss you, Popcorn," he said, meaning it. It had been a long, miserable two-year tour—the biggest fucking mistake of his dumb-assed life. By the time Lisa Arnold had showed up, perky and kind and tough as nails, Crick had been thinking seriously about dancing naked in a minefield, just to make it end.

But Lisa had showed up, and she'd been nosy and perky and in his face... and then she'd found out the one thing Crick hadn't wanted anybody in the Army to know, and he'd been sure he was fucked.

And she'd saved his life instead.

"You won't miss me when you get home and he's waiting for you." She risked a glance off the road—purely against protocol—and in the face of that cute, scrunchy, freckled affection, he tried not to let his anxiety show.

"You think he'll be okay?" He didn't even want to ask her again. He didn't want to think about what life would be like back home if Deacon hadn't been able to pull himself through, hadn't been able to keep himself grounded for the last four months. The man had lived his entire life as a paragon of virtue—until Crick left him and his world fell apart.

Lisa shook her head and frowned absently at something hazy that was ripping through the glare in front of them. "Oh, now baby—you read me the letters. Please, don't—"

The sentence never got finished. The transport in front of them exploded, became shrapnel, and ripped through their bus like a thousand serrated throwing stars, glowing red with the blast.

Crick tried for the rest of his life to forget Lisa disintegrating, shattering in front of him, while he was thrown around like a ragdoll in a drier—a ragdoll made of flesh and a drier made of knives.

Right before his head smacked earth, protected by that damned helmet, he had a moment of perfect clarity.

Oh, goddammit, Deacon—I should have given you more time.

Part 1

Crick

Chapter 1

Honest as a Horse

Levee Oaks, California, thirteen years earlier

WHEN Carrick was seven years old, his mother dated a Bible-thumping bigot who had taken one look at Carrick's straight, dark hair, liquid black eyes, and pale skin and subsequently declared that "the little Mex kid could pass for white, so he didn't reckon it would be too much of a problem raising him right."

"The little Mex kid" had promptly kicked the fucker in the shins and run out of the house. His mother married Bob Coats anyway, but thank the good Lord, he'd never forced Crick to take his name.

Francis was his mother's last name—and he liked it. Wasn't so thrilled with *her*—especially after she married Bob—but the name sounded good. Sounded a hell of a lot better than "the little Mex kid," anyway.

They moved to Levee Oaks, which could loosely be termed a "suburb" of Sacramento but wasn't. Levee Oaks was an odd sort of town—sweet little suburban neighborhoods sat cheek-by-jowl next to horse property. The high school was part of a larger Sacramento district that covered some of the less savory parts of the city, but the grammar schools were all part of an elementary district, and so they behaved like the high school and junior high were on Mars and not worth their consideration. The result was a whole lot of confused junior high students and a high school environment that was known for sending substitute teachers screaming for tequila and a gun permit.

A lot of the residents in Levee Oaks had jobs in the considerably larger city of Sacramento. A lot of the residents didn't have jobs, period. A *whole* lot of the residents attended one of the churches that seemed to sit large on every corner. After Carrick lived through his first flood at the age of eight and a half, he'd figured that the churches were there to keep the water back.

After living through another levee break only one year later, Crick figured the churches were not doing their job and were therefore pretty goddamned useless. This was why he started ditching out of Sunday school, which was how he met Deacon.

Ditching out of Sunday school was not as much fun as it sounded. There were no arcades, no movie theaters—hell, there was barely a 7/11 to haunt, and besides, he didn't have any money, anyway. Mostly what Carrick did, dressed in his threadbare khakis and striped polo shirt, was wander. He'd wander up one narrow road, down one tiny road, and along East Levee Road, and finally, he'd find his way to the levee.

One day, he found his way to the levee and followed it to Deacon's father's horse ranch and fell in love.

At first, he thought he was in love with the place, because it was everything his own home was not. The ranch house was big enough (whereas his mother's house always seemed too small) and painted a whimsical blue, with a nice little patch of lawn and a U-shaped driveway that circled around to the back, where the spread opened up a bit. There was a barn four times the size of the house and two work-out rings, as well as enough sun-browned pasture-land for twenty horses to graze comfortably outside, and enough sun-scorched riding land beyond that so that not all the workouts had to be in the workout rings.

But the house, as nice as it looked, was just a house, so the next thing Crick figured he loved was the horse, because she was—as Deacon said for years—one of the prettiest little fillies he ever did raise. Her movements were liquid-silver, her gait smooth as lube, and her color was a fine, dark chestnut. As Crick grew to love horses he had to agree with Deacon's assessment—even when he thought that 'lube' meant engine grease.

So Crick fell in love with the horse next, but then he found his final love, and that was the boy in the ring, the one guiding that pretty little mare through her paces. His brow knotted in concentration, his face lit with some sort of holy joy—well, he really made the poetry of muscle, sinew, hide, and motion come alive.

Crick looked around and saw that there were a number of folks hanging off the fence of the workout ring, so he wiggled between two kids his own age and stood up on the lowest rail of the fence, the better to look over the top rail and get a better view.

"Isn't she pretty?" the boy next to him whispered, and Crick looked at the horse and thought of wind.

"Yeah," he said.

"Deacon says that if they can breed Lucy Star here and produce a stud, The Pulpit will start rolling in money."

"Deacon?" It sounded grownup but pretty too. In the years that followed, Crick never got tired of hearing Deacon's name.

The kid—a plain-looking boy with straight brown hair and a rather aggressive brow—nodded to the boy in the ring, and Crick found out what real love was all about.

Deacon Winters had been beautiful his entire life. Crick would never see him acknowledge it, even once, which was fine. Crick could do all the appreciating of Deacon's beauty all by himself.

The boy in the ring took off his blue ball cap and revealed brown hair streaked blond by the sun, slicked back against his head with sweat and falling across his brow from what had once been a buzz cut on the top of his head. His face was a very square-ish oval—he had a square chin and high cheekbones and a wide forehead, and wide-set green-hazel eyes that were remarkably pretty, even in the glaring sun.

His face and hands were tanned, but his upper arms under his T-shirt were pale, and even at thirteen or fourteen, he was showing long swathes of knotty muscle in his biceps, chest, shoulders, and across his back. His wrist-bones were wide, because he had a bit of growing to do, and his collarbones peeked sharply through his sweat-soaked blue T-shirt.

Deacon had always thought of food last and horses first—one thing among many that had made Carrick love him even more over the years. Even so, the seeds of that love started at that very moment, as Carrick watched those wide, capable hands carry that horse through her paces like a cloud carried water from the sea to the valley.

Carrick couldn't hardly contain himself, and when he couldn't hardly contain himself, he *never* could contain his damned mouth.

"Geez, that's a pretty horse. Did you breed her yourself? How old is she? Do you get to ride her? Damn, I want to ride her—do you think I could ride her? Are you Deacon? This boy says your name is Deacon and mine's Carrick. Deacon's not anything like Carrick, but maybe your name is Irish, like mine. My name is Irish because my mom is Irish, even though my real dad was Mex. But we don't talk about him, so if I am Irish, and you are too, we could be brothers, right? I wouldn't mind a brother, because my mom's pregnant again and it's another girl...," and so on. Anything—anything—to get that boy to look up at him, to get him to respond, to get someone that beautiful to notice that Carrick existed.

But Deacon ignored him for the next fifteen minutes. He was working the mare, and that was where his concentration went, and that was all she wrote. The two boys next to Crick shifted on the fence and gave him pitying looks before hopping down and going elsewhere. (Crick found out later that they were clients, waiting for their riding lesson, and they would eventually form the background haze of his miserable adolescence.) Carrick was left there—him, his mouth, and the boy of his dreams.

Finally the workout was done, and Deacon led the mare off for water and a good brushing. He looked up at the little nuisance on the fence and jerked his chin, indicating that Crick should follow him.

"You want to ride?" he asked as Carrick trotted up beside him, and Carrick nodded furiously, for once blessedly silent.

"You want to ride, I'll teach you after lesson hours. But you gotta help muck out the stables, right?"

Crick thought that sounded fair. Besides, even horseshit sounded better than Sunday school.

"And another thing," Deacon said, looking down at Crick from what seemed an impressive height. (Crick would grow a good four inches taller, but he didn't know that.) "Please don't talk so much. You'll spook the horses."

Please don't. It was as harsh as Deacon ever got. He didn't talk much—never did. Teachers thought he was stupid until he aced their tests. Riding clients talked at him continuously, trying to get him to break into conversation, but Deacon would blush and turn away. It took Crick *years* to get him to open his heart and spill it out, and even then didn't realize how rare it was that Deacon would talk to anyone at all. But all that impressive silence had its perks.

If Crick wanted to know if he'd ever crossed a line, all he had to listen for were those words, *please don't...* and he'd subside.

Deacon had that effect on a person.

In fact, Carrick would later reflect that Deacon's effect on him was about the only thing that kept Crick alive and out of prison during the next eleven years.

That evening, Parish Winters drove Carrick home, Deacon on the other side of him in the big, steel blue Chevy truck. Crick liked Deacon's dad—he had gray hair, a weathered face, and a sort of sweetness around his smile. Deacon might have had the same sweetness, but he tended to pinch his mouth closed, concentrating all the time.

It didn't matter—Parish saw the heart of his son, and, in that first night, Crick could tell that he saw the heart of a lonely, angry boy as well.

"I reckon we'll take the boy on Saturdays and Sundays," Parish said after Crick's stepdad had opened the door.

Bob Coats had made noises. "Sunday's the Lord's day! Boy belongs—"

"Wandering the levee, looking for trouble? I reckon the Lord would rather we kept him busy, you think?" Parish snorted, and Bob had opened his mouth to argue again, but one up-close-and-personal glare from Deacon's father had shut him down.

"Now you listen here. This ain't the first time I've seen your kid wandering the roads. You wanted to keep him in church on Sunday, you needed to spend some more time with him every other day."

"He's not my kid," Coats denied hotly. "Little Mex bastard is Mel's mistake. But we need him to take care of his sister...."

"Well, you'll have to need him some other days, then," Parish said, his implacable face a testament to his disgust.

"Why this kid, Winters?" Coats asked snidely. "He's pretty enough—is that your thing?"

Carrick had looked up as though shot. It was like Bob Coats had seen directly into his heart and made note of the lovely glow that had surrounded it since he'd seen Deacon. But Coats was purely invested in pissing off Deacon's father, and it worked. Parish grabbed Crick's stepdad by the front of the sweat-stained T-shirt and shoved him against the door.

"You listen here, you ignorant bastard," he growled. "My son is a good kid—he gets good grades, he works his ass off—and he don't ask for nothing but the right to sit a horse. Birthdays, Christmases—that boy's been neck deep in sweaters, because he doesn't want a damned thing. Until today. Today he asked me for Carrick to work at The Pulpit two days a week. And since you don't give a *damn* about that boy, I'm going to give Deacon what he wants and Crick here what he needs." Parish punctuated this speech—one of the longest Crick would ever hear him make—with a shove at Bob's shirt against the door.

"If you want him that bad you can have him!" Coats spat to the side then, and Crick barely missed getting snot in his hair. "But he damned better be here after school to watch the little one for his mom."

"I will!" Carrick swore fervently. He actually didn't mind sitting the baby—Bernice, Benny for short, was a sweetheart with a wicked smile. Until he'd talked to Deacon Winters, his two-year-old sister had been about his best friend.

And so it had started. Carrick's lifelong love affair with horses—and with Deacon Winters—was well on its way.

The next weekend, when Crick was ass-deep in horseshit and still happier than he'd be watching television at home, he asked why. Why'd Deacon put him and his daddy out to rescue Crick from domestic misery?

Deacon had shrugged and grinned at him. His grin was a tight-muscled, sunshine-powerful thing that made Carrick's stomach fly. "You're as honest as a horse, Crick. Loud, but honest. That don't come easy."

So Crick had a quality—a virtue of sorts. He clung to it. There were some difficult years—some damned rough years, in fact—but Deacon had seen honesty in him, and Crick determined that Deacon would never see anything less.

Which was why, that very same weekend, when Deacon put him on the back of a horse and walked that placid, bombproof gelding around the circle with a gait as soft as a cotton ball on a cloud, Crick had grinned fiercely at his hero and laughed. "Dammit, Deacon, it's awesome... but I want to go *faster!*"

Deacon tilted his head back and laughed. "All right, Speedy. Let's try a canter."

And Crick held on for dear life. He never realized that from that moment forward, so did Deacon—but Deacon did manage to drop him some hints.

The time Crick got busted for smoking weed under the high school bleachers in the sixth grade, Deacon had dropped a big one.

At Crick's (panicked, tearful, shameless) begging, the school authorities had called Parish to take him in hand instead of his mom and stepdad, and Deacon had come with him.

If Crick had room for one more request, it would have been that Deacon would never have known about his complete idiocy. The kid who asked him had Deacon's brown hair and eyes, only a little darker, and grooves in the sides of his cheeks, and he had... had smiled at Crick. Had let him in on the joke. Had copied off his math homework and given him some cookies from his lunch in return. It was as close as Crick would ever get to actual popularity—smoking weed hadn't seemed like that big a price to pay.

Then he saw the fearsome look on Deacon's face as Parish's big blue pick-up drove up, and it had seemed like entirely too high a cost.

Parish had needed to deal with the school authorities—and from what Crick figured out, a whole lot of lying had gone on about how Bob and Melanie Coats would be the first ones to know and how a month's worth of detention would be impossible for him to serve, since he was helping at The Pulpit to feed his family.

And while Parish was doing that, Deacon was making a month's worth of detention sound like a dream come true.

"What. In. The. Hell." It was all he could say. Crick stared at his hero as Deacon struggled with words, with breathing, and with the tremble of temper in his hands as he apparently debated whether to strangle Crick or turn him over his knee.

"I'm sorry, Deacon." He tried to be stoic. Oh, he really did, but the tears were slipping out, and his nose was starting to run. Screw Brian Carter and his Oreo cookies—he'd trade them all just to have Deacon's good opinion back.

"Do you know what happens if you smoke weed, get drunk, do stupid shit like this? Do you have any idea?" Crick's back was to the school wall, and Deacon was looming over him, his fist pulled back and cocked like he was going to hit something. Crick didn't quail. Bob tanned his hide at least twice a week—Crick could handle pain, and this time he deserved it.

"I'm sorry…. Please don't say I can't come over any more. Please let me keep working at The Pulpit…."

Deacon let his fist fly—straight at the wall above Crick's head. He grunted at the impact, and Crick heard bones crunch, but Deacon just looked down at him, holding his blood-dripping hand and shaking his head.

"That shit can kill you on a horse. Horses don't know drunk from mean, you don't know a buzz in your brain from a tree in your head—you do that shit, you can't come around no more. That shit'll get you killed!"

Crick looked at the blood on Deacon's hand and cried harder. Without hardly knowing what he was doing, he rubbed the abused knuckles with his thumb. "I won't, Deacon. Please. Just… just please don't be mad at me. Don't…."

"Why'd you do it?" Deacon asked, shaking off the attention as he always did.

Crick hiccupped and yielded to the one virtue he'd ever been accused of having. "He was nice to me, and I was lonely."

Deacon dropped his head with a sigh and carefully repositioned his baseball hat with his good hand. "You gotta hold out for the weekends, Crick. Just remember, you got friends and family from Saturday morning to Sunday night. Please don't make me say you can't come over. Please."

Oh, Jesus. Deacon had said "please."

Parish came out and got them then, and he took his son to the ER at Kaiser in the city without much more than a "Jesus Christ, Deacon—you couldn't lose your temper on a pillow or something?"

When the hand and wrist had been stitched and set in a cast, he'd taken the boys out for ice cream. There had been no mention of school, detention, or the many reasons drug abuse was bad and horses were good. There was just the three of them, eating ice cream and asking Deacon how he was going to hold the reins with the awkward cast on his hand. Deacon shrugged. "That little gelding's so sweet, I just gotta think in the right direction. We'll be all right."

And they were. Crick's troubles were by no means over, but following Parish's and Deacon's examples, that was his last flirtation with substance abuse. Of course, three days later, after Deacon's cast had been replaced with the waterproof fiberglass variety, Deacon took Crick on a trail ride along with Deacon's best friend, wide receiver Jon Levins, and Deacon gave him another reason to never risk losing the best thing in his life.

The Sacramento River could be downright foul in some places, but in Levee Oaks, there were a few tributaries, mostly used for irrigation, that were both deep and clean. One of these ran through the far end of The Pulpit, complete with a big granite rock underneath a couple of oak trees. Deacon called it Promise Rock, and so did Jon, and Crick caught their excitement as they packed up the saddlebags with peanut butter and jelly sandwiches, apples, water, and towels.

The ride itself wasn't long, but it was hot. You didn't wear your swimming trunks on the back of a horse, and it was already in the nineties, even though it was only May. They didn't care. Parish and Patrick, The Pulpit's one permanent employee, were off showing Lucy Star, trying to get up points so Lucy Star's babies could be sold with a pedigree. Deacon had been slated to show her until he broke his hand, so there were no riding lessons and no football practice and pretty much nothing but mucking out stalls and working the other animals until the damned cast got taken off.

Deacon had asked nicely, and he and Parish figured that taking three horses to the end of the property and back counted as working them. The result amounted to a holiday better than going to the zoo or the movies or anything else that Crick hadn't been able to do because step-Bob hadn't wanted to spring for it.

For one thing, Crick got to ride a horse just as far and as fast as he wanted. Ever since his first ride around the little circle, Crick had lived and died for that chance to be free, and the only thing different about this was that there were two other horses in front of him, going mach one with their tails on fire.

It was *awesome*.

Eventually, they had to slow to a canter, which was probably good, because the muscles in his legs were going to give out—it was hard work holding on to a horse in a gallop, even harder if you were going to *ride* him, help him with the lifting of your body and the guiding of your legs and hands and stomach. About the time Crick thought he was going to humiliate himself by asking for a sedate walk, the oak trees they were heading for became clearly visible over the scorched fields that Parish mowed once a year for hay.

A little more cantering and they were swinging off the horses and leading them to the sloped bank of the swimming hole for water, and Crick got a good look at the only place in his life he'd ever held sacred.

Promise Rock was nothing really—a stand of rocks above a wide, deep spot in something less than a river and more than a stream. The rocks were surrounded by oak trees, so the place was shady, and they were sentinel oaks, so there were no scorched grasses in their shade. But the air there, in the shade and by the water, was about fifteen degrees cooler than it had been crossing the field, and they were far enough away from the levee and the roads that the only sounds there were the jangle of tack and the boys' rough, happy breathing now that the ride was done. It was pretty, peaceful, and secret, and for the first time in his life, Crick felt like he was in the center of things. Only this little group of people—and Parish, of course—knew about this swimming hole. There was no trash, no used condoms or soda cups, and no reminders about step-Bob or his little sisters or the classes he hated or the fact that the whole rest of his life seemed to be wrapped up and tied into this crappy little town.

Crick thought that if The Pulpit was his world and Parish was his holy father, then Promise Rock was the church where he'd come to worship.

Deacon had the saddlebags, and he rustled inside them quickly and then threw trunks at Jon and Crick and began to strip off his own clothes to put his on without ceremony.

Crick tried hard not to swallow his tongue.

He'd always known he was in love with Deacon Winters, but he'd figured that was a "normal" kind of emotion that every boy felt for a hero. The boys around him had been talking about girls, and as sixth grade progressed, Crick had assumed he eventually would want to look at them and talk about them too. He had been afraid of that time—because it would mean less of his soul was centered on Deacon—but he assumed it was an age thing and it would pass.

Deacon's skin was pale—especially next to Jon, who was tanned and blond from days in his parents' swimming pool—and he had scars from riding and playing ball and one across his stomach from an appendix surgery, so he was not perfect. But oh God and boy howdy, was that boy beautiful. The tight, knotty swathes of muscle he'd seen the first time he'd seen Deacon had massed out a little in the last two years, but he still didn't eat quite enough. His collarbones stood out vulnerable and delicate from his defined chest, and the hollow between his neck and the slope of his shoulders seemed to be especially tender. He had a flat beauty mark next to his right nipple, and another one low on his collarbone, and Crick tried hard—very hard—not to stare at the same time he was memorizing their positions so he could claim them at some later date. He had to take off his own clothes anyway, or he'd look like a dork, so for a minute that broke his concentration.

He had just skinned off his underwear when Jon said something inconsequential and witty, making Deacon throw back his head and laugh, and Crick looked up instinctively.

Oh God. Deacon was naked, his trunks held out in front of him as he prepared to step in, and Crick got a clear view of him, laughing and nude and beautiful enough to make his heart break.

And his little pecker stood at attention with a rush of blood Crick swore came directly from his brain. He flushed—probably so badly it looked worse than sunburn—and threw on his trunks haphazardly. Without looking at either of the other boys, he gathered his clothes into a knot and dropped them in a little wad up on the rock, then looked up with the most innocence he could muster.

"Can we just jump right on in then?" he asked, and Deacon nodded with a slight smile.

Thank God the water was cold, or Crick might have tried to drown himself in it, just for form.

As Jon and Deacon ran up the rock and leapt in from the height to a shrieking splash in the swimming hole, Crick had time to come to a couple of realizations.

He was *never* going to start looking at girls.

And he would probably love Deacon Winters truly and deeply for the rest of his entire life, in the way that most men loved their wives.

And someday, because Deacon thought he was honest, he would have to take his balls in one hand and his heart in the other and tell Deacon himself.

But not on this day. On this day, he would laugh and splash with Deacon and Jon. On this day, he would laugh at Jon (who was as extroverted and witty as Deacon was not) and watch Deacon on the sly to see his eyes crinkle and his mouth open wide as he laughed.

On this day, he would listen to the older boys shyly talk about their girlfriends and try very hard not to break his heart over it. They were not flirting with each other—and a phantom girl that Crick could not see did not feel like much of a threat.

On this day, Crick would be happy, and he would be good, and he would strengthen his resolve to behave at school so that Deacon would never again have to see the worst of him, the way his mom and step-Bob did.

He managed to make that resolution stick for three years.

Chapter 2

The Hope Express

IN CRICK'S memory, Deacon quarreled with his father exactly once. In a roundabout way, the argument was over him.

The spring before Deacon graduated from high school seemed to be exciting for everyone *except* Deacon. Apparently the mailbox had been bursting with offers and "free money" (as Parish called it) coming in from colleges since February, and the expectation that Deacon would go away somewhere was like lightning in the air. He was an athlete, his grades were top-notch, his counselors, who had sent in most of the forms without Deacon's participation, couldn't say enough good things about him—this kid was clearly destined for great things.

"City college?" Crick could hear Parish's voice clear from the house as he was working Lucy Star's first colt—a showstopper of a horse who had escaped gelding because of his sweet temper and magnificent trot. So far, no one had objected to Crick working a stallion either, although Crick was only thirteen. If Crick had his way, nobody would have reason to—if he couldn't take care of such a docile horse after five years under Parish and Deacon's tutelage, they might as well make him muck out stalls again. As it was, the task now belonged to another boy—Nathan—whom Parish had found sleeping in an empty stall with a black eye. Crick had been mildly jealous at first, but Deacon still treated him like an equal and Parish still treated him like a son, so Crick opened his heart a little to embrace the little shit. Hell, at least he wasn't mucking stalls anymore.

But trust or not, the storm raging in the Winters' usually peaceful and quiet front room was almost enough to make Crick lose all concentration in the ring.

"City college first," Deacon was patiently explaining. "And then Chico State—"

"Oh, and Davis isn't closer—"

"And more expensive!"

"You got a full ride!"

"I don't *need* a full ride!" Deacon shot back, his voice twisting up an octave. "I don't need a B.A. in business to run this place, Dad! I need animal husbandry classes, some EMT training, some computer stuff, some business classes! And I need to *be* here!"

There was a silence, and Crick's entire world screeched to a shuddering, screaming halt. Deacon leave? He'd seen the mail, heard them talk about college, but it had never really registered until now. Deacon was supposed to leave. He had a full ride offer—more than one, from the sound of it. He had a chance to *get the fuck out of Levee Oaks!*

And leave Crick here, in this wasteland, alone.

Evening Star nickered and tried to change direction, almost yanking Crick's arm out of its socket. He remembered that a two-ton stallion was still two tons of trouble if you ignored him and paid more attention to someone else's business—but he still kept his ears as tuned as he could.

"Deacon... son... I promised your mom. I did. She wanted to see you go to school—she wanted everything for you that she never had."

Crick could almost see that grin. It was tight and fierce, just a teeny quirk of the full lips. It said that Deacon was fine—don't worry about Deacon, he didn't need a damned thing.

"Sorry, Dad—all I want is here at The Pulpit. I'm pretty sure that's all Mom wanted, too, or she wouldn't have stayed." His voice dropped gently at the end, and Crick looked up blindly and saw Patrick. Parish's employee and best friend was looking back at him from under a ball-cap hiding wild wisps of hair and sad gray eyes. Nobody mentioned Deacon's mother. Crick had heard that she'd died when Deacon was around five or six—and here she was, as alive and as real between father and son as if she'd lived this whole time, loving Deacon with the same dedication and common sense as her husband.

Patrick jerked his head towards the horse, and Crick took the hint. They were both worried—eavesdropping, worried, and working a stallion that seemed to be losing brain cells with every dusty footfall.

"God*dammit* Even—could you just stay to a fucking canter?" Crick swore under his breath and tried to make sure the lunge line didn't go slack and confuse him again.

"Son," Parish said after a horrible, fraught moment, "don't you want to go off with your friends? Jon and Amy—they're going away down south. Don't you want that? You could play ball for another four years—I know you love it!"

Deacon murmured something too low for Crick could hear, and there was an electric heartbeat in which Even Star's hooves sounded like the thunder of God.

Parish's next words were—on the surface—still protesting. But his tone was resigned and Crick knew—hell, Even Star knew—that Parish had lost and Deacon had won.

"He'll be here when you get back, son."

"We may still lose him, Dad. You know that."

Parish's voice choked, came as close to tears as Crick ever heard it. "Deacon… please… you're young—it may not be what you think it is."

"Dad… please don't." Crick closed his eyes at the magic words, the words that meant Deacon had well and truly won. Deacon's voice dropped too, and Crick wondered at the cost of victory. "Please don't make this any harder than it already is."

After the workout, Crick brushed out Even Star with blind eyes and lackluster strokes. The stallion nickered and almost knocked him against the side of the stall, and Crick pulled out a handful of carrots on instinct, barely saving his fingers from Even's greedy teeth. When he escaped the stall—and a truly amorous horse—he saw that Deacon was standing outside the stable, waiting for him.

Crick couldn't do anything but look at him.

"I don't suppose you didn't hear any of that," Deacon started, a faint smile on his face. His head was ducked in a characteristic attempt to minimize or even acknowledge the sacrifice he was making for… for what? A stray he and his father had picked up? A muckraker with a chip on his shoulder? What a fucking waste of his time!

"You've got a chance to get out, Deacon," Crick growled, feeling like shit. He wanted to throw himself on Deacon's feet and cling, sobbing like his littlest sister, Missy. *Please don't leave me, Deacon, please, please, please* was at absolute war with *You dumb motherfucker, don't screw up your future for a loser like me.*

"I never wanted out," Deacon said quietly. "You can get out when it's your turn." He turned to leave then, fading out into the denim sky as quietly as he'd come. Crick was left gasping in his wake, wondering if this was when he took his balls in one hand and his heart in the other and told the truth.

All I ever wanted was you, Deacon.

But he didn't say it. He was thirteen—what did he know about losing the love of his life?

Seniors pretty much got a free pass on the last week of school, but still, Crick was surprised when Deacon's pick-up truck pulled up in front of the junior high and Deacon's friends, Jon and Amy, unloaded to check Crick out of school.

"Shhh…," Amy whispered to him when he was eyeing them in surprise in the attendance office. "Pretend we're your aunt and uncle…."

Crick grinned at her, and she flipped her straight, dark hair over her shoulder and gave him a perky grin. He'd made his peace with Amy Huerta, Deacon's girlfriend, in the last two years. It helped that she was as pretty and as quiet as Deacon himself. It also helped that besides the dark hair, dark eyes, and café-au-lait complexion, she'd shown a genuine interest in Carrick as a person and not as some pesky little-brother-like-thing that went part and parcel with her boyfriend. He hated to admit it, but it also helped that she was going to UCLA in the fall and Deacon was very firmly enrolling in EMT training as his first step to becoming the perfectly contained ranching businessman.

But that was in the fall. At this moment, the front office secretary eyed the two teenagers with a gimlet eye—and then she took a look at Carrick's hopeful face and sighed.

"Erm… Jon and Amy"—her eyes narrowed—"*Francis,*" she intoned acidly, "you are free to take your *nephew* out early today." The woman rolled her eyes and shook her head. "And by all means tell Deacon 'hi' for me—did you think we wouldn't remember you? It's only been four years for Chrissakes!"

Jon turned a blindingly sweet smile to the woman—a rather round, kind-faced middle-aged mother of three, and bent down to kiss her cheek. "Thank you, Ms. Lacey—you're the greatest."

And with that, the three of them ran laughing for the truck. Jon and Crick hopped in the back and Amy took the front—illegal, yes, but they weren't going far. Deacon stopped at a cattle gate and then took a barely-used service road down a scorched field that *hadn't* been mowed. Crick looked around the field for landmarks and squinted against the hot wind at Jon, whose longish blonde hair was streaming behind him as he turned his nose to the wind like an oversized Golden Retriever.

"Where we going?" Crick called over the jouncing of the chassis and the roar of the wind.

"Same place we always go!" Jon called. "Promise Rock—best swimming hole short of Folsom Lake!" Folsom Lake was nearly thirty miles away—and not easy miles, either. A lot of town driving went on through Folsom, and the river had run fairly high this year, so Discovery Park was dangerous.

"What made you decide to get me?" Crick asked, but he let his grin show that he didn't mind at the least.

"Deac's idea!" Jon called back. Jon and Amy called him "Deac," but Crick couldn't make himself shorten the name. "He said if we were gonna go celebrate, you got to come too!"

There were sodas in an ice chest in the back of the truck, and B.B.Q. beef sandwiches that Parish had made the night before. They'd even packed a pair of Deacon's old swim trunks for Crick, and he was grateful.

They'd been out to Promise Rock a lot of times since Deacon had first brought Crick, and it still held the same breathless holiness that it had that first time. This time, the boys all changed in front of the truck while Amy waited patiently behind it. "I don't know why you're not changing with her," Jon grumbled to Deacon. "It's not like you haven't seen all that before."

Deacon had blushed under his baseball hat and agreed that yes, he had seen it before, but, "It's only polite. Besides," he muttered as he slipped on his trunks, "we're breaking up in the fall anyway."

Crick's heart had done a little summersault in a cheerleader outfit with pom-poms, but Jon had looked thoughtful.

"Why?" he asked, standing up and folding his clothes. Crick tried for a moment to admire his body—long, graceful, tan, and lovely—but next to Deacon's broad chest and pale-marble perfection, Jon was really just decoration. "Why would you break up with her... you two... you really care about each other!"

Deacon nodded, his face pensive and honestly sad. "We do," he agreed, casting that sad expression behind them to where Amy waited patiently, arms crossed, small brown face tilted towards the sun. "We do— but she's going off to be a lawyer, do big stuff." He shrugged and blushed for no reason that Crick knew. "Be a political activist—that sort of thing. My heart's here—you know that."

Deacon looked sideways at Jon, as though they'd talked about this before, and Jon passed the sideways look to Crick as though he should know what it was about. But Crick shrugged, because he was damned if he did, and Jon rolled his eyes and sighed.

"Well," Jon said slowly, with so much forced casualness it was a wonder the word didn't break, "I wouldn't mind, um, looking out for her while we're down there, if that's okay?"

Crick blinked, and it was all he could do not to blurt, *What about Becca?* Becca Anderson had been Jon's girlfriend as long as Amy had been Deacon's. Crick hadn't particularly cared for Becca—she had long gold hair and a pretty face that she was exquisitely vain about. She'd also been less than sly about letting Deacon know that she'd be willing to take Amy's place on any given day, and that had been a shitty thing to do to Amy, Deacon, *and* the guy she was supposedly dating.

Deacon smiled wisely at the boy who had been his best friend since kindergarten. "If you'd wait until you got down there before you made your move, I'd take that as a personal favor, okay?"

Jon flushed and nodded gravely. He understood perfectly, and he seemed to be grateful for the honor.

"Are you guys done yet?" Amy called out cheerfully. "You don't finish soon, and all that's going to be left of me is a puddle of sweat!"

"I thought ladies perspired!" Jon called back, and Amy's laughter was pretty enough to make even Crick's heart break a little.

"That's sweet that you think I'm a lady, darlin'—you don't get your asses in gear, and I'm gonna be a raging bitch!"

Deacon threw back his head and laughed, and Crick found he had to love Jon and Amy because they loved Deacon, and how could you not love someone so goddamned beautiful that he stopped time itself?

The day was golden—one of those days that locked itself into a kid's heart and promised never to leave or even to fade. They swam and played. There was a tremendous water fight, pitting Crick and Jon against Deacon and Amy, which Crick managed to win by climbing up top of one of the boulders near the edge of the water and giving Deacon a full-out body tackle into the deepest part of the pool. Deacon came up sputtering and laughing, and Crick clung to those few brief seconds when their bodies had splayed together, muscle to muscle, Crick's chest to Deacon's waist, for long years before anything better came to take their place.

At the end of it, they sat quietly on the rock, Amy leaning back into Deacon's chest, all of them watching the sunset and talking quietly about the future.

"So," Jon murmured, drawing random patterns on Promise Rock with a stick, "EMT training first, animal husbandry second?"

Deacon buried his nose in Amy's hair for a moment and then looked up and nodded. "I think Parish is hoping that I'll like doing something else *somewhere* else well enough to take one of those deferred scholarships and run with it."

Amy risked a glance back at him. "You sure it won't happen, Deac? You can still…."

Deacon shook his head and rubbed his temple with Amy's. Even Crick recognized the gesture as the beginning of farewell. "No, baby. My heart is here at the horse ranch. I'm sorry." He tilted his head for a moment and rested his cheek on her head while she leaned closer and closed her eyes.

Jon tapped Crick's leg and jerked his chin, and together the two of them quietly wandered off into the twilight.

"He's staying here for you, you know." Jon's voice was unexpected, and Crick looked at him sharply. They were shoulder to shoulder now—Crick had gotten his growth spurt in the last year. He'd grow another four inches, but for now, he was eye-level with Jon and Deacon—and they were six feet at the least.

"I know." He'd heard the argument. "How am I supposed to be worth that?"

Jon stopped and put his face in the air. "I'm not gay—I wish I was, you know that?"

Crick blinked, completely out of his element—even when this *was* his element. "I don't know why you'd wish that," he said from the heart.

"I think I love Deacon more than I'll ever love anyone—even Amy," Jon confided. They hadn't brought beer—as far as Crick knew, none of them drank. Deacon had often joked that they might as well be Mormon, but it just hadn't been a thing that Deacon or his friends had ever embraced. Still, Crick was tempted to lean in to get a whiff of his breath, just for form. Jon saw his discomfort, and laughed.

"I'm going somewhere with this, Carrick, really. See, here's the thing." Jon dropped to the grasses and leaned back, tilting his face up at the stars. He made a pretty picture there—especially to Crick, who had learned the purpose of that thing between his legs and had been enjoying it immensely in the dark of his tiny room. But Crick didn't get hard or shivery or aroused, even looking at this blond movie star under the moon.

"The thing?" Crick asked, plopping down next to him.

"The thing is, I would give anything to be everything to the guy—I'd marry him if my body could go that way, but it doesn't and I can't. Do you understand?" Jon looked at Crick miserably, and it hit Crick. For the first time in his life, he was exactly what someone he cared about needed to be. And then it hit him that he could care about someone who wasn't Deacon or Parish or his little sisters. It was an amazing discovery—but one he would table until later.

Right now, Jon really did need him.

"Deacon's doesn't either," Crick reminded him, and Jon smiled gently at him, as though he didn't get it.

"Deacon is one of those rare individuals," Jon began, trying to sound jaunty and failing, "whose heart takes the lead before his desire, and not the other way around."

Crick frowned, processing. "I don't understand."

Jon sat up and looked at him from under a blond waterfall of hair and then shook his head. "If you think he stayed here to make sure his little brother didn't get in trouble, you've sadly underestimated how much that guy loves you, Crick. That's all I'm saying."

It was a good line for silence, and Crick obliged, but as the two of them watched the sun set—and watched Deacon and Amy have an unbearably private moment from as much distance as they could give—he mulled it over.

He kept mulling it over, too, for the following months, because it gave him a sort of hope that he he'd never dared have before. Hope was an awful thing, Crick had learned. The Christmas when he was ten, he'd hoped that he'd actually get something besides jeans from his mother, or that step-Bob would have even a word of thanks for him for getting Benny, Missy, and Crystal ready in the mornings and feeding them dinner most evenings. He had been sorely disappointed in that hope—but Deacon and Parish had given him a new saddle and a cowboy hat that fit. He'd been stunned and warm all over and had told them so. He learned that hope could betray you—but if you had no hope, life could actually surprise you in the best of ways.

He hated the hope. It made him fear the betrayal.

But the spring of his freshman year in school, he got another reason to hope, and he still didn't know what to do with it.

Oddly enough, it started with a mild concussion—the result of getting his head beat into the pavement by three other guys—and a visit from the local EMTs.

It would figure that Deacon had actually started riding in the ambulance that month.

"Kccerrrristtt, Crick!" Deacon growled while shining a light in his eyes. One of the other EMTs gave Crick some ice for his head and a cloth for the blood coming from his broken nose and then patted Deacon crisply on the shoulder and went outside to treat the three other guys. (Two broken wrists and some lost teeth—no one could say Crick was easy.) "What in the hell made you do it?"

Crick avoided Deacon's all-too-perceptive green eyes. "Dey starbed ib!" he protested, and Deacon lowered the hand with the light and held up both hands in the same way he'd gentle a horse.

"Do you want me to set it now? Or do you want to go home with a broken nose and no way to breathe?"

Crick shrugged, trying to hide the fear. Yes, it had hurt like a rabid motherfucker, why-do-you-ask, and now he was going to feel it again? Deacon placed his hands on either side of Crick's nose and made a sudden thrusting movement with his thumbs.

Crick's body jerked, and he whimpered. Deacon pulled Crick's head in against his chest soothingly. "Yeah—I know—hurts like a fucking jackhammer, doesn't it?"

Crick nodded and tried to think past the aching explosion on the front of his head.

"Now give it a minute," Deacon murmured, pushing him back a little to check out his eyes again. Crick took a deep breath, and Deacon smiled as soon as his eyes widened. Yup—hurt like a motherfucker, but the results were worth it.

"Thanks, Deacon."

Deacon grinned in that tight, knife-edged way and ruffled Crick's hair, prompting another groan as his hand hit some of the bumps and abrasions on Crick's scalp. The grin went away, and some of his bravado went away with it. He looked really worried, and Crick felt like hell for putting that on him.

"You gonna tell me why?" Deacon asked after a moment.

Crick shrugged again and considered lying and then remembered that this was Deacon. They were inside the ambulance, and the fluorescent light washed out the faint freckles under Deacon's eyes and along his nose, but Crick knew they were there anyway. He'd let his hair grow long on top but still cut it short at the sides, and the result was... appealing.

Crick brought his attention back to what he was saying, but it hadn't gotten any easier to tell.

"They... they called names." Well, coming from a high school student, it sounded a little stupid, now didn't it?

But Deacon didn't treat him like he was stupid. He laid that firm hand on Crick's shoulder and asked, "What names?" as though he knew the answer.

Crick looked away.

"C'mon, Crick—it's only got power over you if you give it power. Tell me what they called you."

"It wasn't just me," Crick mumbled, not meeting his eyes.

"Who else?" Deacon asked softly—but he knew.

"It was us... you, me, Jon...."

"What'd they call us?"

Crick looked away and muttered, and Deacon shook him a little. He met Deacon's eyes and said, "Faggot."

Deacon nodded. "And what does that mean?"

Crick blushed. "You know what it means!"

Deacon raised an eyebrow, and Crick blushed some more. "Say it, man—you've got to say it."

"It's someone who likes guys… you know…." Crick was starting to think a broken nose and a nuclear headache weren't so bad compared to this particular conversation, but Deacon, who had always expected the truth from him, was looking at him as though he hadn't ponied up yet. "To… um… sleep with." Okay. There. All done.

Then Deacon threw him a sucker punch. "And is that wrong?"

Crick flinched. "Christ yes! It ain't natural… that's what the… um…." Oh, and now wasn't *this* a little bit of hypocrisy he hadn't counted on? "Um… the church says. And, um… those guys."

"The ones trying to dent the pavement with your head in three-to-one odds? And who lost? Those guys?"

A tiny grin fought its way out of Crick's grasp. "Did they really lose?"

Deacon shrugged. "They won't be forgetting you—but now they'll have casts, so you won't want to provoke them into hitting you either."

Crick's grin got all the way free, and Deacon rolled his eyes.

"Down, boy. Carrick, the first day you wandered into The Pulpit, you were cutting church. The one time you're going to listen to what they have to say in church and it's something like *this?*"

Crick's grin disappeared. "I don't know what you mean."

"Crick," Deacon's voice dropped to *totally and completely serious*, "I really loved Amy—does it make you care any less about what happens to me?"

Crick's eyes shifted. Deacon had mourned her—that had been the truth. He'd lost weight, grown pensive, and more than once, Crick had seen him reaching for the phone to remember that she wasn't at her parents' house anymore. "No."

"Would you care any less about what happened to me if I was breaking my heart over Jon instead?"

Crick looked up, a little panicked. Jon would be a threat. It sounded stupid—and it was—but it felt smart, and he couldn't change that. "Hell no!" he responded to disguise the fact that he was freaking out about it. Deacon's mild expression told him that he knew *exactly* what Crick was thinking, but he also smiled, his eyebrows arching companionably over his green eyes.

"Do you think I care any less about you because you 'like guys'?" Deacon finally asked, and Crick thanked God that Deacon had led him to the answer, because it was a question he'd been afraid to ask. It took a minute for Crick to speak, though, because Deacon's hard, capable hand was on Crick's thigh, and Crick had to remember how to breathe around his bleeding nose before he could answer.

"No," he gasped, conscious of the stillness and intimacy of the ambulance.

Deacon's grin cut through the tightness around Crick's chest. "Damned straight." He leaned back then and made some notations on his clipboard and started to ask Crick if there was someone at home who could make sure he didn't sleep until morning and make sure he took it easy.

Crick shook his head. "No—Benny and Missy get home at three, and I'm already late to pick up Crystal. I was supposed to mow the lawn today...." His vision doubled at the thought of that, and Deacon nodded.

"No worries—we'll get your sisters and take 'em home. Patrick or Dad can watch you, and that way you can nap a little tonight, because they'll be there to wake you up."

The relief at not having to go to the tiny little house with the brown lawn and baby-shit yellow paint job made Crick dizzy. Since the marijuana incident in the sixth grade, he'd taken to spending Saturday nights in Parish's spare room, and, in the silence of his own mind, calling that place home.

He was just about to say "thanks" when the ambulance door opened and Principal Arreguin was there, squat face all stern and glasses steaming with authority.

"We need the boy's parents to come in before he leaves," the man said, giving Crick a scathing glance. Crick was too dizzy to even roll his eyes, and his body was starting to feel like he'd used a street-sweeper to scratch his back.

"I'm on his emergency card," Deacon said with deceptive mildness. He and Parish had been filling those out since the weed incident. As Parish said, Crick couldn't work the horses when his back was too cut up with a belt for him to move.

Mr. Arrequin narrowed his little gray eyes. "I was not aware of that," he said stiffly. "Well, we need to talk about his suspension."

Few things really surprised Deacon—but this one did. "A kid is jumped by three other kids, and *he* is the one getting suspended?" He looked sternly at Crick, as though to ask if there were anything he should know about. Crick shrugged, wondering if it was the head injury but pretty sure it wasn't his fault.

"They pushed me," he said muzzily, trying to look at the principals... both of them. "I was cutting through hallway outside the gym to get to algebra, and they came out of the locker rooms and called me a"—he flushed and looked at Deacon for moral support—"a faggot, and asked me where my faggoty friends were, and then they"—he swallowed, because he hadn't said this part—"called Deacon a horsefucker and knocked me into the wall."

Deacon's jaw tightened. "And that's when you hit them?" he prompted.

Crick shook his head. "There were three of them, Deacon—that's when I tried to get to the quad where there were witnesses. Eddy"—he jerked his chin towards the outside, where the kid with the wide, low forehead and dark buzzcut was probably laughing at his cast and trying to break it over Tomas and Brandon's thick heads—"he tackled me. I managed to get up, but...." He shrugged, pretending he didn't remember the taste of blood in his mouth from where he'd bit his cheek and the jarring of the concrete walkway under his chest and chin. He'd had a terrible moment of panic—there were three of them, and they could kill him. He could have died there, in that nasty little hallway that smelled like gym socks and wet metal.

"I was just defending myself," he finished weakly, and Deacon turned towards the principal with a *Well?* expression on his face.

Arreguin shook his head. "You provoke them," he said sharply. "You do—you know that."

Deacon's eyebrows hit his hairline. "He provoked getting jumped three to one?"

Arreguin scowled. "Look at him—the way he dresses, his hair, the people at his lunch table…."

Deacon looked at Crick with a surprised blink, and Crick hoped his head would explode and he'd die. There were cliques, and cliques had looks. Crick's jeans had become pipe-cleaner skinny, and his T-shirt was tight, baby blue, and cleared his navel. When he wasn't on the ranch, he wore loafers—no socks—and his hair was cut in long bangs. It was the "Alt rock" clique on the outside—Crick and his friends knew what they talked about in their tight knot at lunch.

But Deacon's expression didn't grow dark with disgust, and his brow didn't furrow with disapproval. Instead, he turned a fierce, angry face to his formal principal—the man who had waxed lyrical about what a fine, upstanding American boy Deacon was not eight months before.

"Sir, I do believe you're talking discrimination. I'd hate to think you discriminate against students because of their hair or their clothes, wouldn't you?"

Not even Arrogant Arreguin could mistake the threat in that tone.

Arreguin blinked and backed out of the back of the ambulance a little. "He's trying very hard not to fit in," he said stiffly.

"Last I heard, 'fitting in' wasn't a state requirement," Deacon replied, his jaw hard. "And getting beaten for 'not fitting in' was considered a hate crime, with required prison time—am I right?"

Crick made a sound of surprise, and his principal flushed. Deacon looked over his shoulder and rolled his eyes at Crick. "You have to learn more on this job than how to stock band-aids," he said with a little smirk, and then he turned back to the man who had the potential to make Crick's life a living hell for the next three years, three months, and two days.

"So, sir—can I take Crick to where he can get some rest and some medical attention, or am I going to have to call the sheriff and report a hate crime?"

Arreguin glowered at the both of them with terrible distaste. "I never would have thought you were the type to 'not fit in' yourself, Mr. Winters," he said snidely, and Deacon gave one of those fierce, tight grins—this one with no humor in it at all.

"Being a 'type' is a kid's game, sir—I thought that little ceremony last year was about how we get past all that. Now if you'll excuse me, Crick's about to toss his breakfast."

Which Crick did, as Deacon wrapped an arm around his shoulder and held the emesis bucket for his puke.

By the next evening, Crick's dizziness had (mostly) cleared—but his seething anger had not.

His sisters had spent the first evening with them, and Crick had enjoyed watching Parish deal with the three rambunctious little girls. It was a lot funnier when their chaperone/entertainer/chef/bath attendant was someone other than Crick.

When the three of them had finally been put down in Deacon's bed—he would be on shift 'til the wee hours of the morning—Parish woke him up and sat him up, then flopped next to him on the couch. They watched television for a bit so Parish could see that Crick wasn't going to pass out, and then he carefully set the alarm clock on the end table for the next hour.

"Don't know how you do it, son—that's a whole lot of busy for a boy with as much on his plate as you got."

Crick blinked. "I just… I don't know… I have to. They needed me."

Parish laughed and slapped Crick's thigh—gently; Crick looked like hell. "Well, they adore you, you know? All night it was 'Crick's hurt!' and 'Be good to Crick!' Benny wasn't going to let me out of her sight until they saw that you were asleep on the couch."

Crick would have rolled his eyes, but it hurt too much. "Benny's smart," he murmured. "If only she could control that mouth of hers."

Parish nodded sagely. "Yeah—she's got a temper. I reckon her father has something to do with that."

Crick's mouth quirked. "I don't know—I'm the one who just got his ass kicked in a fight."

Parish turned Deacon's intense green eyes on him. "Boy, not all the stuff that happens to you is your fault. Those girls came here without one word of worry about mom and dad—that says something bad about them and good about you. Your folks didn't object—not once—to just turning their whole family over to people they claim to hate. That does the same. And those boys—whatever was in their craw, you being you had nothing to do with it. You were handy. They had violence, and you looked like a good place to punch. It was not your fault."

Crick rubbed his eyes. Oh God, his head hurt. The ache was subsiding, but he had refused pain relievers, and now he wished he hadn't.

Suddenly Parish's hand was under nose with a couple of Tylenol and a glass of water, and Crick's eyes filled with tears.

"You and Deacon are my best family," he said, not sure if it was the concussion or being tired or the fact that Deacon's father was the nicest person on the planet.

"Boy, we feel the same about you," Parish told him, watching carefully as he downed the pills, and Crick felt tears overfill his eyes and drip a little down his cheeks.

"It wasn't right, what the principal said about Deacon," he murmured, because this had been weighing on him hard.

Parish grunted. "Deacon didn't mention that part."

He could almost feel the painkillers working, and his eyes closed in a little bit of chemical bliss. "Deacon was amazing," he murmured. "Deacon can take care of anything."

"Yeah?"

Crick tried to give as clear account as he could, but what he said obviously hurt.

"That man… spent Deacon's entire four years trying to get him to play more football for him. Now he's graduated and has his own opinions, and he's got to go and get nasty? Redneck… asshole gives rednecks a bad name."

Crick was getting dreamy, but he didn't care. The Tylenol had kicked in, he was still a little goofy from the head injury, and hiding his hero-worship was not going to happen. "Deacon gives 'em a good name," he murmured. "Showed that fucker what for. Made him look like an ignorant doofus. He was like Superman, you know?"

Parish's voice sounded troubled. "Crick, Deacon's only human. He's got his weaknesses same as anybody else. You need to remember, he can only do so much, take so much on himself, okay?"

Crick opened one eye to see Deacon's father running his hand through his graying hair, and it suddenly occurred to him that Parish was over fifty. Sure, he looked hale and hearty and still worked as hard as any two under-aged stable-boys, but he wasn't young. Deacon was his only child—and Parish looked worried about him.

"Don't worry," Crick said, trying to be the grownup he knew Deacon needed him to be. "I won't ever do anything to hurt Deacon."

Parish blew out a breath and worked the remote. "Go to sleep, boy," he urged roughly. "People hurt each other all the time just by being. What matters is that when you hurt someone, you do what you can to make it right."

Good advice, really. Too bad Crick wasn't thinking about it the next night. His sisters stayed home the next night—Parish shamed Crick's mom into taking some time off work to watch them, if she wasn't going to put herself out for Crick. Crick was off coma-watch, but he was still woozy and sore, and mostly he spent most of the day plying the remote control and doing the dishes because he felt guilty for being an imposition. When he was done or bored with all of that, he took to sketching in his sketchpad. The one teacher at Levee Oaks High that he *didn't* hate had told him he was good at art, and he had a notebook to sketch anything and a notebook to sketch special things, and he wanted to practice, since he had time to sit.

And when he wasn't doing that, he was seething.

Just seething.

Principal Arreguin—the guy hadn't said two words to him his entire freshman year, and then he showed up to accuse Crick of starting something? He gave Deacon shit for sticking up for him? Fucking Levee Oaks. Redneck—sure as shit, Parish had fucking nailed it. Levee Oaks, redneck capital of the fucking world.

Crick's eyes suddenly narrowed.

Boy, didn't he wish the whole rest of the world knew about that.

The water tower was right in the center of town, right next to the community center and the bike trail and the four (count 'em!) feed stores and small grocery center that tided people over between bigger trips to Safeway and Wal-Mart, which were around ten miles away. But at nine o'clock at night, after Parish thought he'd gone to bed and before Deacon got home, they had already rolled up the sidewalks and put up "Do Not Disturb" signs on the main thoroughfare, so no one saw Crick climb up the damn tower with a bucket of red paint left over from the last time they'd painted the barn dangling from one hand.

By the time he was halfway up, he was convinced this was his worst idea ever. He wasn't completely healed, his whole body trembled, and his head was pounding like it was going to blow brains all over the tower and the paint would be unnecessary.

By the time he got to the top and looked down, he was sort of hoping he'd fall on the ground, hit his head, and die, because it would hurt less than climbing back down.

But dammit, the guy had insulted Deacon, and it just couldn't stand.

With grim, determined strokes, Crick started painting.

He hadn't counted on the ambulance rolling through town around one a.m. and Deacon pounding out of the passenger side, swearing loud enough to wake Sheriff Cooper, who lived out by the levee too.

"God*dammit,* Crick!" Deacon took the rungs on the ladder two at a time, scrabbling up the side of the tower like a fucking spider, and Crick eyed him with the closest thing to dislike he could summon for a guy he'd loved since he was nine.

"Couldn't say that, Deacon," Crick mumbled. He let the paintbrush slide into the bucket, sat down heavily on the platform, leaned on the railing, and stared at his shoes. If he vomited from here, what sort of radius would it cover? He had a feeling he was going to find out. "Can't let him say that to you."

Deacon got to the top and shook his head, his face working between exasperation, pity, and humor. "Couldn't let who say what to me?"

Crick turned bleary face towards him and wondered why his head hadn't fallen off his neck. "Principal. Bastard. No one talks that way to you."

Deacon looked up at his handiwork and rubbed at his temples. "So you decided to paint 'Rednek Captl o th Wurld' to get him back."

Crick heard the inflection of the misspelled words and frowned, tilting his head on his shoulder to see. "My spelling was supposed to be better." He'd made the letters a foot tall—it must have skewed his already blurry vision.

Deacon let a giggle escape him and put a tender hand on Crick's head. He frowned and pulled it back. "Crick, you've got a fever, *and* you don't have a coat. Fuck. Fuck this all to fucking shit. If the whole town wakes up and sees this, you will never go to school here again. *Jesus*, why didn't you say anything?"

Crick leaned his cheek against the cool bar of the railing. "You weren't there, Deacon. I'm no good when you're not there."

"Boy, someday you're going to move away from here and you're going to have to learn how to be good. But not right now. I'd like to see you through school first."

With an angry sigh, Deacon pulled out his cell phone. "Dad, yeah, we've found him. Is Patrick still there? Look, could you do me a favor and have Patrick run the portable air compressor and a gallon of that white paint we have in the garage out to the middle of town? No. You don't want to know what he did. Maybe when he graduates from high school I'll tell you, and you can have at him then." Deacon's voice dropped with concern. "No—he's not all right. I think we can chalk a lot of this up to a smack on the head and a fever... and Crick just being Crick. Yeah, don't worry. Patrick'll see me when he gets here. I'll be careful. Love you too."

Patrick had to stand behind Crick and hold on to the bars to walk him down the side of the water tower. Deacon stood up there and hooked up the air compressor, watching them anxiously until Patrick had escorted Crick into the ambulance. Deacon's partner, Jake, worked two jobs to keep up on his alimony, and he was in the back on one of the gurneys, napping. Patrick settled Crick down, had Jake give him some more Tylenol, some water, and a blanket—it *was* early March— and left them both sleeping in the back of the bus while he helped Deacon.

Crick's last fuzzy thought before he faded off to sleep was that he had somehow managed to fuck up the act of fucking up, but he couldn't seem to put a finger on how.

By the time Deacon and Patrick had put the last coat of white over the red and crept down the ladder, dawn was a frosty hour away, and Crick's teeth were chattering from a combination of fever and the cold of the still vehicle. He heard Deacon's voice as the car started up and the heater came blessedly on, and then a heavenly warmth engulfed him, along with the smells of horse, spicy shaving cream, paint fumes, and clean male sweat.

"Mmmm...," he murmured. "Smells like you, Deacon."

"That's because it's my coat, jackass."

Crick held it closer and rubbed his face against the fuzzy lining. It was Deacon's paramedic's parka, and the outside was slick nylon, but the inside was all soft and squishy and Deacon.

They got him to The Pulpit, and Deacon had John drop him off and found a substitute for work the next night. Three days later, after Crick was conscious, no longer throwing up, and fever-free, there was an ass-reaming of epic proportions, but since he could barely sit up and was still overcome with remorse, he still had a little ass left when it was done.

But Deacon's lecture and Parish's exasperated, sorrowful face were never what he remembered about that night—or never what he remembered first, when he thought about it.

His clearest memory from the night he almost got expelled from Levee Oaks—the school *and* the town—was of Deacon sitting next to his bed as the sun came up, singing softly to him because he was whimpering with fever.

"I never knew you could sing," Crick muttered, and Deacon's soft laughter chased him into sleep, along with a soft, almost imperceptible kiss on his temple.

Ah, gods, hope. Our savior and our tormentor, the price and ferry pass for the dreams that carry us to the future.

Chapter 3

The Cost of Breaking Promises

THE art room was absolutely empty at four o'clock on a Thursday afternoon, but the supply closet attached to the back of it was not.

Mrs. Thompson, the art teacher who had inspired Crick to draw, trusted Crick and Brian Carter to clean up, and they had. They wouldn't betray that trust—they loved her. She was the one teacher who really understood them, believed in them, and who knew them for what they were and didn't judge.

But that didn't mean she'd be thrilled to know that after they'd cleaned up and the custodian had come by to sweep and mop, the two of them had sneaked into the supply closet to do what they were doing now.

They sat across from each other, their knees up in front of them in the cramped space, their pants around their ankles and their cocks in their hands. Crick's head was thrown back against the row of tempura paints no one used, leaving a hair print in the dust, and he was thinking brokenly that calluses felt *wonderful* on the underside of his cockhead... especially that one... that kept catching... right...on that...fucking... spot....

"Crick," Brian's voice panted in the dark, hot silence, and Crick pulled back from what might have been a humdinger of a climax to see what Brian wanted.

"Crick... watch this." Carefully, Brian took the hand he *wasn't* masturbating with and popped his finger in his mouth, getting it good and wet. Then, with difficulty, because his body was quivering and he was fighting his own orgasm as hard as Crick was, he lowered that hand down between his legs. Crick's hand slowed down, and he watched in fascination as that finger traced a path between two testicles covered in wiry brown hair to the tickly place between Brian's balls and his asshole... and then, as Brian struggled with the awkward position, it just... popped... in....

"Urrrgghhhhhh." Brian's orgasm was strangled, because they were trying to be quiet, but it was powerful nonetheless. Crick watched, wide-eyed, as the other boy's cock erupted into a heavy ribbon of come, and another, and another, and then his own body shivered, and he closed his eyes and leaned his head back and—

And a hot, wet mouth engulfed him, strong young arms wrapped around his waist, and his entire body ran fire as he came.

And came and came and came.

Brian couldn't swallow all of it—a sloppy trickle slid down Crick's testicles and underneath, coating his crease and slithering by his hole, just to tease. Crick looked in shock at his friend, who grinned back at him.

Brian had shaggy blonde hair and an appealingly round face—complete with apple cheeks sprinkled with freckles—and for a moment, Crick wanted to kiss him more than he wanted to do anything in the world. He even lowered his head, a gentle, dreamy smile on his face, when he suddenly wondered what Deacon was doing just then. He stopped and jerked back and could have kicked himself when Brian turned away, hiding his hurt.

"I'm sorry," Crick muttered, pulling his pants up because Brian was doing the same.

Brian tried to shrug like it was no big deal. "It's okay. I just thought... you know...."

Well, of course he did. They'd been friends, they'd come out to each other in quiet conversation—for all Crick knew, they were the only two gay people in Levee Oaks, period. For most of Crick's sophomore year, Brian had been giving him rides in his little red Toyota—hell, he'd even been out to The Pulpit for dinner.

Deacon had told Crick that Brian was a nice young man.

And now, when things had progressed past the *I'll show you mine if you show me yours* stage, Crick was backing out.

"It's not you," Crick said softly, leaning forward to put his hand on Brian's shoulder. He owed him that much. "I... I thought we could. I thought… I thought I could feel that way about you, but I… guess I don't."

"So what—now we're just friends?"

Crick hoped for the best and wrapped his arm around Brian's chest from behind. Brian leaned against him, his shoulders stiff and stooped and miserable.

"Well… *yeah.* Dude, do you have *any* idea how important that is to me? Any idea at *all?*" He spoke with all his passion and the honesty Deacon had burdened him with, and Brian's body relaxed just a little against him.

"Then why?"

Crick leaned his face into Brian's hair, thinking about how wonderful it was to touch another human body like this and how horrible it was that this wasn't quite the one he wanted.

"It's stupid," he mumbled. "*I'm* stupid. I'm… I'm sort of in love with someone else and I thought I didn't have to be, but I just can't make my body think it's…."

But it was no use. As his words sank in, Brian's whole posture stiffened, and he pulled away angrily.

"You're right," he snapped, pushing himself awkwardly from the dusty floor. "You're stupid, and I'm even stupider—more stupid—totally fucking moronic—whatthefuckever." He kept his back to Crick, but his hand rose to his face, and Crick could hear his voice break. Oh Christ. *No, Jesus, Brian, don't cry….*

"Brian, I still care a lot about you." Crick scrambled up, wishing he could salvage this somehow but pretty sure jacking off with a guy and then telling him you were in love with someone else equaled a classic Crick fuckup, times three. Oh God. He'd tried to get over his thing with Deacon, he really had, and Deacon had seemed to approve, but it wasn't until he'd seen Brian's face, beautiful, hopeful, but so not for Crick that he realized….

Hell. Realized that he was still just jack-fucking stupid.

"Save it," Brian turned his head to the side and wiped his face across his shoulder. "I should have known—I thought you wanted a boyfriend, but seriously—who could ever be as good as Deacon-fucking-he's-a-god-Winters!"

Crick closed his eyes—nice to know that being "honest as a horse" also meant being as easy to read as one as well. "I'm a total fool," he muttered, wondering why he couldn't seem to change that.

"Well I'm worse of a one, because I thought you could really love me," Brian said sadly, and Crick reached out again. It would be good, he thought wretchedly, if they could just go back to where they were before they'd ended up in the art supply room. They'd been friends—he hadn't been joking. He'd really loved having a friend.

"Brian...."

"Go to hell." Brian never did turn around. He just stalked out of the little cupboard room, leaving Crick alone with the smell of acrylic paint, dust, and come.

"But Brian...." Crick took two steps out, and Brian let fall the curse of doom.

"And get your own fucking ride home!"

Crick sighed and watched him go. Well, shit. So much for getting home when the girls did—it was a good thing Benny was getting good at helping Missy and Crystal, because if he walked fast, he might make it home in time to get them dinner.

He did walk fast, but it was still a long walk, and he had time to wonder if he should call Parish and ask him for help. He decided against it for a couple of reasons. For one, Parish would want to know what happened, and Crick didn't have it in him to spill the beans. For another, Parish would want to take care of the girls again, because ever since Crick got his head beat in, Parish had taken to dropping in on them and spoiling them rotten before step-Bob got home to drink. He also did it to give Crick a break of his own, for which Crick would love the man forever, but he was not up to explaining to his mother and step-Bob what Parish was doing there on this particular day.

But the final reason he didn't call Parish was that he didn't want to talk to Parish. He wanted to talk to Deacon—he *really* wanted to talk to Deacon.

Did something grow bigger in your chest because you didn't let it out? He had to know. Maybe if he let this thing with Deacon out into the air, then it would get smaller, or weaker, or he could stomp on it and kill it or something, because right now it was wrecking him. There Brian had been, a perfectly good boyfriend with his *mouth on Crick's cock,* and

Crick had driven him away for a pipe dream, a betraying hope that Deacon might someday love Crick the same way Crick had loved him forever and ever amen.

He really needed to tell Deacon and have Deacon tell him that he'd grow out of it so that maybe, he finally could.

That thought kept his feet on the ground and his head in the clouds and his stomach in a field full of butterflies for the whole trip home.

He got home, fed everybody, herded them into the bath, and dressed them. When he was done, he did a load of laundry so the girls would have clothes for the next day, cleaned the kitchen, and, just when his mother's hand touched the knob of the front door, he retreated to his tiny room with a sandwich and his sketch book. It was his evening routine, and all the better to ignore her quiet whining about her job or the way her eyes would dart to the door in absolute fear of step-Bob.

It also kept him out of step-Bob's way, so he didn't have to duck shoes for the nightly drinking game of shit-on-the-Mex-kid.

So he sat in his room and opened his special sketchbook, the one he'd held to his heart for the last year, and told himself he was going to rip out every last picture and burn it.

But he couldn't, because they were of Deacon, and they were his best work.

Deacon working a horse, his forehead a knot of concentration and irritation. Deacon leading a horse with a kid on its back, his face relaxed and soft, laughing without inhibition. Deacon, sitting under the oak trees at Promise Rock, the necklace of shell beads making his vulnerable young man's shoulders seem to stand out just that more sharply. Deacon, giving that fierce, tight grin from under the bill of his ball cap, the shy smile that dared Crick to smile back at him.

Ah, gods. Crick closed the book with a hand that trembled and set it down on his end table, then turned off his light and lay down to think about sleep. He tried to concentrate on Brian's expression as he'd jerked away, the better to make himself feel like shit, but the last thing behind his eyes as he drifted off was a fantasy of Deacon, turning his face up to Crick for their first kiss.

He woke up to a frenzied pounding on the front door and Deacon's frantic voice, calling his name.

"Crick... Crick... dammit, Crick, if you're in there, I just need to see you for a second!" Deacon's voice was breaking and hurt, and Crick scrambled out of bed, tripped over six different things in the dark, and still got beat to the door by his step-Bob.

"Boy," Bob sneered, his breath so foul that Deacon took a step back, "I don't know who taught you manners, but it's three o'clock in the goddamned morning. Nobody sets foot in my house this fuckin' early...."

"Stuff it," Crick muttered, pushing past step-Bob and into the cool night air. The door slammed behind him, and he couldn't give a shit because Deacon was embracing him tightly, reaching up a little because Crick had grown in this last year, and holding him like he'd never let him go.

"Oh God..." Deacon gasped. "Oh God. You're okay. I saw that car... I did, and... Jesus...."

Crick frowned and backed up. Deacon was wearing his EMT uniform, and the ambulance was parked on the curb. "What car?" he asked hazily, and Deacon wiped his cheek with the back of his hand like a little kid and tried to get a hold of himself.

Crick could see when it happened, because Deacon closed his eyes, grabbed Crick's arms, and tilted his forehead to meet Crick's, and for a moment, they just stood there, breathing steam into the cool spring night.

"I'm so sorry, Crick," he murmured. "I'm so sorry. I thought you were in it. This last month if you haven't been at The Pulpit, you've been in that red Toyota with Brian. And tonight, we...." He straightened and crushed Crick to him, and Crick went willingly, putting his head on Deacon's chest because, oh God, oh God, he knew what was coming. Brian, driving off in such a snit.... He hadn't been a great driver anyway, and there were so many places on the levee for a car to go wrong....

"Brian," he whispered.

Deacon sighed into his hair. "Yeah. They found his car about an hour after the wreck... he was already"—heartbeat—"dead. Crick, I'm so sorry...."

"Brian. Oh God." Crick started to tremble. Brian, who had been pissed off and broken-hearted because Crick couldn't even kiss him after he'd put his heart out on the line. Oh Jesus... Crick's friend, Crick's true friend who had let him copy off his math homework and worked English projects with him and helped Mrs. Thompson clean up after Art Club and… "Brian… oh Deacon… it's my fault. Oh God." His chest was going to explode. It was going to flat-out disintegrate like fireworks on his front lawn. He couldn't breathe, he couldn't breathe… oh God….

Deacon helped him sit down on the ground, the cold seeping through his sweats, but damned if he cared. He sat there with his head between his knees, breathing so hard he had spots in front of his eyes while Deacon rubbed slow, soothing circles on his back and told him not to talk until he could do it without sobbing.

It didn't matter.

The whole awful story tumbled out, because this was Deacon, and Deacon loved him unconditionally, and God, sweet, dear God, Crick needed to know somebody still did.

When he was done sobbing and talking and sputtering through spit and snot and tears, Deacon leaned Crick's head on his chest and rubbed his cheek on his hair.

"You have such a good heart," he murmured. "God, Crick—you didn't do anything wrong. You just tried to be honest, that's all. Sometimes people hurt each other, just by being. It's not your fault."

"I could have at least kissed him," Crick murmured, seeing Brian's happy, hopeful expression, the absolute sunshine of joy. He'd killed that. He may not have killed Brian, but he'd killed that moment with his dumb, self-centered crush.

Deacon made a sympathetic sound. "Crick, you did your best. Man, sometimes that's all you got. You were the best friend you knew how to be, but you weren't ready to be lovers yet. Nobody can hold that against you."

"I can," Crick muttered against his chest, so glad, so infinitely grateful that Deacon was there, Deacon was alive, Deacon understood.

"Please don't," Deacon asked gravely, and Crick shivered. There it was. The words of finality from the hero he loved.

"I'll do my best," he promised, and he did.

But it was hard, damned hard. It was hard when Mrs. Thompson called him aside and asked him if he was all right, and hard when she asked if he knew what happened, why Brian had been alone. It was hard when step-Bob had grunted "Good riddance" when he returned home the next day after Deacon took him to The Pulpit to spend the night with

Parish because nobody wanted him to have to go back inside and deal with step-Bob's bullshit.

It was especially hard at the funeral, when Crick outed himself in front of half the goddamned town.

That hadn't been his intention. His intention had been to go and pay his respects to the guy who used to goof off during lunch with him, and Deacon was at his elbow, just for good measure. He walked up to the coffin and saw the pallid, dead flesh doing a poor imitation of his friend and murmured, "I should have taken you up on that kiss, Brian," just loud enough for Deacon to hear, but no one else. Deacon took his elbow then, and they turned around to find themselves face to face with Brian's mother.

She looked half-crazed.

She was a licorice-thin woman with big blonde hair and a big bust line who had spent most of Brian's life looking for a daddy to replace the one who hadn't stepped up. Brian had thought she was beautiful, but she didn't look that way that night, because people in pain, people grieving, often had red eyes, a red nose, big bags under their eyes from being sleepless, and an air about them that was more than a little bit insane.

Crick could respect that. He looked pretty much the same.

"I'm so sorry, Ms. Carter," he mumbled, and her face twisted into something ugly.

"Is it true?" she asked. "Tell me it isn't true. Tell me you and my boy weren't... being all perverted this whole time. Tell me you weren't riding around this town, doing the nasty behind my back! The whole town is saying it... tell me it isn't true."

Crick looked helplessly at Deacon, who gaped like a fish back. Of all things....

"Jesus, lady," Deacon said. "Of all things to be worried about, this is what you grieve?"

"I ain't talking to you, Deac!" she snapped with so much venom that Deacon blinked. "I'm asking this dirty little Mex kid if he touched my baby!"

"No," Crick said numbly, wanting to give her whatever comfort he could manage. If her problem was that Crick was Mexican, well, he could put her mind at rest. "Brian and I were friends. We had the same classes, and we both liked art, and we had to be gay in this dumb town, that's all. We were never... you know, together."

He was unprepared for the crack of her hand across his cheek, or for her to scream "Faggot!" in his face with full force and spittle.

But by the time Deacon pulled up in front of his house after a tense, sorrowful, and silent drive, the numbness had worn off, and he was a little bit prepared to find all his belongings slagged on a blanket on the front lawn.

"You stay in the car," Deacon said quietly. "I'll start packing. Here." He pulled out his cell phone and handed it over. "You call Parish and tell him to get your room ready. He's been waiting for this to happen since you were nine."

Crick made the call and left a message, watching distantly as Deacon started to stack his books together. He saw a white flutter, and Deacon lurched after it as it flitted across the yard like a hurt bird. Crick realized what it was and belatedly threw himself out of the truck to get it before Deacon did—and before it became public property in general.

Deacon got to it first.

He stared at it blankly in the glare of the headlamps and then blinked. A faint smile touched his square-jawed face, and he put the paper gently in Crick's hands.

"That's real good, Crick," he said, his voice kind. "Goddamned beautiful, in fact—but you've got to know, it's not really me."

It was a picture of Deacon, sitting on Promise Rock, from Crick's perspective, sitting below him. He was looking out over the water, his chest bare, his shell necklace—the one that Crick had given him for Christmas five years ago—making him look vulnerable somehow. Crick had drawn what he saw—he couldn't be responsible for the aura of kindness, of strength, of beauty that seemed to surround Deacon without his knowledge.

"Of course it's you," Crick said, puzzled and a little relieved. Deacon thought it was good. "You remember that day."

Deacon looked unhappy and turned to picking up Crick's clothes, wrapping them in the comforter from his bed. "Crick, someday, you'll get the hell out of here, and you'll see that I'm just a guy. I'm not that special. I'm not the man in the picture. I'm flattered...." He stopped for a moment, and a shudder seemed to pass through him. "I'm more than flattered.

I'm...." He looked away, and for a moment, he looked unbearably young and terribly vulnerable. "I wish more than anything I could be the guy you drew there. I wish more than anything I'd never have to let you down, but...."

He looked at Crick beseechingly, and Crick wished they were having this conversation in broad daylight, because he couldn't for the life of him read Deacon's face. It looked something like hunger, and it looked something like denial, but mostly it looked like hurt.

"No one could live up to that picture, Carrick. No matter how bad I wish I could always be your hero."

Crick turned a naked face to Deacon, not caring if he sounded or looked weak, not caring if Deacon wanted him or wanted a little brother or just wanted a stable muckraker.

"Just promise me you'll always love me, Deacon," he said rawly. "Just promise you'll never throw my stuff on the lawn and tell me I'm not good enough. You want to be my hero, that's all you got to do."

Deacon smiled a little, something shadowing his eyes that Carrick couldn't even guess at. "Sure thing, Crick—as long as you promise to write us when you get the fuck out of here. Is that a deal?"

Crick swallowed and nodded, leaning into Deacon's strong hand on his shoulder. It didn't occur to him that Deacon expected him to leave. It certainly didn't occur to him that such an occurrence would break Deacon's heart.

Someone once called fate "the only cosmic force with a tragic sense of humor," and Carrick would have agreed. Once again, the thing, the big obvious thing that didn't occur to him at the outset, managed to make its presence known in the most painful way possible, with Crick as a witness.

Chapter 4

Making Promise Rock

IN THE middle part of Crick's senior year, it all looked golden. Thanks to living at The Pulpit, Crick's grades had improved, he'd submitted his portfolio to some art schools down south, and he was even looking to get some scholarships to help him out. Parish and Deacon had surprised the hell out of him on his eighteenth birthday in January when they'd presented him with a bank account that they'd been adding to since he was nine years old. (How they'd gotten his social security code from his mother was a story neither of them would discuss, but he would be forever curious.)

"Did you think you were working for free all that time, boy?" Parish had asked with a laconic smile on his long, weathered face. "We may be running on a shoestring, but we do manage to pay our muckrakers a little something!"

"A little something" was enough for a couple of years at school, and Crick had wanted to cry.

So he was unprepared when, about a month later, Patrick skidded the truck into the high school parking lot during passing period, jumped out, and cast wild eyes around the milling students. He just lucked into seeing Crick before he disappeared into the art building, and Crick ran down to him, heedless of the stares.

He'd gotten used to stares and whispers in the last two years—but no one would touch him, not anymore. The mystique of having a "boyfriend who died" managed—just barely—to put a blanket on the rampant homophobia running through Levee Oaks High. It had been a lonely two years, but since Crick went home every night to The Pulpit, he'd been able to bear them just fine. In fact, he'd have said they were the happiest of his life.

"Patrick." The man's round, creased face was red and blotchy from tears, and his habitual baseball hat was missing, leaving patchy, sparse hair flying in the February wind. "Man—what the hell's wrong?"

Patrick shook his head, unable to speak, and Crick started to panic.

"Oh God—Patrick, is it Deacon? Has something happened to Deacon?"

Patrick passed a hand in front of his eyes and shook his head again— this time a definite "no."

"No, boy—I was hoping you'd seen him, that's why I came by. I...." He looked apologetic, but it was clear his heart was broken, so Crick was ready to forgive him anything. "This is a hell of a way to tell you, Crick, but I'm so worried about Deacon, and I wanted him to tell you himself, but now I just want to know he's okay!"

Crick knew this feeling—oh sweet Jesus, he knew this feeling. "Oh God, Patrick... what happened?"

Patrick swallowed and nodded absently at Crick's art teacher, who had come outside to see what the deal was with the stranger on campus.

"It's Parish, Crick—he was working Evening Comet this morning and he just...." Patrick's voice broke completely. "He just dropped. I called the ambulance and Deacon got there and there was his father, and... Crick, he was dead—hell, before I got to him he was dead. Just gone."

Crick's vision went sort of an icky pewter gray, and he heard Ms. Thompson talking to him from the bottom of a well. "Where's Deacon?" he asked from that same well, and Patrick's weathered hand clamped on his arm and sat him in the open side of the truck.

"That's why I'm here, Carrick—that boy.... You see, the coroner got there, and they got Parish on the gurney and Deacon...." More tears. When he was nine, Crick would have said this man couldn't cry, but he sure could laugh. Now he wasn't sure if Patrick would ever laugh again. "Deacon said 'Daddy?' and it was the same voice he used when his mama was put on that same damned bus. Then he... he was just gone. Jumped on the back of that three-year-old. Damned horse was just milling around the yard, I was so tore up. It's been an hour. Crick... I'm so worried."

Parish? Deacon's dad—the first person to ever stand up for Carrick for anything at all? The man who'd greeted him every morning with coffee and breakfast—hell, even just Pop Tarts—and asked him what he was doing that day?

And to watch him and Deacon talk—about horses, about movies, about the state of the world—it was like a textbook on hope, about what family should be to each other.

"Oh Jesus," Crick mumbled, climbing out of his own misery for the first time in his life. "Deacon. Patrick, we've got to find him!"

Lucky for Crick, he had an idea of where to look.

Patrick had a key to the gate of the adjoining property, and as the truck jounced along the rough track towards Promise Rock, Crick tried to man up for whatever he might find there—even if what he found was no Deacon.

But Deacon was there.

They saw the horse first, and Patrick shoved the truck keys into Crick's hands as they walked around the irrigation stream toward the narrow end, where a little bridge sat for convenience. Since Crick had been there mostly in the summer, he couldn't remember ever using the bridge—when it was a hundred and five degrees in the shade, it was easier just to swim across—but he sure was grateful for it now.

"I'll take Comet back," Patrick murmured. "He's going to need you."

Crick doubted it. Deacon needed a grown-up. A mother or a father or... hell, anyone but Crick, who had been successfully fucking up his own wet dreams since he'd been having them.

Still, Deacon looked happy to see him when he hoisted himself up to the top of the boulder and plopped his ass down on the cold granite.

"Hey, Crick," he said with a faint smile. "Getting out of school again?"

"Yeah." Crick swallowed, hard. "You know—slacking as usual."

Deacon nodded, still staring off into the vacant field on the other side of the swimming hole. It was green with the winter rains, which had been plentiful, for once. It had almost flooded this year—always a worry in this area of Sacramento—but the rains let off at the last moment, and everybody had let out a collective sigh of relief. Didn't mean they weren't due, just meant they weren't due this year.

"In about a month," Deacon said absently, "this whole field will be a riot of flowers… those yellow ones that make the air smell good. I love that time."

"Me too," Crick told him. He had the field of flowers in his sketchbook, but since he had done it in charcoal and not watercolors, it didn't really sing.

"My mother drank herself to death, did you know that?"

Deacon's voice was so remote and empty that it took a moment for the words to sink in, and Crick's lungs almost froze with sudden pain. "No," he said, looking at Deacon in horror. "I didn't know that."

Deacon nodded. "Parish was starting the ranch, and he was working a job to make the payments and then coming home and working the horses and… and she would get so lonely."

"She had you," Crick said, not sure how you could leave a baby like that, no matter how lonely you were.

"I was little—Parish said I was pretty self-sufficient. I could dress myself, make a sandwich, it was no big deal. And she was good about it. Waited until I was down for a nap or when I went to bed, and then she'd just… drink. Steadily, for about three hours and Parish got home and she'd be passed out on the couch. And then she got sick—her liver started backing up, and she ended up in bed. We didn't have health insurance then—and, you know, she wouldn't stop drinking."

"Oh God, Deacon… I'm so sorry, I didn't know." Crick had always had sort of an idealized vision of Deacon's late mother—her picture on the mantel had been a dreamy, soft-focus female version of her son. He'd thought she'd died of cancer, or pneumonia or….

Or anything but the same thing that made step-Bob throw whiskey bottles at him when he wasn't quick enough to duck.

Deacon shrugged like it was no big deal, like everybody knew and Crick hadn't had to find out on the worst day of their lives. "Yeah… well, the thing is, after Parish came home and found me in the stables, I kept asking him when he was going to go away. I figured if she could, then he could, and I just wanted to…."

A hiccup then. A real, honest to God hiccup of humanity, a sudden closeness to that distant, nobody-home voice.

"Just wanted to know, right? So I could be ready, because I wasn't ready that time. Parish told me... he said he would stay with me as long as he possibly could. Until God dragged him away by the heels, kicking and screaming the whole time."

Jesus fucking Christ. Crick pushed himself up on the rock and reached a tentative hand to Deacon's thigh. He was not prepared for Deacon's death grip on that hand, but he did scoot up closer so they were touching shoulders. Deacon tilted his head a little—Crick had finally reached that four inches taller than his hero—and Crick sighed as his shoulder took up a little bit of that weight.

"The bastard didn't drag him off, Crick... he took him by surprise. You know that's the only reason Parish would leave us, right?"

Crick nodded and wiped his wet cheek on Deacon's sun-streaked brown hair. "Yeah, Deacon. He got ambushed. Wasn't fucking fair."

"No," Deacon's voice finally cracked. "Wasn't fucking fair at all." Deacon wiped his face on his shoulder, and Crick held up a hand to brush the tears off his cheek. Deacon captured Crick's palm and held it to his face with a shaking hand, rubbing against it like a skittered colt. "Oh God, Crick... you're the only family I've got left. You're like the only person on the planet, tethering me to its crust... and you're going to have to leave me too."

Deacon broke completely then, and Crick held him, weeping over Deacon's head as he came completely undone. Oh God... Crick thought he knew pain, and he thought he'd learned a little about death, but nothing, nothing at all had prepared him for this.

Deacon needed him. Needed him completely, in a way that had nothing to do with Crick's teenage crush and everything to do with family, and dammit, Crick needed to man up.

Crick rocked his brother softly for a long time, and when the storm of sobbing had passed, Deacon lay still, his head in Crick's lap, shivering in the February cold and the terrible chill of grief. By the time Crick made him sit up, made him move so they could take the truck back to The Pulpit and deal with all of the awful detritus of death, the hope for Deacon's love had been put quietly to sleep in Crick's chest, like a giant sleeping off a magic potion of grief.

Next to that sleeping giant was the slumbering hope for Crick's future in art school, because he'd be damned if he went off and rode the whirlwind when Deacon was left home, lost and alone.

Two years later, in this same place, Deacon looked at Crick with a sudden slyness, a sudden heat in his eyes, and that giant woke up, screaming to get laid.

Part II

Deacon

Chapter 5

Promises Made

JON and Amy got married at Promise Rock in April, when the fields were full of wildflowers and the air was gentle and sweet and the winds sweeping across the valley weren't too brutal.

Deacon stood up with Jon, of course, and Amy's best friend from UCLA stood up with her, and the minister was young and perfectly willing to balance on the top of the rock for the brief, simple wedding ceremony.

They could have had a larger ceremony—both their parents had money—but that was not what they wanted. They wanted their friends, their families, and people they knew, and they wanted it someplace special to them. Jon had first kissed Amy during a break from school at Promise Rock, and Deacon had been pleased—more than pleased—to give them a wedding in the place that meant so much to all of them.

The day before, the whole bridal party plus Crick had spent hours hauling out chairs and running streamers, placing vases of flowers, laying that fake lawn stuff, and basically "girling the place up," as Crick called it, and the result was their favorite place in the world, given a little bit of glitz and romance by the care of friends.

Amy looked beautiful—her dress was white satin, clean and elegant, draping her tiny, vital body like a queen. She had a kiss on the cheek and a smile for Deacon that morning, but now, at the ceremony, she only had eyes for Jon.

And Jon, whose movie-star dimple and oval face had only gotten more handsome in the past six years, looked besotted and tender and basically like the happiest man on earth. The two stood together barefoot (the better to balance on the rock) under the shade of that big old oak tree and repeated the old rituals that bound people together in this part of the world. Deacon watched them with a smile that felt like it split his body and shone outward until the middle of the ceremony, when his attention wandered, and he caught Crick.

Crick was looking at him with such a dark, powerful yearning, he woke a hunger that Deacon hadn't felt in his belly since he and Amy had last made love under this very tree.

Deacon's breath caught in his chest, and the heat, which had seemed mild and spring-like, suddenly washed his face and his chest and—oh dear God—his groin. That wash of heat purged away the last two years, which they had spent living together like brothers. It scoured away two years of being roommates, taking care of each other and The Pulpit. That one look put an entirely new perspective on two years of simple things like eating breakfast together, breaking horses, working around Crick's schooling and shifts as an EMT, and basically existing in companionship and family, and took Deacon back to the torturous two years before his father's death.

He'd wanted Crick so badly it had hurt like knives and shamed him like poison at the same time.

Yeah, he'd known about Crick's crush, but Deacon was older—he knew that what you felt in high school didn't necessarily last. That was why he'd kept Crick at arm's length, treated him like a little brother, kept his love and support unconditional and independent of everything but Crick's being Crick. And Carrick had seemed happy with that—especially after Parish's death had rocked their world.

And Deacon had been so not ready to start dicking with the one family member he had. It had been a good two years—with the exception of Crick's stop-gap profession.

"What in the fuck?" Crick had come home with the registration papers in hand, a done deal, about a month after they'd scattered Parish's ashes over all corners of The Pulpit. Deacon hadn't been pleased. "You gave up art school for this*?"*

Crick shrugged, as though his entire life hadn't been focused on getting the fuck out of Levee Oaks. "I deferred my scholarships—I've got a couple of years. It wasn't a good time to leave, Deacon. Don't tell me it was. You had to quit your job, give up your schooling. It was worth it. So's this."

Deacon thumped Parish's Stetson on his thigh. The hat had replaced his habitual ball cap and was the one thing of his father's he'd kept out of sheer sentimentality. "This isn't what Parish would want, Crick. He was so proud of you—he wanted you to live your dream, man—you know that."

Crick looked at him with hidden hunger then, and Deacon looked away. "This family, this place, it is my dream. Deacon, don't tell me you can do this by yourself—I know better. Please let me stay."

Deacon sighed. "It's a done deal, then. But don't tell me I didn't warn you it's a damned thankless job and the last thing you're going to want to do with yourself."

Crick shrugged. "I'll be here. It'll be fine."

And it had been. Deacon had been right about Crick not being happy as an EMT. Deacon had loved it—the adrenaline, helping people, being the first folks there on the site. He wasn't a talker, but he had a way of smiling and being quiet in the right places, and people responded to that.

Crick once showed up at a crash site and said, "Holy God, no wonder the guy didn't make it!" right before the victim opened his eyes and said, "I'm still alive, jackass, now help get this fence post out of my chest!" They'd laughed for a long time about that one, but Deacon had renewed his campaign to get Crick to take those scholarships and go back to school with a vengeance.

And right now, on this day, with a sweet breeze and the joy of friends, that look from Crick sent the whole issue right out of Deacon's head.

God, it had been so long since someone touched Deacon's whole skin. He jerked his attention back to the wedding ceremony—it was almost time for him to pull out the ring—but that look, that dark, boiling look from Crick, sat low in his stomach for the rest of the day.

Even Amy noticed it as they were dancing on the little floor of AstroTurf to music from a portable stereo-system plugged into a generator in the back of the truck. The tune was "Always and Forever," and the gentle irony of the song was not lost on either of them.

"So," she asked innocently, "has it happened yet?"

Deacon turned his eyes from where Crick was talking uncomfortably with Amy's parents and looked at his best friend's new wife with affection—and puzzlement.

"Has what happened?" Crick was pulling at his collar, never a good sign.

"You and Crick—you know, that whole reason you didn't follow me to school." Her voice held no rancor, but Deacon couldn't let the misconception stand.

"Darlin', you know very well The Pulpit was the reason I didn't go away to school." He smiled as he said it, inviting her to smile back, and she obliged.

"I know Crick was at The Pulpit, sweetheart—and you're avoiding the question, so I'll guess that 'No, it hasn't' is the answer." Amy grinned cheekily, and Deacon leaned forward and kissed her softly on the forehead.

"Crick was meant for greater things than this town, Amy. But then, so were you, which is why I can't understand why you came back." Amy and Jon were setting up their own practice in civil rights law right on Levee Oaks Boulevard, and Deacon was still flummoxed as to why they thought that was a good idea.

"Deacon, if any place on the planet needed someone to fight for civil rights, it would be Levee Oaks—you and Crick of all people should know that."

Deacon blinked. "Amy, I love you, but I'm not following you."

Amy shook her head. "Yeah, but I bet if that thing that should have happened two years ago had happened, you'd probably know *exactly* what I was talking about."

That flush came back, the agonizing flush of arousal coupled with the wealth of words that Deacon could never say in any given situation, just pushing at his tongue.

Amy's cheeky grin grew exceedingly gentle. "Has he figured it out yet?" she asked.

"Figured what out?" Crick had freed himself of Amy's folks and was now drinking punch with Patrick, both of them looking as though they'd rather be wearing anything but the fitted suits that Deacon had insisted on buying for them. Crick looked damned good in his, though.

"Figured out that when it looks like you're being all 'manly and mysterious', you're really just being shy."

Deacon actually stumbled. He recovered, picked up the next step in the box pattern, and glared at her. "No," he said in abject horror. "No. I didn't think anybody had."

The absolute pity on her face was enough to make him want to go run behind the rock and hide until the crowd went away. "Jon clued me in, you know. When you and I were dating and I kept thinking I'd said something wrong. He told me that you were just afraid of speaking your mind. You got over it, mostly, with me. I just didn't know if you'd gotten over it with Crick."

Deacon looked miserably at the boy, who had just said something to Patrick to make him spit out his punch. "I talk to Crick," he said with a pathetic attempt at defensiveness.

"Yeah, but does he know he's one of the few?"

Deacon thought about the two of them, side by side, watching television as Deacon went off about baseball until Crick patted him on the shoulder with incredible good nature. *I get it, Deacon—Dodgers bad, Giants good. Can we watch* Smallville *now?*

Deacon shook his head. "Crick's Crick," he muttered. "We get along all right." He always could talk to the kid when he couldn't talk to anybody else, even his father.

Amy threw back her head, her filmy veil fluttering in the slight breeze, and groaned loud enough to get Crick's attention. "Jesus, Deacon, you're killing me. Jon, here, you dance with the stubborn asshole."

With that, Amy whirled around to her father, who caught her in surprise and left Jon and Deacon staring at each other in shock. And then Jon put his hands up in the female's position and made Deacon's mortification complete.

"C'mon, big man—you owe me one last dance before you send me off into the arms of the woman who mended my broken heart."

Deacon gaped like a fish, and then, to the encouragement of hoots and hollers around them, put up his arms and took his best friend up on the offer.

"Jesus, you jackass," Deacon swore, grinning in spite of himself. "What're you trying to do, make her jealous? Dude, you've *got the girl!*"

Jon's expression sobered, and Deacon got one of those uncomfortable flashes again, made more uncomfortable by their close proximity. "Deac, you know damned well that if I could have made her jealous this way, we'd be having a very different wedding."

What was it with the two of them? Were they trying to kill him with mortification?

"You were damned young," Deacon muttered. Jon had come on to him—twice—in junior high, in this very place. Deacon had responded, actually, with some enthusiasm because he'd figured out when he was very small that both kinds of bodies held a serious fascination for him, but Jon had backed out. Gotten cold feet before they could do more than brush lips. Deacon had been willing to let both moments slide—moments from their childhood, when kids didn't know a damned thing about themselves. But apparently they had meant something to Jon.

"Yeah," Jon said, not blushing even a little bit. His hand, held loosely in Deacon's, was dry. "My spirit was willing, but my flesh wanted something with breasts. But I still love you, man. And I'm starting to worry about you."

"If you're going to worry, worry about me breaking an ankle. You don't follow worth shit." It was true—Jon had put his feet in the wrong position twice, and "Always and Forever" was a little worse for the wear.

"Yeah—but I bet Crick would bottom for you just fine."

Then Deacon *did* stumble, and he broke off the dance. "I'm getting something to drink," he muttered, not wanting to have this conversation anymore.

"Then I'll come with you." Together they exited the makeshift dance floor where about five other couples were dancing happily, and a patter of amused applause walked them to the punch table. Crick wasn't there anymore, Deacon thought, feeling grumpy. He missed Crick's easy conversation, the fact that his tongue didn't just knot up in front of Crick, the fact that Crick didn't expect him to say any more or anything more meaningful than he already did.

"I'm just saying that he makes you happy," Jon said quietly when they were situated with the punch. "He makes you happy, and he's loved you forever…."

"And he put a promising career in the arts on hold to help me out," Deacon said seriously. "So fine. He wants to, fine. But he needs to still go away to school, because I'm not going to have him kill that dream for a case of hero worship that just ain't gone away yet."

Jon downed his drink and sighed. "Okay, Deacon. I see what you're saying. But if you think hero worship is what makes that boy's eyes shine, then you're not paying the right kind of attention."

And with that, Deacon's best friend left to dance with his wife, and Deacon was alone until Crick came up alongside him.

"They were determined to have their two cents, weren't they?"

Deacon rolled his eyes, and Crick, who knew his expressions, laughed heartily. "So, what'd they say?"

Deacon couldn't make himself say *They want me to fuck you until you* have *to shut up!* So he just looked at Crick sideways and shrugged. There must have been something in the look he hadn't been planning on, though—some heat, some speculation, some sort of "Hey boy, you look damned good in a suit!" —because Crick blushed.

"Really?" he asked softly, and then Deacon blushed.

"They think I'm going to turn into the lonely old cat lady when you finally pull your head out and go off to school," Deacon muttered, tasting the punch. Too much sugar. With a sigh, he grabbed a bottle of water from the bucket of ice instead.

"When we all know The Pulpit would become a den of iniquity, featuring all girls all the time, right?" There was an edge to Crick's voice, an irritation and a jealousy. Crick had never asked him straight on about his sexual preferences; he'd just assumed that since Deacon had loved Amy, they only went one way.

"Or boys," Deacon said mildly, wondering what had possessed him to say this out loud. "I'm equal opportunity. You know that."

Crick sputtered and started choking on his punch so badly that Deacon turned to him directly and started pounding on his back. "Stupid kid," he grumbled. "You'd think they started putting fish bones in soda or something."

"Eleven years," Crick growled. "Eleven years we've known each other, and you think that little tidbit might have slipped out before now!"

Deacon's temper pricked this side of irritated, and he gave Crick a sideways glance that was nearly hunted. "You knew," he snapped.

Crick snapped back, "I hoped!"

"Mmm," Deacon grunted, swigging his water in the sudden heat of Crick's body six inches away from him and throwing out fire like a careless promise. "I wanted you to have a bigger life than me," he said at last, a little bit of despair in his voice. That want had faded, grown dim and far away, eclipsed by the want that built day by day in Crick's company. Deacon had seen his body—long, tall, lean, and beautiful. He had stringy muscles, a narrow waist, and that lovely pale brown skin. He'd even seen Crick naked in passing and knew that his cock was long and slender, with a little mushroom of a head, and he was pretty sure there was a birthmark one side, but he hadn't seen it long enough to be sure.

Deacon wasn't a saint, and he wasn't a monk, and his one sexual fantasy for the last two years had been Crick's body in any imaginable position—usually with Deacon on top and inside of it.

"What do you want now?" Crick asked, suddenly much too close to Deacon's ear. Deacon closed his eyes, allowed his body to soak up Crick's smell. He'd used Deacon's shaving cream and aftershave this morning, but it just didn't smell the same. On Crick it smelled spicy and exotic, and Deacon tried to open his eyes and concentrate on the dancing—Dire Straits was playing "The Ballad of John and Mary," one of Deacon's favorites.

"Same. Thing." Deacon said it through gritted teeth, because it was damned close to a falsehood.

"You're lying," Crick whispered, seeing right through him as he always did. Crick's long-fingered hand was suddenly on the curve of Deacon's backside through his slacks, and Deacon tried to risk a glance behind him to see if anyone was looking, but he turned the wrong way and ended up eyeball to chin with Crick instead.

He was still the prettiest goddamned kid Deacon had ever seen, with a lush lower lip and a wicked slash of humor at the sides of his mouth. Deacon risked a glance up, knowing that Crick's eyes were still that fathomless shade of brown. Only now they were a man's eyes and they were filled with a man's heat, and Deacon had a sudden wish for a horse and an open field, because this here was too much sex and too much emotion for him to deal with gracefully.

"Not entirely," he whispered helplessly, just inches away from Crick's full lips.

Crick's mouth quirked. "You are the stubbornest asshole I have ever met."

Deacon's eyes narrowed. "You haven't met my asshole yet," he snapped, turning sideways again. "Much less had enough experience to make a comparison."

He'd meant to drive Crick away, to piss him off, but Crick took a step behind him, and Deacon could feel the kid's long, slender erection through their clothes and almost saw spots, he was breathing so wrongly.

"Goddammit, Deacon," Crick muttered, a little bit of desperation in his own voice now. "That sounded something like a promise!"

Deacon sighed, some of the heat taken out of him as he looked back on his own words. "This," he muttered, moving his hands restlessly, "this is why I don't talk. There is not much I can't fuck up when I open my mouth."

"Goddammit *all* to hell," Crick whined in his ear. "That sounded like a promise too!"

Jon caught Deacon's eye meaningfully from across the little meadow, and Deacon smiled weakly back. Christ if his resolve wasn't in tatters around his feet. He turned to Crick miserably, so torn he could barely meet the man's eyes.

"The only promise I've ever made is to never turn you away," he said after a moment, searching Crick's eyes for some clue what to do next.

Crick blinked, obviously thinking hard. "You've kept that one," he said softly, his voice so full of hope it hurt.

Deacon shrugged, blushed, and muttered, "I always will," before turning around and walking away. Jon found him on the other side of Promise Rock, the side in the sun, half an hour later when it was time for pictures and cake eating and garter throwing and what-all.

"What happened?" Jon asked, obviously worried.

"I think I just gave in," he said, turning his face up to the mild spring sunshine. It wasn't too mild, though—he was sweating inside his dark wool suit.

"You're not sure?"

Deacon shrugged. "It's up to him. He knows I'll love him whatever. He wants it to change, it'll change."

Jon kicked his foot in its shiny leather shoe. "That's sort of passive, isn't it?"

Deacon turned a hunted face to his best friend. "Won't be if he makes a move. It's his future we're fucking with here, Jon. We're not having a roll in the hay—we're having a relationship, dammit, and those are hard for someone like Crick to walk away from."

On that note, Deacon turned to walk back around the rock fall towards the shady riverbank. He pretended not to hear Jon when he said, "And damned impossible for you."

Chapter 6
Promises Broken

DEACON and Crick were on for cleanup. That was part of being the hosts, but they didn't mind. The day after the wedding it only took two trips to clear out the chairs and the dressings and the stereo equipment, and the third trip was for the AstroTurf.

It was Crick's idea to go swimming before they left that third time. He had Deacon drive the truck out while he fed the horses and then rode Comet out to meet him.

He didn't tell Deacon that he'd packed the truck for a picnic, but Deacon figured it out when he saw the ice chest and the blankets and the backpack full of clothes next to him. He shook his head, amused. What, did the kid think they were going to have a love tryst on that damned rock? Now wouldn't *that* be comfy.

Still....

Deacon was showering the night before, using the bathroom that adjoined their two bedrooms, since neither one of them had found the heart to move in to Parish's room yet. There he was, clean, wet, wrapped in a towel, brushing his teeth, when he heard a noise at the door.

"I'll be out in a sec," he said absently. The two of them had shared a house for four years. If Crick had eaten too damned much cake and needed to blow up the bathroom, he could use the bathroom attached to Parish's room. It was only polite.

So he was surprised when the door opened and Crick stuck his head in curiously.

Deacon frowned at him in the mirror. "What?"

Crick had smiled cheekily. "We haven't been out to swim this spring. Want to go tomorrow?"

Deacon shrugged. The water would be cold, but the day would be warm. If they brought extra towels, he didn't see why not. "This couldn't have waited?"

Crick eyed him up and down, and Deacon looked at his own reflection to see if there was anything wrong with him. Square jaw, small nose, compressed mouth: check. Wet brown hair, parted in the middle, long on top, short on the sides and back: check. Body—well, it was his. He had a wide chest and a narrow waist, but his bones weren't as long as his father's had been—if he ever got a beer belly, he'd be built like a fire-hydrant, that was for sure.

Deacon turned a bewildered face towards Crick. "I ask again—what?"

Crick smiled, his eyes at half-mast, his mouth looking like cherry almond fudge ice cream. "Checking to see if that mark's still there," he said, and Deacon caught sight of the stork-bite next to his nipple and flushed.

"Yeah, my body ain't perfect. So what?"

Crick's smile grew wider and even more decadent. "There are parts of it I promised myself, that's all," he said smugly. "I was just making sure they're still where I left them."

He sashayed off then, leaving Deacon with goose-pimples, a hard-on, and an acute knowledge that resolve only got you so far before human weakness picked up the fare.

"Yeah," he called belatedly, trying to come up with something that didn't sound lame. "Well, maybe they got plans of their own!"

Crick's laughter, drifting down the hallway, did nothing to ease his mind.

Today, jouncing the truck over the rough cattle road on the vacant property next to the irrigation stream, Deacon couldn't do anything but shake his head. Their normal evening routine of sitting side by side on the couch, reading or watching television, had been entirely too tense for his peace of mind. He'd taken his book to bed early, entirely conscious of Crick's hand following his ass as he walked away.

The truck jounced one more time, and the blankets fell off to reveal a queen-sized air mattress and a little air compressor, and Deacon found himself laughing in defeat. Okay. So Crick had planned a seduction. If he showed even a whisper of follow-through, Deacon would have him laid out and splayed out, his body open and begging and ready. It would be fun teaching that boy that you couldn't seduce a predator, you had to just lay down and take his teeth and claws on your flesh.

They made short work of the AstroTurf, and Deacon reached for the backpack for his swim trunks, only to have Crick rip it out of his hand. "Nope," he said, his brown eyes as merry as Deacon had ever seen them. "You can't have them. No swim trunks for you!"

"I'm not swimming naked," Deacon growled. A man had his limits.

Crick stood up to his full height and tried to use his shoulders to pressure Deacon into the truck. Deacon lowered his head and glowered, and Crick took two steps back, stopping at Deacon's triumphant grin. Deacon raked his eyes up and down over Crick—the boy was shirtless and wearing low-rise jeans, his hipbones guiding the eye appealingly to what lay under the snap.

He looked up and saw that Crick was flushed as he licked his slightly parted lips uncertainly. Deacon looked down and saw that the jeans were a bit tighter than they had been a minute before, and he looked in the middle and saw Crick's nipples, pebbled and tight from nothing more than Deacon's eyes on his body.

Deacon swallowed and tried not to get too lost in the moment. Crick had plans. There was an air mattress and a picnic and whatever was in that backpack that Crick didn't want him to see.

"You get sand in your creases," Deacon said, his voice low and rough. "I was, um, under the impression that was uncomfortable."

Crick smiled. Crick didn't know it, because Deacon had never told him, but Deacon had spent nearly half his life working for that smile. With all his burdens and his troubles, the three little sisters he'd never let out of his life, and the step-father who'd sooner beat him than talk to him, Crick's smile was still as bright as the day. Everything that was hope and kindness was in that smile. There were some drawbacks to it—it was fearless, and since Crick hadn't yet looked before he leapt, there were times when that smile sent Deacon to his room along with cold shivers and his arms wrapped around his knees. But for the most part, there wasn't much Deacon wouldn't do, wasn't much he wouldn't hazard, to be able to see Crick through life still able to smile like that.

"Swim trunks it will be," Crick said through the warm, fuzzy glow of stupid that had somehow made shit of Deacon's resolutions. With a little rummaging, he handed Deacon a pair of trunks Deacon was reasonably sure was Crick's and not his, but he wasn't going to press the point. "Now go change and get in—I'll set up the food and shit."

Deacon rolled his eyes and let his own tight grin slip out. "Boy, you set up shit next to my food, and I'm taking the horse and leaving you to deal with the AstroTurf alone."

Crick laughed. Deacon smiled and Crick stopped laughing, but Deacon managed to walk away and change before either of them could find out why.

The water was cold, but it was refreshing and they'd both been working hard. By the time Deacon pulled himself out, Crick had set up the air mattress and the blankets and had some sandwiches and sodas in the middle. Deacon was willing to play along. For one thing, he was hungry. For another, well… it seemed to be Crick's fantasy. Deacon figured Crick would learn soon enough that he wasn't a saint or a hero or whatever was going on behind those pretty brown eyes, but the least Deacon could do would be to let Crick have his day.

"Good stuff," Deacon muttered around a mouthful of barbecue, and Crick preened a little under the praise.

"Made it myself." He had, too. The house had smelled like barbecue for the last five days. It was one of the few things that Parish had tried to teach Deacon that he'd never taken to. He was glad Crick had the knack of it.

"I'm appreciative." Deacon finished his sandwich, wiped his mouth, and disposed of his trash in the little grocery bag that they'd wrapped the sandwiches in. Then he stood and rinsed off his hands at the edge of the swimming hole, Crick at his side. When he stood up again, Crick was right there, kissing distance away, his whole heart in his eyes.

"Do you ever want to kiss me, Deacon?" he asked, and Deacon could tell that he'd rehearsed the speech, trying to make it sound sexy and seductive, but what it sounded was uncertain and wanting.

Deacon thought that the second combination was probably the one that did him in for good.

"All the damned time," he muttered. He brought up his hand and traced the silk of Crick's collarbone from his shoulder to the center of his chest. The finger kept moving, slowly, down between his pecs to right above his tender, corded stomach. Crick sucked his stomach in, making a little whining sound in the back of his throat, and Deacon smiled up into his eyes. There was still a little bit of barbecue sauce on the corner of Crick's mouth, and Deacon wiped it off with his thumb.

For that moment, that suspended moment, Deacon thought about giving Crick the lecture again, the one that said that this didn't mean Crick wasn't going to school, the one that said "Don't put all your dreams on hold because of me!" Then Crick's pink tongue came out and caught Deacon's thumb, and it was Deacon's turn to suck air in through his teeth. Crick sucked that thumb into his mouth and teased it with his tongue, and every coherent word zoomed right out of Deacon's hyper-aroused brain.

Leaving his thumb where it was until the last moment, he hauled Crick's mouth down for a kiss.

Oh God. He tasted like barbecue and river water and... and *Crick,* and Deacon couldn't stop kissing him. Their tongues met and tangled, and Deacon pushed at those narrow shoulders until Crick started to back up the hill. He stepped on the air mattress and caught the hint, sinking down to his bottom, and still Deacon pushed him back relentlessly.

"Do I want to kiss you?" Deacon muttered, kissing down Crick's jaw line, nipping at his ear, nuzzling the flesh of his throat. "Do I want to kiss you?" More kisses, these on a direct course to Crick's nipples as Crick made incoherent "ah" noises into the still-shaded air around them.

Deacon moved down to Crick's tender stomach with its promising trail of brown fur below the navel and started licking the skin there just to feel Crick convulse around him. Crick's hands struggled for purchase in Deacon's wet hair, and Deacon slid out of his fingers like an inquisitive, voracious otter and moved downwards. He teased for about a second and a half, sweeping his tongue under the elastic of Crick's Hawaiian swim trunks before grabbing the waist and dragging them down, leaving Crick completely exposed to the air.

Deacon propped himself up on his elbows and took a moment to appreciate that sweet stretch of flesh. Crick's body was so long and so lean, such a pretty color of pale brown, with hardly a blemish or a freckle anywhere except his shoulders, which burned almost every year.

Deacon met Crick's eyes, a limpid, helpless brown, and reached out a rough-callused finger towards his erection, watching as those eyes grew enormous, anticipating, wanting—so hungry Deacon had a moment of doubt that he could feed all that hunger, and then he was so hungry himself, he thought that maybe he could.

Deacon's finger found that beauty mark, almost lightning-shaped, and he grunted in satisfaction and then again as Crick arched up toward that single touch, begging. But Deacon knew a little something about this from his own hands on his flesh, and he kept up that one finger, stroking the underside of Crick's cock, investigating the tenderness of testicles and the fur in between, skating playfully across the slickened head and torturously across that delicate, shiver-inducing little stretched cord of flesh that once attached the foreskin.

Crick groaned when he did that, so he did that again.

And again.

Crick started to plead with him, gibbering, begging, "Please, Deacon, please, please, please, pleasepleaseplease," and Deacon, who was used to having no words at all when Crick talked all over the place, loved that he didn't even have words for what he wanted. Deacon didn't need words to know what Crick wanted, and when a half-spasm of pre-come spurted across Crick's stomach, Deacon raised his head and engulfed that beautiful, swollen cock with his mouth, taking it as far back into his throat as he possibly could and holding it there as Crick lost control with a strangled "Auuughhhhh." It was sweet and bitter and thick, and Deacon swallowed and swallowed and swallowed.

Not all of it, though. He couldn't. When he looked up at Crick to smile wickedly into those brown eyes, he was very aware that Crick's come was dripping down his chin.

"Now that *that's* over with," he panted, "we can take things a little slower."

Crick pushed up on his elbows and stared at him stupidly. "Slower?"

Deacon smiled, and he knew it was a dreamy, devious sort of smile. "Crick, the things I've got planned to do to you... I don't want to rush them."

Crick groaned and flopped down backwards. "I thought I was seducing you!"

Deacon popped Crick's cock into his mouth for a playful clean up and then started investigating the inside of Crick's thighs with his lips, teeth, and tongue.

"Nope," he muttered, positioning himself between Crick's spread thighs. He pushed at Crick's knees then, and Crick's body was spread out in front of him. Some of the come had dripped down the crease of Crick's body and was there, at Crick's opening, waiting to be played with.

Using that one wicked finger, Deacon obliged.

"Ahh... God... Deacon... I didn't know you'd done this before." Crick's voice cracked as that finger slipped inside him and circled, stretching so gently, Crick could barely feel any resistance.

Deacon pushed himself up to peer at the boy he'd loved forever and make sure this point was clear. "I haven't," he said, nodding earnestly. "I don't have a fucking clue what I'm doing." He ducked his head then and pushed his tongue where his finger had just been, liking the keening groan Crick made so much that he pushed it even farther.

"Could... have... ah, God, Deacon you're killing me... fooled me... *fuck!*"

Deacon had gone back to using his fingers again, and that was when he found that little walnut-sized swelling right there inside. He rubbed it again, and Crick's body arched and flailed, and Crick all but sobbed.

Deacon grinned. Good. He had a plan now. Licking carefully, using as much saliva as he could, he coated two fingers and eased them right on in. Crick made a negative sound then, and Deacon pulled out so quickly Crick almost came right there.

"Wait," he panted, and Deacon did, while Crick reached for the backpack next to the bedding. He rifled desperately for a minute, and Deacon got bored and started drawing the alphabet, right there on Crick's anus while Crick called him all sorts of horrid names and upped the search as fast as he could.

What he came up with surprised Deacon and delighted him too.

"Cherry lip gloss?" It was Vaseline, actually, the cherry flavored lip balm, and Crick threw two tubes of it at him as Deacon grinned from between his legs.

"I chickened out at the drug store—I was gonna buy lube!"

Deacon chuckled and squirted one of the little tubes onto his fingers, sighing a little. "Mmm... it's warm," he said before he eased both fingers inside of Crick's body. Crick moaned, and Deacon spread his fingers, scissoring them a little, and Crick screamed but in a good way.

Deacon raised his body up then and kicked down his own trunks, and he moved up so they were chest to chest. Crick reached out a hand and grazed Deacon's erection—it was as long as Crick's but fatter, and it was so hard that even Crick's soft touch made it ache.

"Gaaawwwwddd." Deacon buried his head in Crick's midriff and tried to get control of himself. Dammit, he wasn't a kid to go shooting off with just a touch, and Crick stroked his hair until he knew he wasn't going to lose it before he was buried inside the love of his goddamned life.

The first touch of his cock to Crick's asshole made them both stop and tremble for a moment, but Crick was prepped and stretched and ready, and Deacon didn't have a whole lot of control left. Crick swallowed, leaned up, framed Deacon's face, and kissed him.

This time, his body poised at the threshold of something irrevocable, Deacon accepted the kiss. It went on and on until Crick's hands were pushing against Deacon's back and Deacon's shoulders were trembling with the terrible state of arousal and want.

"Please, Deacon?" Crick panted. "Please… we need to…."

Yeah. Deacon pulled back and placed himself tenderly where he needed to be. There was a little resistance—not much, he'd been too thorough for that—and Crick threw back his head and begged some more.

Oh God. He felt heavenly. Crick's body wrapped around Deacon's cock was…. Crick spasmed around him, and Deacon almost came. God, it was perfect. Deacon thrust some more, easing his way in, and Crick pulled his legs as far wide and as far back as he could get them. He closed his eyes and breathed then, shifting, begging for more with every quirk of his hips, and Deacon looked at him in this moment, their first moment of possession, because he never wanted it to end.

But it had to. He had to move, he had to thrust, he had to bury himself deeper and deeper into Carrick Francis's willing body, and Crick loved it, whimpered for him, begged him, told him it was wonderful. Deacon's hips started thrusting harder and harder, and Crick pulled his legs to his chest and howled. His cock spat come again, coating their bellies, making their sweating bodies slicker and stickier, and maybe it was that, or maybe it was the way Crick's head was thrown back and his body was so open and vulnerable, or maybe it was that he hadn't had sex in forever and it was just *time*, dammit, but Deacon's vision went black, and he groaned and buried himself in the hollow of Crick's throat and in the haven of Crick's body and came.

And came and came and came.

Even moments when time stops have to end. Deacon slid out of Crick's body in a floppy sort of way, and he rolled over to his side, pillowed his head on Crick's shoulder, and stared bemusedly at the dappled green oak-leaf sky above them like a stained glass canopy. For a few minutes, there was nothing but the sound of their breathing, growing a little less frantic until it was lost in the slight breeze of the afternoon.

"Love you, Deacon."

"You too, Crick."

"So," Crick laughed a little. "Does this mean I can stay?"

Deacon frowned and wondered if "stupid" was a lasting condition or if he'd shot all his brains out with his load. "Stay where?"

"With you—you know—no more of this 'when Crick leaves' bullshit."

Deacon frowned harder and moved his hand down under him to sit up. "It ain't bullshit, Crick. You've hated this place your whole life. You'll never be happy here unless you go out and see something of the world. That don't mean…."

Now Crick was standing up and yanking his trunks back up with unnecessary force, and Deacon was wondering what in the hell had just happened that he was not aware of. "Oh, I know what it means. It means I go away to art school and you sit here and wait for me like some sort of goddamned monk or a martyr."

"I'm not a martyr if I'm happy to be here!"

Crick reached over to the rock where he'd laid down all his clothes and starting dressing over his swim trunks with hard, rough movements. Deacon wondered in sort of a panic when he'd stepped out of happy afterglow and into Crick going off half-cocked. He also wondered if he should start across the swimming hole for the truck to get his pants, because if Crick was going to take off across the field on the horse, he'd want to beat him back to The Pulpit to have this out.

"Well I'm happy to be here with you!" Crick shouted, throwing on his boots without socks, and Deacon held out his hands, trying to appease this monster argument that had blown out of nowhere.

"Crick, please don't…." *think I don't want to be with you.*

That was what he was going to say. He knew it was what he was going to say. It was the thing that had been in his heart since Crick had first put art school on hold for him. It seemed like the simplest of ideas, that phrase, the most obvious thing in the world.

Crick looked like Deacon had pulled out a gun and shot him.

"Oh Jesus," he muttered. "You're just like Bob—you're going to send me away!"

Deacon was horrified and shocked, and he stood there, his mouth gaping, trying to summon up the magic words of "Oh Christ, no!"

He managed them, but by that time, Crick was up on the damned horse and roaring across the field, and Deacon was running barefoot over the little bridge to throw on his clothes and go stop him. Whatever was going on in that jump-the-gun head of Crick's could only make this whole shit storm worse.

He left it all there—blankets, ice chest, fucking AstroTurf and all— and stopped barely long enough to pull on his jeans, T-shirt, and boots. Apparently he left his common sense in the wreckage of Crick's lost virginity, too, because he jumped in the Chevy and floored the fucking thing without even his seatbelt.

This was a problem when he hit the pothole in the shitty road, broke the axle, and got thrown headfirst into the windshield at twenty-five miles an hour.

Chapter 7

Dreams Like Shattered Glass

DEACON came to in a hospital bed, feeling like at least six kinds of fool. Carrick was right beside him, looking at him as though he'd grown a second head.

"It doesn't mean we can't be together." Deacon's mouth felt like gum and cotton balls, but he was pretty sure he said it right.

"Deacon—Jesus, are you okay? You scared the shit out of me! I thought you'd be home, and then you weren't, and when I got back from town you weren't there and then...."

Deacon focused his blurry eyes and scowled. "What'd you do in town?"

"You weren't wearing a seatbelt!" Crick accused.

Deacon supposed he should be ashamed of this. "I guess I'm lucky to be here," he said warily, but he didn't feel lucky. Crick was looking like he had a three-hundred-pound horseshoe to drop on Deacon's aching head.

"What did you say?" Crick asked, handing him some water in a cup.

Deacon took a sip and felt a little better. "I'm lucky to be here?" Crick wasn't meeting his eyes. Oh fuck. How bad was it that Crick couldn't meet his eyes?

"Before that, when you woke up." Crick's shoulder-length hair was stringy from running his hands through it, and Deacon tried and failed to figure out how much time had passed.

"I said you going to school doesn't mean we can't be together. Lots of visiting, lots of texting... hot weekends. It's only San Francisco or L.A., it's not the ends of the earth, you know?"

Crick sat down heavily, and that shoe-dropping feeling turned into a nuclear-bomb-dropping feeling. "Yeah," Crick said, his eyes glazing a little, and Deacon, with his aching head and the weakness in his arm (what *was* that anyway?) fought the urge to cry.

"Crick?" How bad was this going to be? Was this 'I sold your favorite horse' bad? Was this 'I slept with someone else right after I crawled out of your bed' bad? How bad was it?

"I probably should have stuck around long enough for you to say that, huh?" Crick said, and then he tried a smile like moldy cottage cheese.

"Crick...." Deacon tried to sit up, grunted in pain, and realized that his arm and shoulder were plastered. Must have broken the damned thing in the wreck. Shit. The truck. He'd have to get it repaired. Later. "What did you do?"

Carrick managed to meet Deacon's eyes then, and his own were red-rimmed and bloodshot. "We'll talk about it when you're better...," he tried lamely, and Deacon felt himself grow angrier.

"We'll talk about it now!"

"We can't change it," Crick muttered. "They made me sign six kind of things that said I couldn't change it."

Deacon's worry actually started to outweigh his personal body discomfort, and given that his brains felt like they were running out his ears, that was saying something. "Jesus H. Christ—Carrick James Francis, what in the fuck did you do?"

Crick didn't get mad at him back. He just sat there and stared at his hands with eyes so lost it was clear they didn't quite believe what he'd done either.

"Iraq," he said randomly.

Deacon had never felt so lost. "Tibet?" he tried, wondering if this was some sort of new awareness test for concussed patients.

"I'm going to Iraq, Deacon. I signed up at the recruiters'. That's where I was in town."

"You did what?" There was literally an ocean roaring in Deacon's ears—he truly wasn't certain he heard right.

Crick shrugged, the kind of shrug he used to use when Deacon asked how things were at school and they were pretty fucking shitty but Crick didn't want to admit it. "I... I, um... you know. I figured if you wanted me to see the goddamned world, I'd see it. I... I didn't know you were planning to be a part of that." All of it was said without emotion. Matter-of-fact. Like an alien surgeon ripping out Deacon's heart and analyzing it as it lay bleeding on the stainless steel tray.

Deacon's vision turned the color of tarnished silverware, and he fell heavily back on the hospital bed. His lips went cold, and he started to shake.

"Jesus, Crick."

"I'm so sorry, Deacon."

"Why would you... why would you think...."

"I... you kept pushing me away, and then... I don't know. I figured today was some sort of spectacular goodbye!"

Deacon was upset enough to try to sit up again and hurt enough fight a spinning room when he did. "Goodbye? You dumbfuck kid! I was finally giving in! Why would you ever think I'd shove you out of my life like that?"

Carrick turned a few shades paler and said, "Because you're the only one who hasn't, Deacon. I guess I figured I was due."

Deacon had no answer to that. If Crick hadn't trusted him after... after four years of living like brothers, after most of a lifetime of Deacon being there to pick him up.... Iraq. People got killed in Iraq. Deacon couldn't go there to bail him out—he'd be far away, unable to touch, like his mother or Parish or....

The wrenching, ripping sensation in his chest made him howl when a broken arm and broken collarbone and a concussion had barely made him blink. He tilted his head back and let out confusion and anger and pain, and when his throat was done making the noise, the echoes still pinged off the stainless steel bed frame and the beige tile and the taupe walls.

"Carrick... Jesus. What... what...." His voice was going to break, he knew it. "What have I ever done to you...." There it went, two octaves, and he wrenched it back under his control. "What have I ever done to you that you would hurt me like that?"

He didn't wait for an answer—he couldn't. He just turned his gaze blankly at the wall beside him as tears slipped helplessly down the creases of his eyes and wished the goddamned truck had been going ninety when he'd hit that pothole. He'd worked enough shifts as an EMT to know what that looked like, and it was a damned sight prettier than how he felt now.

Oh God, was it only that morning that he thought his one dream, his one incorruptible dream of what he wanted in the whole world, was finally his with the glory of a stained glass window? And now here he was, broken, and that dream was shattered shrapnel, cutting the hell out of his heart.

He may have fallen asleep, just bleeding into the air like that, because Crick spoke, and he startled, and the hurt gnawed his chest just as fresh and as savage as it had been when it all sank in.

"Please, Deacon," he said quietly. "Please?"

Deacon almost didn't turn, but eleven years of giving Crick what he needed was a hard habit to break. Crick was sitting with his head down, looking beat.

Shit.

He'd spent the last eleven years of his life telling Crick no fuck-up was too bad for Deacon Winters to love him. What kind of promise was it if it couldn't stand up to this?

"What?" he asked quietly, and Crick reached out and gingerly wiped Deacon's wet cheeks with his thumb, cupping his face with a long, callused hand as he did it.

"You promised you'd always be my home. I… I fucked up. I didn't believe you today. Please don't… please don't kick me out now."

Oh God. "Crick, you're…."

Crick nodded and rubbed his face on his shoulder. "I'm going away, I know. But I've got two weeks, and…." Finally, finally, Crick sounded as young as the thing he'd done. "I'm so scared. Please… please let me know I've still got a home when I get back."

Fuck. Fuck, fuck, fuck, fuck, fuck, fuck, fuck.

Deacon sighed and wiped Crick's cheek as Crick had wiped his. "How long 'til I get out of here?" he asked, wondering about all that shit he should have wondered when he first woke up.

"You'll be out tomorrow, and back in two days for a fiberglass cast. I asked."

Deacon nodded. It sounded about right. He was suddenly tired, and his whole body ached fiercely, not just his head. "On our way home tomorrow, we'll stop and get some paint and some bedding and shit. We can move into Parish's room before you go."

"I'll get it," Crick said hesitantly. "What do you want?"

Deacon smiled a little, faintly, sadly, and with enough weariness to sink a ship. "It's your room too, Crick. Pick out what you want."

Crick nodded, but he didn't move. He seemed to be crying a little harder now, but then, so was Deacon. "Aren't you going to be in there too?"

"Yeah," Deacon said, closing his eyes because he had to. "But you'll be gone. Make it remind me of you."

A thick silence fell then, the kind with a lot of stuff that would be said later, and some stuff that might never be said. Crick eventually began to nod off. Deacon scooted to the side of the bed and reached out with his good hand and leaned him into the pillow. Crick put his arms under his head and regarded Deacon soberly.

"If you can love me after this, you can probably love me after anything," he said softly, and Deacon grunted.

"It all hinges on whether you come back to me, Crick. I guess I'll forgive you anything but dying."

Two and a half weeks just flew by, and there was not a blessed thing Deacon could do to stop them.

For one thing, there was a lot to be done. Besides the normal stuff of making the ranch work, there was the process of Crick disengaging from his life in Levee Oaks and Deacon dealing with his damned foolishness and the car wreck. Crick worked hard to find a replacement for his ranch work, and they lucked out. One of Parish and Deacon's former muckrakers was out of high school and looking for a job with flexible hours to get him through college.

Edgar was a good-looking kid, and Deacon thought Crick might have been a little jealous, but the boy was one-hundred percent devoted to his girlfriend, so he wasn't.

They managed to paint and fix Parish's room—or rather Crick did—in the two days after Deacon got home from the hospital. Deacon supervised from his position of enforced rest. When Crick was done, Deacon looked around at the soothing tones of sage green, pale lavender, and ivory, and shook his head.

"You don't like it?" Crick asked, the apprehension clear on his face, and Deacon turned a twisted look to the man who had slept next to him for three nights straight. They hadn't made love again, not when Deacon's body was still a mess of bruises, but they had lain beside each other and touched softly. It was hard to do when every touch stung like goodbye.

"It's awesome, Crick." A smile broke free, but it was a broken smile. "It's just hard to believe you've got enough butch in you to cover for two years."

Crick looked back at the room again with big eyes and covered his face with hands spattered in dry paint. "Oh Christ. I'm gonna get the shit beat out of me, aren't I?"

Deacon stepped into him and started brushing that long hair back. "Naw... once they cut your hair, you'll fit in with the other grunts, I swear."

Crick looked at him hopefully, brown eyes peeking out from between paint-spattered fingers. "You think?"

Deacon shrugged a little. "It's not like you'll be wearing a pink T-shirt that says 'I joined the Army to get away from my gay lover'!"

Crick's horrified expression was eloquent and pitiful. "Look, Deacon...."

Deacon blushed and made to turn away.

"No, dammit—Deacon, you can't believe that."

"Forget about it," Deacon mumbled, embarrassed. It had been a joke, really, but Crick was reminding him that it felt like the truth.

Crick caught his shoulders in his long-fingered hands then, and suddenly they were both aware that Crick was taller than Deacon, and that yes, they had been lovers not more than four days ago.

"Deacon—what happened was me. Do you hear that? It was all me. I'm a fuck-up—"

"No more than me!" The embarrassment of wrecking the truck was something he wasn't sure he'd get over.

"You were provoked. I've been a fuck-up my whole life!"

"That's a *lie*!" God, Deacon felt this in the pit of his stomach. Passionate? Yes. Impulsive? Yes. But a fuck-up? No. Crick was all potential, all amazing potential, from his art to his sense of responsibility to the way he seemed to love Deacon without reservation.

Crick looked at him wryly, and something in Deacon's face made him shake his head. "Well the parts of me that aren't are all because of you and your dad and the fact that you gave a big fat crap about me. I...

what I did, what I'm doing… it's a piss-poor way of paying that all back, but it's not you. It's not your fault. I jumped the gun and ran out and did the most dumb-assed thing possible." Crick swallowed and looked away, and Deacon was reminded—yet again—of how young he really was.

"Don't worry about it, Carrick," Deacon said gently, cupping his chin. God… barely any stubble at all. Twenty. Crick was twenty—what kind of damned fool would take his signature on a piece of paper signing his life away and think that he meant it?

"Deacon Parish Winters, do you think I'm going to worry about anything else in the next two years?" Crick asked bitterly, his lips twisting as he used Deacon's full name.

"All I want you to worry about is coming back," Deacon said with some force, and Crick looked at him sadly.

"Deacon, don't you ever get mad at anything?"

Deacon felt it then, the pressure of anger behind his lungs. It almost suffocated him, but he shoved it back into hiding, beat it back until it cowered, made it sick with itself, snarling and rabid.

"I'll be mad when you're gone."

That night, Crick didn't just lie next to him and touch. That night, Crick scooted forward and kissed him with the same passion and drive Deacon had kissed Crick with back at Promise Rock. Deacon was surprised—and then he wasn't thinking much at all, because damned if the kid couldn't still scramble all his synapses in one thrust of his tongue. Deacon went from rubbing Crick's chest with his good hand to sliding it down the back of his boxers, and Crick got even closer and did the same.

Crick hit a bruise—the one across Deacon's abdomen—and Deacon sucked in his breath. Crick scooted under the covers and kissed it, and then one across his hip, and then Deacon's boxers got shucked off entirely.

"How're we going to do this?" Crick asked, nuzzling Deacon's groin, and Deacon sucked in a breath when Crick opened his mouth and took him, partially erect, completely into his mouth.

"We're doing fine," Deacon panted, and Crick rolled over behind him and started rifling through the end table. "What the hell's in there?"

"There's a sex store on Auburn Boulevard," Crick mumbled, popping his body back under the covers. Deacon rolled gingerly to his back and tried to see what Crick was doing, but by the time he maneuvered his cast around the blankets, Crick was done. He popped out of the blankets and got on his hands and knees, bending over Deacon's body with a long-limbed grace. He put his mouth back on Deacon's cock and busied one hand behind his backside, and the other—now decidedly slippery—wrapped around Deacon and started a firm, manly handshake with Deacon's firm, manly body.

"Gaaahhhh," Deacon managed before his tongue shorted out. Crick started doing things with his tongue on the head of Deacon's cock that made his entire body shiver, and then he started doing things with his fingers to Deacon's shaft and his balls that made him grab Crick's head with his good hand and start convulsing way sooner than he wanted to.

"Stop," Deacon begged. "Gonna come."

Crick stopped so abruptly Deacon flopped out of his mouth with wet smack. "No, no… can't do that. I've got plans," he ordered frantically. His hand went behind him again, and this time, Deacon saw his face contort into the fine lines of pleasure and pain as he moved. Crick's entire body relaxed for a moment, and he dropped something on the end table and turned around, lying on his side so his backside was nestled against Deacon's hard-on.

His ass was slippery, dripping with lube, and as Deacon's fingers moved to position his cock, he realized that Crick's hole was dilated too.

"What in the hell…?"

"Plug," Crick gasped. "And now it's out. And I need you in. Please, Deacon, please, please, please, please… *augh*… thank you thank you thank you thank you…."

Oh geez… the thought of Crick prepping himself… *pleasuring* himself that way, amped Deacon's arousal up another six or so notches. He thought of Crick on his hands and knees with his ass in the air as he sucked Deacon off and of that thing inside him, stretching him….

"Hold still, Crick," he rasped. He was lying on his good arm, and he carefully put the cast on Crick's hip to anchor him still. It only worked because Crick was so eager to keep Deacon's flesh in his own body, but he managed to work his hips harder and faster, and Crick helped by slamming back into him with every thrust until their breath grew thicker and thicker in the dark.

"Grab yourself," Deacon panted, because he couldn't do it. "Grab it… hold it… stroke it… c'mon, Carrick, jack yourself off for me."

"Nnnnnggggggh…."

Oh. Damn. Was that hot. Carrick started to tremble, to convulse, to climax, and his hole spasmed around Deacon, and then Deacon let go inside of him, burying his face in Crick's shoulder and groaning as his body turned itself inside out in orgasm.

The quiet afterwards was sated and textured with the smell of their sex.

"Interesting trip you made there, Crick," Deacon murmured, and Crick started to laugh.

"Not every idea I get into my pointy head is fucked up," Crick murmured, and Deacon wrapped his arm—cast and all—around Crick's chest and all but purred into his ear.

"I knew that, you know. In fact, Crick, I'm counting on it."

Two days before Crick left, they had Jon and Amy and Patrick and Crick's little sisters to the house to see the newly painted living room (because Crick had a taste for it now and couldn't seem to stop) and to have dinner and to wish Crick good fortune on his travels.

Jon was so angry you could have iced soda on his ass, and Amy wasn't far behind.

"He did what?"

Deacon was outside feeding the animals while Crick and his sisters finished dinner. Deacon couldn't begrudge them their time together— Benny, especially, was looking like Crick's absence would hurt. Benny had grown into a precocious young woman with brown hair dyed a rather spectacular shade of rabid cranberry, a terrible mouth, and a habit of sneaking cigarettes behind the stable. The fact that Crick needed Deacon as muscle to pick his sisters up to take them to the movies or the park once a week didn't bode any better for their adolescence than it had for Carrick's.

"You heard me," Deacon muttered, adding some oats to Even Star's mix. The stallion had won himself a pedigree, and now his only job was to stay fat, happy, and to get laid as often as possible. Sadly, it was usually with the mating dummy, but still, Deacon reckoned the horny bastard did his duty by them and earned his oats.

"We're here to see him off because he joined the Army." Amy repeated it again as though she hadn't understood it the first time. Well, that was fair. Deacon hadn't understood it either.

"Yes." Well, that was everybody. Deacon turned to lead them out of the barn and go inside and smelled cigarette smoke. Damn. He'd have to hang out and make sure Benny didn't burn the place down.

"Deacon," Jon said patiently, as though Deacon hadn't just seen the look he'd shared with his wife. "You crashed your car and Crick joined the Army. There has *got* to be more to it than that."

Deacon blushed. "There is," he said quietly. "There was a conversation that zigged when it should have zagged, and all of Crick's issues jumped in with two feet, and he thought I was telling him to piss off when I was telling him to go to school but come here on the weekends and see me, and, well, Crick being Crick...."

"He joined the Army." Amy said it like it was finally making sense to her, but Jon was looking closely at Deacon in a way that made him uncomfortable.

"Deacon," Jon said charitably, "which one of us do you want to stay and finish this conversation, and which one of us do you want to go escort Benny to the house and make her put out that butt?"

Deacon's blush took over his full body, and Amy kissed him on the cheek, saying, "That's my cue to go ride herd on Benny," before walking out of the barn with a wave.

Deacon watched her go with a sigh and turned to Jon with a small smile. "My life could have been so much easier if I'd followed you to school."

Jon nodded and took a seat on a hay bale, and Deacon sat on the bale next to him. "I think Crick will make you happier...." He stopped and shook his head. "Or I think he would have. Or... whatever before this happened."

They were lying in bed that morning, Crick with his head pillowed on Deacon's hard stomach and staring at the walls.

"I'm telling you, Deacon—kittens are the way to go. Fuzzy kittens— it'll be awesome."

Deacon snorted. "Wouldn't you prefer Impressionist paintings or a hunk-of-the-month calendar? Because that would be a sure-fire way of completely gaying out this room."

Crick rolled over to his stomach and looked at Deacon wryly. "I hate to break this to you, oh mighty testosterone bearer, but we are *gay."*

Deacon raised an eyebrow. "Speak for yourself. I'm bi. You're gay." *He was met with rolled eyes and Crick's outstretched tongue, which made him laugh. "Okay, okay, okay... since I'm not having 'bi sex' with you, I'll concede. In this bed, with you, I am a living, breathing Easter parade, are you happy?"*

Crick blinked. "Right here and now?" he asked seriously, and Deacon nodded. "I've never been happier in my life. But we still don't know what we're going to put on the wall."

Deacon lifted his good hand and stroked Crick's hair out of his face, knowing it wouldn't be there much longer to do that. "When you get back, draw me a picture—Lucy Star, Even Star, Comet Star—whichever one, you know? Make it big... and I know you'll put your whole heart in it. We'll hang it there, 'kay?"

Crick grimaced and looked away. "Talk about being gay, you big, queer bastard—I swear you just made me all verklempt."

Well, that made two of them.

"He does make me happy," Deacon said softly to Jon now. "When we are past this, I think he will make me seven kinds of happy." Truth and a bitter lie, and Deacon couldn't tell when one started and the other stopped.

Jon looked at him, and Deacon kept looking at the stable in front of them. It was three times the size of the house, clean and airy, with skylights and a neat, double-line of stalls. It smelled like hay and horse and very rarely like horseshit (at least in too great a quantity), and of carrots, since there was always a bag of them on the door to use as a treat. Deacon had fond memories of watching Crick as a gangly kid in this barn. He used to sing to the horses—he couldn't hold a tune for shit, but he'd sing pop songs and rap to them as he was mucking out the stables, and sometimes he'd even tell them jokes.

In the here-and-now, Deacon hauled in a razor-blade breath as he realized where that goofy kid was going to be in a few days.

"It's the getting through that's going to suck," Jon said with some sympathy, and Deacon shrugged stoically.

"I'll manage."

Jon put a hand on Deac's shoulder and pulled him in, and Deacon found himself resting his head on his best friend's shoulder in the quiet of the barn. "You promise me you'll ask for help?" Jon asked quietly, and Deacon made a neutral sort of grunt. Jon sighed. "Yeah, asking for help isn't your strong point. Don't think I don't know that, Deacon."

"I do fine," Deacon muttered, and Jon laughed without any humor at all.

"Mm-hmm... remember freshman year? You ended up in frickin' Pre-Calculus, oh-mighty-genius? You stayed up until the wee hours of the fucking morning to study, then you got up in the morning to work the horses, then you went to football practice, then you came home and fed, and then you stayed up into the wee hours to do it all over again. Do you remember the outcome? Hmmm?" Jon picked up hay straws and shredded them during this speech, and by the time he was done, he had a prickly yellow mess all over his dark wool work slacks and Deacon's cast, which was resting between their bodies.

Deacon shrugged and tried a quick, fierce grin. "Yeah, but as far as I know, you can only get mono once. I was fine before school started up again." He had just been getting better when Crick had walked up to The Pulpit and made him think beyond his own misery and weakness.

Jon pushed Deacon's head off his shoulder to stand up and kick the bale of hay. "That's not my point and you know it. You're here alone now, Deacon. Don't think I don't know that. You're doing a dangerous job in an empty house, and I swear, if Crick hadn't called me to figure out the insurance on the Chevy, you'd be trying to weld the axle together with a soldering iron and bubblegum."

Deacon flushed. "I was waiting for a call back from the company," he muttered, and Jon turned to him and swatted his head.

"You were waiting to be screwed by the world's dumbest insurance company. God, Deacon—when are you going to learn that the world doesn't have your sort of integrity? And that's my point. You don't know it, but Crick has been managing those sorts of details here...."

"Don't think I don't know it!" Because he did—he told Crick every day that he was grateful.

"Yeah, well the point is, you never ask for shit. Crick does it because he loves you, but you just hate to admit that Deacon Winters, God's gift to quarterbacks and quarter horses, is not an island unto himself!"

Deacon was still looking past him and into the barn itself. He actually really loved this barn. His father managed to build it a little before Deacon's mother died—before that, the horses had stayed in a simple line of plywood stalls. But once the barn had gone up, their horses— and the horses boarded at The Pulpit—had one of the finest barns in the area, and one of the largest. It was big enough to house three tons of hay, twenty horses, and two hands, although Patrick only stayed over when the mares were in foal. It had also housed one lonely little boy, trying desperately to show the world that he was big enough not to need anyone, even when he was tired and hungry and lost.

And it had housed Crick. Clear as day he could remember grooming the horses in one stall and hearing Crick singing—Green Day's "Time Of Your Life" was never going to be the same, that was for sure—but Deacon had loved hearing him anyway. The barn was suddenly not such a bastion, guarding him against loneliness, but a common room, where the people Deacon loved most visited.

He hadn't asked for that, but it sure had saved his life.

"I hear you," he said blankly, not seeing the gentle spring evening or Jon's concerned face. He was lost instead in another day, hot and sunny, with honey-thick sunshine dripping through the skylights and Crick's off-key adolescent voice cracking enough to startle the horses.

Jon sighed, knowing he hadn't made so much as a dent in Deacon's determined self-sufficiency. "Dammit… just… just promise me you'll ask, would you?"

Deacon sighed, because he probably wouldn't and they both knew it, and then tried a grin, but something about it only seemed to make Jon sad. "Here," he said at last, standing up and stretching. "Let's go inside before Crick burns the whole thing and spends the rest of the evening apologizing."

Dinner was a success of sorts—Crick claimed he was happy with the outcome, everybody wished him well, and Amy even shed a couple of tears. In the car as they were dropping off the girls, Benny told him to fuck off and die, and then she hugged him fiercely and told him that he'd better fucking come back, and neither of them had the heart to chide her for swearing. Crick watched the girls walk down the broken walkway to their home and looked at Deacon with a sudden horror.

"Christ, Deacon—I think they need me."

Deacon hadn't been able to look at him as they'd pulled away. Fucking dumbshit. Of course they did.

After that, the next two days were spent in a horrible normalcy. In the end, as it turned out, goodbye was only a matter of walking away from each other like it didn't matter, like they would see each other again in hours, like they hadn't spent the last two weeks making love like honeymooners and the last eleven years in each other's lives like family. Just that simple, really.

They kissed, long and hard and heartbreakingly, in front of the car as they were loading it with the single duffle that comprised what Crick was allowed to bring with him, and that was the end. They were hetero-brothers, casual friends, as Deacon dropped him off in front of the recruiters' in the warming chill of a May morning.

"Let me know when your leave starts," Deacon said roughly from the car window.

"I won't have time to come back and visit…," Crick started softly. It wouldn't do to get too upset, not here when the front walk was all military. Deacon knew his own face was a rather passive mask of neutral concern, but all of Crick's love was staring out at him from his expressive brown eyes. Deacon was pretty sure that, for both their sakes, he had to get the hell away from him before they fucked Crick large by their eyes alone.

"I'll be there," Deacon said firmly. "Just give me the dates when you got 'em." And then, because he saw the bus coming, "Take care of yourself, boy. I'll write."

Crick nodded and wiped at the side of his nose with a shaking finger. "You'd better." He mouthed, "Love you, Deacon," and Deacon mouthed, "Love you back." Then Deacon pulled away.

He drove to The Pulpit and fed the horses, then went inside and cleaned up after breakfast. It was Tuesday, so he went into the study to gather the bills and fucked up and glanced inside their newly refurbished bedroom. The green, ivory, and lavender pillows all lay heaped at the top of the bed, and the comforter was bunched up at the foot. The sheets smelled like their sex the night before.

Deacon wasn't sure how long he stood there, fighting the impulse to just lay on that bed and smell Crick on the sheets, but when he finally made it to the study to do bills, he had a hell of a time seeing the figures through the blur in his eyes.

Part III

Letters Through the Looking Glass

Chapter 8

An Abrupt Change of Plans

CRICK hadn't been thinking too clearly when he signed up at the recruiters' office. The fact was, he had some very specialized skills that the Army would be *very* interested in acquiring, and he hadn't tried to capitalize on them at all.

Four weeks into boot camp at Fort Benning, he was called into his CO's office, honestly wondering what in the hell he'd done now.

It wasn't that he got into trouble. Deacon was right. Once he got his hair cut and put on fatigues, he was like every other grunt—a little taller, a little ganglier, and his hands and feet tended to get in the way more often than not, but there was no pink T-shirt, there was no big banner, and since nobody asked him to decorate, his "gayness" or lack thereof never came into question.

But he was never going to be soldier of the year.

Crick was pretty fit going in—he worked the horses every day, flung hay, fixed machinery, helped maintain the property, and, in general, kept up with a very physical job. That, and Deacon pretty much pushed his ass out the door three times a week to go running with him in the cool of the morning along the levee road. The physical conditioning was intense, but it wasn't going to kill him, and it was pretty much what he expected, so he could deal.

He could even keep his mouth shut—which surprised the hell out of him.

The problem seemed to be guns. Crick and guns were not friends, and he couldn't really say why. He and Parish's shotgun had formed a working relationship based on a mutual hatred of rattlesnakes, and although Deacon had the bright idea of buying a couple of potbelly pigs to keep the fuckers off the land, Crick had wasted his share of them before Porky and Petunia had come to live at The Pulpit. Crick had learned to clean it and to disassemble it and basically how the damned thing worked, and playing with M-16s had not been on his list of fears when he'd arrived on the base to have the drill sergeant scream in his face.

But the first time he'd disassembled the gun and put it back together, he had stared blankly at the table.

"What *is* your *problem*, Private!"

Crick had been ignoring mean people most of his life. Listening for the meat of what the drill sergeant wanted and ignoring the acidic sauce meant to break down his sense of self was a lot easier than his last two years of high school, that was for damned sure.

"There's a piece left over," he said, puzzled.

"What?" The drill sergeant had been truly at a loss and suddenly human—a man in his forties, a career soldier who was proud that the boys in his charge left Fort Benning able to defend themselves as well as six weeks of intensive training could prepare them to do. A gun with a piece missing was a bad thing in terms of survival.

"What the hell is that?" The drill sergeant almost mumbled to himself. "I've never seen that piece of metal before in my life…."

Crick and the drill sergeant had missed lunch, still stuck in weapons practice, trying to figure out where the little bit of metal fit into the now re-disassembled M-16. They never did figure it out—Crick's weapon had to be replaced because they were too afraid of firing it. This time, the sergeant breathed like a dragon down Crick's neck to make sure he didn't break something or take something apart that didn't need to be taken apart, and this time the M-16 seemed to go together just fine.

But it shot three feet to the left.

They hadn't believed Crick at first. He'd sat behind the hay bale and fired the damned thing at the way-off target, same as everyone else, but his target remained as pure as a virgin's dreams. (Well, maybe that was a bad analogy, Crick reflected as the drill sergeant spat it into his face—his own dreams as a virgin had been just as filthy as his dreams now, only a wee bit more desperate.)

"I'm firing into the target!" Crick had protested, and the private next to him said, "The hell you are; my target's shredded!"

The drill sergeant had looked at Crick with narrowed eyes, as though maybe this was all his fault. "Let me see your weapon, Soldier!"

Crick handed it over, and target practice stalled as the drill sergeant aimed that fucker and pulled the trigger... and the remains of Private Compton's target shredded under the onslaught.

The drill sergeant grunted, put the safety on, commandeered Private Compton's gun, and asked Crick to shoot at the target. Finally—*finally*—Crick's target got some penetration, and Crick, for one, was relieved for the poor thing. He knew how it felt.

The drill sergeant looked at Crick's gun and then looked at Crick, a sort of reluctant sense of attachment in his pewter gray eyes. "Son," he said like he was mulling something over, "do you have any particular skills that might be of use to this Army?"

"Skills?" Crick asked, feeling dumb.

"Skills, son. What did you do before you joined up?"

Crick smiled. This was easy. "I was an EMT, Sergeant, when I wasn't working the horse ranch."

Crick managed to surprise the guy twice in six weeks—someone told him later it was a record. "Anything else you can do?" he asked faintly.

"Draw, Sergeant."

"Draw?"

"Portraits—that sort of thing. I was going off to art school before I"—he grimaced—"before I lost my fucking mind and ended up here." Wasn't that an old joke? The guy got his heart broke and joined the Foreign Legion?

"Portraits." The drill sergeant shook his head. "Christ all-fucking-mighty. Boy, you need to report to the CO tomorrow after breakfast, hear me? Skip weapons training...." The man shook his head and looked at the gun as though it might just jump out and bite him. "By all means, you're relieved of weapons training, you hear?"

Crick shrugged. The guy barked orders with a voice made strong and gruff with twenty years of practice. Yeah, sure—he heard.

The next day he marched as crisply as he could (although he heard drill sergeant's voice in his head screaming something about "meandering") through to the CO of new recruits and confronted the man behind his military-neat but over-stacked desk.

"Sir!" He saluted smartly—in his effort to look as un-gay as possible, he'd elected to do as many things "smartly" as possible. Saluting was fairly easy, as far as that went.

Captain Roberts (as the little plaque on his desk said) was a thirty-ish man with blond hair, brown skin, and pale eyes—and right now those pale eyes were fixed on Crick with the same sort of pained exasperation his drill sergeant had.

"Son, am I to understand you signed up for the Army and neglected to mention your EMT training or your horsemanship experience?"

Crick shrugged and nodded. "Yes, sir."

The captain took a deep breath. "Did you not know these things would maybe, I don't know, benefit you when we're fighting a war where camels are a form of transportation?"

Crick wrinkled his nose. Parish and Deacon had actually taken him to a circus once, because hot *damn*, had they done his birthdays up right, and he'd gotten a close-up view of a camel. "About the only thing camels and horses have in common, sir, is that people ride them." Because it sure as shit wasn't the smell, the attitude, or the fact that the fuckers spit worse than a redneck with chaw.

"What about the EMT experience?" The captain drawled, his lips quirking up in reluctant appreciation.

Crick flushed. "No, sir, it did not."

The captain's eyebrows raised to the roots of his beige-ish hair. "Not even a little?"

Crick blushed harder. "Sir, I had three art schools throwing money at me for two years. Let's just say joining the Army was not the clearest bit of thinking I've ever done."

That was met by a scowl. "Don't tell me you were drunk—if your recruiter signed you up drunk, you'll have the option of a discharge, free and clear."

"No." Crick shook his head and sighed. How to word this, how to word this…. "I was actually offered the thing I wanted most in the world, by the person I most wanted it with, and because I am a retarded asshole, sir, I thought I was being kicked to the curb."

The captain was looking at him now as though he had confessed to being a space alien, and he felt a sudden pressure to scream *I'm gay, dammit, let me the fuck out of here!* But he didn't.

"And so you signed up for the Army?" said his puzzled CO.

"And so I signed up for the Army, sir," Crick replied.

The CO blew out a breath. "Well, son, the fact is, you have enough training as either a medic or in animal husbandry to rate a promotion to second lieutenant when you're through with training. We could hold it over your head and say you didn't sign up for it, so you're stuck being a grunt until you work for it, but we need both of them too damned badly. The question is, which one do you want to be?"

"A medic or a… a…." What was the word for it?

"Camel jockey?"

"Isn't that a racial slur?"

"Not when we need them so damned bad. In fact, you should know that a few of the boys from your hometown signed up for that gig, if that helps make the decision any easier."

Crick wasn't sure if the bolt of abject horror that shot through him was apparent on his face. He had *come out* to his entire hometown. The *last* thing he wanted was to face any of those assholes again. A sudden memory trickled into his brain like sweat down the crack of his ass. His squad had been double-timing it through the barracks when they'd passed another squad doing jump-ups, and a familiar face had startled as he passed. *Eddy? Eddy Fitzpatrick?* He'd dismissed it at the time, but now he had no doubts that one of the people who would be there to greet him at the animal husbandry barracks in Iraq would be the guy who helped beat the shit out of him in the ninth grade.

"Medic, sir," he said, "smartly" turning to "sharply" at the memory.

His captain nodded, almost as though he understood. "Fine, Private. Medic it is. Consider yourself an officer upon completion of your training."

"Sir, yes, sir!"

"And if nothing else, it will keep you as far from any sort of firearm as possible as a member of this man's Army. We're a superstitious lot, here, Private—I'm not fucking with our mojo, no matter *why* you and the M-16 seem to be at odds."

Crick let a smirk show through, and the captain managed to hide his own. "I hear you, sir. Am I dismissed?"

"You may go." The captain turned to make some notes on Crick's paperwork, and Crick pivoted to leave. He was stopped at the door.

"Private?"

"Sir?"

"Will she be waiting for you?"

Crick couldn't hide his surprise. "Sir?"

"The girl… the stuff… everything you wanted in the world when you thought you were going to be kicked to the curb—will it still be there when you get out?"

Crick didn't know what his expression was, but he knew he felt naked and exposed, and he didn't give a shit. "That's the plan, sir."

The captain nodded. "I'm glad to hear it, son. Now double-time it back or you'll miss chow, and you're a little on the thin side as it is."

That night, he had a precious fifteen minutes to write to Deacon, and he used it.

> Deacon—
>
> I've posted the dates in June when we're on leave before
> shipping out. It's only three days. It's hot as hell and twice
> as wet—we may not want to plan on doing much while
> you're here. Otherwise, things are fine. I mean things suck,
> but I expected them to suck so it's not much of a surprise.
> In fact, I even got a promotion….

Crick wrote three letters while he was at Fort Benning, and Deacon knew them all by heart. He'd gotten into the habit of writing a short paragraph to Crick every night and then finishing up the letter and sending it off. Stupid stuff—how the horses worked, what Patrick had said, whether or not Jon had called. He tried to see Crick's sisters twice but had been turned away at the door both times. It galled him, but step-Bob was right—Deacon had no blood claim to the girls, just an obligation to Crick.

The last time he'd been there, planning to take them to the movies, Bob had been there with a couple of drinking buddies to run Deacon off. Deacon had taken one look at the array of pipes and chains on the Coats's living room coffee table—as well as the meaningful looks of step-Bob's cronies—and said, "You should be ashamed of yourself, you useless fucker. You don't want me coming around and trying to be a parent to your kids, you need to get off your ass and do it yourself."

He hadn't quite dodged the eight-inch length of lead pipe that went flying towards his head, and the girls had peered anxiously at him through the back bedroom window as he'd driven away, trying to staunch the bleeding in his temple. That had been two weeks before his flight to Georgia took off, and he wasn't sure what to tell Crick about his promise to look after the girls, and he really wasn't sure what to tell him about the fact that Patrick had wrecked Crick's Gremlin (fucking useless car, but Crick had loved it) when the damned thing had *lost a tire* while taking the back roads to Wheatland to broker a deal for Even's stallion spunk. They were going to have to buy another car, but worse than that, Deacon's vow to keep home *home* for Crick was unraveling one broken promise at a time.

> Crick,
>
> I'll be there—here's the hotel name and the number. I would imagine you can just walk right on up and knock. I've got some good news and some bad news for you. The bad news is that you've got a brand new Hyundai Hybrid to drive when you get back from Iraq. The good news is step-Bob's fucking useless toe-licking friend can't throw worth shit....

Deacon opened the hotel door carefully. Crick hadn't needed to say anything—they were in the middle of fucking Georgia, barely a mile from Camp Benning—if anyone saw them, Crick would be toast. Crick rushed in and closed the door, and they stood for a second, looking at each other cautiously.

"You look tired," Crick said at the same time Deacon said, "You got thinner!" and then Crick's goofy grin spread over his narrow, high-cheekboned face, and Deacon shoved him back against the door. His cast was off, and he used his thinner, paler hand to cup Crick's cheek while his good hand held Crick by the collar. They stood there, smiling and panting, and then Deacon smoothed shaking hands through Crick's cropped hair and claimed Crick's mouth with everything in his soul.

Much later, they lay tangled in the sheets, naked, sated, and still breathless, with Deacon's arm wrapped around Crick's chest and Crick's head on Deacon's shoulder.

"Your new haircut?" Deacon murmured against Crick's short, sweat-soaked hair.

"Yeah?"

"Hate it."

"Me too. First thing I'm doing when I get back—growing that shit out."

Deacon laughed a little, and Crick shivered under his gentling hand. "I'm hoping you'll have some shit to do while you wait for that to happen."

Crick laughed too, and Deacon suppressed a whimper because he'd *missed* that sound.

"So how'd you get promoted?" Deacon asked to keep the sadness at bay.

Crick told him the story—the one that didn't come through in the letter, and when they were done laughing, Crick turned over to his stomach and grew sober. "So, this is what you define as 'bad aim'?" He fingered the still-healing cut above Deacon's left eye.

Deacon winced a little and shrugged. "He was trying to knock me out. He failed. Damned straight I called that bad aim!"

Crick's face went unaccountably sad. "Now see, Deacon, this is what I'm afraid of."

Deacon wondered if he looked as puzzled as he felt. "You worry that step-Bob's asshole friends are going to randomly bonk me with lead pipes? 'S'okay, Crick—I think this was a one-time gig."

Crick rested his forehead on Deacon's chest for a moment and choked on a strangled laugh. "No, idiot. I'm afraid horrible, horrible shit is going to go down while I'm gone, and you're going to write it off with, 'Yeah... it was no big deal. Everyone gets their dick ripped off in a hideous farm equipment accident! And they always swell to six times their normal size and turn green after they're reattached. You worry too much, Crick! I'll let you know when I'm really hurt'!"

By the time he was done, Deacon was convulsing with laughter, and Crick was repeatedly socking him on the arm.

"It's not funny, Deacon! Goddammit! Take this seriously!"

Deacon looked at him and rolled his eyes. "Trust me, man. I take getting my dick ripped off *very* seriously! Especially now that I remember how to use it again!"

Crick finished off with one final smack on the arm and threw himself back against the pillows and scowled. "That's not what I'm talking about, asshole, and you know it!"

Deacon rubbed that dark, short hair again, kind of liking the way it prickled against his palm but not enough to want it to stay this short. "Then what *are* you talking about, baby?"

They both froze for a moment—it was an endearment, one they hadn't used before, and Deacon froze to see how Crick took it. He imagined Crick froze to taste it on his ear for the same reason.

Crick pulled the hand that was rubbing through his hair and kissed the palm gently, with a little bit of tongue, and Deacon found he was getting all squirmy again. "Please call me that again sometime," he said softly, "but right now, listen to what I'm saying. I'm leaving you alone, Deacon. I know I'm about the only soul on the planet you talk to besides Jon, but Jon isn't going to be there every day like I was. It kills me to think of things getting bad—really bad—and you there, alone, not able to tell a soul. If you can't even write it down—not even to me—where will you be, Deacon? I just want to know you'll be okay while I'm gone. If you're not honest with me, I'm not sure you'll be okay when I get back."

Deacon sighed at the end of this little speech and threw himself back against the pillows and crossed his arms over his chest self-protectively.

"You know what kills me to think about?"

Crick rolled over to look at him, but Deacon kept his gaze fixed firmly on the yellowing plaster ceiling of this less-than-opulent hotel. "Please tell me—baby."

"I worry that you won't come home. I worry that you'll be thinking about some dumbass complaint I make about my day-to-day bullshit, and you'll make some sort of fatal error, and then there will never be a time for you to come home and for things to get better. So tell me...." Deacon pinched the bridge of his nose hard to make the congestion in his head stop, to make the sadness go away until Crick was no longer there to be burdened by it. "Tell me what you want, Crick. I would rather push all my funky bullshit off until the end of the term, so when you get home you'll get it all, than to not have you come home at all, or to... to...." Fuck. Fuck. Fuck. *Say it, Deacon, make it real for him too, you spineless bastard!* "To have the worst happen on either end, and have you think it's all your fault and that you ever let me down. That right there is my worst worry, Carrick. So I'll make molehills out of mountains all I want, because once you're home, once I've got you back, odds are pretty fucking good they'll really be molehills, okay?"

Crick nodded, sniffled and sniffled hard, and Deacon finally looked at him and cursed himself because he made Crick cry. He reached out his arms, and Crick went willingly, sobbing his heart out on Deacon's chest while Deacon rubbed his back. He may have let a few tears slip, but not many. Carrick needed him—he could be anything, do anything, while Carrick needed him to be strong.

The three days went by so fast. They ordered in, took lots of showers, and used an entire bottle of lube. Crick was surprised that Deacon brought condoms (since Deacon had been celibate since Amy, and Crick had been celibate until Deacon) until he caught Deacon shoving them in Crick's duffel bag.

"Deacon!" Crick whined, and Deacon could tell he felt like a little kid.

"Crick!" Deacon whined back.

It was the night before Crick had to be back, and they were packing so Crick could get up in the morning, shower, dress, and walk out the door. Deacon would leave a few hours later, after Crick had taken the bus back to base.

Deacon had a towel wrapped around his waist, and Crick was wearing his boxers, and Crick came up behind him and started playing with the knot at Deacon's hips. "You really think I'm going to just wander into someone else's bed after this?"

Deacon's lips quirked up in spite of himself, but he didn't turn into Crick's long arms yet. No. Crick wouldn't just "wander" into someone's bed. "You actually saved your virginity for me, Crick. Do you have any idea how rare that is? If you were a girl, we could have sold you for extra cows or something." He stared thoughtfully—and a little too hard—at the zippered pocket where he'd shoved the condoms. He'd give anything for that pocket to never be opened.

"Then why...."

Deacon couldn't look at it anymore. He turned into Crick, and, rarity of rarities, rested his head on Crick's chest, because Crick was taller and it only made sense. Crick hadn't taken a shower since the last time they'd made love (fifteen minutes earlier), and he smelled tangy, like sex and sweat. Deacon put out a tight little tongue and tasted the sweat from a chest so hairless it might as well have been waxed.

"You're going to be a long way from home, farmboy," Deacon murmured, like they both didn't know this. "And there's going to be a big part of yourself that you're not going to be able to tell *anyone*. If you... if you get a chance for someone to hold you... to give you comfort... hell, just to know that part of you...." Deacon looked up, proud of his dry eyes until he saw Crick's stricken face. "Just take it, Crick. Think of it as a gift. It won't have anything to do with me—I know that." He wrapped his arms around Crick's waist and pulled him in tighter. "It will just be loneliness. I can't stand to think of you lonely, Carrick. It just...." It just broke his heart way, way worse than thinking of Crick with someone else.

Crick nodded, breathing hard into his hair. "I won't use them, you know."

"Please don't hurt yourself keeping that promise. Just let them be."

The next morning they both woke with the alarm, and after Crick shut it off, they spent a minute—just a minute, Deacon looked—lying in the morning stillness with Crick's arm wrapped around his chest and Crick's warm breathing against Deacon's cheek.

"Stay in bed," Crick murmured. "I want to think of you all soft. You smile at me different when you're in bed."

Deacon looked over his shoulder and, well, smiled. "How's that?"

"Any other time, your smile's all tight and busy...." Crick punctuated this with a hard kiss. "When you're in bed with me you smile sweeter... it's the one time you look most like your dad."

Deacon knew his mouth fell open in surprise, and Crick took full advantage of that and kissed him, hard and thoroughly and well enough to short out Deacon's brain and take the hurt away. He must have done it on purpose, Deacon thought with a little bit of bemusement, because by the time his brains were unscrambled, Crick had hopped out of bed and was halfway to dressed.

"You're not going to take a shower?" Deacon asked, feeling muzzy. Crick had topped the night before. He'd asked to. *I want to know all of you.* And now Deacon's body ached in unaccustomed places, and his heart ached all over, and he wasn't sure if he could make his body move fast enough to catch the new, improved, quick and efficient Crick as he charged through his morning routine.

Crick flashed a broken grin. "I want you on my skin as long as possible."

Deacon blushed, and Crick's broken grin fixed itself a little. He'd pulled on his T-shirt and his fatigue bottoms, and he leaned over, fully dressed, and kissed a space on Deacon's pale chest. Deacon had a classic farmer's tan, and he looked down and realized his skin was blotchy with his embarrassment.

"You blush all the way across your body," Crick said in wonder. His slow smile held a whole other kind of magic. "I knew you did it during sex, but… wow. I made you blush all over!"

Deacon caught his breath and blushed even harder, while Crick laughed delightedly. "Oh God!" He couldn't recall ever in his life ever feeling so naked, and he sat up and pulled his knees up under the covers and buried his face in his hands.

Crick managed a kiss on the hair at his temple in spite of all that. "It's perfect," he said softly. "It's like a gift. I get to take it with me—I'm the only one in the world who knows."

Deacon peered at him through his fingers. *Oh, Carrick, you're the only one in the world who's ever known me. How could you doubt it?*

Crick grinned and then threw on his boots and cast a panicked look at the clock. He was taking a bus back to Benning, and he was cutting the time close as it was. In moments, he'd thrown his duffel over his shoulder and was coming across the bed for a last kiss.

"Smile for me, Deacon—please? Let me take that with me too."

Even in the awfulness of the next two years, Deacon often thought that smile was the bravest thing he'd ever done. "Love you."

"Love you back." And then there was a tender, bitter kiss and he was gone. Deacon listened to his footfalls disappear down the corridor and the slam of the door leading to the outside stairs.

Then he rolled over to where Crick's warmth and smell were evaporating from the sheets and buried his face in them and howled sobs like an infant until he could barely breathe.

Chapter 9

An Elephant Across the Ocean

YEAH—Crick had heard it, and it was the truth. A whole lot of being in the Army was hurry up and wait. He'd been there for three months, and he'd treated one helicopter crash, a whole lot of heatstroke, and a hat full (or, well, more than that) of dysentery and nary a bullet wound. He assumed this would change, but he wasn't really looking to hasten it along any.

Saying Iraq was hot was like saying the sun was hot. It was such an understatement it needed to be said again and again and again with a whole lot of force just to believe that this much suckage was not in the imagination.

Crick was stationed near Farah, and he hadn't the faintest fucking clue where that was in relationship to anything else in the whole rest of the world, and he told Deacon so in his first letter home.

Deacon's reply back had been horrified.

> Jesus Fucking Christ, kid—if you don't know where you are, you don't know what to expect!

That particular letter had come with a care package of snacks and books (Deacon sent two of these a month—it made Crick very popular with his unit), several general maps of the Persian Gulf, and CNN reports of where the latest fighting was.

And whether Deacon had planned to send it or not, it had also come with a fucking truckload of worry.

For all the shit he didn't say in his letters, the shit he did say was gnawing at Crick's stomach worse than the two-day-chili trots.

> Forgive the writing. I broke my fucking hand again when
> Shooting Star threw me. I may have to ride your horse for
> a while if I can't keep my goddamned seat.

Deacon's horse, Shooting Star, was a prickly tempered mare, and Deacon was about the only one who really could ride her. But even so, Deacon hadn't been thrown from a horse in Crick's memory, and probably before—that horse all but rolled over and simpered for Deacon when she usually bit, kicked, or generally despised all the rest of the human race. What in the hell was happening if Deacon couldn't keep his seat? Of course, Crick's favorite riding horse, Comet, was as sweet as they came, and Crick was glad his gelding was getting some attention, but still… it was troubling. But not as troubling as the letter that came a month later.

> I tried visiting before your folks got home—Missy and
> Crystal told me they hadn't seen Benny in a while. I think
> she's been hanging out with the kids in front of the liquor
> store. I'll see if I can't hunt her down next time I'm there.

Okay. Two things there making Crick *very* uneasy. The first was that Benny was missing.

The second was the bit about the liquor store.

"So?" said Crick's transport driver, Private Jimmy Davidovic. Private Jimmy drove, Crick tended the casualties in the back, and together they got them back to the medical facilities outside of Farah. If the fighting—or the dysentery or the heatstroke—was really bad or any farther, Crick got to ride the Black Hawk, which on the one hand was seven shades of cool, but on the other scared the hell out of him, mostly because one of his first ops had been a helicopter crash, and it had looked like a year of Blood Alley all in one mangled knot of metal, body parts, and blood.

"So Deacon doesn't drink," Crick said as they were trudging across the camp to the chow tent. They had missed lunch doing a transpo. Hopefully there was something they could grab that wouldn't make them need medical attention themselves. Deacon's letters tended to be very... general. Crick didn't mind on the one hand—it meant he could share letters from "his friend at home" without worrying about what the rest of the unit would think.

On the other hand, he was dying for something—anything—that would let him know Deacon was really okay, and, yes, really thinking about him. This "news from home" shit was starting to chafe Crick like wet underwear.

"What—so he had more than a beer a night and needed a refill?" Jimmy was saying, and Crick looked at him with all of his irritation in his scowl.

"He doesn't drink, period," Crick snapped, more worried than ever. He didn't drink. He hadn't ever gotten drunk. As far as Crick knew. Before he'd left Deacon all alone.

Fuck.

Jimmy looked at him and shrugged. "Jesus, Crick—how bad can it be? I mean, he's still writing and still sending you cookies! That makes the guy better than half the wives here—he gets any more forthcoming, folks would suspect something between you two!"

Crick shot Jimmy a look of pure and honest disgust. He was starting to attribute the fact that the Army wasn't picking up on his gayness more to the fact that people in general were dumber than camel shit than to anything else. If it walked like a soldier and talked like a soldier and dressed in fatigues, it wasn't going to want to fuck another guy. Bullshit. Crick had spotted three "like-minded" guys in his first month. The fact that they hadn't started their own little club was probably because they had nothing in common besides the one thing they couldn't talk about, but that didn't mean that Crick didn't want to just spit whenever Jimmy or someone else went off with the not-so-subtle innuendo.

"I'm telling you, Jimmy—the guy doesn't drink."

They dropped it for the moment, but Crick couldn't help be haunted by the last time they'd been joined together. Crick had been inside Deacon, liking the feeling but more interested in seeing if Deacon liked it. He'd been watching Deacon's face curiously, loving the shifting dark of his green eyes and the pouty concentration of that full lower lip. But looking at Deacon's face that day, he'd seen more than just passion. He'd seen… wonder. Surprise. A shy sort of ecstasy. Playfulness. The same starry-eyed, happy regard that Crick knew shone out of his eyes when he was looking at Deacon.

It had taken him three months to ask himself why he kept pulling that memory out like a crime scene photo to be looked at again and again. It hadn't been the best sex they'd ever had—Crick was uneasy as a top. He liked Deacon there just on general principal. But now, looking at Deacon's last few letters, the ones that sounded the oldest, the most tired, the reason hit him.

Deacon had looked young then. He'd looked young because he *was* young. He was young and vulnerable and as new to their awakened love as Carrick was. And Deacon had the weight of The Pulpit on his shoulders, and, he felt, the weight of Crick's happiness. Crick had spent so much time looking up to the "older" Deacon that he'd forgotten that Deacon had never really had a youth himself.

Until he'd been lost in Crick's arms.

Oh God. What in the hell was going on at home?

Deacon—

Nothing going here—after that helicopter crash in the first month it's been all about the barf and the shit and the heat. Yanno, I used to think sliced bread was the bomb—now I've got a serious hard-on for the ice-packs that fit in our helmets. For the army, that's some decent thinking right there.

Gotta tell you, buddy—I'm starting to worry a little. So far, you've fallen off your horse, broken your hand, gotten sick more in three months than you have in twelve years, and wrenched your shoulder doing something you didn't want to explain. I know you said you'd save all the bad shit for when I get back, but I'm starting to worry that I'll come through this with nothing worse than a tan and there'll be nothing left of you to come home to.

Please Deacon, write me something real. I've got more worry here with radio silence than I'd have with the plain truth, even if the plain truth is something awful.

Crick

Chapter 10

Something Real

THE truth—the plain truth was that the night Deacon got back from Fort Benning, Jon brought a bottle of Ketel One vodka to The Pulpit and got Deacon drunk for the first time in his life. And Deacon stayed that way pretty much for the next three months.

He learned to play it smart. After his mare threw him when he downed two shots of tequila with a sandwich for lunch, he decided to take a lesson in how to be a functional alcoholic from his mother. He woke up, threw up, downed a handful of painkillers with a liter of water for the hangover, had crackers for lunch, some protein for dinner, and as much of whatever he had in the house as it took him to pass out for dessert. He didn't even seem to be getting a beer-belly, which, if he'd been sober or thinking, he might have been sort of proud of. In fact, he seemed to be losing weight, which made his morning runs easier as well.

Patrick may have looked at him narrowly when he tossed his cookies behind the barn every so often, and Jon had been leaving increasingly frantic messages on the phone that Deacon hadn't really wanted to return. He'd broken his hand when he got thrown, wrenched his shoulder when he rode a horse into the side of the barn as a result of a hangover, and had developed a serious shake in his fingers if seven o'clock rolled around to find him sober. In spite of all that, he was starting to see the attraction. Was there any price too high to pay for that long, lovely slide to oblivion when the house rang with silence like a cathedral rang with bells?

Write me something real.

Okay, well, shit, Deacon thought on the way to the liquor store, that might be too high a price to pay.

The liquor store was barely legal distance from the grade school, right along the main Levee Oaks drag of M street, and the first time he'd gone with the intention of buying enough alcohol to make him drunk for a week, he'd felt mildly guilty and a whole lot deviant—but not today.

Today, he stood in front of the liquor store for at least fifteen minutes, feeling his body starting to shake with just the proximity of all of that lovely alcohol. Deacon didn't discriminate—if he had something spicy for dinner, he'd rather not drink tequila just because the rebound was a little more unpleasant, but other than that, he liked to switch it up. Jack was good, Stoli better, Tanqueray even better than that. He had no experience with mixers, but since the taste wasn't the point, he didn't think he should start now.

Write me something real.

His hands started to shake harder, and his forehead popped out in the cold sweats. The thought of telling Crick that he spent his days dreaming about clear poison was enough to keep him there, leaning on the hood of his car, for the rest of the night. Crick had asked for something real. If this was the only real he had, he had to fix it, because that was the shittiest reality he could burden Crick with, and he refused to do it.

"What's the matter, Deacon? DTs so bad you can't make it to the store?"

Deacon blinked and tried to focus his darkening vision on the owner of the voice. "I'm not going to the store," he said faintly. "I thought I was going to, but I can't." His vision cleared, and he got a good look at the girl.

"Benny?" he asked, surprised. She looked like hell. Her face was lean and dirty, and her teeth looked like they hadn't been brushed in a while. Her hair was still dyed that shocking red, but it was stringy and knotted around her face.

"I'm surprised you recognized me," she sneered. "You've walked right by me now for a week!"

A week? "I looked for you," he told her, his voice feeling far away. Oh God—all that time spent worrying about her, fretting over Crick's little sister, and she'd been right *here,* with a front row seat to him flushing his life down the toilet? Fucking Christ.

"When?" she asked, and even with his vision swimming, he could tell she hid a lot of desperate hope behind that angry word.

"For two months," he said, seriously. "For two months I sneaked by the house to bring dinner for Crystal and Missy. For two months I asked after you. They'd tell me you'd stopped by but they never knew when."

"Why'd you stop?" she asked suspiciously, and Deacon had to look away.

"Your mom caught me there—threatened to call the cops. Called me some sort of sex deviant." God, that had stung. Melanie Coats could barely clothe her own children—they'd been cooking their own dinner since Crick had left—and one glimpse of Deacon feeding her kids peanut butter and jelly sandwiches, and she was mother of the fucking year. Deacon found he could look Benny in the eye about this matter after all. "I didn't really have a choice, Benny. I'm no one to your family, really."

Benny looked stricken, and with that look, her shoulders collapsed, and her hands tightened in her pockets, and her oversized hooded sweater got tight against her middle, and Deacon got a look at the thing that maybe made Benny run away. *Oh Christ—Benny. What are you, fourteen years old?*

"My brother loves you," she said through a tight throat, tears making tracks of clean grime down her cheeks. "How can you be nothing?"

Oh God. *My brother loves you.* Deacon swallowed, fought nausea, and swallowed again. "It's been hard," he said softly. *Write something real.* That there was the most honesty he'd spoken since Crick had left him in Georgia.

Benny reached out and took his sweating hand in hers. "Yeah," she said softly.

"You told your parents yet, Benny, or did you just decide to run away before they kicked you out?" He said it kindly and without judgment, and she seemed to appreciate the honesty.

"Well, Deacon, you're not the only one who went to the wrong place for comfort when my brother left." She glanced at her swollen stomach with troubled eyes. "I'm not eating enough," she said apologetically. "I want to, but my friends can only put me up a night at a time."

Deacon nodded. "You're welcome at The Pulpit, Benny. You always are."

Benny looked at him with a sort of bitter betrayal. "I won't live with another drunk, Deacon Winters. Bob is bad enough."

Oh God. She must have been so desperate, only to see him walk blindly past her, bent on easing his own misery. "I'm officially on the wagon," he said, trying to say it like he wasn't two minutes away from tossing his cookies and running screaming through the door of the liquor store just begging for something, anything, to ease the pain of withdrawal.

"I'll believe it when I see it," she snapped, and he guessed he must look every bit as desperate as he felt. But he wasn't going to let Crick's sister down—hell, what he'd been doing for the last three months was bad enough. He couldn't walk away from her. Dammit, the girl needed him.

"I'll bring you proof," he said quietly.

"Proof how?" Okay, fine. She had the right to be suspicious.

"I'll find something. You need to go to your parents' first. Eat. Bathe. Get your shit together. See if you can't get them to enroll you in independent study or something—it'll be easier if they do it and a pain in the ass if I try. What's today, Sun... Sunday?" That shiver had been hard, dammit. Fuck. He didn't have long before he had to be home, alone, someplace where this shit could work its way out of his system without witnesses.

"Yeah, Sunday." She looked at him like she knew what his damage was, and he gritted his teeth and stood up a little straighter.

"You go do that. I'll even drive you to your folks and stay outside to make sure they don't do anything too drastic. You put up with their screaming and their bullshit for four days. I'll be back on Friday for you and your shit. I'll have proof. I swear to God."

"Swearing's easy," she said, so obviously miserable for something to believe in that he wanted to just take her home right now. But he knew—had a bone deep feeling and *knew* what was around the corner for him, and he refused to let her be a witness to that. If he had his druthers, no one would.

"All right then. I swear to Crick." He stuck out his hand and she took it, wincing a little at the clamminess of it.

"You going to make it, driving me home?" she asked uncertainly. "You look pretty fucked up, Deacon."

"I'll make it," he promised, and then he tried the truth—he'd been good at it once. "But it's gonna be close. Get your ass in the truck, Benny, and remember not to tell them about the baby until I come get you on Friday. I'll be ready then."

He got her home and waited for her "all-clear" wave at the window. Her face was taut and angry, and he swore to himself again not to let her down.

He blew chunks twice on his way home and barely managed to get himself out of the car and into the bathroom before he lost it again, with nothing more than stomach acid for company.

The next morning, he was huddled in the bathtub, naked under a blanket, resting his head on the toilet seat from a kneeling position. His soiled clothes were wadded in the corner. He heard Patrick calling his name into the front door as he had every morning for most of Deacon's life, and called out hoarsely.

"Patrick—man, do me a favor, would you?"

Patrick had been their hired hand, Parish's best friend, and Deacon's only extended family for most of his entire life. Deacon figured that facing him from under that blanket was about the bravest thing he ever did.

"Jesus Christ, Deacon—are you okay?"

Deacon wrapped the blanket tighter, figured he was about done puking for the next thirty seconds, and slumped back into the bathtub. "Patrick, do me a favor, would you?" he repeated. "Could you give Jon a call and tell him I need some fucking Valium?" His lips were cracked, he realized. He was so dehydrated they were bleeding. "And a glass of water would rock the house."

Facing Patrick had been bad. Facing Jon was worse.

"Deacon?" Jon came to the edge of the bathtub warily about an hour later—as well he might be wary: Deacon had thrown up most of the glass of water about two minutes before Jon walked into the house.

"What's left of him," Deacon chattered. *Please, Jon, please, just put the fucking Valium on the sink and let me deal with this alone.*

"Jesus." Jon sounded legitimately shaken. "Deacon, what's wrong with you? You look like you've got the mother of all bugs—what's Valium going to do?"

Deacon's vision flirted with black and then resolved itself to gray. "Valium is a benzo." Deacon shortened the name because he wasn't sure he could say it all, but otherwise he thought his "textbook voice" did him proud. "It's used to treat alcohol withdrawal symptoms, reduce mortality, and will hopefully keep me from thinking my skin is crawling off my bones... so, did you bring any?"

Jon handed him a tablet from what looked to be a little brown bottle and filled a cup by the sink with some water for him. Deacon downed them both and rested his head on the cool toilet seat for a moment while his body decided if it was going to accept the offering of the Valium or make his life complete by yakking it back up.

"It's Amy's prescription," Jon said numbly. "She was really freaking out during the bar exam. She doesn't take it anymore. Did you say alcohol withdrawal?"

"God, you're quick." Oh... Deacon's stomach was emptier than step-Bob's soul. All it took was a little bit of chemical grace to bestow a miracle on him. With a sigh, Deacon relaxed a little, sank to his ass in the bathtub, and leaned his head on the side of the tub instead of the toilet.

"But, Deacon, you've only been drunk once in your life... three months ago."

"Yeah," Deacon admitted, wishing he could die of embarrassment quickly instead of dying of the DTs slow. "Welcome to the hangover."

Jon blanched and sat down on the floor and then grimaced. Deacon hadn't exactly been right on target with all his shots. "I did this to you?"

Oh fuck. "Don't be an asshole. *I* did this to me. It runs in the blood—it's what my mom died of, I should have known better." Woohee! There went that little bit of information. Go Valium!

"Oh God...." Jon looked like that made him feel worse. "Deacon, you didn't tell me...."

Now he was starting to sweat a little... and his sweat smelled putrid, like living in his own vomit and diarrhea hadn't been enough. "I didn't tell anyone," he murmured. "Parish barely told *me*. It's not your fault, man— the only person who knows is...." Deacon couldn't say his name. Not in this condition. Oh Jesus... how was he ever going to look at Crick again?

"Crick." Jon said it for him and then shook himself earnestly. "Hell, Deacon—we've got to get you into a program or rehab or something. Twenty-eight days and all that shit. I'll book you a spot—my treat."

"Fuck that," Deacon muttered. "What day is it?"

"Monday, why?"

"Because I need this dump cleaned up by Friday, that's why. Crick's little sister is coming here to live, and I need every bottle out of here and something pink in Crick's old room, and I need to"—Oh crap, the nausea hadn't left for good... *Fight it... fight it... there we go*—"I need to give a passable imitation of a human being by then."

"Crick's little sister?" Jon sounded downright dazed. "What in the hell...?"

"She's pregnant, Jon." Deacon wondered if his psyche could take a recitation of his wrongs again, and then he figured, why the fuck not? Wasn't there something about an alcoholic coming clean? "I passed her going into the liquor store for a week, and didn't see her. I... I promised I'd give her a place to come home to, since I let her down so bad."

An after-shiver passed through him then, and he convulsed a little around the blanket and then stabilized. It felt like maybe the worst of it had passed—at least until he couldn't live without the Valium again.

"Four days?" Jon was looking at him like he was crazy. Well, he was a functional alcoholic—didn't crazy come with the T-shirt? "Where are we going to start?"

Deacon sighed and made to push himself up in the tub. He wobbled, his hands down on the side of it and his ass in the air, and then he pushed off against the wall and stood. Well, he was used to his vision being black anyway.

"How's about a shower?" he asked, trying to sound confident.

Jon nodded, and stood up himself, grimacing at the what-all he had sat in. "I get it after you. You got any clean clothes?"

"Loads," Deacon told him. It was the truth—he'd been wearing the same clothes for days at a time. Who needed to use the clean ones in the drawer? Unselfconsciously, because Jon had seen his shit before and didn't give a fuck, he let the blanket slide down, and he gave it a weak-armed pitch to the corner where his soiled clothes were. "And if you could burn all that, I'd take it as a personal fav—"

"Holy fuck," Jon whispered, staring at him, and Deacon's head felt like it weighed six thousand pounds. He didn't think he could look down at himself, so he yanked the curtain shut and turned on the water blindly. It was freezing when it came out, and he almost screamed. His skin was hypersensitive, and it was all he could do not to double over and resume his position huddled on the floor of the bathtub, shivering under the spray. Jon was still outside, and Deacon heard him sit down heavily on the toilet so he could start taking off his shoes. When he spoke again, his voice sounded strange, even over the sound of the shower.

"Deacon, you're all... you're all bones, dammit—when in the fuck was the last time you had a meal?"

"Jon...."

"No, man—I'm serious. You couldn't call me? You broke your fucking hand or something?"

Deacon actually felt a laugh push at his chest. "Yeah, I broke my hand—and wrenched my shoulder, and I think I might have broken my nose on the doorframe one night, but I must have set it before I fell asleep...."

"*Stop it!*" Jon yelled, and just when the water was starting to get warm, he wrenched open the curtain, and Deacon was there, in the middle of every bad nightmare he'd ever had. He was shivering, naked, and he'd fucked up. His life had spiraled out of control, and there wasn't a person he could sob on for refuge because he'd managed to lose everyone he cared about just by being alive.

Feebly, he pulled at the shower curtain, trying to get some privacy so he could wish he was dead, and Jon just kept it open, looking at him.

"You couldn't ask for help? Dammit, Deacon." Jon's voice broke for real, and if Deacon thought he'd felt like Death shit him out and served him as the dog's breakfast before... well, now he knew how it felt when the dog threw him back up and buried him in guilt. "Why didn't you call me sooner?"

Deacon didn't answer. He reached for the shampoo and dropped it instead, and Jon put his hand on Deacon's shoulder and stopped him from bending down.

"I'll get it," he snapped. "If you bend over you'll fall down."

It was probably true, so Deacon let him.

"You still didn't answer my question." Heedless of the water on the floor—it needed a good washing anyway—Jon kept the shower curtain open and soaped up Deacon's hair while Deacon stood there like a child. He wondered vaguely why there was nothing sexual about their situation, but he missed Crick so bad, he couldn't bring himself to care.

"What question?" Oh… damn. Damn. That was another person touching him. It suddenly didn't matter if sex was involved or not—it was human contact. Deacon kept his eyes closed and hoped Jon couldn't see what was shower and what was not as it slid weakly down his face. Human contact. Human touch. It was almost as good as booze—who knew?

"Why didn't you call me sooner?"

And now Deacon was *really* glad he had his eyes closed. "Because I didn't want you to see me like this," he whispered. Suddenly Jon's arm was around his shoulder, getting sopping wet down through the dress shirt that Jon had been wearing when he walked in.

"Too bad, Deacon," Jon murmured, and Deacon clung to him, completely ashamed and unable to stop himself. "You're one of the blessings of my life—hell, you're one of the blessings of my marriage, do you know that? I get to see you however you are, whatever shape you're in. You'll always be a blessing, okay?" Jon's whole body was in the shower now, completely clothed and wrapped around Deacon like a friendly, warm blanket. Jon seemed to be crying some more, and Deacon didn't feel quite like such a pussy as he gave into his weakness and leaned on his friend.

"All things considered," Deacon mumbled against his friend's sodden chest, "I bet you're wishing we'd sprung for the fancy silverware as a gift instead."

"Nah," Jon mumbled against his shoulder. "We got two of those from Amy's parents. We've only got one of you."

Deacon had some sort of fantasy about getting out of the shower, grabbing something to eat, and getting started on the house. Jon barely managed to get him dried, dressed, and into bed where he could sleep off the violence of his body's withdrawal. He woke up towards the evening and pattered out of the bedroom, looking around the house like it wasn't his.

"What," he muttered, "did the house fairy visit? Who cleaned up all the bottles?" He rounded the hallway corner to the living room and almost turned back around and went back to bed. "Awww, fucking Jesus."

"Good morning to you too, Deac," Amy said dryly, glancing at him over her shoulder. She was standing in the kitchen, working on something at the stove. "What, did you think Jon wasn't going to tell me?"

The living room was spotless—not an empty bottle or old plate of food in sight, and someone appeared to have dusted as well. The kitchen wasn't looking bad either, but there were four big Hefty bags by the door to the porch, waiting to carry the bottles to the recycler.

"I was sort of hoping you'd stay away out of sheer disgust," he mumbled with complete truth, feeling his eyes water again.

She put the spoon down and turned her little brown face towards him, and he saw her eyes widen and thought longingly of going back to bed. "No," she said, her voice a little broken. She scrubbed at her cheek viciously and turned back towards the stove. "I may beat the shit out of you at a later date, but you're not shaking us that easy."

With a sigh, Deacon came all the way into the living room and perched himself on a stool at the counter that divided it from the kitchen. Without even asking, she filled up a glass with water and set it down in front of him. He drank greedily, and as she filled it again, he asked, "Where's Jon?"

"Feeding the horses," she said shortly, and he hopped off the stool with a guilty little thump.

"Shit—I've got to go help him."

"Sit the fuck down, Deacon." The words came out like a whip-crack, and Deacon glared at her.

"I've been feeding the damned horses my whole life."

"Don't care." She turned towards him again, and she'd given up on keeping the evidence of tears to herself.

"Aw… dammit, Amy." He moved in to the kitchen to pat her on the back. "Don't cry. Man, I'm just not fucking worth it…."

"You just shut up, Deacon Winters," she sniffled, launching herself at him in a stealth and attack hug. He hugged her back, and she choked a sob as her hands felt his shoulder blades cutting through his worn T-shirt.

Then she pushed away from him and turned back to the stove. "Shut up, sit down, and for Christ's sake eat something. You look like hell."

"I'm fine," he lied as pulled the stool around from the counter, and if he thought she was mad before, he'd never seen her really angry.

"Fine?" her voice cracked. "Fine? Deacon, remember when I got drunk after the game that one time, and you held my head while I puked on my shoes?"

Deacon held back a chuckle. "You got drunk a little, our senior year," he admitted.

"You didn't judge me. Not once. You worried, you fretted, you *begged* me not to let Crick see, but you didn't judge." There was a splat, and then a huge bowl of Mexican chicken soup was shoved roughly at him over the cutting board. The spoon got thrown in with a plop, and then a hunk of cornbread with butter. She glared at him, and he got the hint and started to eat gingerly, and then with some more enthusiasm as his stomach promised to behave.

"You were just being a little wild," he mumbled through a mouthful of El Pollo del Soleil. It was really very good.

"And you were just being a lot sad!" she snapped. "Did you think we were going to hold it against you, that you got sad?"

He didn't have an answer for that. The enormity of being drunk for three months, of lying to Crick and Jon and Amy, of letting down Benny—well, it just didn't seem to be covered by "sad."

"And you thought you'd do it all yourself," she muttered, trying to get him to respond. He still wouldn't look at her, so he guessed she figured she'd try another tack. "Do you remember my friend, the one I brought home from college?"

"Karen?" he asked—there had been a couple of girls Amy had introduced him to, but Karen had been the most memorable.

"The one you took to the hospital because she was bleeding from a botched abortion?" Amy snapped. "Yeah, Deacon—that's the one. Did I tell you she went into med school?"

Deacon shook his head. "No."

"Did I tell you that she tells people to this day that you're the one who inspired her? She says that anyone who could be so kind to someone so piss-stupid has to make you want to do something better with your life."

"Oh Jesus." What part of this was supposed to make him feel better when he could barely hold a spoon without shaking and his body was already begging him for one more fucking shot of whatever the hell he could find?

"Well she sent me a prescription for Valium because I asked and mine isn't strong enough. What she sent should be enough to last you through detox, but she thought I was kidding when I told her how much we guessed you weighed. She put her med license on the line to do that, Deacon, and I didn't even ask her to. She volunteered for you, because she says you saved her life—man, that's one person. One person you touched, and you hardly knew her. You and Parish—you've had over sixteen muckrakers, and Crick may be the only one you kept, but the others owe you both a helluva lot. You're going to take a lifetime of being there for the whole rest of the world and just...." She'd been a whirlwind of activity through this speech—dishing out two more bowls, pouring milk for the three of them from groceries she and Jon had apparently bought, throwing stuff into the sink with undue force. But now she just froze in the kitchen and looked at him with red-rimmed, haunted eyes.

"Just shit it away in a bathtub alone?" she sobbed, and Deacon put his soup spoon down and went to comfort her again. Her tiny little body shook against his and he tried a tentative, "I'm sorry."

"You could have died, Deacon," she said against his chest. "She says that with all the weight you've lost, with how much you must have been drinking... if Patrick hadn't called us in a fucking panic, you could have *died*!"

"Thank you," he muttered. "Thanks for coming... you know, bailing me out."

"Don't thank us!" she ordered, even though the sound was muffled against him and she was clinging to him hard enough to make him stagger. "Don't thank us... just don't do it again. And I don't mean don't drink—relapses happen. People fuck up. Just don't... don't make us scrape you up off the floor to help you, Deacon! For God's sake—"

"Shhh," he hushed, and Jon walked in at that point. Deacon looked up and gave a little jerk of his chin for Jon to come take over comfort duty, and the big asshole wrapped his arms around Deacon's back and Amy's tiny shoulders instead.

"What she said," Jon murmured, and Deacon, surrounded by his friends in a way he didn't know he could be, muttered broken promises back.

"I'll ask for help... I swear. I won't ever make you do this again."

They broke up the little group hug eventually, and Jon and Amy stood in the kitchen and ate while Deacon kept his spot on the stool. He had dropped his spoon twice when he heard a rather meaningful clearing of the throat.

"I believe you're slacking on that little resolution," Jon said, half teasing, half angry.

"I'm not," Deacon muttered, but he was trying to keep his teeth from chattering. "I don't want to get too depend... too depend... too dependent on the fucking Valium."

Jon fiddled with the bottle in his pocket and slapped a tab in front of Deacon on the cutting board, next to his milk, then turned around and stalked out of the kitchen.

Deacon sighed and downed the tablet, then turned a rather disgruntled face to Amy. "This is going to take a little bit of work," he said thoughtfully.

Amy raised her eyebrows and took a bite of soup. "So's a teenaged girl—are you sure you know what to do with one around the house? Especially a pregnant one? Now?"

Deacon shrugged. "I don't know a lot about teenaged girls," he conceded. "But I know a lot about you. And I know a lot about Crick. She may be built like you, but you know, she's wired exactly like Crick."

Amy laughed a little and conceded the point. "I think you're right—but I think I'll come by to help anyway."

"That would be much appreciated." Deacon tried another bite of barley and chicken and realized that even though the Valium had kicked in and the nausea had faded, he was still full. He pushed it away and sighed. "It will help with the good faith thing, too. I told her I'd have proof that I would be there for her. I think maybe having you guys around will help prove it."

Amy took Deacon's bowl and put it in the sink thoughtfully. "Have you thought about a program, Deacon? You know, twelve steps, that sort of thing?"

Deacon thought about it and shivered. "Amy, I have enough trouble asking you and Jon to come here and help. Do you really think I'll get all excited about testimonials and complete strangers?"

Amy nodded. "I guess there's no halfway for you, either. I mean… one drink is off the wagon—there is no moderation."

"Not in my family," Deacon agreed. "If I've bought a bottle, it's a pretty sure sign I'm in trouble."

Jon stalked back in with a sheaf of papers in his hand and the bathroom scale under his arm. Apparently he'd been to Deacon's computer in the study.

"Stand on this," he barked, and Deacon sighed. Really—how much more humiliating would an AA meeting be anyway? He stood and looked surprised and then mortified. Jesus… he knew his sweats had been sliding off his ass and even his underwear was baggy, but….

"You're six feet tall and…." Jon's jaw tightened, and his movie-star prettiness burned away in the heat of his anger and concern. "Six feet tall and one-hundred and thirty-five pounds. Fuck."

Deacon didn't have anything to say to that, really, so he waited for Jon to continue.

"Here," Jon muttered. "I looked it up. Here's your body weight—Jesus Christ, Deacon, you couldn't have sprung for the beef jerky with the Jack Daniels?—and here's your height and here"—he pulled out a highlighter and circled the number—"is the maximum and minimum milligram dosage for Valium per day. The info I got says you should be taking it for about a week. That's a week for you to take somewhere between these two numbers—and you have now officially taken the minimum dosage. Are you good now? Is your machismo fulfilled? Can you just give yourself a fucking break and recover?"

"Yes, Parish," Deacon said humbly—and when Jon glared at him and saw the glimmer of humor in his eyes, he promptly smacked him upside the head.

He had one year, eight months, and fourteen days to go.

Crick—

I'm sorry—you're right. I haven't really been all there for
you, and I should have. I hit sort of a rough patch there
for a while—let's just say that any alcohol is too much for
me, and leave it at that. This box is late too—there's a
reason for that, but it's not important now—there's too
much other shit to talk about and I want to get to it.

Now brace yourself—I've got some good news and some
difficult news, but mostly it's good news. We hope you'll
think it's good news.

We found Benny (or rather, Benny found me), and she's
no longer obligated to put up with step-Bob because she's
going to have to put up with me. She's moved into your
old room. (We cleaned out the last of your, um, calendars
under the bed, btw—fucking subtle, Crick. And so fun to
explain.) Anyway, she gets your old room, and in
February, her baby gets mine. I sincerely hope you had no
illusions about moving back to that room, btw, because
you've got your choice of colors—pink, purple, orchid,
fuchsia, mauve, rose, violet and lavender—with a little bit
of off-white thrown in for fun. The house is probably
freaking out from all the estrogen. One more girl and the
front windows are gonna grow tits.

Your sister is settling in fine, mostly. We've had to spend
some time getting to trust each other, but Amy and Jon
have come by to help. She didn't want to write—she's
sort of embarrassed, although I told her you'd just be glad
she's okay. (I know I am.) I gave her a camera for when
the baby comes, and she took a lot of pictures instead—
she wanted me to tell you that they're her letter, and she
knows you'll know what she's saying. She's thought long
and hard about whether to keep the baby, Crick—I don't
know what you'll say about this, but in the end, she said
that you and I were the reason she's keeping it. I told her
that the baby would always have a home, and so would
she. I hope that's okay—and if it's not, you'll just have to
make it home to bitch at me about it, right?

The next care package—and the next letter—will come a
lot sooner, I promise. I can't promise to not let you down

again, but I promise to try my hardest not to. Take care of yourself, Carrick James.

Deacon

It didn't say enough. It didn't say that Deacon's body felt dead and senseless without Crick beside him. It didn't say that he dreamt of the taste of Crick's skin and woke up breathless because Crick's breathing wasn't in the house. It didn't say that one night, after he got Crick's next letter, he woke up in the darkness, scared awake in his own bed, with his own come splashed across his belly and tears he didn't know he'd shed stinging the creases in his eyes.

Because that was just about too real, even for Crick.

Chapter 11

Lessons From Walkabout

CRICK didn't know that the package was a week late at first because he was busy getting lost in the middle of the fucking Iraqi desert.

He swore it wasn't his fault.

A convoy had broken down ten miles from camp and been ambushed. Crick was flown in to help triage, and Jimmy met him with transpo to get the least wounded back if the choppers couldn't hold them.

The chaos on the chopper had been replaced by chaos on the ground, and all Crick knew was that when he got to the ground, the whole fucking world seemed to be eighteen-year-olds calling him Second-goddamned-Lieutenant.

Crick managed. He'd done large-scale trauma before when a Greyhound bus carrying elderly casino patrons had gotten rammed by a semi on Blood Alley back home. There was considerably less panic and screaming here on the ground, even if the background noise was bullets and could kill you.

Crick himself felt safe—a bunch of those eighteen-year-olds surrounded him with flak-shields, and he managed to triage and treat, and together they got the most critically wounded on the Black Hawk and sent it back to camp, where a doctor with more bars than Crick would try to put them back together again.

This left Crick and the kid with a bullet in his leg hunkering down in the shade of a tank and wishing the M-16s would shut the fuck up. He was beginning to think getting shot was a serious possi-fucking-bility.

It was maybe the first time he'd been happy to see Jimmy since the two of them had been assigned together. Of course, the minute they got out of sight of the convoy, the armored van—which had apparently taken a bullet in the oil pan—gave up the fucking ghost and went tits-up.

Jimmy had done a considerable amount of bitching then—he wanted to sit tight with the van and hope for a rescue. Crick was not particularly sure that Jimmy had caught on to the general urgency of the combat site. Those boys had been settling down for the long haul, waiting to fight out the rest of the afternoon and hoping that the Black Hawks would be back in time to bail *them* out. Crick didn't like their chances of living bullet-hole free if they stayed there, broiling in the sun.

Finally, it came down to stars and bars. As a medic, Crick had one, and as driver, Jimmy had squat. Crick rigged a travois out of a sheet, gave the poor bleeding private a backpack full of ice packs and medical supplies, grabbed his own backpack full of water with some of those freeze-dried food packets, and made whining-like-a-girl Jimmy grab some more water and the guns.

"Why can't you carry the guns?"

"Because I'm dragging the fucking patient, asshole!" Crick declined to mention that his luck with the M-16 had gotten no better in the past five months. The M-4 he could handle just fine—but the M-16 was still giving him no goddamned joy at all. He was the only person in the unit to have one jam during a firing session. Twice.

They had just managed to haul Private Blood-loss up the nearest rise when Crick saw them—what appeared to be a squad of the bad guys, marching down the middle of the road like they either a) were heading to go wipe out the unit Crick and Jimmy had just left, or b) owned the country (and Crick was still trying to figure out whether that was true). Either way, he and Jimmy managed to haul ass off the road before they were spotted. It was a minor miracle.

And it got them lost.

Not too lost, though. Because of Deacon and his goddamned maps and CNN reports, Crick actually had a working knowledge of his immediate geographical area, thank you very much. But they still had to travel rough terrain, on foot, dragging a wounded man behind them.

Their first night out, Private Blood-loss (also known as Andrew Carpenter, a polite young man from Georgia with skin the color of an Egyptian sky at night) almost got bitten by one of the nasty little sand-colored vipers that came out in the dark to hunt. Crick had seen the thing crawling up on Carpenter's travois and had thrown one of the used ice packs behind it. The snake turned to strike, and Crick threw another ice pack, and the nasty two-foot slither of death might have gone on his own way, but Jimmy lost his tiny fucking mind.

Grabbing his rifle *by the barrel,* he threw the butt end at the snake as it was escaping, once, twice, three….

"God-fucking-dammit, Jimmy, you asshole—*you haven't even put the safety on!*"

"Wha?" Jimmy looked up, completely lost in his kill-the-snake insanity, and Crick, who had been sitting in front of Private Carpenter with his hands over Andrew's head in sheer instinct, stood up slowly, like Jimmy was the snake, and put out his hands.

"Private Davidovic, before you use that lethal fucking weapon like a club from the barrel, would you please be so considerate as to *put the fucking safety on?*"

Jimmy looked down at his weapon and smiled greenly. "Holy shit, Lieutenant. It's a good thing you weren't doing that—it would have blown your goddamned head off!"

Crick looked at Jimmy and then looked at Andrew, who was looking at Jimmy, and then he just shook his head and sat back down, looking gingerly for another goddamned snake. *Dear Deacon,* he thought in his head, planning the letter already, *I'm finally starting to believe you when you say I'm not a fuck-up. I have met a real fuck-up, and if I was him, I'd be dead.*

The next day, they saw a camel spider, and it took some fancy talking from Crick to keep Jimmy from shooting the damned thing as it skittered under the brush. No amount of screaming, "Goddammit, they're not fucking poisonous!" worked, and Crick finally had to resort to, "Private, I order you to stand down!"

Wow. It was like turning off a switch. As Jimmy stood there, rifle lowered and looking at him expectantly, Crick said with exaggerated patience, "Jimmy, where are we?"

Jimmy blinked. "I have no idea, sir."

Crick nodded. "I have a little idea. Enough to get us to camp. Not enough, however, to keep us alive should you bring every insurgent hiding in the fucking hills down on our heads with rifle fire for a thing that is ugly and yet not deadly. Now, I want you to put the safety on that thing and give it to Private Carpenter until I say so." He pitched his voice to the soldier on the travois, who had stopped bleeding and started shivering with fever, but who was still hanging in there. "Private Blood-loss, how you doing back there?"

"I'm conscious, sir."

"Do you think you could do better with this fucking gun than Jimmy here?"

"Fuck yes, sir."

"Excellent." And away they went.

They rationed the water and used the ice packs to line their flak jackets and helmets until they lost their cool, but after three days of rough terrain, they were flat-the-fuck out of anything wet and anything cool and of patience in general, but that wasn't the worst part.

The worst part was that their MREs, the magical little foil packets of tasty stew that were supposed to sustain them and to remain good in temperatures up to 120 degrees Fahrenheit, had apparently gotten hotter than that in their trek. Day three had been taken up by mad scrambles to crap behind the nearest stray boulder (after checking for snakes, of course), and their dehydration was getting to be a serious thing. Poor Andrew hadn't been able to make it to the nearest boulder, given his wound and all, and spent a good twelve hours being dragged through the desert in his own defecation.

But finally—before Jimmy could say "Good Christ, it's hot!" or "Where the fuck is camp?" or, Crick's personal favorite, "I'm thirsty, Lieu," one more time and make Crick have to shoot the guy himself, there was camp, visible in a space between two boulders. They could make out the helicopter pad, the big-assed medical tents, and their own barracks. Crick's favorite landmarks were the shower and the chow tent, but he wasn't picky—after the last three days, it all looked like the pinnacle of civilization to him.

Except for the fifteen-foot-long fucking cobra, staring at them from the middle of the two boulders.

"What is it with this place and snakes?" Crick wondered aloud. "I mean, for fucking real... I've dealt with rattlesnakes all my life, and they're not pretty, but... but these things... it's like they think they own the fucking place."

Poor Private Carpenter gave a shivery little sigh from behind him. "Yeah… give me a cottonmouth any day."

Private Jimmy dropped his end of Carpenter's sling so he could grab the M-16, and as Crick stumbled from the weight shift and saw where Jimmy was going, he threw out a foot and tripped the guy.

Jimmy went sprawling, landing about ten feet from the snake, which was rising slowly, in that creepy, sci-fi way that cobras had, so that his hooded head was about six feet off the ground and the rest of his fifteen-foot body was coiled around him.

"What in the fuck!"

"Back up slowly, asshole. Very. Very. Fucking. Slowly."

For once, Jimmy did as ordered, and when he got back to where Crick was, he glared at his commanding officer—who, Crick thought irritably, had been hauling his ass out of shit left and right in the last three days—and snarled, "Why in the hell did you do that?"

"Jimmy, where's the snake?"

Jimmy looked over to the creepy six-foot tower of death making threatening noises. "Right there, sir."

"And what's beyond 'there', darlin'?"

Jimmy blinked and said, "Camp, sir," with no real comprehension.

"About how far is camp, Private?"

Jimmy shrugged, completely non-plussed. "I don't know, Lieutenant—about half a mile?"

"And what is the range of an M-16 rifle?"

This took a while. It was painful. Finally Private Carpenter rasped, "It's over three thousand feet, asshole. If it wasn't for the fact that you'd probably kill someone, I'd ask Lieu to let you fire at the fucking snake so we could attend your court marshal with popcorn!"

Crick laughed throatily, snake or no snake. That there was a really appealing thought. "Private, you make it with us back to camp, and I swear to God, we'll go someplace where popcorn is served."

"I'd settle for any movie with Beyonce in it, sir."

"Austin Powers it is, Private."

"That's sweet and all," Jimmy snapped sullenly, "but first we've got to get past the fucking snake."

"Carpenter, we still got those hard plastic ice packs?"

It was a matter of throwing the ice packs at the snake and distracting him—and then making Jimmy serve as bait. Once the snake's attention was on Jimmy, and he was backing away slowly, Crick circled around and grabbed a mid-sized boulder—it weighed about thirty pounds—and dropped it solidly on the stretch of snake between the coiled body and that slinky, wily head that was thinking very seriously about going after Jimmy.

And then jumping away before that furious, flailing head could sink some of the world's deadliest venom into Crick.

Jimmy ran and grabbed another rock, and then (carefully, thank God) dropped his boulder on the snake's head. When they were sure that it was pinned, they pulled out Crick's Army-issue serrated blade and cut through the stretch of snake trying to writhe between the two boulders and left the damned thing in the sand so they could stagger their way home.

An hour later, Private Carpenter was in surgery, getting blood, fluids, and antibiotics injected into him while he got the shrapnel yanked out, and Crick was freshly bathed, lying on a unit bed next to Jimmy as they got pretty much the same treatment, minus the blood and the surgery.

Their CO wandered by to congratulate them on living, and Jimmy said, "Hey—I wanted to stay with the transpo—don't blame me for that fucking nightmare!"

The CO eyed him with a sincere dislike. "That fucking nightmare saved your ass, soldier. We found your transpo—what was left of it after it had been hit by a ground missile. Now if you don't mind, I'm going to pull the curtain here and give Crick a field promotion."

"Oh Christ!" Crick swore. "The last fucking thing I want to be is promoted."

His CO smiled a little. "This one just comes with some extra cash, Crick—you're not quite ready for an extra bar yet."

"Thank God."

The Captain nodded and set down the burden he'd carried into Crick's curtain-shrouded "room." "Something like that—here, I brought your lock box with your stuff, and you got another care package while you were gone. I'm afraid the cookies are about pilfered, but your letters and books have remained unmolested."

"Oh joy!" Jimmy called from the other side of the curtain. "I can hear him get all gay over 'Pastor' or whatever his name is!"

Crick might have panicked a couple of months ago, but now he was fairly sure it was just Jimmy being a world-class moron. "Better gay than stupid, jackass!" he called back, and Captain Somers actually laughed.

"Amen to that, Soldier. Hey—when you write your family, be sure to tell them we'll be rigging up the big-screen and the satellite near the holidays. It won't be private, but if your family has a computer, you'll have a chance to see them. We'll be picking time slots by rank, so you'll have a good one."

Crick stared at the big manila envelope that had Deacon's letter and what looked to be some photos in it, feeling his throat lump up. "I'll ask them," he rasped, swallowing his absolute yearning to see Deacon again. "I'll ask him when a good time to call will be."

The captain nodded and went to leave, but he remembered something else. "Son, your leave is coming up after Christmas as well— you get a month of it altogether. Now, I know your first instinct is going to be to want to go home, but" —as Crick looked up at him, his heart in his eyes—"I wouldn't."

"No?" Crick's voice felt like it came from far, far away.

"No." Captain Somers's face got oddly gentle. "I've seen boys like you—the ones who want to go home so badly they can taste it. Very often, when they get there, they can't come back—and if you do that, you fuck yourself, son. You never *can* go back if you just go AWOL in the States. I'd suggest you take a week, go to Germany maybe, and put the rest towards early release—you think about it, okay?"

"Yes, sir," Crick muttered, swallowing hard on his disappointment. But still, he had a letter....

> Crick,
>
> I'm sorry—you're right. I haven't really been all there for you, and I should have....

Crick read for a while, lost in the letter, and then he went back and read it again and tried to see the things Deacon wasn't telling him, and then he opened Benny's packet of photos and tried hard not to cry.

Most of the pictures were of Deacon.

A close-up of Deacon, rubbing noses with Crick's horse, Comet. Deacon's eyes were half-closed, his lashes fanning his cheeks, and oh God, there was that smile as he looked at the horse. It was the same smile he used in bed with Crick—the gentle, sweet smile that made him look young and a little vulnerable. Crick turned the picture around, and Benny had written, *I asked him to think of you.*

Crick closed his eyes and savored the pain—the pain of knowing Deacon felt like he failed, the pain of his little sister setting up to make a difficult life even harder, the pain of knowing that Deacon had stepped in when he couldn't and helped her out. But mostly, the pain of having Deacon right there in the picture, not quite close enough to touch.

When the pain had worked its way into his bones and sat sweetly on his tongue, he looked through the others, just as slowly.

Deacon, working Lucy Star in the ring, his fierce, tight grin of concentration back, his UC jersey flapping around his body like a sail. The caption read: *It's the only time he looks happy.*

Deacon, standing next to Benny—her arm was around him tightly, and she was looking impudently at him as though she'd coerced him into the shot, and he was smiling at her with an exasperated roll of the eyes. Her stomach was swollen—Crick guessed she was around four months now—and Deacon looked dwarfed by his tiny sister and her uninvited little guest. *He really is my hero, you know.*

Deacon, standing between Jon and Amy. Crick didn't know what the conversation had been, but Deacon was scowling, Amy was challenging back at him, and Jon was looking obstinate. There was another picture in the sequence, when they were all relaxed and laughing, but still, there was something wary about Deacon's eyes that Crick couldn't figure out. And then, on the back, *They threatened to show you how much weight he's lost. He didn't like that—he doesn't want you to know.*

Oh. Oh fuck. Crick was such an idiot—so damned blind. He sorted the photos back to where Deacon was wearing the UC jersey, opened his lock box, and took out his "Deacon" sketchbook.

It had been risky bringing it—he knew it was risky. The pictures were all of Deacon—and none of them were gender-preference neutral. But if he was going to be six zillion miles away for two years, he was damned if he was going without his sketchbooks—and that included the one filled with the person he loved the most.

And now it paid off, because after only a little bit of flipping (he had the pictures memorized), he had it. A picture of Deacon wearing the UC jersey while sitting on Shooting Star's back. He was fighting to keep his seat as the horse got uppity.

It was a sketch, and Crick's hormones had been raging, but Deacon's shirt still stretched slightly across his chest.

It most certainly did *not* flap around his body like a sail.

Oh geez… how much weight *had* Deacon lost? Crick picked up the photos—glossy from the processing—and continued looking. Deacon, asleep in front of the television, his wrist bone prominent as he leaned his head on his hand. *He watches your favorite shows, even though I don't think he likes them.*

Deacon, leading Lucy Star to the water trough, a child getting lessons on her back. *He's as good with kids now as he was with me when I was little.*

And then, pay dirt: Deacon, sitting on Promise Rock, elbows leaning on his knees, looking pensively into the sun-dappled-green-shadows overhead. It was almost the exact same pose Crick had sketched him in when Deacon was a teenager, with more sadness and less sun. *He doesn't know I shot this one. He's gained about ten pounds since I moved in, but you should know how bad things got before I came along.*

Crick caught his breath. Oh God. Deacon.

Let's just say that any alcohol is too much.

He wasn't just lean or rangy. He wasn't "thinner." He was emaciated. He'd been six-feet, two hundred pounds of solid, lean muscle, and now he was prominent clavicles, countable ribs, a sunken stomach.

And he'd gained weight?

Oh Deacon—what have you done to yourself?

Crick had no idea how long he sat there, staring at the photo and dashing his cheeks. Jimmy's voice broke into his reverie, and for a moment, he honestly wanted to strangle the kid.

"Lieutenant—you okay? I was only kidding about the going gay thing—there's nothing wrong at home, is there?"

"Nothing I can fix from here," Crick said back, hating that his voice cracked. For a second, he thought about pouring his heart out, going next door and showing the pictures, just to have someone else look at them and know what he was feeling.

But Jimmy wouldn't do that—Jimmy might get him a dishonorable discharge, but he wasn't going to look at the pictures of Deacon and know, just by looking, that this was the mess you left when you broke someone's heart.

I'll be mad when you're gone, Deacon had said. Crick hoped so. Crick hoped Deacon was kicking the furniture and cursing his name, because this… whatever was in these pictures, it was worse.

> Deacon,
>
> I think you should know that you saved my life this last week—a couple of times, actually. I was literally wandering the fucking desert, facing poisonous snakes and a private who needed shooting more than any man I've ever met, and the whole time, you were in my head, saving my ass.
>
> You and your damned maps were the only reason I knew where I was. Your internet research kept us from snake bites and attracting enemy fire, and your goddamned common sense kept us from drinking all our water on the first day and not setting watch and a thousand other things I can't even put a name to. It was your voice in my head for three days telling me to watch out for the snakes and only fire a gun if I have to and that dangerous things come out at night. It was your voice talking to a wounded man and telling him to stop fussing about dying and start fussing about living goddammit and it was you—swear to god it was you, Deacon—who kept me from shooting the asshole next to me for just being an asshole.
>
> And when I get back, I find out that you're not just saving my life, you're saving Benny's—I haven't seen her look that happy since she was three. She's made a mistake and fucked up, and I bet you haven't told her she's a fuck-up, not even once, because you don't do that. You don't judge people on their fuck-ups. You just have faith in us for the shit we do well.
>
> Stop being mad at yourself for whatever you think you fucked up. The drinking hurts me—not because you did it, but because I wasn't there to help you through it. I know you're probably comparing yourself to your mom right now—because you never talk about it, but it probably lives

inside you, and it took me a while to know how that shit lives and breathes inside you when everyone thinks it's gone. It's not. I can't imagine what it was like to be you, when she was sick and after, alone with her in the house after she'd passed away, but trust me, Deacon—you haven't done that to us. You're still hanging on for us.

You're telling yourself that you let me down—I let me down, and I broke your heart and I'll have to live with that, but it's not your fault. You're telling yourself Benny was your fault when she's probably the first one to admit it was her own damned fault—you taught her the facts of life same as you taught me, when she was a little girl on the back of a horse. Don't think I don't remember—your blush didn't fade for days.

You told me the only thing you wouldn't forgive me for would be not coming back. The only thing I can't forgive you for is if you're not there to come back to. Please, Deacon—take care of yourself while you're taking care of Benny. And for Christ's sake, eat something. You're scaring the shit out of me.

I love you.

Crick

Chapter *12*

The Name of the Thing

DEACON was starting to be very, very glad that he had chosen a man to love for the rest of his life, because he was pretty sure living with a woman would have been the end of him.

"Good God, Benny—what the hell is this shit? It looks like someone got shot and died in here!"

"Oh geez... sorry, Deacon!"

Benny stuck her head inside the bathroom, and Deacon hurried and zipped up. There was a bathroom with full bathtub and shower adjoining Parish's room—Deacon thought he really needed to get in the habit of going in there to take a leak. Benny had no respect for personal boundaries, and if Crick had "gayed up" their room, Benny had "girled up" this entire half of the house.

Deacon moved to the sink to wash his hands. "Seriously—what is this shit? It's even on the walls."

Benny grinned from underneath a towel turban on her head, and then pulled the thing off. "It's 'blood-garnet burgundy'—I'm dyeing my hair!"

Deacon blinked and looked at the red streaks on the walls. "That's hair dye? Benny—what are the odds of that shit getting off the walls if it dries?"

Benny blinked. She had big blue eyes under dark (okay, "blood-garnet burgundy") hair, and the effect was gamine and appealing. It was always disconcerting to see the bulge in her belly that meant she had gone past "gamine" adolescence and straight into adulthood.

"Oh crap... I'll go get the towels and the cleaner right now, Deacon. I'm sorry. I didn't realize it was all over. I swear, I'll get it to come out or I'll paint the walls again or...."

"Don't sweat it, Shorty!" Deacon called before she blew a lung or something. She talked as fast as Crick had at that age, and she was so eager to please.

The afternoon he'd showed up to get her from her parents, she'd been sitting outside their front door with a pillowcase full of clothes, an old ragdoll Deacon happened to know her brother bought for her with money he'd borrowed from Parish, and a black eye.

Deacon had seated her in the car with Amy and told Jon to wait for him in the truck and then went to knock on the door.

Bob Coats opened the door with a sneer on his face, and Deacon cold-cocked him and shut the door. He stalked back to the truck without looking at anybody, hopped in, and told Jon to drive. When the cars had started and Benny couldn't really see from the car to the truck, Deacon moaned in pain and massaged his shoulder. He didn't have the weight to hit like that anymore, and he was still weak, sleepy, and shaky from the Valium regimen that had helped him pull through the worst of the DTs. He'd expected more of Benny's stuff, and he hadn't been in any shape to drive, which was the reason he'd given Jon and Amy for having the two cars.

The reason he'd given Benny was closer to the truth. *It's not just me there for you, Shortness—I've got back-up in case I let you down.* She'd started crying and thrown her arms around his neck, saying, *You showed up, Deacon. You're already my hero.*

Which was funny, because her hero had to roll around in the front of the truck in pain for a good ten minutes, but he still resolved to stay a hero for her. That resolution—plus Jon and Amy's help—had made the first week work just fine.

Jon and Amy had their own lives, though—and so did Deacon for that matter. After another week of babysitting, Deacon's friends left them to return on a weekly basis for dinner, and Deacon and Benny were left to fend for themselves.

As it turned out, they did all right on their own.

Benny was enrolled in independent study. Deacon took her once a week to turn in her completed packets and pick up new ones and to take her quizzes, and he had no worries in the school department. Deacon told her it was because she was smart, and she told him it was because she didn't have the moron exposure in independent study that she had in regular school. In the meantime, she cleaned the house, took the business phone calls, made vet appointments, and did whatever else needed doing.

As Deacon remarked more than once, she was stunningly competent.

Deacon would go out, feed the horses, work them, give the riding lessons, prep the likeliest horses for show, move the animals about in their pastures, care for the gestating mares, get Even Star to exercise his now famous super-come-blowing-money-cock, and everything else that needed to be done outside, and Benny would stay inside and make the business run like clockwork.

It was the same stuff that Crick had used to do on his off-shifts, but Benny had the time to treat it like a real job. She wrote herself a schedule, did all the horse ranching stuff in the morning, worked on her schooling in the afternoons, and by the time Deacon came in at dinnertime, she'd made him something to eat as well.

Deacon found the whole thing a little spooky, and he told her so.

"It's not right that a girl your age should be so organized. It's damned weird. Have a slumber party or something."

Benny had looked at him searchingly, afraid that she'd done something wrong. "I'm... I'm sorry... should I, um do something different? Did you need something else?"

Deacon smiled at her, his heart shattering a little as he remembered Crick at this age. "You're doing great, Benny. Just...." And oh, the irony, because he could hear Jon's voice in his head even as he said it: "Just don't forget to ask for stuff. Don't forget this is your home too. You're getting a little big for your old clothes—remind me, and I'll take you shopping. We can get stuff for the baby too. You're...." He'd had to trail off because she'd started to cry. Damned female hormones—that was the only reason for it.

She'd launched herself at him, still crying, and he muttered, "You're Crick's family, Benny. How'd you expect to be treated?" But she hadn't been able to answer him.

So finding the bathroom covered in hair dye was actually not a bad thing, he reflected now. It meant she was comfortable—it meant that maybe they could bicker over the television, and she'd ask for some kid shit for Christmas, and that maybe he'd come in and get to microwave something because she got lost in a book or something. (He took her to the library once a week—he was always surprised at how much that girl could read.)

She came back, and he was opening cupboards in a search of one of those stupid little things that could mean so much in the course of your day.

"What're you looking for?" she asked. "Let me find it so I can get in there and clean the place!"

"Lip balm," he asked, a little embarrassed. He'd been putting on weight steadily, but he was still thin enough that he got dehydrated easily. He moved out of her way, and she reached into one of the fiddly little drawers next to the sink and pulled out...

A little tan tube of cherry-flavored Vaseline.

Deacon took it from her numbly. "Where'd we get this?"

She shrugged. "We had some and ran out. I got it at Wal-Mart the last time you took me shopping."

Deacon nodded and gripped the thing tight in his palm, his good mood and cheerful irritation completely gone. Without another word he turned and left the house.

"Where are you going?" she asked when she heard the door open. "It's almost time for dinner!"

"Forgot to feed Comet!" he muttered back. It was the best answer he could come up with, since, for the first time in nearly three months, what he really wanted was at least a fifth of anything that would club him over the head and make him lose consciousness.

Comet Star was the ugliest horse Parish Winters had ever bred. Someone had given him a brood mare in lieu of payment once, and she had been sixteen hands, gangly, dish-faced, swaybacked, bony-hipped, and the attractive color of fresh yellow baby-shit.

But *damn* was she sweet. Her name was—appropriately—Sugar, and they still used her as a riding horse for beginners. She was what Parish termed "bomb-proof"—it would have taken nothing short of a grenade launch to startle that horse, and if only beginners were riding her, they'd never be on long enough to figure out how uncomfortable she really was to ride.

Comet was sired by Even Star, which was like taking Sugar's disposition and adding a big dollop of honey and chocolate. His father's genes had given him some nice conformation—he wasn't swaybacked, and his hindquarters were as round and as handsome as Even's—but his face was still dish-shaped, and the squishy tan color hadn't gotten a shade darker since he'd been born. (He was listed officially as "buckskin"— Parish always said that if a self-respecting buck woke up that color, he'd donate his hide to ladies' fashion as revenge against God.) Sadly enough, breeding for a sweet nature was out of style, so Comet had been gelded— but since he'd promised to grow to seventeen hands, they'd kept him.

Parish had known at the time that Crick would need something big enough to ride.

Deacon had the presence of mind to grab some carrots from the burlap bag hanging on the door, which was a good idea, since Comet liked to nuzzle. He stood there for a couple of minutes, nose to nose with the big doofus, just breathing in horse. Why was it that horseshit and sweat and hay could smell so much like home?

Comet lipped the carrots from his hands and whuffled against Deacon's shirt. Deacon stroked his sensitive nose, and for a lost space of time, it was all the comfort he needed.

"Who needs Jack Daniels?" he asked rhetorically, because it sure as shit felt like he did. "I've got you, you big pussy. We'll make do until he gets back."

"I brought you dinner," Benny said behind him, and Deacon turned and saw she'd set a bowl of stew on a hay bale along with a big glass of milk.

"Sweetheart, you didn't have to do that."

"Yeah, I did," she said back, making herself comfortable on another hay bale. "You were coming out here to stay for a while—you can't afford to miss a meal, Deacon. Not right now."

"Well look who's practicing to be mama," he said, but he said it with a smile, and she wrinkled her nose at him.

"I need practice. I didn't have the best role model in the world, you know."

Deacon sighed and gave Comet one last nose bump, and then he moved back to eat his stew and try and be the person Benny needed. "You had Crick—he'll do."

"I had Parish and you too," she said. "Tell me—did Parish ever yell at you?"

Deacon remembered the day he told his father that he was giving up college to stay and make sure Crick had his shot. "Once," he murmured, taking a bite of stew.

"Now see!" Benny was legitimately upset, and Deacon wondered what it was he'd done now. "I made you all sad again!" she sniffled, and Deacon scooted over and reached out to loop an arm around her shoulders. One of the things he and Benny had enjoyed about living in proximity was that they were both "off limits"—she was too young and too pregnant, and he was too old and too in love with her brother, so there was no sexual tension between them. They were, for the most part, genderless beings to each other, and as such, Benny could sit on his lap and he could hug her to his side, and together, they could cling to each other like children. There were no misunderstandings, there were no inappropriate moments—there was only humanity and human comfort. It was, Deacon could admit to himself, one of the reasons he'd come out to talk to Comet and not gotten in the car and driven to the liquor store.

Benny wasn't going to be like this if he let her down.

"Shortness, you cannot be responsible for everything that makes me sad. I'm a recovering alcoholic, remember—shit had to pretty much be under my skin to begin with." She leaned into him and sniffled some more and muttered something about "fucking hormones," but he didn't call her to task for her mouth any more than she ragged on him.

"It was the cherry Vaseline, wasn't it?" she asked, and then continued without waiting for an answer. "What—did you guys use it as lube or something?"

Deacon almost choked on his own tongue. When he was done saying intelligent shit like "Ulngursrsnlgggg," he managed, "The things you know about sex… for the love of crap, Benny, could you try to pretend I'm a virgin or something so you don't kill me?"

But Benny was laughing instead of crying now, so he figured it was worth a little bit of embarrassment on his part. "It *was!*" she crowed. "Omigod! That's soooooo *sweet!*"

Deacon had to laugh—he wasn't sure when gay couples had become romantic in the under-twenty women's crowd, but Benny sure seemed to think he and Crick were fashionable. Well, good for her. He imagined they'd be facing enough challenges when Crick got back without worrying what she thought about the two of them.

"Yeah," he said quietly, able to live that memory for a moment without the bitter, Crick-less aftertaste. "It was."

They were quiet for a moment—nothing but the whuffling of horses and the shifting sounds that indicated large animals settling their bones for the night. The sun had set—it was late October, after all—and it was getting a little chilly. Deacon shed his jacket with some maneuvering and threw it over her shoulders, and she let him.

"What happened, Deacon?" Her voice was so quiet, and he was so… needy, to talk about Crick, that he couldn't find the fancy word-dance that he'd used when Jon asked him.

"Well, we were out at Promise Rock and"—he gave her a brief, tight smile—"freshly out of cherry lip balm, and Crick asked me if it was forever. And I tried to tell him it was."

"I don't understand," she said softly.

"Benny, you've lived with me for two months, and you haven't stopped waiting for me to yell at you or get drunk or throw something."

"Yeah, so?"

Deacon leaned his head back against the horse stall and remembered Crick's face that day, the way it closed down before Deacon could finish his sentence. "Well, your brother never stopped waiting to come home and find his shit on the front lawn. I was trying to give him forever, and he thought I was throwing his shit on the front lawn. By the time we got it all sorted out, he'd already joined the Army—as a pre-emptive strike, sort of."

"To cut you out before you could do it to him," Benny said like she understood.

"Yup. And you know the rest." The rest was him falling apart. In spite of Crick's (extensively re-read) letter, there weren't enough good deeds in the world to erase his complete shame of those first months.

Benny sighed and rested her head against him, as happy in the quiet as he was. "I don't know how you could forgive him," she said quietly, and he looked at her in surprise.

"Well, I haven't yet. Why do you think I drank so much?" Her shock was palpable, so he gave her a sweeter—and ultimately more important— truth. "But I will, Shortness. I have no choice. He's Crick. How do you not love your brother?" He didn't wait for an answer but shook his head instead. "It's damned impossible. Forgiveness will happen—I can't live with anything else."

She chewed on that for a while, and then, out of the blue, said, "Deacon, what's your middle name?"

He laughed a little. It was a family joke. "Parish."

"Like your Daddy?"

"Yeah—and his middle name was 'Preacher', which was my grand-daddy's name, and his middle name was 'Pastor', like his daddy. It goes back to, like, before the Gold Rush." He was getting sleepy, and she was getting heavy as she leaned on him.

"Are they all, you know, religious?"

"Yup. That's why Parish called the place The Pulpit. Which is really funny, since I don't know if any of us have stepped foot in a church since back before the Civil War. Why'd you want to know?" Her hair smelled harsh, like dye, but the rest of her felt like a child, in spite of what she was carrying in her belly. He wanted to protect her—hell, he wanted to raise her. He had a sudden inkling as to where Parish got his drive to collect muckrakers. There were just too many children in the world who needed a daddy. Parish gave what he could, and he'd taught Deacon to do the same.

"I wanted to name the baby 'Parish'," Benny said unexpectedly. "I figure it can be a girl's name too—I was hoping your middle name would be something, you know, unisex or whatever, but it's better. That way I can name her after you too."

Deacon's throat caught. "That's wonderful, Benny—Parish would be so proud." He didn't add that he wasn't worth a namesake. This was his daddy they were talking about.

"Yeah," Benny sighed, "but naming a girl 'Parish Deacon' would probably get me put up for child abuse."

Deacon chuckled. "Very probably. What's your middle name, Shorty?"

"Angela... but I don't want to name her after me. That's like a curse."

He grasped her chin with his fingers and made her meet his eyes under the drying mop of "blood garnet" hair. Her narrow, gamine face was earnest, and thankfully filling out after the last two months of steady food and comfort. "Then name her 'Angel'—for hope. 'Parry Angel'. It's a very pretty girl's name, you think?"

Oh gods, her smile was as goofy and as charming as Crick's. Her eyes shone with tears, and she rubbed her face on his shirt. "If I ever have a boy I'll name him Deacon Carrick," she threatened, and he laughed.

"Talk about child abuse—I'd call the authorities myself!"

A week later, Crick finally wrote with his time slot for their "holiday visit." He'd asked for early, because there was a good chance he'd be able to use the equipment again in the rotation, and they were slotted to visit a little after Thanksgiving. He also wrote with the news about his leave, which didn't surprise Deacon in the least. *Stay,* he wrote back. *Hell—take two weeks, get a Euro-pass, go to Paris and Munich. Visit museums, take tours—do all that shit you talked about when you were planning to go to art school. Find the shit I'd want to see—you can take me back later. (Do anything, anything, but don't come home just to leave me again, because I'm weak, Carrick, and it would kill me all over.)* He didn't write that last part—but he was sort of proud for being honest enough to think it.

Thanksgiving came—Jon, Amy, Patrick, Benny, and Deacon. They set a place for Crick, just because. It was a good day—laughter, generosity, kindness. Crick got a chance to call towards the evening—with someone else in the room, of course.

When Deacon heard Carrick's voice over the phone, his knees actually got weak, and he had to sit down. He forgot later what they talked about—it seemed sort of superfluous, really, to be talking at all. Their letters kept them caught up on the news, and the small shit seemed just too small for their first conversation in six months. But they muddled through, and Deacon passed the phone around. He looked up sharply when he heard Jon say, "I'll never forgive you," but Jon waved him off and finished the sentence in private. The phone finally came back to him, and Crick only had a few minutes left.

"Crick, you're taking care of yourself, right?"

"Yeah, Deacon—I promised I'd come back. I wasn't joking about your voice in my head, making sure that I do. I won't leave you twice—I promise."

"Good," Deacon murmured, wondering how the kid had read the part of the letter he didn't send. "It's all I want."

"You need to ask for more from life," Crick muttered bitterly, and then, before Deacon could protest, he said quickly, in a broken voice, "Look, I've only got a few seconds and you know… you know what I'm thinking. Please say it. I need to hear it."

Risky words from Crick, with someone listening on his end. But then, Crick had been writing *I love you* at the end of his letters for months, while Deacon—mindful that Crick's letters could be read on Crick's end—had been writing "take care."

"I love you, Carrick—I'll love you forever. Take care of yourself and come home and don't ever break my heart again." The room around him went silent, and he didn't give a shit. Crick needed to hear it, and that trumped all of the embarrassment in the world.

"Backatcha, Deacon. I swear, once was enough." His voice caught, and he finished up with, "I'll see you next week on the computer."

"We'll be there."

And then they both said, "Goodbye." Deacon looked up at the silent room and felt a delayed sense of mortification. "I'm… I'm gonna go outside and check on the horses," he muttered, which was an outright lie, because they all knew he'd checked on them an hour ago, right before dessert.

"Don't go, Deacon," Benny said softly, coming up and wiggling her way under his arm. "Stay here and cry if you have to—but don't go off and be alone. Not tonight."

Deacon sighed and looked around him, and he saw his friends looking back with concern. All he wanted was to be alone for a minute, but he guessed they'd all be gone in a couple of hours, and then there'd be enough aloneness to swallow him whole. For Benny's sake, he managed a tired, weak, and watery grin. "Men don't cry, Shorty—we get choked up. And if I'm going to get any more choked up, I need some more goddamned pie."

A week later, he and Benny were dressed like it was church and waiting in the tiny study that adjoined the master bedroom. They were going to see Crick.

Crick—

I know there's the possibility that letters will get read when they shouldn't, so burn this one if you have to. I'm looking forward to actually seeing you, even on the computer, but I'm afraid too. Mostly I'm afraid all the shit in my heart is going to back up against my tongue and I'll just stare at you, so damned glad you're alive that the whole moment will be shot to hell.

You need to know that I want to touch you. You need to know that I want to say a thousand things that are meaningless and perfect in your ear. You need to know that I dream about your eyes and your crooked grin and that a thousand times a day I start a conversation with you about something stupid and I'm heartbroken when you're not there to say your bit. You need to know I love you—I'm still mad, but I promised you I wouldn't be mad when you get back, and I'm starting to think I can keep that one, so don't worry about it. I love you—that's the important thing. I'd die for you, and it kills me that you're in a place where you might die for your country and I can't save you. I'm glad you're hearing my voice in your head to keep you safe—I hear your voice in my head to keep me from losing my fucking mind.

You need to know all these things, and then you need to file them somewhere in your head for later. We're not half done yet, baby. Neither of us will make it if we break our hearts the way we've been doing. I need to live in the moment for Benny. You need to live in the moment for me.

When you get home, the floodgates will open and the flood will clear the pain and it will be just us, shiny and new, with our hands on each other's skin and our bodies touching so tight we'll be able to hear each other's thoughts. When you get home we can be lovers.

In the meantime, we'll see each other on the computer and pretend to be like brothers. Now that your CO has given his stamp of approval, we'll text or 'tweet' (thanks, Benny) and we'll talk in code like we've been doing, and you need to know that you are still loved. And you need to hold it close to your heart. There's a reason you didn't try to back out of your signature on the recruitment papers, and there's a reason I didn't try to make you. We need to hold to that—it's who we are and it's one of the reasons I think we can love each other through anything. I know you're homesick, Crick, because it doesn't feel like home without you. Let's just hold on so you can come back home in peace.

(And, as off-topic as it may seem, I need to add that if you're anything like me, you are hornier than a goat in the springtime. Just sayin', in case you were worried about that end of things—don't.)

Remember that song at Jon and Amy's wedding?

I need you, like I want you. Always and forever. I want you like I love you. Always and forever.

Consider that a promise.

Deacon

Chapter *13*

A Mistake in the Night

CRICK memorized that letter. Then he pilfered from the supply closet and laminated the pages in layers of clear tape, folded it up, and added it to the pictures of Deacon in his wallet. If someone wanted to steal his shit and out him to the U.S. fucking Army, let them. Let them explain why stealing his wallet was better and more honorable than what Deacon had written. Crick was all ears.

He had his wallet in his pocket like a talisman when he stood in front of the computer and wondered what Deacon would see.

"Jesus, Crick—your chest is like three-feet wide!" Deacon's surprise was obvious—Crick hoped his delight was only there for Crick himself to see.

"Yeah, big brother," Benny chimed in—what color was her hair, anyway? Damned bright was what it was! "You're looking pretty yummy over there."

Crick laughed at Deacon's look of disgust. "Ewww, Shorty. Just, ewww."

"My God, Benny—your hair's probably visible from space," Crick said, laughing. They were cute together, in a big brother-little sister sort of way. Crick's chest was suddenly open and happy, when he'd sworn the tightness would strangle him through the whole conversation.

"And if you can't see my hair, you can probably see my stomach," Benny told him, embarrassment clear on her rounding face. She turned sideways in a form-fitting pink-and-black striped knit shirt and showed off the burgeoning life inside.

Crick nodded. "What are you now, five, six months?"

"Six months—she's due in February, a little after your birthday—but I'm naming her Parish after Deacon and his daddy, so just don't get any ideas." Deacon's hand tightened on her shoulder, and Crick could see—even on the small screen of the computer—that she patted it as it sat there.

"Parish Deacon?" Crick asked in confusion. "Sounds like child abuse to me!"

The two of them laughed, the sound so spontaneous that Crick knew it must have been a joke between them as well. "Parish Angel," Deacon told him softly, probably reading the hurt on his face. "Parry Angel—we figured it sounds girly enough to maybe match her room." He rolled his eyes and faked a gag reflex with enough dryness that Crick could laugh again—but it didn't last.

"Did you get my birthday card, Deacon? I tried to send it on time." Deacon had turned twenty-six in late November. Just one more reminder to Crick that his lover—the hero he worshipped—was awfully damned young for all of that.

"Deacon!" Benny punctuated the exclamation with a smack on his arm. "You didn't even mention it was your birthday!"

Deacon blushed so dark that Crick could see it over six thousand miles away. "Didn't seem important," he grumbled, and Crick got a good enough look at his face in profile to see how much weight he hadn't put back on yet.

"It's everything," Crick told them seriously. "It was the twenty-ninth, Benny. You make sure you take him out for ice cream or something. He's not putting on nearly enough weight."

"It's bad enough that your sister cooks with cheese!" Deacon protested half-heartedly, and Crick was able to forget the pain and the worry for the two of them as they teased each other—and him—for the next twenty minutes where he could see. Deacon still looked good, in spite of the thinness. His cheekbones were sharper, and he looked wearier than Crick was used to, but that square-jawed face was just as gruff when he scowled and just as sweet when he smiled—even when it was that fierce, tight grin that he used anytime *except* when they were in bed together.

And his eyes… still that remarkably pretty green, still thoughtful and now….

Had they always been that sad? Crick thought maybe they had been—he'd just been too callow to see it.

The time was over way too quick. Crick almost wished they'd spent it stuttering, staring soulfully at the screen, unable to think of a thing to say. It would have seemed longer that way.

Before it was done, Deacon checked to make sure Crick had gotten his early Christmas present—a shiny new BlackBerry so they could text and Twitter.

"Benny set me up. If we want it to be private, we have to block *everybody,* and not use any terms that get a lot of attention, which shouldn't be so hard on you—I guess I'm under 'DP'…." He stopped when Crick burst into raucous laughter.

"Benny—you precocious little shit—you didn't!"

Benny blushed. "I swear, Crick—it didn't even occur to me until he told me he was getting hits from porn-IDs."

Deacon blinked, those big, pretty green eyes wide and guileless, and it hit Crick and hit him hard. *He's not just young—he's innocent.* "What in the hell does it mean, people?" Deacon growled, and Crick had to talk through a lump in his throat.

"It means 'double penetration', Deacon. It's a porn term."

Deacon blinked again, and his mouth opened, and then he turned a bright, computer-console-defying purple. "Jesus—I'm gonna be fighting off those porn people for the next eighteen months. I hope you two are damned happy about this."

Crick looked at him softly—Deacon, his sweet little virgin, or damned close to it. "Yeah, Deacon—actually, I haven't been this happy about things in about six months." The private in charge of the media operations was giving him the "wrap-it-up" signal, and Crick fought the urge to tell him to fuck off because he wasn't nearly done yet. Instead he said, "Guys, I've gotta…."

Deacon swallowed and looked grim. "Merry Christmas, Crick, if we can't talk before. I'll be on Twitter every night, nine o'clock sharp, so that's seven a.m. your time, right?"

Crick nodded, suddenly feeling the huge gift of technology in the little techno-pink thing that Benny had picked out for him. "It's perfect. I can't give you any real details," he cautioned, and Deacon nodded.

"Understood—we're only interested in four letters. If that's all you've got time for, that's all we need."

I'm OK. "Understood," Crick said back. "Deacon—I've got your letter in my wallet."

Deacon looked startled and then resigned. "I meant it all." Code. It's what they had, and it allowed them to say goodbye.

Crick was walking out of the tent, and one of the privates called out to him. "Hey, Crick, where was she?"

Crick turned around, looking puzzled. "She?"

"Yeah—rumor has it, you're in love with a girl back home—it's why you don't… you know…." Look at the smuggled porn, hound any woman who was assigned to the base, jerk off in the bathroom to the sex pictures Private Compton's uninhibited wife kept sending him, regardless of regulations.

"Yeah," Crick muttered, blushing. He knew. "We're sort of putting that relationship on hold until I get back. That there was my family. They're all I need."

It took a while to get used to the Twitter website, and for a while, their posts were stilted and dumb. But after a while, Crick got almost as quick with his thumbs on the teeny keyboard as Benny seemed to be, and Deacon was catching up. It never did take the place of letters, for which Crick was sincerely grateful. Every so often, he would tell the truth, which was that his heart was bursting out of his skin with the hiding and the being careful—he'd even borrowed some porn and visited the bathroom, just to make everyone think he was het, which he had to put down as one of the most asinine things he'd ever done. So he would threaten to lose it, and Deacon would write him another tender, painful, real love letter, and he would tape it up to keep it safe and put it in his burgeoning wallet.

But even those didn't ease the pain when, in February, his phone buzzed in his pocket.

DP @Crick—prettiest baby ever. See the link.

And God, was she. Benny looked tired and older and so scared as she held the wrinkled little goober, but the goober herself had big, blue eyes, the same shape as Benny's and Crick's. There was a shot, taken by Benny, with Deacon's big hands around that tiny body. Deacon looked... happy. There was a joy shining from him as he looked at that baby, and Crick knew, without a doubt, that he'd missed something important, something huge, and that his sister had given Deacon something he'd never be able to, even if it was just until she got her shit together and left.

Crick @DP—you're already in love, I can tell.

DP @Crick—she's got your eyes.

And Crick had to fight back tears. Ah, Jesus... *Deacon, don't get attached. The little goober will only break your heart. It must run in the family.*

Crick @DP—Don't let her break your heart.

DP @Crick—It's stronger than it used to be. It'll stay strong enough for all of you.

Crick @DP—gotta go. Give Benny and Parry Angel my love.

And you, Deacon. Take most of my love for yourself.

So Crick was in a bad way when his two weeks' worth of leave finally went through—especially because by the time he was actually on the plane for USO Germany, it was Jon and Amy's first anniversary.

The minute he got to base, he checked out and had the really bad fucking fortune to meet Private Jimmy as he stood in front of the base. He was waiting for the bus that would take him to Berlin, the train, and eventually to Paris. Deacon said he should go—following that bit of advice was the least Crick could do, since once he got back to The Pulpit, he didn't intend to go anywhere again without Deacon by his side.

"Hey, Lieu—where you off to?" It sounded innocuous enough, but Crick must have been really desperate for any sort of human contact whatsofuckingever, because eventually, that little greeting ended him up at a strip club in Berlin. "C'mon, Crick—give me a send off! I'm going home to work a McJob, probably, and this could be the last time I see the world."

As Fraulein Wundertits shook her thing to the techno-industrial music in the converted warehouse, Crick had to ask himself if this was what Jimmy had in mind. He certainly couldn't ask Jimmy—the music was too goddamned loud. There was a buzzing in his pocket, and he pulled out his phone. It was Benny.

@Crick—Naked with something hot yet?

@Benny—Not tonight, Shorty. Heart hurts.

@Crick—Deac's too. Comet's brushed to a sheen.

@Benny—I'm on leave and I'm not home.

@Crick—Think we don't know that, jackass?

@Benny—Go away, some chick's shaking her tits and I'm pretending to care.

@Crick—Do something I wouldn't do. It'll make Deacon happy.

@Benny—HA!

@Crick—He thinks of you alone. It hurts him.

@ Benny—I can't have this conversation now. Tomorrow.

@Crick—Tomorrow.

"Who's on the horn, Crick?" Jimmy had to lean forward and shout in Crick's ear, and Crick shrugged. He was tired, heartsick, and incredibly lonely, but not even that could make Jimmy's gap-toothed, sandy-haired, square-headed face interesting enough to even consider.

"My sister."

"Well, tell her you're busy—look!"

Crick looked. There was Fraulein Wundertits, looking suggestively at him from the doorway to the dressing room behind the stage. She was pretty, she had a nice smile, and she was wearing a red silk dressing gown. Crick sighed. Maybe this would be good cover—he could go pretend to be heterosexual in order to give up pretending that he was interested in showing poor Jimmy a good time.

"I should go talk to her," he screamed over the pounding techno-industrial-metal of the club, and Jimmy grinned.

"Don't do anything I wouldn't do!" Jimmy yelled, and Crick sent back a sincere, "I wouldn't count on that, Private. Good luck in the States!" before he grabbed his duffel and made his way through the throng of people circling the stage. In a minute, he was all cozy, snuggled back into the hallway with a pretty girl.

"Hello, GI," the girl said in an appealing—and strong—accent. "I have a... a deal for you, you like?"

He looked at her and had to smile—she was very pretty. Her face was small and round, with enormous blue eyes—heavily made up with attached lashes—and her hair was up in a beguiling, two-toned ponytail. He figured if he was straight, he'd bend her over here and now, but he wasn't.

"I'm sorry," he said. It was quieter in the back stage; he didn't have to scream. "You're very pretty"—and now he smiled with incredible embarrassment—"but you're not really my type."

He spotted a door at the end of the dark hall, slung his duffel over his shoulder, and turned to walk towards it when he felt her hand on his sleeve. "American?" He turned and smiled politely again and was totally blown away when she said, "You are more my brother's type?"

Crick knew his jaw had dropped, and then it was suddenly twenty degrees hotter in his casual fatigues. "Um…."

Her smile was both gentle and ironic. "You Americans—you make these things so hard. Here—my shift is over, let me change."

He thought she'd just let him stay out in the hallway, but apparently, now that she knew he wasn't interested in her, she wasn't interested in keeping up pretenses. She dragged him back into a dressing room only slightly bigger than an airplane toilet, dropped her silk robe, and started pulling on clothes while Crick squashed himself against the door like she was a wet dog.

"What's the matter, American? Afraid you'll catch girl cooties?"

Crick wondered if he'd ever be able to explain this to Deacon and then thought maybe Deacon would laugh his ass off. Deacon, at least, would know what to do with a naked German chick who'd come on to him.

"I just don't know if I'm up for a random hook-up," he said apologetically. "Your brother may hate me on sight!"

The girl shrugged. "If he hates you, he may like your cash. If he likes you, it will be no charge."

"But I'm not interested," he tried to protest, but she reached around him and opened the door. He fell out into the hallway, and she grabbed his hand and hauled him after her.

"Sure you are. You have the loneliest eyes I've ever seen."

Oh geez, he looked so hard-up that random strippers were picking him out of a crowd and hooking him up with their brothers? Wonderful.

It had rained the night before, and the girl's platform heels smacked lightly on the wet pavement. Crick could see neon signs reflected in the black puddles, and he had a slightly disjointed feeling—what in the fuck was Carrick James Francis doing here, in this alien city, with this very determined stripper?

"Um… what's your name?" he asked, and she laughed.

"Anke—why does it matter? You're not going to screw me!"

"It seemed polite," he mumbled, and pretty much determined that, after he explained to her brother that this was a big misunderstanding, he'd ask for directions to the monorail. He understood it went all night.

Anke didn't live far. He had a decent bead on where the main thoroughfare was from the strip club, and he thought he might find his way back there and then to the train, when she hauled him up about six flights of stairs to a small, seedy apartment at the end of a concrete hallway. She didn't knock but dragged Crick into a small kitchen-cum-living room and then went down a hallway about six inches wider than she was and knocked on the door to his left.

"Stefan!" she called. "Stefan—wake up. I brought you home something."

"Ist es 'was zum essen?" came a voice, and she turned the knob and stuck her head in.

"That's up to you. But he's American, so speak English, *bitte*." Anke backed out of the hallway and looked at Crick with a bright smile. "The rest is up to you, American. If you shower in the morning, don't use all the water." And then she ducked into the room across the hall with a cheery wave.

"Dammit, Anke—it's my night…." A head appeared in the open doorway, and then two very blue eyes turned towards Crick. "Hello. Danke, kleine Schwester!"

"Bitteschön, Stefan—sei süß. Er ist einsam."

"Lonely," the boy said with an even heavier accent than his sister. "Ja, das kann ich sehen."

Crick was starting to wonder if he'd had "lonely" tattooed on his forehead when he was asleep—first Private Jimmy, and now random brother and sister in back-alley, Berlin.

"Look, Stefan, is it? Yeah... I'm sorry... I didn't mean for this to go so far. If you could just give me some directions back to the monorail...." Crick started backing slowly towards the door, feeling both sheepish and surreal. Then Stefan came out, wearing a pair of boxer shorts and not much else, and Crick stopped backing out.

Oh, he was pretty. Not as pretty as Deacon, but, well... God. It had just been so long since he'd been able to even *look* at a man that way. Stefan's muscles were small but well-defined. He was tall—not as tall as Crick, but a little taller than Deacon, and besides the white-blonde hair and the blue eyes, he had a sweet little oval of a face and full, pouting lips. Pretty. Pretty and wearing boxer shorts.

Out of nowhere came the thought that the condoms Deacon had given him were still in his duffel bag, and he gave his pecker a stern talking-to before looking up to tell Stefan "no" again.

Stefan had moved, and those pretty blue eyes were right in front of Crick.

"You are lonely, American—it's my night off. Come—all we have to do is sit on my bed and talk. I will not bite." A grin—a quick, fierce, tight little grin that made Crick's chest hurt—and then he added, "Unless you want me to."

Crick shook his head. "It's... it's been a long time since I've talked about him," he said. "He's... he's waiting for me."

Stefan nodded like he'd seen it before. "American military—it makes things hard, I know. Come. Do you have a picture?"

Crick found he was digging for his wallet before they even got into Stefan's room. Stefan's room was a mess—clothes, food boxes, scraps of paper with phone numbers—but Stefan cleared off a spot on his bed without embarrassment and patted it for Crick to sit down. Crick pulled out the pictures of Deacon that Benny had been sending. The one where he was asleep on the couch with the baby was more recent, and he was looking a little less like a famine victim in that one. The one where he was nose to nose with Comet was still one of his favorites, and a new one where he was sitting on a horse and grinning self-consciously into the camera showed him off at his best. But he didn't stop there—he pulled out all of them, and the letters too.

Stefan's grin was faintly ironic. "It's a good thing it is my night off—there's no room in that wallet for cash!"

Crick blushed. "I keep the cash somewhere else," he said, and Stefan laughed. It was a nice laugh—a few hard breaths, a round, rolling sound, and then he moved his attention onward.

"He's very pretty," Stefan said, looking at the pictures. "His eyes are sad, like yours."

"He's been in my life since I was nine," Crick tried to explain. "It's hard being apart."

Stefan reached out and put his hand on Crick's as it was lying there on the bed. "You think he wants you to be this lonely? You want him to be so lonely?"

Crick closed his eyes. "I... I just want so bad to talk about him," he said.

Stefan closed his hand on Crick's, and Crick found he was squeezing it back. "What's your name, American?"

"Crick."

"Crick?"

"Short for Carrick."

Another one of those fierce, tight grins, and Crick's heart started pounding in his chest. "And what's his name?"

Crick closed his eyes so he could save the sounds in his mouth when he said them. "Deacon. Deacon Parish Winters."

"He's a good man, this Deacon?" Stefan asked gently, and Crick kept his eyes closed and nodded, even though he could feel the puff of Stefan's breath on his face when he spoke. "A good man will forgive you, Crick. If my sister saw your loneliness in the middle of a dance, I don't see how he couldn't."

Stefan's breath was very near—it wasn't sour, exactly, but he hadn't brushed his teeth since he last slept either. But he didn't smoke (and it felt like most of Germany did) and he didn't have alcohol on his breath, and he was... warm. Warm and male. Crick put out his hand and splayed his fingers across that smooth, bare chest.

"I just wanted to say his name," Crick protested, feeling his loneliness burn behind his eyelids and blur at the fringe of his lashes.

"Then keep your eyes closed," Stefan murmured, touching lips with him. "Keep your eyes closed and speak his name."

"Deacon," Crick breathed, just before Stefan's mouth claimed his.

Crick got up quietly the next morning and put on his boxers, taking care not to wake Stefan as he did so. He cleaned up the condom wrappers and threw them in the trash and went into the miniscule bathroom and gave himself a GI shower with a washcloth and some of Anke's scented soap. When he was done, he dressed in his fatigues from the day before, since they weren't much the worse for wear, put on his boots, and bent and kissed Stefan on the cheek.

"Thank you," he murmured brokenly. "You... you were very kind."

Stefan opened lazy eyes. "Guilt, American?"

Crick shrugged as though it was no big deal. "It goes in the collection bucket."

Stefan snorted and waved him off with a dreamy smile. "At least now you're not so lonely. Enjoy Paris, American. I very much enjoyed you." And then he closed his sleepy blue eyes and fell back asleep, and Crick crept out of the tiny little apartment like the criminal he felt like.

In the daylight, he could see the monorail from the window of Stefan's room, so he started marching toward it in the chill morning. He reached for his BlackBerry six times on the way, because it was his time to chat with Deacon and it was habit, before he remembered that he wasn't sure what to say.

You're honest as a horse, Crick.

Shit. That long-ago virtue finally made up his mind for him.

Crick @DP—Woke up next to a mistake in Berlin this morning. The things I'll do just to say your name out loud.

There was a pause. A longer pause than usual, and Crick wondered if he could please, just please, die enough for his heart to shrivel and cease to beat, because he knew Deacon would never speak to him again.

DP @Crick—It's not a mistake if it saved your life.

Crick stopped short right there on the sidewalk, which was getting busier by the minute. In that one moment, Crick finally got it. If he hadn't believed before, he was now a true believer. He would *never* come home to The Pulpit and find his shit out on the lawn.

Crick @DP—Save my life? It really did.

DP @Crick—Then tell me you at least used a raincoat—a good soldier keeps his gun clean!

Crick closed his eyes tight, opened them, kept walking, kept texting.

Crick @DP—Squeaky clean. Don't want my gun dropping off when it needs to shoot more than blanks.

DP @Crick—That would piss me off too. I still love you—no worries.

Crick @DP—I'll worry 'til I'm home.

DP @Crick—Yeah. Me too.

Deacon,

Paris was everything it's talked up to be—especially in the springtime. I've sent some sketches I made—common stuff, the Arc, the Tower, small cafes, the Seine. It's almost like an obligation—young art student comes to Paris, bad art ensues.

About the mistake in Berlin—you gave me "permission" before we left, and I thought you were crazy. I underestimated how smart you are about people. I wasn't lying when I said I'd do anything just to say your name, and the mistake knew it. It always surprises me to find kindness in the world outside of you. I was lucky to find it that night.

But the good news is, I got back to base and got to actually pick out my new driver. I guess they felt like after Jimmy, maybe the army owed me. There was one girl standing in the ranks—she reminded me so much of Amy, and she smiled. (She wasn't supposed to—they were supposed to be at attention.) I figured any girl ballsy enough to smile, well, she and I should get along okay. Wouldn't it be something to find kindness (okay—whole different type of kindness) somewhere else out here?

I like the Twitter thing—any technology that gives me instant forgiveness can't be all bad. Of course, it's kind of like the M-16 thing—it all depends who's behind the button.

I love you. I want to shout it sometimes. I know you worry about our letters and texts getting read—shades of WWII, haunting us still, I guess, and I'm well aware that nothing's safe on the internet. I worry too. You need to know that when I say it, when I ask you to say it, it's because my lungs feel full of dark water, and seeing it or writing it lets me breathe.

I'll love you forever.

Crick

Chapter *14*

Marching On

THE first year was incredibly hard, but they found a rhythm to living without each other. It hurt like losing a limb or eyesight or the ability to breathe, but it was doable. At least, that was what Deacon told himself when he got the message about Berlin.

He'd been up late that night anyway, taking his turn with the baby. Benny never expected him to get up with her, but Deacon liked that part. It was late, the house was quiet, and it was just him and this tiny little person that he had yet to disappoint. So there they were, Parry Angel and Deacon, listening to Deacon sing to The Eels, when Deacon's phone buzzed in his pocket.

"I've finally stopped pretending that I didn't break your heart," Deacon finished crooning, and the baby gurgled. She liked his voice, and he liked making her smile, so it was all good. He pulled out his phone while balancing the baby, read the message, and promptly dropped the phone.

His heart was racing, which was a helluva thing—he'd been expecting this for a year. *Anything, anything, but don't let Crick be lonely*—wasn't that what he'd said to himself? He recovered the phone and ignored the cold sweat on his palms. It was time to pony up.

DP @Crick—It's not a mistake if it saves your life.

He believed it, but that didn't mean that when the conversation was over he didn't slouch down the couch while holding the now-sleeping baby, and sniffle into her flannel blanket.

Benny came out of her bedroom, yawning. "Why didn't you wake me, Deacon? It was my turn!"

"I like doing it," he murmured, but she was a smart kid. She flopped down beside him and leaned into the side that wasn't holding the baby, snuggling like the child she was.

"What's the matter, Deacon?"

He thought about lying to her but didn't. This was what Jon was talking about when he said "ask for help"—it would be nice to learn something before Crick got back.

"Your brother just texted. He's—he *was*—lonely."

She was quiet for a moment, digesting. "But he's not anymore?"

Deacon's lips twisted a little. "He wasn't last night."

And she knew what that meant. "Oh."

He shrugged. "I'll live. We'll live. I'm glad he's not so lonely." He remembered the text—*There's not much I wouldn't do to be able to say your name.* "We at least get to talk about him. He doesn't get the same thing."

Benny nodded against him. "Look—do me a favor. Tell him I said 'good going' or something like that. But don't tell him that I want to beat the shit out of him for doing this to you, okay?"

"Why can't you text him yourself?"

Benny sniffled against his shirt and wiped her face on Parry Angel's blanket like he had. "Because I told him to do this, but I'm pretty sure he knew I was kidding, and now that he's done it… I'm not as good a person as you are, Deacon, and I'm so mad at him for doing this to you…."

"Shhh." He calmed her then and eventually put both the girls to bed. Then he pulled out the phone.

DP @Crick—Benny says 'way to go'.

Crick @DP—That girl's priorities are screwed up.

DP @Crick—You'd be surprised how level-headed she is. Night, Crick—I love you.

Crick @DP—You are up hella late. Night Deacon. Love you too.

"So," LISA was saying, "does this place have any season besides 'hell, prior to freezing'?"

Crick looked up from his sketchbook and squinted at her against the sun. He was parked right outside his barracks, enjoying the early morning shade and the good light before the desert remembered that it hated human life with a passion and tried to fry them all like chicken.

"It rains for about two weeks in December, and everything gets moldy except you. But I've sort of tried to block that out."

Crick's driver wrinkled her nose and plopped her pert little bottom down on the sand next to Crick's chair. "I'm so bored."

Crick had to laugh—it was the way she said it. Lisa had been funny and tough in the last month or so, and she had a capable head on her shoulders, which Crick highly appreciated after dealing with Jimmy. He recognized this as an overt offer of friendship, and damned if he could afford to turn one of those down.

"I've got boxes of paperbacks in my barracks. Want me to bring them out for you?"

She turned a winsome smile on him and batted her eyelashes. Crick laughed and stood and stretched. He set his sketchbooks down on his chair before he went into the men's barracks tent and fetched one of the boxes of books that Deacon sent regularly.

He was completely unprepared to find Lisa looking at his sketchbooks when he came back.

"These are really good," she murmured, leafing through the one on top—the "public" sketchbook, the one that he replaced on a regular basis as it filled up with whatever he was working on at the moment.

"Thanks," he said, setting down the box and trying not to panic. The Deacon book was right under the public book, and he thought maybe, if he reached out his hand, she'd hand them over without... without....

"Wait, no, can I look?" She didn't look up for his answer. In a way, it was flattering—she just assumed that his work was good enough that he wanted to share, but then, to his horror, "Ooooh... who's he?"

That was the first one, when Deacon had been younger and Crick's work was rougher. Her fingers, which had been busy, flipping through the pages of rough sketches of things like camels and tanks and the far-off mountains in the morning, suddenly stilled, moved reverently, slowly, as though she felt what Crick had felt as he'd been working.

She reached one of the sketches toward the end and stopped. It was one Crick had made in the hotel in Georgia of Deacon asleep on his side, the comforter rucked up around his waist and one arm stretched out above his head. The other arm was tucked between his chin and the mattress, and his hair—long on top, short on the sides, which hadn't changed—was tousled and falling in his closed eyes. His expression was almost peaceful, for Deacon. Crick's breath caught just looking at the sketch—he looked vulnerable and young, and Crick often wondered if the man he went back to would ever be that man, right there in the sketch, that he had left.

The look Lisa turned towards Crick now was eloquent and compassionate. Crick finally moved, his hand resuming normal speed instead of sluggish slow motion, and took the books from her unresisting grasp.

"I... um... I don't usually show that one around too much," he muttered with a green smile.

"What's his name?" she asked, surprising him, and he figured that if he was fucked royally, he might as well enjoy it.

"Deacon. Deacon Parish Winters."

She blinked. "Do you ever just call him 'Deac'?"

Crick shook his head adamantly. "Never."

"Why not?"

He closed his eyes and felt foolish and answered anyway. "I like to say his name."

Lisa reached out gentle hands then and took the sketchbook from him. He resisted at first, but she said, "You know, Crick, you might want to let me keep this one in my lock box. It can't be all that safe in there."

It wasn't, in fact. They'd busted two men for stealing in the last three months—Crick had been lucky, and he knew it. But still, Crick looked at the book like he was giving his newborn child to a teenager to babysit. "I... I like to...."

"How 'bout we meet here after assembly most days—you bring the paperbacks, I'll bring" —she smiled sweetly—"Deacon, and we can be... you know...." Her face was suddenly a little bit uncertain and almost as desperate as Crick had felt before he'd left for Germany. "We can be friends?"

Crick nodded and gave her his best smile. "I could definitely live with that, Popcorn."

"Popcorn?" she asked, smiling that cute little scrunchy-freckled smile.

"You are just so damned perky!"

The little ritual of meeting in that spot to talk about books or home or to just give each other shit lasted until Crick's last day in Iraq. Besides Deacon's letters, he figured those moments were the other thing that just about saved his life.

Crick @DP—At the risk of sounding like a teenaged girl, I've got a friend.

DP @Crick—We could send you some make-up and pink slippers if they make you more comfy w/the idea.

Crick @DP—Do you enjoy being a dick?

DP @Crick—I'm less of one when I get to use mine.

Crick @DP—ROFL now fuck off.

DP @Crick—No, tell me about your new friend.

Crick @DP—She's my driver. She saw my sketches and thinks you're hot. And she wants a human to talk to. It's a win/win.

DP @Crick—And she's a 'she'. I win too.

Crick @DP—I've thought of that, but no more mistakes for me anyway.

DP @Crick—I can live with your mistakes—no worries.

Crick @DP—I don't need to make mistakes when I have someone to talk to, so backatcha.

DP @Crick—This is one helluva conversation to have at 140 chrctrs a shot.

Crick @DP—Think of it as minimalist love poetry. I love you dickwad.

DP @Crick—I love you too, Gidget.

Crick @DP—Who?

DP @Crick—Neverthefuckmind.

Benny @Crick @DP—I love you both, but you're both dicks.

DP @Benny—get lost, Shorty!

Crick @Benny—Jesus, Benny, get out of our conversation, wouldja!

Benny @Crick@DP—*ROFLMAOSTCAYUAL*

Crick @Benny@DP—I'm afraid to ask.

DP @Benny @Crick—'And Yakking Up A Lung'

Crick @DP—Jesus.

DP @Crick—Welcome to my world.

Benny @Crick @DP—bye guys—love you both.

DP @Benny We love you too, now let us sign off!

Crick @DP—I love you different.

DP @Crick—Me too.

Deacon didn't know the young black man at the door, but the guy smiled winsomely at the pudgy nine-month-old in Deacon's arms, so Deacon liked him on sight.

"Hi—I'm, um, Andrew Carpenter... I don't know if Crick told you about me?"

Deacon blinked. Damn... it had been in one of his early letters, but Deacon had been dealing with other shit then, and....

"Lieutenant Francis, um." Andrew grinned brilliantly, the gap in his white teeth doing nothing to make him seem any less trustworthy. "He might have referred to me as Private Blood-loss?" And with that, the young man held out a jean covered ankle that was obviously prosthetic, and the lightbulb went on.

"Private Blood-loss!" Deacon was delighted. "Come on in! It's great to meet a friend of Crick's!" He turned his head over his shoulder and called out "Benny! We've got company for dinner. Throw on more cheese, darlin', I know you're dying to!"

"Will he settle for another steak?" she called back cheerfully, and Deacon turned a smile at Andrew. "Steak good?"

"Steak's great!" the boy said enthusiastically, and Deacon laughed and ushered him in out of the early November rain.

A couple hours later, after Benny and Deacon had heard the whole of Crick's walkabout from the point of view of the guy being hauled around the desert, Deacon couldn't remember when he'd laughed so hard or felt so proud of Carrick.

"Jesus, Private...."

"Andrew, sir."

Deacon rolled his eyes. "Deacon, Andrew—anyway, that's not the version we got from Crick."

"No," Benny added, "but we did get a whole lot of Crick wanting to shoot, strangle, or bludgeon Private Jimmy to death—and now we know why!"

She poured Andrew a glass of milk, since that was what they were drinking, and they all took a collective breath. Parry Angel gave a little squeal from her high chair. She was eating pasta and vegetables, only mashed, and was wearing an attractive little halo of it around her fat, pink cheeks and even mashed into her fuzzy brown hair. Benny looked at her and sighed.

"You know, I was going to feed her, but no, Uncle Deacon had to let her play with her food!"

Deacon blushed. He was pretty damned indulgent, and he felt bad. "Here—I'll clean her up before I go feed for the night...."

Benny slapped his hand and laughed. "Stop it—I like bath time! Besides, you took her three nights running. She's going to forget she has a mama!"

Parry Angel gave another squeal and started banging on her high chair shelf, excited by all the by-play, and Benny gave Deacon another shooing motion with her hand. "Go! If Comet doesn't get his extra carrots, he starts getting cranky!"

Deacon held up his hands in mock surrender and moved toward the entryway to get his coat.

"Sir... Deacon," Andrew said, rising, "can I come out and see the horses?"

He did more than see them—he helped feed and asked about care and, in the end, leaned over the half-door and fed Comet his carrots. Deacon let him—their last muckraker had needed to move on to college, and Deacon had yet to find another lonely kid to help them out with the small stuff. Muckraking was like laundry—it never stopped, and it only got uglier if you let it pile up. He moved around in Shooting Star's stall for a bit, getting rid of the horse crap in the wheelbarrow they took out to the compost pile out back. They sold the compost to a local fertilizer company—another one of the small ways the ranch made money. Horses took a lot of food and a lot of care. Everything from boarding, breaking, and training other people's animals, winning show prizes, giving riding lessons, and regular donations from Even Star's wonder-cock helped to keep The Pulpit in the black. The animals they bred and broke themselves made up the bulk of their income, but it was all part and parcel of a successful business, and it was a life that Deacon wouldn't trade for the world.

Deacon pushed the wheelbarrow out of the doorway and closed the door behind him, turning around to find Andrew holding out a couple of carrots. Since Deacon had been heading for the carrot bag anyway, he took them thankfully and offered Shooting Star her treat. She took it and tried to take a couple of Deacon's fingers with them. Deacon shoved her head away with authority.

"Greedy old bitch—that shit doesn't play with me, never has."

Deacon moved to take the wheelbarrow then, and Andrew grabbed the handles instead. "Where do you need it, Deacon?"

Deacon was a little surprised—helping to feed was one thing, but hauling horseshit was something completely different. Deacon was quiet for a moment as they walked out to the compost pile far behind the barn, and his "Crick sense" started to kick in.

"Private Carpenter, is there something you'd like to talk about?"

Andrew dumped the wheelbarrow, after having—apparently— proved that his prosthetic wasn't going to hold him back from any chore.

"Sir...."

"I'm just a guy, Andrew—Crick's the officer."

"You're a CO, sir—anybody can see it. Please, just let me.... I've been in the military for two tours, right out of high school. That's three and a half years, sir, and they just cut me loose. I'm...." Andrew put the wheelbarrow in its customary spot, leaning it against the stable wall.

"I'm at a loss, sir," Andrew said at last, looking at Deacon in the dark. "I... I had nothing going for me in my hometown, even less now." He indicated his leg. "Crick—he came by and visited when I was getting ready to be moved out, and… he just made this place sound perfect. And he's right. It's perfect. And I'm lost."

Deacon blinked. "Andrew—are you asking for a job?"

Andrew shrugged. "I know you can't pay much—I saw some cots and rooms in the stalls, and a little shower cubicle back behind them. If no one's using them…." He shrugged and looked away, the gesture showing Deacon how very much he needed a place, a haven, and Deacon wanted to oblige. But first, a little bit of truth.

"Look, Private…."

"Andrew."

"Andrew—we're short a muckraker, and I've got no problem feeding you and giving you a place to stay and a meager-assed salary, but first…." Oh God. Deacon had always known Crick was fearless, but coming out to a stranger was a first for him. He took a few steps out toward the nearest open pasture and looked up at the full November moon powering its way out around the big, dense gray clouds that had dumped on them all day.

"Andrew, Benny's got Crick's old room, and Parry Angel's got mine. It's a three-bedroom house. Where do you think Crick's going to sleep when he gets back?" Well, that was one way to approach it. Deacon kept his eyes on the moon for a while, wishing Levee Oaks wasn't quite so close to Sacramento so he could see more stars.

He heard Andrew grunt when the situation sank in. "I assume he's going to sleep in your room, with you, sir."

Deacon turned and looked over his shoulder. "Our room. The kid painted it for us before he left. Still want that job, Andrew?"

Andrew met his eyes and nodded, no doubt whatsoever. "Absolutely, sir."

"Kid, you're going to have to stop calling me sir."

DP @Crick—Met a friend of yours today. Had a totally different take on wandering around the desert.

Crick @DP—Lies, all lies. How is Private Blood-loss?

DP @Crick—Helping your sister with the dishes and getting ready to move into our stables.

Crick @DP—That's damned nice of you, Deacon.

DP @Crick—He's a nice young man. And he's apparently very liberal.

Crick @DP—Liberal?

DP @Crick—He knows where you sleep.

Crick @DP—That was brave of you.

DP @Crick—You taught me everything I know.

Crick @DP—Bullshit. I model everything you taught me.

DP @Crick—Go away. I have to find a space heater and a sleeping bag.

Crick @DP—Say it first.

DP @Crick—I love you, Carrick James. You make me proud every day. I miss you enough to scramble my brains—howzat?

Crick @DP—Incredibly humbling. Love you back. Crick out.

"Dammit, Deacon, you're losing weight again!" Crick was appalled—it was their Christmas computer visit, this one landing square on Deacon's birthday, and Deacon looked like hell.

Deacon gave him a tired smile. "Sorry, Carrick. I... It's been a rough month."

"Where's Benny and the baby?" Crick hadn't realized until this very moment how much he'd wanted to see the baby smiling, active, in something besides the myriad twitpics that Deacon sent to him on a daily basis.

"They're at the hospital, getting fluids—I'm sorry, Crick—I told you we were getting sick... it got bad this morning." Deacon scrubbed at his face with a hand that shook so badly Crick could see it through the computer. Off range, a voice said, "Deacon, dammit...."

"He's got a half-an-hour, Drew," Deacon said with grim patience. "I'm not going to waste it."

Crick felt his helplessness at the far end of the world. It hit his chest like a posthole digger hit hardpan, and he got a terrible surge of fear and adrenaline. *This must be how they worry about me all the time.*

"What do you all have?" he asked, and he noticed that Deacon didn't deny that he was just as sick as the girls.

Deacon shrugged. "Fucking flu. It's gotten a little less virulent since you left, but…." His whole body shuddered—Crick assumed it was with fever and fear. "The baby—it hit her the worst. It's…." Deacon's voice choked and he squared himself up. "If you don't mind making a little peace with a higher power, Crick, this might be the time for it."

"What about you?"

"I'm fine."

"You're AMA, asshole!" Andrew barked from off camera. "Don't lie to him, dammit—he should know."

Deacon shot him a glare that was weakened with illness and worry. "They're gonna turn me loose tomorrow anyway," he snapped. "I may as well be here now." He turned back to the camera. "Don't listen to him, Crick. He's worried, that's all. He's gotten sort of attached to us this last month. It's sweet that he doesn't want us to leave."

"I should be there," Crick said numbly, the weight of the last eighteen months crashing on his head.

"You're goddamned right you should be!" Deacon said harshly, almost out of nowhere, and Crick's head snapped back in shock. Deacon scrubbed his face again. "I'm sorry. Dammit—I'm sorry—I don't want to yell. I… you know, it doesn't matter if you're home or there in the middle of the fucking desert, Crick, if you're not here to hash it out, we've got to make it all good. So it's all good. You understand?"

Crick's face was cold, and his stomach was knotted. He'd had a bad feeling when Benny and Deacon's texts had gotten terse. They'd said there was illness, but they hadn't mentioned the fucking apocalyptic plague there in his home.

"You should have told me how bad it was," he said at last.

"We didn't know until this morning," Deacon told him, and Crick had no doubt he was being honest. "Besides, Carrick, there's not much you can do anyway. I'm just as glad you're not here to get it, if you must know the truth."

They talked some more, and Crick promised to try and get a hold of another time slot so he could see the baby. At the end, he could do nothing—he could only look at Deacon, haggard face and bleary eyes, mouth "I love you," and hope nobody saw. Deacon mouthed the words back, and Andrew's dark hand appeared to haul him physically away.

Crick staggered out of the tent feeling like shit twice and practically ran over Lisa on his way.

"Hey, Crick, how's the family?"

Her chipper voice sort of tapered off as she saw his shell-shocked face, and when he rasped, "Sick as hell," she grabbed his arm and took him to the commissary for an ear and a beer.

To say that they "waited" for news during the next two days was like saying that the guy on the roof of his house during a flood "waited" for rescue. When Crick didn't get any texts at all the next morning, Lisa found him huddled in the ambulance as it sweltered in the truck bay, his arms wrapped around his knees as he rocked himself back and forth.

"Whatcha doing, Lieu?" she asked cautiously.

"Praying," he muttered. "I suck at it."

"You're doing it wrong," she said flatly. "I'm not big on church, but I'm pretty sure you're supposed to do it with a friend." And she sat across from him for a half-an-hour in the broiling heat while he muttered, "Please, God, let them be all right" and not much else into the echo of the bus.

The next afternoon, Crick's phone buzzed for the first time in nearly three days.

Benny @Crick—Me and the baby are back at home and fine.

Crick @Benny—Thank God. Deacon?

Benny @Crick—Hospital won't let him out. He's conscious now though.

Crick @Benny—CONSCIOUS?

Benny @Crick—Dumb bastard shouldn't have snuck out. Christ he's stubborn, Crick—only listens to you.

DP @Crick @Benny—Bite me, little sister, Im fine.

Benny @DP—I'm not talking to you until you're home, asshole. Dammit, Deacon, you should be asleep.

DP @Benny @Crick—Din't want Crick to worry.

Benny @DP—Tough. We're all worried. Drew's worried, Patrick's worried, Jon and Amy're worried.

DP @Benny—KEEP AMY AWAY—she's pregnant!

Crick @Benny @DP—Was anybody going to tell me?

DP @Crick—busy wk ere notim e

Crick @DP—Sign off, dammit. Sleep. Get better.

DP @Crick—wan seeu gain

Crick @DP—I promise. Deacon, I promise, okay? Go to sleep.

DP @Crick—night.

Crick @DP—Night, Deacon. Love you.

They got another chance to talk at Christmas, and Deacon did what he could to not look like death warmed over. Christ, the flu had leveled them all this year. He'd sent Patrick to his sister's place for the month because the elderly man hadn't gotten it, and Deacon wasn't sure if he'd survive it if he did.

Deacon and Benny had been too wiped out to do more than decorate (with a lot of help from Andrew), so thank God for the Internet. Deacon had given her a credit card to play with, and she'd invited him in on the fun. Between the two of them—with some help from Crick, who had his own money to play with—they bought out half the Toys-R-Us catalog, and they'd spent a whole lot of time in the last two weeks wrapping the packages that had landed on their doorstep. Deacon had also spent a little bit of time spoiling Benny rotten—T-shirts with her favorite movie, a Jack Skellington book bag, a gift certificate to someplace girly where they could dye her hair instead of having her dye the entire bathroom.

Between Benny, Crick, Jon, Amy, Patrick, and Andrew, he'd answered "What do you want for Christmas?" about six thousand times a day. He'd finally asked for an iPhone and music because it would give them something to spend money on, and he couldn't say the only thing he really wanted, because everybody knew that anyway.

What he got—besides the iPhone—was a laptop, which was pretty awesome in its own way, because he used it in the living room to show Crick the baby. She was sitting determinedly up, her wide, smiling mouth open and drooling, and playing devotedly with something pink, plastic, and noisy.

Crick was appropriately charmed. "She looks like she's doing okay," he said over the sound system. "She's… God, Deacon, she's really big."

"She's put on some weight since the hospital," Benny said earnestly. "We were worried—none of us ate for, like, days."

"Except for me," interjected Amy dryly from the back of the room. Deacon looked at her and grinned—she was pretty round for two months along, but Jon couldn't stop doting on her. It was damned cute.

"And you, Deacon?" Crick asked anxiously, and from behind him—hard to see in the shot—came a female voice.

"Oooohh... make him take off his shirt and see!"

Deacon blushed, probably to his toes, and Crick said, "Um, no. That... that's for me."

"You must be Lisa," Deacon said dryly, setting the laptop down on a cleared spot of the kitchen table. "Pleased to meet you." Amy and Benny had cooked for days, and the residents of The Pulpit had done their best to eat, in spite of still catching up from the flu. A cute, round, freckled little face with blond bangs escaping a perky ponytail peered around Crick's shoulder.

"You're Deacon," she said back. "Crick's been so worried."

Deacon blushed some more. "Well, the baby and Benny had it pretty rough there," he dodged. "I'm glad Crick had someone to lean on."

Lisa tapped her wrist, and Crick nodded and then said, "Deacon, take me into the other room, would you?"

He'd spent a long time watching the baby play and talking to the family—they both knew that, so nobody objected, and the chatter kept going as Deacon took the computer into the bedroom and propped it on the dresser by the still-empty wall.

"Did you get the...."

"Yeah, Deacon, I got the care package and the presents. No worries, okay? I just need to see that you're okay."

Deacon shrugged. "I'm tired, but that could be just staying up late and wrapping presents," he tried with a grin, and Crick shook his head.

"Look—Lisa's got the media guys outside with some eggnog—take off your shirt and sweater!"

"Crick...." Oh God. That blush was all the way back.

"Please, Deacon—I just need to see you're not like... you know. Like you were when Benny got there."

Deacon sighed. He wasn't—but not by much. The shirt and sweater came off, and Crick sucked in his breath, and Deacon sighed in the now-cold room, unable to look Crick in the eyes. "I'm not much of a pinup," he said with an attempt at humor.

Crick murmured, "Deacon, please look at me."

Deacon looked up, and across the ocean, across the so-so picture quality, and across the nineteen months of separation, he saw Crick's eyes, those brown, open, sweet eyes, on his body. "That's mine," Crick said now, gruffly. "That's mine. You promised it to me—you need to take care of it. You hear me? You eat good and you drive safe and you watch yourself on that mean-assed mare of yours, and you make sure that's waiting for me, you hear?"

Deacon smiled—the soft smile, the one Crick said he only used in bed—and Crick smiled back. There was a ruckus from behind Crick, and Crick said quickly, "I love you."

"Love you back."

"Merry Christmas."

"Merry Christmas."

And then he was gone.

DP @Crick—Dammit, now I'm all horny.

Crick @DP—All my stuff's in the drawer.

DP @Crick—Can't use it. It's yours.

Crick @DP—That shit have a shelf life?

DP @Crick—Maybe I should throw it out and not test it.

Crick @DP—Only if you're going to replace it!

DP @Crick—I'll wait until you get home.

Crick @DP—Hold on, baby. I'm coming.

DP @Crick—And sadly, I'm not.

Crick @DP—Not yet, anyway.

DP @Crick—Heh heh heh heh heh...

Crick @DP—Deacon?

DP @Crick—mmmm?

Crick @DP—You're still a little mad at me, aren't you?

DP @Crick—Less every day.

The ambulance had rolled into a deep spot in the desert, the two patients hadn't survived the tumble, and Crick and Lisa were back to back, cradling their M-16s and listening for enemy fire.

"Sorry 'bout the wreck, Lieu," Lisa said, her voice taut. They'd pulled themselves out of it, checked each other for injuries, radioed for help, and grabbed their guns. That had been about an hour ago, and Crick's belly quivered as he thought that his life might actually depend on him firing that damned M-16.

Goddammit, he'd made it to the baby's first birthday and his twenty-second. He'd promised Deacon—he just wasn't about to break that promise, that was all.

"Not your fault, sweetheart," he muttered. It hadn't been. A shell had hit right in front of them. She'd swerved and managed to save both their lives. It was a shame about the Marines in the back of the van, though— Crick hadn't lost many patients, and it rankled that he lost these two to a combination of traumas.

"You say that to all the pretty women you get wrecked with?" It was a shitty attempt at humor, but he gave her points for trying.

"Only the ones that keep me in the closet," he looked back and told her honestly. "Fuck!" Whoever it was over her shoulder, he wasn't friendly. Crick aimed, fired, and hit. His one and only shot in the war, and he never even dreamed about it, barely even remembered it happened. Before Lisa had a chance to check her back or see what or whom he'd shot at, they both heard it, and the scattered gunfire over their heads stalled out.

"Sound like a Black Hawk to you?" she asked, her tight little fighting smile fierce and hopeful.

"Hey—think we've got enough practice praying to make that stick?" he asked breathlessly, looking overhead. Together, like children and only partially kidding, they started to chant, "Please God, let that be a friendly. Please God, let that be a friendly" After a few rounds of distinctive air-to-ground fire, there it was: a Black Hawk, landing on the ridge above them—cannyagimmehallefuckinlujah, amen.

It wasn't until Crick and Lisa were safe back on base, holding shaking hands over a couple of off-duty beers, bruises, abrasions, and all, that Crick checked his pocket to contact Deacon. Holy shit—his BlackBerry was gone. Shit. Shit, shit, shit, shit—it had been there after the wreck—it must have come out when he'd belted himself into the Huey. He could get it back, maybe, but when?

"Jesus, Lisa!" He was panicked. "I've got to get a hold of him. He'll be watching CNN—he'll see all the fighting and I won't be on the horn—he'll think I'm dead!"

It wasn't until the next evening, when both he and Lisa tried for time on the satellite phone and were denied because of weather conditions, that his CO called him in to watch CNN to see the flooding in northern California. That was when Crick realized that Deacon might possibly have some other shit on his mind.

Chapter 15

Broken Levees, Dead Horses, and Driving While Gay

DEACON'S body ached, and he couldn't remember the last time he'd slept. It had started raining steadily in November and kept it up through December and January, but this last month... well, the ground was already saturated, and February had pummeled them like God had gotten drunk and was pissing on Nor-Cal for sport.

Deacon had spent three sleepless days loading up the back of the truck with sandbags and either schlepping them to The Pulpit to bank up the levee side of the ranch and build an inner ring of bags around the house or to the National Guardsmen, helping to bank up the levee itself. It was late now—Crick's calling time, actually—and he hadn't called in three days. Deacon was starting to think of the storm as a blessing, because it meant that he didn't have to think about it, didn't have to watch CNN and see what might be happening at the far ends of the earth, didn't have to imagine Carrick, dead, mutilated, or suffering—he could just load sandbags and try to save his fucking home.

Which was what he was thinking when the truck gave out on the way back home from the sandbagging site at the fire station, right smack-dab in front of Sandy's Bar.

A bar, God? Really? I haven't heard from Crick in three goddamned days, and You park me in front of a bar? I'm seriously starting to think Crick was right about You, ya big fucker.

Deacon looked up at the sky as he said it, and since the rain kept pissing down, silver against the black, he figured that God could give a shit about what one Deacon Winters thought about his grand-and-fucked-up plan.

He tried to call Jon for a jumpstart—it was the alternator; he knew it because the damned thing had been threatening to quit all week—but the storm was wreaking havoc with the satellite reception and cell service was down. He figured he could go inside and use the payphone and call him—he'd call Benny, but she wasn't there. She was visiting her grandmother in Natomas, mostly to keep the old bitch from threatening them with Child Protective Services because Benny was living with a man eleven years her senior. Patrick was still up at his sister's in El Dorado Hills, and Deacon was thinking seriously of sending Benny, Parry Angel, and even Amy, Jon, and Andrew up there if the storm didn't get better by the next day. If the levee broke, there might not be enough of The Pulpit for the sandbags to save.

Fuck. He sighed and rested his head on the steering wheel of the vast and ancient Chevy. *Okay, Deacon—you haven't even wanted a drink since before the baby was born. Go in, get a soda, call Jon for a jumpstart, and get the fuck out of here.*

And it should have gone that way too.

He walked in and was mildly surprised at how many people would brave that weather to come and get drunk and watch CNN. He eased his way into the bar and looked blankly at the row of once-familiar labels at the back and then looked at Sandy—a three-hundred-pound bearded biker who fed about a thousand cats from his trailer behind the bar—and asked for a soda.

"A soda?"

Deacon smiled faintly and nodded. "Seven-up would be great. I gotta go make a call...."

"Deacon? Deacon Winters, is that you?"

Deacon turned and blinked. "Becca—Becca Anderson?"

Jon's old girlfriend was there, looking a little worse for the past ten years—her hair was dyed now instead of natural, and she was one of those women who got lean-skinny as she aged instead of comfy and round. Still, she was tiredly pretty for all of that.

"Deacon!" she squealed, giving him a wholly unwanted—and very personal-feeling—sort of hug. He smiled politely and tried to disentangle himself. He hadn't been blind to Becca's attempts to get between him and Amy—he'd just never wanted to hurt Jon by telling him that Bec was a skank whore, that was all. He'd been relieved when Jon told him that he'd had a longtime crush on Amy at the end of their senior year. It meant that his friend's taste had improved and that the odds of his heart getting carelessly ripped to shreds were considerably diminished.

"Good to see you, Bec," he lied, and then he looked up and nodded when his soda arrived. He took a drink and sighed a little—the sugar tasted good—and set the drink down again.

"I gotta go make a call," he murmured, and Bec shook her head.

"Stay a while, sweetie. What are you doing here anyway? Did you know that boy?"

Deacon's heart literally ceased to beat. "Boy?"

"Yeah, hon." Becca nodded at the TV, where CNN was showing scenes of the stepped-up violence around Kuwait. "You know—that one boy, he used to get riding lessons from you? A couple of years younger than us... you know...."

"Crick," Deacon said faintly. His vision was black. His goddamned vision was black and he couldn't fucking breathe.

"No—not that kid. Eddy something...."

Deacon took a breath, and it tasted like sour milk. "Eddy Fitzpatrick," he said, but his vision was still black, and his hands were still shaking, and he wasn't sure if he could stand.

"Yeah! That's him—you remember that kid?"

Deacon remembered that he'd once beaten the crap out of Crick, and he thought maybe he was a bad person, because he couldn't bring himself to give a shit that he was dead. "A little," he muttered, not sure if he could even talk right. "That's too bad. If you'll excuse me, Becca?"

He made it to the bathroom in time to throw up. Oh God. He'd thought... of course he'd thought it. The fucker hadn't called him in three days. Jesus! He cleaned himself up with shaking hands, and when his vision had cleared enough to get him out to the little vestibule in front of the men's room, he stopped at the payphone and left a message on Jon's home phone, wondering where the two of them were this time of night.

Crap—that meant he was stuck in the bar. Oh *hell* no, he thought viciously. He was three miles from home. He could fucking walk and at least let the horses out of the stables if the water threatened to get any higher. So he managed his way up to the bar again and smiled gamely at Becca.

She smiled back, and he registered the predatory look on her face just as he raised the glass to his mouth.

He could smell the gin about a fraction of a second before it hit the back of his throat. He tried to tell people that when they told him that the rest of the night wasn't his fault. He tried to tell Jon, so Jon would know that this was his fuck-up and no one else's. He tried to tell Benny, so she could get mad at him for breaking his promise. He tried to tell Crick, so he could assure Crick that they were even for Berlin, not that Deacon had been keeping a tally anyway.

He tried to tell them all, but they didn't believe him. He hadn't eaten or slept in three days, and he'd just had a nasty scare and lost whatever was in his stomach to keep him going. The alcohol on his tongue was like the goddamned elixir of life, and even as he gulped down the gin and tonic that Becca had substituted for his soda, it slammed through his nervous system like a freight train.

He barely remembered setting the glass down or Becca's voice, stretching wonkily like taffy in his head as she told him not to worry, she'd get him home just fine.

He woke up before dawn, sitting up like he'd been shot and then groaning as he fell back down. *Christ, please, if I promise to go to church, maybe once with Parry Angel and Benny all pretty for you, could you please let my head fall off? Please?*

Becca's low chuckle next to his ear told him that maybe that was more mercy than he deserved, and then his phone started to buzz, and as he scrambled over the edge of the bed for his pants (was he *naked*? Oh *shit*. He was *naked*! And there was a… oh, *ewww*… at least it was a condom, and it was still on his pecker, but it was *used*), all he could think of was that if he'd let himself get hungover the first time he'd ever gotten drunk, it might not have lasted for three months straight.

"Benny?" he mumbled, "I thought you were still at your granny's!"

"Yeah, well, the visit started with how the baby would be better off with her and ended with how all gay people were going to hell, so I made her take us home. Deacon, where the hell are you—it's four in the morning, and the shit's hitting the fan outside!"

"The truck broke down in front of Sandy's...."

"The *bar!* Oh God, Deacon, you didn't...."

"Yeah, Benny. Yeah, yeah I did. But you don't have to worry, honey. If you'll let me tell the story, I swear it was the last goddamned drink I will *ever* have in my fucking miserable life." He stood up and thunked the condom into the trashcan by Becca's bed—which was practically in the living room of her tiny apartment—and then reached for his jeans and underwear (still together, actually) and pulled them up while keeping the phone on his ear.

Benny was quiet for a moment, and Deacon prayed for real and sincere that she wouldn't take that baby to her grandma's big-assed house in Natomas and never speak to him or Crick again.

"I'm not throwing away all you've done for us because of one relapse, Deacon. I swear, man—what kind of ungrateful bitch do you think I am?"

Deacon closed his eyes and thanked God sincerely. "Benny, you're the best goddamned sister on the entire planet, you hear me? I love you like you were my own kid—and I will never let you down again."

"You haven't let me down now, Deacon," she muttered, her voice cracking a little. "Just how do we get you home so I can hear that story?"

He sighted his shirt at the foot of the bed and looked down at his skinny body to see Becca had left hickeys on his stomach on the way down to his... *God...* he closed his eyes against the nausea and hoped to hell that Crick had a better moment waking up in Germany than he was having right now.

"Call Jon again—he might have been taking Amy to her folks' house, but if he's still there, have him meet me outside of Sandy's with some jumper cables and some faith. If he can't make it, send Andrew if you can—he's in the house, right?" It was a hell of a night to sleep in the stables.

"Yeah, he's here. And so're Jon and Amy—their house has about two feet of water right now. The Pulpit's still good."

Hey, speaking of good—he'd left his socks in his boots. Even in the dimness of the tiny, crappy apartment, he could see them at the entryway.

Well, good to know his mudroom manners didn't desert him when he was drunk enough to sleep with Becca Daniels.

"Well, I want you and Amy to get the baby ready to travel—call Patrick's sister in El Dorado Hills, and I'll have Andrew take you both."

"We're not leaving—"

"The hell you're not. You've got babies, both of you, even if Amy hasn't had hers yet. You've got bigger things to think about than the horse ranch, so you just man up and get ready to get yourself someplace safe, okay?"

"Fine," she snapped, and he breathed a sigh of relief.

"Okay, Shorty—you get someone to the truck with some jumper cables, and I'll get back and tell you the story before I go. It's a side-ripper, trust me."

"How're you going to get to the bar?" she asked suspiciously, and he looked at Becca, who was looking at him bemusedly from her side of the bed.

"I'm going to run like hell," he told her, meaning it, and hung up.

"Oh come on, Deacon," Becca said, laughing in that sultry way that had made her so very popular in high school. "You had yourself a good time. I mean, the sex was over pretty quickly—you must have been damned hard-up—but you enjoyed yourself!"

Deacon blinked at her as he was shrugging on his denim jacket. It was still sopping from four days sandbagging, but it was better than nothing, and he sure as shit wasn't leaving it here.

"How in the hell would you know that?" Oh God, where was... okay. His Stetson, hanging on the edge of the chair. He snagged it while he was waiting for her answer.

"Well, sugar, you told me you loved me!"

Deacon blinked. "That's unlikely," he said, like his inner eyeball wasn't looking for some cortex bleach with the very thought.

Becca was so outraged she dropped the sheet, and Deacon held his hand up in front of his face out of sheer instinct. "You sure as shit did!" she shrieked. "I had your dick in my mouth and you said 'I love you, Bek', plain as day."

The world went so still it was almost like the storm stopped. "Crick," he said through a sandpaper throat. "I said 'I love you, Crick'."

"You did not!" She gathered the sheet up, which was a pure relief, and Deacon nodded, because this was maybe the one thing he *did* remember from the night before.

"I did too—how drunk you gotta be, Becca, to think I said Bec instead of Crick?"

"Crick? Isn't that a boy's name?"

Deacon nodded and tried not to laugh hysterically. "Oh yeah."

"Crick? Seriously, isn't Crick that gay Mexican kid who used to shovel horseshit?"

Deacon knew the truth in the pit of his stomach, and he wasn't going to sugarcoat it for Becca Daniels. "That 'gay Mexican kid' is serving our country right now, you rank whoring bitch—and he's a better human being than you've ever been."

"Oh my God!" Her scream followed him as he turned and stalked out the door. "You're *gay*? Does that mean I've got AIDS now?"

"Only if you gave it to me!" he yelled back as he slammed her door.

She lived about two miles from the bar, and Jon was waiting there, his blue Mercedes giving off steam as its motor purred and Deacon trotted up in the wet, rainy dawn.

"You wanna tell me what happened?" Jon asked. Deacon grunted and lifted the hood of the battered truck, hooking up the jumper cables that Jon handed him before he answered.

"Not particularly, but if you want to pull up a chair and some popcorn, I'll give you the whole show when I 'fess up to Benny." He looked at the truck with a sigh and turned his back on it, leaning against the fender for a minute while it charged.

"How about you give me the unabridged version," Jon suggested inexorably, and Deacon tipped back his head, letting the rain wash his face clean, because it wasn't like he wasn't wet through anyway.

When he was done talking, Jon actually had the balls to laugh. "I love you, Crick," he chuckled. "Damn, Deacon—that's just fucking precious."

"Shut up," Deacon growled, and Jon just kept chuckling.

"How drunk did she have to be to think you said 'Bec' instead of 'Crick'?

"Did I mention the shutting up?"

"Yeah, but I'm ignoring you. Dude, it's just good to see you can still fuck up like the rest of us."

"Oh, and three months of being drunk didn't count?" Deacon reached inside and turned the ignition, relaxing just a little when the engine caught. He had two tons of sandbags under a tarp over the back that would do him no good at all if the fucking truck wouldn't at least get him home.

"Yeah, but you've been living the last eighteen months like you're trying to atone for killing somebody." Jon stopped talking when Deacon glowered at him.

"Can we stop talking about this?" he growled, and Jon shrugged, looked at the sky in the grey light, and sighed.

"Yeah, man—for right now, I'll let you slide." There was a crack of thunder overhead, and both of them shuddered. Over the sound of the rain and the truck's engine, the roar of the river could be heard as it danced a disastrous can-can with the levee banks.

Deacon unhooked the jumper cables and held his breath. After a few moments, it looked like the alternator was on good behavior, and he gave the cables back to Jon with a grateful nod.

"I'll meet you at home. Are you and Amy ready to drive up to El Dorado Hills?"

"We were thinking a hotel in Rocklin's closer—Amy'll spring, so don't worry 'bout that—but she's driving Benny and I'm staying at The Pulpit." Jon slammed his own hood shut and rolled his eyes at Deacon's scowl.

"What are you going to do at home?" he asked, hesitating at his open door. "You should be with Amy."

"Instead of defending your home? Screw that, Deacon. You're going to need help, and I'm tired of waiting for you to ask for it. I'll follow you to make sure you get back okay." Jon slammed his door with unnecessary force and waited for Deacon to pull onto the main thoroughfare and drive to the levee road that would take him home.

And it was a damned good thing too, Deacon later agreed, because Jon was a witness when Deacon got pulled over.

Deacon saw the lights and sighed, hand-rolling down the window as the officer approached. Oh. Oh shit. "Morning, Jason," he muttered, fighting the temptation to bang his head against the steering wheel. "You got nothing better to do right now when the river's threatening to cut loose?"

Jason Gresham—school bully, local sheriff, and Becca's on-again, off-again boyfriend since Jon had cut her loose.

"Morning, faggot," Jason said with a sneer, and Deacon's eyes actually crossed.

"So, Becca gets me drunk, takes me home and fucks me, and then calls you when it goes wrong?" In retrospect, it was probably not the most diplomatic thing he'd ever said—in fact, he had to admit it was downright Crick-worthy. And so were the consequences. Jason's hand, slamming Deacon's head into his own steering wheel, was particularly merciless— and so was his baton as he started to bash in the headlights on the truck.

"Hey, Jason!" Jon called, just when that little extendable billy club was going for Deacon's front window. "Smile for me before I send this photo to my wife!"

Deacon looked up blearily and wiped the blood out of his eyes. "What took you so goddamned long!" he snapped, opening the door so Jason didn't think about going after Jon.

"I was making sure we had satellite feed," Jon apologized. Then he focused his iPhone square on Jason. From Deacon's angle, he got a nice moving shot of Jason folding up the baton and stalking right at Levee Oaks's premiere defense attorney before Deacon kicked the back of his left foot over the back of his right and sent him sprawling.

"You two fuckers are under arrest!" Jason growled as he hauled himself furiously from the mud, but Deacon and Jon were already behind the wheels of their vehicles.

"You want to arrest me, asshole, you know where to find me!" Deacon snapped, and then the two of them pulled away, gunning as fast as they could in the pissing rain for safety.

Benny tended to the cut on his head when he got home, and he told the story again—the abridged version this time, without the icky condom and the pathetic fact that he'd called out Crick's name when he came.

Benny was still young enough to think the world was fair—at least to grown-ups—and she didn't deal with the story well.

"So she switched your drink?" she said, throwing the first-aid kit back together with unnecessary force. "That cunt-whore switched your drink, and you're talking like it was *your* fuck-up?"

"I knew at the first taste, Benny—she didn't hold a gun to my head to make me swallow."

"*So-the-fuck-what?*" Benny spat, wiping her eyes with the back of her hands. "Sorry, Deacon—sounds a lot like the night Parry was made to me. Just because you're not a little girl...."

Deacon blinked past the pain in his head and grabbed her hand, wondering when his life had turned into an emotional Escher print. "He got you drunk?" he asked, feeling a little ill. Maybe he should eat something... and then his gorge rose, and he thought, *maybe not.*

"We're not talking about this now," Benny muttered, turning away, and Deacon looked around the kitchen helplessly.

Amy shrugged and murmured, "She's right—we don't have a lot of time before the next storm system rolls in and shit gets really ugly, and you guys need to unload the sandbags. Besides, Crystal managed to sneak a call in—step-Bob hasn't done jack about the flooding, and the girls are standing on the goddamned beds. If we're going to go fetch them...."

Deacon groaned. One goddamned thing after a fucking other. "Okay, here's the plan, the new revised version. Jon, you and Andrew unload the sandbags and shore up that section closest to the levee. Amy, you stay here and mind Parry. Benny, you come with me, we're going to collect your sisters, and if your mom's still telling them I'm some sort of deviant, they may be flat-out afraid of me. Jon, I'm taking your car. If anybody else has any fun stories about getting drunk and waking up with strangers, I'd advise you to shut the fuck up and save it until fucking June, am I clear?"

"So the story about Private Jimmy and the camel will have to wait, sir?" Andrew asked drolly, and since his voice was the driest thing any of them had seen in a week, it wasn't such a hardship to laugh as Jon threw him the keys.

Deacon had to cold-cock the sonovabitch to get in the door, and step-Bob fell with a splash on his front room floor. However, Crystal and Missy trotted willingly out when Benny called them, and that was a plus. They didn't seem scared of him either, which was pretty damned nice as well. Deacon and Benny had been keeping tabs on them—visiting after school when their parents weren't home—but still, it was rewarding to watch them hug their sister.

"Is he going to be all right?" Missy asked, prodding her groaning father a little with her toe.

"You didn't need to hit him that hard!" Melanie Coats accused, bending down to tend to her husband in the six inches of dirty water. Deacon was so used to ignoring the two of them, to thinking of them as obstacles, as thorns in Crick's side instead of human beings, that he didn't need a whole lot of prompting to wash his hands of them now.

"Probably not," he growled, shaking his hand out with a grim smile, "but it was pretty damned satisfying. C'mon, girls, the water's only getting higher."

"You're just going to leave me here?" Melanie wailed, and Deacon made a rather fascinating discovery about himself. His compassion for strays only went so far.

"You've sided with your husband for Crick's whole life," Deacon said without even the tiniest bit of pity in him. "There's no reason to stop now." With that, they loaded up the car and left.

When everyone was rounded up and gathered back at home, it was hard watching them all leave for Rocklin—it was such a crapshoot. Stay at The Pulpit and hope the sandbagging worked, or drive through the storm to someplace safe and hope the car didn't get stopped or flooded. Fuck. It was certainly not the easiest decision Deacon had ever made. But the power was already off—although the old phone in the kitchen worked—and the roads were already three inches under. If they were going to leave, they needed to leave right the fuck now. Deacon found he was enough of a caveman to want the women-folk safe while he stayed and battled the mastodons.

Which was why, after getting Parry Angel strapped into the car and her port-a-crib and shit loaded in, as well as a suitcase of Benny's with extra clothes for the girls, Deacon was shocked and plenty dismayed when the car started to pull away and Benny hopped out.

Amy honked twice, and Benny waved, and Deacon and Jon walked up to her, their mouths open to chew her out, when she turned a tear-ravaged face to them both.

"Amy's keeping the baby safe, assholes—this here's my home." With that, she stomped toward the house and called, "Go finish with the sandbags, Deacon—I'll move all the important shit off the floor."

"Well," Deacon said, and they moved their bodies into a soft run because the river was getting louder, "I got nothin'."

Jon smacked him on the back of the head and kept on moving. "You've got us."

The next two hours felt like swimming through quicksand. Andrew would throw a bag to Jon, who would hand it to Deacon, and Deacon would shore up the four-foot, two-hundred yard stretch of low-lying pastureland that faced the levee road. The truck had officially died when they'd parked it, so the sections of sandbagged fence that were farthest away had to be trekked towards, and Deacon was off on the far end of the pasture when he saw them.

"Oh *fuck!*" He turned and sprinted back towards the house, going off at an angle from the truck because that was the quickest way.

"Deacon—Deacon, what the hell!" Jon called, and Deacon paused and turned around, watching his feet as he went.

"Fucking rattlers!" he called out. "The pasture over must be flooded!" It had been vacant for years, and unlike Deacon's property, it didn't have the two potbelly pigs to kill the varmints in an eco-friendly, circle-of-life sort of way. The half-dozen or so adolescent rattlesnakes that Deacon had just seen did not look interested in hearing why rattlesnakes shouldn't eat the horses—they were just as freaked out as every other living thing in this neck of the woods.

"There's a whole fucking family of them! All the horses are out in pasture, Jon—including the babies! I need the goddamned shotgun and a shovel—the fuckers are heading towards the barn!"

Because the barn was high ground, and all of the pastures circled it. Fuck.

"Deacon—man, the levee looks like she's gonna go!"

"Man, throw some sandbags around them if you can, finish unloading, and get the hell back to the house! I'll be back in five with Comet and take care of it!"

"Great," Deacon heard Jon grumble, even as he threw his body into his sprint. "Bad cops, floods, rattlesnakes… when's God gonna give us a plague of goddamned locusts, just for kicks?!"

"He's saving the locusts for my birthday!" Deacon yelled, and then he kept all his wind for running.

By the time he splatted through the wet garage to get the shotgun out of the gun safe, a shovel from the barn, and a bareback pad for Comet, Andrew and Jon were already halfway back to the garage.

"I trapped most of them," Jon called across the rain as Deacon rode by, "but one or two got away—be careful, Deac!"

"Will do!" And then Comet was picking up a cautious canter while Deacon kept his eyes scanning the ground. Thanks to the rain, the grass was long and green—once he saw the irregular movement under the rain-flattened grasses, the tan and black snakes were pretty easy to spot. He hopped off Comet and nailed the first one he saw with the shovel, chopping at it until the shovel came up red and the thrashing in the grass stopped. He brushed the grass back with the shovel and cut the head off of the poor thing with the shovel blade and then buried it right there while Comet waited like the patient creature he was.

In a minute, Deacon was back up on the horse, looking unhappily at both the threatening sky and the levee, which was starting to crumble and spill water. The bareback pad shifted uneasily, and Deacon adjusted his seat and grimaced. Those things just never felt as secure as a good, solid leather saddle, at least not to Deacon, but he'd been in a hurry and hadn't wanted to bother. That didn't mean he wasn't hoping that Comet kept up his record of being the world's most placid horse.

Together they kept riding, and the heavens kept threatening to crack. The thunder and lightning were getting worse. Deacon took this as a good sign, because it meant that the weather was changing in some way, but the clouds over his head were roiling and black, and he felt like the last man on the planet under them. There were enough oak trees scattered about the property that he didn't feel *too* exposed, but still—the way his day had been going so far, getting hit by lightning would be the cherry on the shit-sundae.

He found Jon's little circle of sandbags—Jon and Andrew had done a good job, even crushed one of the buggers between bags—and Deacon got off Comet and started hacking at them with the shovel, thinking that maybe he could get this finished and get up behind the second row of sandbags that were banking the house and maybe get warm and dry. He'd given up feeling his hands, but he was pretty sure that he had blisters forming from being wet under his leather gloves for so long and then chopping at the snakes like a madman, and he was starting to dread clenching the reins to steer the damned horse.

He finished the grisly job and rested his hand on Comet's flanks to keep the gelding calm. The thunder and lightning were getting closer and louder, and the shushing roar of the river felt like it was right at his feet instead of two hundred yards away. Just to check, he looked up from the sandbag circle of dead rattlers and kept his eye on the shored-up levee across the road. The water was high, dammit—dangerously high, and he saw some sandbags squelching their way down the sides. *Please, God... please, could you pay back that dead-truck-in-front-of-the-bar stunt by not flooding the house just now? Plea—*

God rewarded him with the subtle sound of rattling practically right under Comet's feet and a horrific crack of thunder directly overhead. Comet did what horses did, but what he'd never done, even as a baby, even as a yearling—he reared up on his hind legs in a panic, and again and again as Deacon reached for the reins anxiously. *Damn... don't let the dumbassed horse get snake-bit, please, please.* Another crack of thunder and the horse actually threw Deacon down as he reared back, and Deacon found himself face to face with a pissed off rattlesnake and, thank God, with a shovel in his hand.

The snake drew itself back to strike and threw itself into the shovel instead, and Deacon scrambled up to smack the fucker on the head before Comet could trample the poor dumb human in his way. He got the snake once, twice, in the back with the blade, and Comet squealed and reared and then came down hard on his forelegs and then... Oh God. Oh God. What in the fuck was that sound? It was a sick snapping, a squelching thud, followed by a scream that shred Deacon's eardrums. He had spent his whole life around horses, and he had *never* heard a sound like that. Oh Christ. Oh holy fucking Christ....

Comet reared up again, and there was the heavy thudding of his back legs as he scrabbled for purchase, struggling to do anything but put his weight on the leg that… Deacon almost couldn't look at it. He'd seen death and snapped limbs in humans, but never on a horse. Oh Jesus—that was his foreleg and *it was snapped in two!* That was his metacarpal bone, sticking out like a dagger, and the rest of the useless foreleg, flapping on the ground, held only by a strip of skin. And the damned horse was trying to stay off it but he couldn't do it, couldn't walk upright like a human, and he came down on the bone stump and snapped the upper radius bone with a sound not quite as loud as the thunder above them. His shoulder rolled to the ground, and he came to a quivering halt, squealing and thrashing on his side.

Deacon could do nothing but look dumbly at Crick's horse, panicked, in agony, and doomed.

Crick's horse. Easygoing Comet, who had kept Deacon sane while Crick was gone… and Deacon was going to have to… Oh God.

Comet screamed, a terrible sound that felt like it cracked Deacon's own ribs, and Deacon closed his eyes and swallowed. He had to take care of that. He had to take care of that right now. Comet had been a friend, and his friend was panicked and in pain, and there was no way to cure a leg that had been broken off like that, not in two places, not in the thick part of the thigh.

Deacon swallowed again and manned the fuck up. Lucky for both of them, Comet had rolled onto his right side, and the shotgun was on his left. Deacon was tempted for a moment to run and get the bolt-action rifle—the wound would be cleaner, and the corpse would be prettier—but one look at Comet's pathetic panic made him knock that shit off.

A pretty corpse would be for Deacon's benefit, not for Comet's. Either way, death would be instantaneous, and, if Deacon held the shotgun right there, under Comet's jaw….

"Easy, boy," Deacon murmured, not wanting him to go thinking the world was all chaos, wanting him to have some peace before he made the dark journey. "It's all good. You know, Parish'll be there—I know you miss him. Parish, my mom—they tell me she liked horses." He thought it, he did, but he wasn't going to promise Comet that Crick would be there, not when Deacon needed him so badly on this end of things, so he just patted the horse some more until the animal's squeals stopped. Comet finally lay there, eyes rolling, heart thundering, breath coming in pants, and waited for Deacon to make it better.

Deacon positioned the gun, patted Comet's nose one last time, then stepped back and pulled the trigger and made it all better.

Carefully, he put the safety on the gun again, set it down, and grabbed the shovel that he'd dropped when Comet had crashed to the ground. And then he began to dig.

Common sense told him it was insane—the ground was saturated, and it didn't matter how many shovelfuls of dirt he was moving, it would be a giant puddle of mud. Even if it was six feet deep and eight-by-ten feet wide and long, it would still be an armpit-deep puddle, and he would have to shovel quicklime on it. That was always a bad idea so close to the levee, but damn… he'd be goddamned if he sent his friend to the rendering plant to be made into dog food by strangers.

He was swearing and didn't know it. He was cursing and shouting as he dug, screaming and spitting, and he couldn't seem to stop any more than he could stop the relentless, rhythmic motion of the shovel in the mud.

"You fucking bastard… you goddamned dumbass… how the fuck am I supposed to keep you safe, you just run off and do something stupid like that? You should have trusted me, motherfucker, you should have trusted me, I have never let you down, I will never let you down. Goddamned, motherfucking, sonofafucking dumbassed cuntwhore bitchfucking cocksucking bugger… fucking hate you… I fucking hate you, goddammit. How could you leave me like that? I got nothing… you go off like that and I got nothing. I'm just fucking left here, and it's like being left in the desert when you're gone, you hear me? You bastard, you hear me? I got nothing… *I got nothing*! Well, fuck you. Just fuck you… just *FUCK YOU, CRICK, JUST FUCK YOURSELF, YOU'RE GONNA GO FUCKING LEAVE ME LIKE THIS!*"

Somewhere in there he'd stopped shoveling mud and started beating the horse with the shovel, and his foot hurt like he'd kicked something. It was probably Comet's poor abused body, but he couldn't stop, couldn't stop, couldn't stop….

And then a groan… a crumbling rumble from the direction of the levee stopped him.

He turned toward the sound, squinted against the rain, and saw it. The sandbags came tumbling down like they weighed nothing, and there was a crack in the earthen part of the levee, and then another, and then the lip of the damned thing washed away. In a quick and ponderous roll, a four-foot-tall, fifty-foot section just disintegrated, and all that water heaved its way towards the inadequate sandbag shelf that Deacon had spent four days putting up between the place he loved and the wrath of God.

"Oh really?" Deacon screamed at God. "You want to play? You want to fucking play? I haven't heard from Crick in four days, and you think this is what's going to do it? Have I mentioned you can fuck yourself?" The water swelled up, ran into the ditch by the levee, overflowed, and powered its way across the road.

"You're gonna wreck my walls, right? *Do you think I give a shit? Try me, motherfucker! Just fucking try me!*" He was standing in front of Comet's ill-advised grave and hopping up and down, shaking the shovel at the water as it rose… rose so fast… came up over the sandbags, and heaved its way onto the lowland pasture.

"That it? Is that it, you bitch? I can fucking swim, motherfucker!" The water rose up to Deacon's ankles, and he couldn't seem to make himself care, couldn't seem to want to run away. He just stood there, daring God to fuck with him one more goddamned time.

And God tried—the water rose, came up to his knees, his thighs, his hips… and then crested, there at his chest. Deacon was freezing; he couldn't breathe. His feet came off the ground for a moment, and he was pushed backwards as the water battered at him, threatened his home, sucked out his breath and his hope and his anger and all the bitterness that he'd been tamping down like sour bile for the last twenty-one months, praying it would go away, go away before it soured his love for Carrick forever.

The flood stayed there as he struggled for footing, struggled for breath, dared God to take him, dared the world to just fuck him over one last time….

And then the water receded, falling down the slope that led up to the house and running down the blacktop of the levee road on either side, leaving his lower pastureland flooded, but the house, thank Deacon, it left alone. Deacon was left, panting, his throat sore, his hands bloody under his gloves, his whole body shaking from cold, from wet, from grief, from reaction, right there in front of the body of a dead horse—and a big glorpy hole in the ground.

Comet slid into it first, the ground under his vast body weakened by the water as it ran and took the mud away, leaving a fragile shelf. Deacon had worked hard and fast in his frantic time digging the grave, and Comet sank a good four feet right before the ground behind Deacon's boots gave in for the same reasons, and he fell right on top of Crick's dead horse, ass first, in the liquefied mud.

He floundered for a horrible, *horrible* second, his body giving out, reminding him that he hadn't slept, hadn't eaten, hadn't cared for his flesh and bone, and for a moment, he thought he was going to die there, in this mud pit, buried alive with a dead horse and what was left of his sanity. At least he'd see Crick again. And then his feet hit Comet, and he pushed himself up. His feet slid down Comet's rump, but his knees finally hit something solid, and he pitched himself forward onto the solid, saturated ground and turned his head to the side and gasped like a fish.

All right, God, I'm done sparring. I'll see you next flood, you pussy-assed bitch.

He might have lay there until he died of hypothermia and embarrassment, but two pairs of strong hands seized him, one on either side, and pulled him up, helping him to climb out of the mud pit that was now officially Comet's grave.

"Heya, Jon," Deacon sputtered, and Jon shook his head at him, at a complete loss for words.

"Jesus, Deacon," Andrew said from his other side. "Did you know the levee broke? Why didn't you get up to higher ground?"

"'Cause me and God were having a conversation," Deacon mumbled with as much dignity as he could muster. "I called him a pussy-assed bitch, and he told me he didn't give a shit. It was a draw."

Jon took Deacon's arm and slung it around his shoulder. "Deacon, where's your horse?"

"Crick's horse." Oh, Christ—that hadn't changed. "Crick's horse is dead, Jon. He broke his leg and I shot him. And then I dug a pit, and God thought he'd do me a solid, and buried the poor bastard. Crick's horse, Crick… they leave. They leave me. It's what they do."

Jon and Andrew looked behind Deacon into the pit they'd pulled him out of, and Jon left Deacon's side for a minute to grab the shovel, which was still at the side of the mud pit. Gingerly, he probed the liquid mud with the shovel and grimaced when it hit something solid with enough give to be a body.

"Jesus," Jon muttered. "No wonder you're off your rocker. God really had it in for you today, Deacon."

Deacon felt suddenly lucid. Cold and weak, but lucid. "I haven't heard from Crick in four days, Jon."

Jon nodded, and touched foreheads with his friend. "I know, Deac. We're praying for him, right?"

"I think God's too busy beating the shit out of me to listen."

"Yeah, well, you're still standing, champ," Jon told him dryly.

"Only because you're here to help me up," Deacon told him with so much reverence and gratitude that even Jon couldn't find a witty comeback.

"Took you long enough to lean on me," was all he could manage, and there was no response to that. Together he and Andrew wrapped their arms around Deacon's waist and started to urge him up to the house in what felt like the longest walk of his life.

They dragged him into the tiled washroom by the kitchen and started to strip off his clothes. Jon invented new swear words when they saw his blisters, and his toes would be bruised and black for days afterwards. Andrew had just brought him a blanket—clean and dry, because the double layers of sandbags had worked, dammit, they had!, and the only water in the house was what they'd just tracked in themselves—when the phone rang.

"Oh my God," Deacon said in wonder. "I keep forgetting that damned phone works." His head hurt. It was pounding, in fact, and he couldn't decide if it was the muddy, bruised cut on his forehead or the lack of food or the lack of sleep or even the hangover…. Maybe it was all of it, but for a moment, all that seemed to matter was that his brain was threatening to ooze out his ears.

Benny barged into the mudroom then, the old-fashioned cord from the kitchen stretched as far as it could possibly go.

"Jesus, Benny, give a guy a little priv—"

"It's Crick," she said breathlessly. "It's Crick. He left his BlackBerry on a helicopter, and he got to use the satellite phone to tell us he's okay."

Deacon grabbed the phone from her before she could finish and let the cord pull him back against the wall of the mudroom. His feet slid from underneath him, and he flopped abruptly on his ass, chuffing into the phone.

"You're okay?" he asked dreamily. "Please tell me you're okay."

"God, Deacon—I'm fine. You sound like hell. Benny was worried sick. What happened?"

The laughter was uncontrollable, bubbling up from some bitter place in his gut, and he couldn't seem to stop it. "What happened?" he giggled. "Damn, Crick... that's the fifty-bazillion dollar question. How 'bout ask me what didn't happen? Or let's narrow it down a bit... maybe the best and the worst of it... how's that sound?"

"Deacon." Crick's voice went very quiet. "You're scaring me."

"Backatcha, baby," Deacon said, suddenly sober. There was a heartbeat of silence, and he tried to pull something coherent from his aching head. "Let's just say I almost drowned in a mud pit with your dead horse, and because I thought you were dead too, it was just about the best part of my day."

"Oh God... Deacon I'm so... so...."

"Don't say it," Deacon told him, surprising himself with how mild he sounded—how mild he felt. "Please—not because it'll make me mad, because I'm not anymore." And that also was a surprise, because it was the truth. "I've got all the mad out, okay? The mad's all gone, and I'm clean and shiny inside, right? You don't ever have to apologize again... that part's over, hear me?"

And oh, God, it was true. Standing in the pissing rain, shrieking at God, daring the world to fuck him just one more time—it had scoured him right out, and he had no room in his heart left for bitterness or anger. Crick was there, Crick was on the other end of the phone, and he was alive. Deacon was cold and naked and alone on the floor, and all that mattered was that Crick was alive.

"Okay, Deacon," Crick said, sounding lost and a little confused. "What do you want me to say?"

"Mmm." Deacon's whole body relaxed just hearing his voice, and he slouched down on the floor a little more until his head was resting on one arm and he was holding the phone on his opposite ear. "Just talk to me, baby. Just tell me what happened, tell me you're all right again. Tell me about your day."

And now that voice, that dear, dear, far away voice, was gentle and sweet, almost rhythmic. "The thing was, we got caught in some fire and the bus rolled. We're fine, some bumps and bruises mostly, but we were there, ass to ass, waiting to be rescued, and we heard the Black Hawk, right?"

"Mmm-hmmm," Deacon mumbled, content to let Crick's voice wash over him. The story wasn't exactly comfortable, but the moment was pure comfort, and it soothed him, eased him, let his mind stop raging at the world, let his body settle itself down to rest.

He didn't even feel Benny's hands as she picked up the phone and told Crick he was asleep, and he certainly didn't know to pose for the photo she sent Crick over the phone when he'd recovered the damned thing a week later. The picture was of Deacon, fast asleep on the floor of the mudroom, smiling slightly as he dreamed of Crick's voice in his ear.

Chapter *16*

Unnecessary Business

IT TOOK two weeks for the six-page letter that explained the entire shit-in-the-blender day to arrive and another week for the follow-up letter, and three days for Crick to get through the whole thing, because some of it was just so awful he had to walk away.

Crick—

I almost had to write this to you from the county lockup—it's a good thing I'm friends with the best defense attorneys in town.

Crick chuffed, reading it again. County lockup—*Deacon!*

Anyway, it turns out, Driving While Gay is NOT illegal, just like Jon said, and so Becca's boyfriend got to get fired and go to jail, which I have to say was kind of fun to watch. Jon almost got a contempt of court slapped on him when the judge asked if I really was gay or not—seemed to think the question was intrusive. The judge explained that if I was, and Jason knew it, then he'd be arrested and all sorts of bad shit, and if I wasn't, it was just trash talk and a grudge for sleeping with Becca. The fun part was when the guy asked why, if I actually were gay, would I be sleeping with Becca. Explaining the doctored drink and the equal-opportunity pecker was just damned embarrassing, let me tell you. But all in all, it's no big deal—you came out at a funeral, I came out in court, and together, we're town legend. Go us.

Crick thought about Deacon and his incredible shyness. "No big deal"—right, Deacon. Crick knew the man—he probably went home and slept with the horses after that just to wash away the mortification. He'd never been ashamed of his sexuality—it wasn't that—it was the being open to the public that would hurt him and hurt him deeply.

But I'm sorry about the Becca thing. I've got no excuses here. I should have spit the gin out—and probably thrown it in her face too. You know, I keep thinking about that picture you drew of me once—the one where I look like a god. Some god. I'm sorry I'm such a mess—I'd give anything for me to be the man you thought I was. I just hope I'm still the man you want to come back to.

Crick read that passage, and then read it again. A week after he'd called home and found Deacon half dead and the place barely standing, the pilot of the Black Hawk that had bailed him and Lisa out of the shit had returned his BlackBerry. Crick had given him a box of paperback books for his trouble and spent three days Twittering in every spare moment with Benny to make sure Deacon was okay.

Now, he took out the damned piece of irritating technology and pulled up the picture Benny had sent him right after the whole thing went down.

Deacon was asleep—naked to the waist and asleep on the mudroom floor. He'd wiped some of the mud off his face, but there was a line of it back against his hair, and his hair was stiff with it as it dried. His head was pillowed on his arm, and the pose was a lot like Crick's sketch from the hotel room in Georgia, right down to the expression. His body was skinny and battered, and Crick could see the bloody blisters on the palms of his hands from the sandbagging and the shovel as well as the bruise and cut on his forehead from that bastard cop, but his face as he slept… it was peaceful. There was a faint smile on his still-handsome mouth, and Benny had told him that he'd fallen asleep with Crick's voice in his ear.

No, Deacon wasn't a god. He was just a man, stubborn and flawed, shy with everyone but the people who loved him, tough, compassionate and hammer-and-nail practical, and brave—so brave—to take on the world, to carry The Pulpit and all the people who looked to him on his shoulders.

He wasn't a god, but he was still the man Crick had left in the hotel in Georgia, if a little worse for the wear. He was better than a god. He was Deacon.

Your mama came and got your little sisters after the trial, which was too bad. We had them set up in Benny's room, and got a bed for Benny in with the baby, and I think they enjoyed themselves. I know Crystal is looking to take the same path as Benny if something doesn't happen soon—unfortunately, Driving While Gay may not be an actual crime but it doesn't make you really popular with the social workers either. We had a tough time convincing them that Benny and the baby would be better off with me and not a foster family—that was a pretty nasty scare right there.

Oh Christ. Deacon loved that baby, loved Crick's sister—they were his family. Crick wanted to howl. He should be there. If he were there, she'd just be living with her brother and his boyfriend—dammit, he should be there!

But they got to stay—Benny kept threatening to run away and I think she scared the social worker a little. Scared me too—damned kid. She's smart and capable, but Jesus, Crick—so much like you.

The whole shebang has hurt our business a little—a bunch of people tried to pull their animals out of the stables and not pay us. Again, Jon saved the day—apparently there's a reason for that contract, right? But still—that money'll be gone in a couple of months, and we're going to have to find a way to replace it. Benny put up a website (here's the link if you want to check it out) and we've been shipping Even Star's Wonder Sperm all over the country instead of just to local farms, which is good because some jackass started a rumor about 'horse aids'. Swear to Christ, Crick, sometimes I see why you wanted to get the fuck out of here so bad. We've got yearlings I can sell, and we had a fairly big batch of newborns (another reason it took me so long to write—you know that season, you're up to your chin in laboring mares and afterbirth) that are promising, but I need to keep a few to train up to stay solvent next year. Anyway, forget it. Not to worry. You'll be home in four weeks, and it will all be golden.

Crick took a shuddering breath. Funny thing about time—his first months had crept by. The next big chunk of it had flown. These last two weeks had stretched strangely, like a hallway in a horror movie, and Crick wasn't sure he could make it to the end.

I'm sorry about your horse, Crick. It wasn't his fault—between the lightning and the snake, he just did what horses do and came down wrong. It wasn't his fault. When the ground got drier, we brought in the backhoe and buried him right, with some quicklime and a marker. Had to kill two more snakes that day—I swear, if I had the littlest bit of capital, I'd buy that vacant property next door just so I could turn the pigs loose and keep the rattlers away.

Benny's text on the matter had been more succinct. *Every night he starts for the door to give that damned horse a carrot. I swear, Crick, it's like losing you all over again.*

Crick had loved Comet—his even temper, his sweetness. He always swore that if Deacon were a horse, he'd be just like Comet, only better looking. He knew—hell, Deacon had told him—that the horse had gotten him through the worst of Crick's absence. How could the damned stupid animal have deserted them when Deacon needed him most? Crick asked the question and then cringed at the irony.

It's weird, Carrick—I gave up school for The Pulpit, but after almost losing it to the flood and getting you instead, I think God and I have come to an agreement. If it's a choice between you and The Pulpit, I'll take you, alive and well, any day.

Jesus, Deacon, Crick thought, *learn to ask more from life, would you?*

Only one more care package between now and you coming home. I'm almost afraid to say that. Feels like it will jinx it somehow. But I'll say I love you, Carrick, just to make sure you keep your head above the dark water, okay?

I love you,

Deacon

The third day after he got the letter and Lisa came to their spot and found Crick staring at it with shaking hands and red-rimmed eyes, she read the letter herself.

"He seems to be taking it pretty good, Crick," she said quietly. "I mean, the guy may seem to be the master of understatement, but it sounds like they're getting through okay."

Crick pulled out his BlackBerry again and showed her the picture.

"Ohmygod."

"Benny says they got him to shower, and then he slept for twelve hours."

"Well, he was recovering...."

"He woke up to go to jail. It took Jon two days to get him out."

Lisa made a "humph" sound and then looked at the picture again. "It doesn't say anything like that in the letter."

"Benny texted me. I'm telling you, Lisa—he's not okay. He's not. And if he is, then *I'm* not." Crick shoved his hands through his slightly-longer-than-regulation hair. "He had to go through all of that alone...."

"It sounds like he had family with him," she said gently, and Crick turned a tortured face towards her.

"He didn't have *me*!" Crick wailed. Lisa rubbed his back then, and he fought back the pressing sobs and prayed that nobody would come and see him like this. He wasn't even afraid of being outed in the Army anymore—fuck, he'd done his term, he'd served his time, he'd lived up to his word. It was just that, in the last two years, he'd come to appreciate Deacon's quiet strength, his ability to power on through with what he had. It felt like he'd shame Deacon to the bone if he got outed because he was sniveling like a girl.

"Look, Crick—have you asked the Captain if you can call him? You know, family emergency or something like that?"

Crick nodded and took in another gulp of breath. "I already had my 'family emergency' call. They're not going to lose the house—yet—nobody's pregnant, and unless my wife's about to file divorce papers, it just doesn't rank."

"Really?" Lisa asked archly, and Crick looked at her. She had a look on her face he'd never seen before. If he had had to put a name to it, he'd have called it "wicked."

Crick @DP—Lisa's going to call you in fifteen and pretend you're her boyfriend, about to break up with her.

DP @Crick—WTF WTF WTF?

Crick @DP—I NEED TO HEAR YOUR VOICE. This is the next best thing.

DP @Crick—Dramatic much? I'm fine.

Crick @DP—I don't believe you.

DP @Crick—Here, look at the picture.

The bastard took a picture of himself leaning back against the arm of the couch and holding the camera out as he balanced the sleeping baby on his chest. He was smiling toothily at the camera, but Crick wasn't buying.

Crick @DP—You've lost weight again.

DP @Crick—Dammit, did Benny rat me out?

Crick @DP—Didn't need to. Now do me a favor and just talk to her, okay?

DP @Crick—'Hi, Lisa, I miss Crick, I'm horny as hell, do you want details?'

Crick @DP—Fuck you. Take this seriously. She's got a list of questions and a scale of 1-5...

DP @Crick—They really don't give you enough to do there, do they?

Crick @DP—1=emotionally repressed and in agony, 2=emotionally repressed and in pain, 3=not taking the question seriously

DP @Crick—I'll save you a lot of time. They're all gonna be 3.

Crick @DP—4=possibly dealing but still in pain, 5=will be fine. A cumulative score of less than 20 on ten questions will...

DP @Crick—Are you insane?

Crick @DP—lead to Crick outing himself in front of his entire camp for a dishonorable discharge and an instapass home.

DP @Crick—That's not funny, Crick.

Crick @DP—I'm not laughing, asshole. Not even a little tiny bit. Pony up and be honest.

DP @Crick—Honesty's your schtick—mysterious is mine.

Crick @DP—'Mysterious' gets you a 1. I'm not shitting around here, Deacon. I've got two months and you need to be there when I get back.

DP @Crick—I promised, didn't I? You're not the only one who depends on me—I'll be fine.

Crick @DP—The fact that you're being all emotionally repressed and stoic still gets you a 1.

DP @Crick—I haven't even answered a question yet!

Crick @DP—but you're taking me seriously now, aren't you.

DP @Crick—Honestly, Carrick James Francis, have I ever taken you as anything less than a threat to my heart and my sanity?

Crick @DP—*sulk* You say that like saying my full name makes me weak in the knees or something. You're not all that.

DP @Crick—LOL if I'm not all that, maybe you can spare me the psych eval?

*Crick @DP—She's going into the tent now to call. Don't be scared.
I just really need to know you're okay.*

The phone rang, and Deacon sighed. Benny looked at him from her
spot on the couch and held out her arms for the sleeping baby.

"He's just worried."

"After two years, you think he'd be over this."

"Yeah, but your two years were rougher than his."

The phone rang again, insistently, and Deacon went to answer it.
Lisa was on the other end, playing "wounded girlfriend" to the nines, and
Deacon had to laugh—if nothing else, he knew she was a class-A friend.

"Please, Deacon, please… tell me you're not going to marry that
horrible Becca Anderson!" She sounded like she'd managed to work up a
few tears even, and Deacon almost choked on his tongue.

"Oh Jesus—sweetie, you tell Crick that's the *last* thing I'll ever do!"

She sniffled a little and gave a convincing little hiccup. "Are you
sure, baby—she is your type too!"

Deacon gave a long-suffering sigh. "You tell him that just because I
switch hit doesn't mean I'm going to sign on with the devil himself,
okay?"

"But baby… you *did* end up in her bed, didn't you?"

Oh Christ. If this was question number three, he must really be hung
up on this subject. "Tell Crick that I said 'I love you, Crick' during a
really critical moment, and she thought I said 'Bec' and was about to pick
out curtains. I was obviously not in my right mind. Do I have twenty
points yet?"

She covered a snort with a sob, and Deacon had to give her points—
she was enjoying this a lot more than he was. "I'm just worried, that's all.
I mean, you did just lose someone close to you."

Ouch. "Yeah," he said softly. "Losing Comet hurt."

"But you're not being honest with me, sweetheart—you gotta tell me
how much!"

"Can't we just skip this question?" He looked furtively at where
Benny was eyeing him with no discretion whatsoever. It was like being
double-teamed by the two of them, and he had some glimmer of what his
future might hold. He was going to be laid out and filleted like a trout on a
daily basis—welcome to marital bliss.

"We skip a question, Deacon, and Crick follows through," Lisa said quietly, totally and completely sober. "I've read your letters and I've seen your pictures, and I haven't said anything to Crick, but if you were mine, I'd be AWOL right now. He's been a big boy over here, and I may be the only person who really knows him, but the only thing keeping him together is the thought that you'll hang in there. I need to know it's the truth. So tell me, how're you doing about Comet?"

Deacon was getting irritated because it was better than getting grief-stricken. "I kicked the shit out of his cooling corpse I was so mad at him for leaving—how's that, Lisa? You really want to pass that bit on? I'd rank it as one of the worst fucking moments of my life, right next to being stuck in the house with my dead mother when I was little—by all means, see what that bit of trivia does for his mental state, shall we?"

"Mmm," she murmured, as though looking at something. "I'm not sure this scale was a good as we thought it was—that's either a one or a four—I can't figure out which."

"Make it a four and then you only have to ask one more question?" he asked hopefully.

"I'll make it a one, and you still have to answer all of them," she said sweetly, and he laughed in spite of himself.

"I take it your witnesses are gone?"

She faked tears again. "I was just... so... you know...."

"Girly?" he supplied, and she laughed again. He liked her laugh—it reminded him of Amy.

"Yup. You do know the Army, my friend. Okay—next question. How was the trial, really?"

Deacon caught his breath and banged his head softly against the doorframe. "Abso-fucking-lutely morti-fucking-fying."

A real laugh slipped out, and she covered with a big hiccup. "Dammit," she giggled into the phone. "I'm giving you a two on that one, just for cracking me up!"

"I deserve a five—I'm going to live."

"Nope. A one for resorting to humor instead of an honest emotional response. Here's an easy one—how much do you weigh?"

Deacon sighed. "I have no idea."

"That's skipping the question, Deacon—I've got three more minutes, and if we're not done because you're stalling, Crick's going to follow through."

"One-sixty." It was one-forty-five—Jon had made him get on the scale that morning like some sort of goddamned prison warden.

"And that's a one for lying. If you're one-sixty, I'm five-ten. You've got one more chance on that one, buddy, or I'm covering for him while he gets the fuck out of dodge."

"That's a court marshal, Lisa," he said through a dry throat.

"That's how much we give a shit. One minute and three questions."

"One-forty-five."

"Eat something, dammit. What are you going to do if Benny and the baby have to leave?"

Deacon made a sound like he'd been gutshot. "Send Crick our address from Canada," he said, so stunned by the brutality of the question that he said what he'd been thinking from the get-go.

"Wow, Deacon—your first five. Next question—how bad are the finances?"

Deacon whimpered. He actually whimpered. "In the fucking toilet, are you happy?"

"One more. Crick wants to know if it was worth it—all this pain he caused you, all this shit you've gone through alone. Was it worth it, Deacon? Would you do it again?"

Deacon closed his eyes, saw Crick's face on that one day, when they were merged and moving and the whole world was green-filtered sunlight and the wonder of each other's skin. Saw Crick in Georgia, *It's like a part of you only I can see.*

"In a heartbeat," he rasped. "I'd do it twice, just for that handful of days. Tell him that, okay?"

"Deacon, they're back," she whispered, and then, in her "acting voice," said, "It's okay, baby. I just needed to know you love me.... No, no, you don't have to worry, I won't do anything I'll regret. Just hang in there... it won't seem that long, I promise."

"Tell him I love him," Deacon said brokenly.

"I love you too, baby. I wouldn't change a goddamned thing."

Crick @DP—So, how you doing.

DP @Crick—Go the fuck away. I'm not talking to you.

Crick @DP—Was it really that hard?

Benny @Crick—He said go away. He's out at the stables right now—whatever you did, it was too goddamned rough.

Crick @Benny He was falling apart. I needed to see how bad.

Benny @Crick—You could have just sent Jack the Ripper—it would have been easier on him.

Crick @Benny—You expect me to just let him lie to me? Blow sunshine up my ass about how he'll be fine?

Benny @Crick—He HAD some pride about holding it together, asshole. Nice of you to rip that away like a stuck bandage.

DP @Benny—Log off, darling. The boys need to talk.

Benny @Crick—Hurt him again and I'll give Melanie your e-mail and tell her you have money. I'm so mad at you I could rip your balls off.

Crick @Benny—OUCH.

DP @Crick—She's very protective.

Crick @DP—So. Am. I.

DP @Crick—I'm not five, Carrick. How are you supposed to look at me like an equal when you treat me like a child?

Crick @DP—I wasn't treating you like a child...

DP @Crick—You couldn't let me have my illusions of holding it together? You couldn't let me pretend?

DP @Crick—Except for those two weeks, Carrick, pretending's all I've done in life. It's kept me together fine. You just rip that away?

Crick @DP—I don't want you to 'pretend you're fine' Deacon. I want you to BE fine. I want you to BE WONDERFUL. I want you to have the whole world, dammit!

DP @Crick—The world is overrated, Carrick. All I want—have ever wanted—is The Pulpit and you. I'd settle for you.

Crick @DP—You don't deserve to have to 'settle' for anything.

DP @Crick—I didn't deserve to have my heart dissected in an ambush.

Crick @DP—I don't deserve to have to pick through your emotional denial to see how you really are.

DP @Crick—Well I'm NOT fine right now. Are you happy?

Crick @DP—No.

DP @Crick—I'm sorry, Carrick. I know you mean well. If you were here, asking these questions, I could deal. But using a go-between...

Crick @DP—She's all I had.

DP @Crick—Well my pride was all I had.

Crick @DP—I wish you could see yourself like I do. You'd see that you've never had anything to be ashamed of in your life.

DP @Crick—I've got to go. I still love you. Talk to you tomorrow.

Crick @DP—Running away, Deacon?

DP @Crick—Damned straight.

Crick logged off and put it in his pocket, sighing. Lisa looked at him from across the commissary table and raised her eyebrows.

"He didn't take it well?"

"I damaged his pride. If you'd have asked me before, I would have said that wasn't a flaw of his."

Lisa patted the back of his hand. "You've got some of that, Crick. Just talking to the guy, I think he's got a lion's share."

Crick yawned and stretched and wished he were home. "We'd probably argue about this at home too, you think?"

His partner laughed and took a dainty sip of her diet soda. "I think you two are well matched, but even the best couples fight." She gave him a winsome smile. "Don't worry, Crick. Reading your letters, seeing your texts—it's enough to make me believe in love. Twu Wuv ith what bwings uth together today...."

Crick laughed and grinned at her. "Popcorn, you are like a reward for something good I didn't know I did."

"Punky, you are like the big sister I never had."

They both laughed then, and Crick started to plan what he'd do with Deacon's scrawny, half-starved body while they were waiting for Crick's hair to grow back and Deacon to put on some muscle. Mmmm... best thought of the whole day.

Chapter 17

Consequential Truths

Crick @DP—Whatchadoin?

DP @Crick—Bills, what else?

Crick @DP—Money still tight?

DP @Crick Would you settle for 'we'll live' and not bitch about details?

Crick @DP—Have you learned nothing?

DP @Crick—Please, Carrick. For me? My head's killing me, and I'm trying to get creative with numbers.

Crick @DP—Since you asked so nicely, okay. Wanna know what I'm doing today?

DP @Crick—If it won't gross me out, piss me off, or make me buy a ticket for forward area, sure.

Crick @DP—I'm training a replacement.

DP @Crick—ooooowwwwooooohhh BABY! Talk dirty to me some more!

THEY managed to sell two of the six yearlings, and Even's wonder-cock was getting a hell of a workout, but still, money was going to be tight. Deacon was getting good at figuring out what bills needed to be paid immediately and which ones could be put off until later. Little things became a pain in the ass—the burlap bag with carrots was replaced with store-bought, because the farmer's market suddenly wouldn't sell to Deacon in spite of the fact that Parish had been one of the founders of the community endeavor. They had to haul the fertilizer to a farm in Woodland because the one in Levee Oaks was suddenly full up.

But Deacon believed firmly that it was small shit—miniscule, gnat-biting bullshit, and it was okay. Benny planted a carrot garden while Parry Angel played mudcakes next to her, and Deacon's new connection in Woodland got him two boarders to replace the five that had been pulled after the "Driving While Gay" trial started. It was okay—everything had to be okay.

Crick was coming home.

Still, having to do the weed whacking by himself instead of hiring a service was a pain in the ass, and he was heading into the stable to get his third bobbin of nylon line when Andrew squealed into the driveway, barely missing the pigs.

He'd been picking Benny up from Amy and Jon's house. Amy, who had always been so tiny and so vital, was not taking to the pregnancy thing well. She'd started bleeding right after Deacon's trial and had been on bed rest ever since. Benny went over three times a week to keep her company, clean the house (although she said that two people made zero mess compared to the three single people and the baby who spent time at The Pulpit), and cook dinner. Jon tried half-heartedly to tell Deacon that all the care was unnecessary, but Deacon had laughed evilly.

How hard is it to accept a little help, buddy? Consider it my legal fee. Because of course the two of them hadn't charged Deacon a red cent. And that was it—Jon had shut up and gratefully accepted Benny's help, and Deacon, Andrew, and Patrick had all pitched in to take up the slack on the business end of things. Once a week, Jon or Deacon made dinner, and they ate at Jon and Amy's instead of The Pulpit—and Amy tried not to get all weepy on the lot of them because sometimes, family really was a blessing.

But apparently not today.

Today, Benny was ripping Andrew a new asshole as they got out, and she continued to rip it as she got Parry Angel out and grabbed the bags of groceries and the craft supplies that she'd bought to help keep Amy entertained. (They had both taken up knitting with a passion, and, so far as

Deacon could tell, had produced enough scarves to be measured in acreage instead of feet.)

Deacon, who had never heard her speak sharply to Crick's Army buddy, actually dropped the weed-whacker and walked over to help her with the groceries, just to see what her damage was.

"I swear to God, Andrew Carpenter, if you ever do such a dumbshit thing again, I will never, ever speak to you, not even at your goddamned trial."

"There's not going to be a trial, Benny," Andrew snapped back. "If there was a trial, that fucker would have to own up to what he did to you—"

"And what if he did!" Benny turned to Andrew in tears. "What if he decides to own up and gives them one more reason to take Parry away from us? Did you ever think of that? No—you wanted to be my knight in shining armor so bad, you forgot that maybe there was a fucking reason I never brought this topic up!"

"Whoa!" Deacon dropped the groceries and took Parry out of Benny's unresisting grasp. "Benny, Andrew, you put the shi—stuff in the house"—Parry Angel had been getting pretty good at repeating things now that she was fifteen months old—"and I'll put the baby down for her nap. Then, when you two have cooled off, we'll have a little chat about this. Unless"—Deacon looked seriously at Andrew—"you think the police will be here before then?"

Andrew shook his head and turned his head over his shoulder and spat. "He's a coward, sir—he doesn't want his daddy to know what he did anymore than he wants the rest of the world."

Deacon nodded. "Well then, we've got time. C'mon, Angel, you ready for a song and a bottle?"

The baby nodded and patted his cheek with chubby little hands and then laughed. "Deek deek!"

Deacon laughed into her face, blew a bubble on her neck, and looked meaningfully at Benny and Andrew, who obeyed his order and started working together in glum silence.

When the baby had her bottle and a book and a song from Deek-deek, he found that Benny had made sandwiches. She and Andrew were standing in the kitchen. They were quiet, but that was an improvement, so Deacon got himself a sandwich and thanked Benny politely.

After he'd taken a couple of bites, he said, "So I take it this is about Parry's father?"

Benny nodded and looked away.

"Okay—Benny, you and I will talk in a minute, okay? You want to go… put away your yarn or something, and then come back?"

She looked gratefully at Deacon then and nodded, a miserable little smile on her face as she hurried away. She was wearing jeans and one of Deacon's T-shirts, and she looked her age, which was barely sixteen. She was so competent sometimes, Deacon forgot she wasn't as grown as she tried to be. He sighed and looked at Andrew.

"Okay, Private, it's your turn to talk."

It was simple enough. Andrew and Benny had come out of the grocery store, pushing the cart and flirting with the baby, when Benny had stopped dead right in the middle of the sidewalk and shut her mouth, turned the cart around, and started a really roundabout way to the car, which was only a few spaces down from the front.

Behind them, what had looked to be a college kid with blond hair and blue eyes and a permanent sneer had called out, "Hey Benny—want some tequila? I'm dying for a blow job, sweetheart!"

Benny had turned a mortified, stricken face to Andrew, and that was when the young Private had lost his mind.

"You don't talk to a girl that way," Andrew muttered. "I don't care what you've done with her—that's just six kinds of wrong."

Deacon pulled a steep breath—he had to agree. "So that's when you hit him?"

Andrew nodded and looked uncomfortably at Deacon. "It wasn't until Benny was pulling me off of him that she told me he was Parry's father. Deacon…." Andrew shifted uncomfortably. "Deacon, that kid was damned near as old as I am. I'm twenty-two. If he's Parry's father, and he got her drunk, that doesn't just make him a slimeball, that makes him a…."

"A criminal… yeah, I know. Thanks, Drew—I think I'll be calling Jon after this, but first I've got to talk to Benny." Deacon took another bite of his sandwich, and Drew turned to leave. Deacon cleared his throat for a second. "Um, Andrew?"

"Sir?"

"Two things. The first thing: if the cops come to get you, we'll bail you out ASAP. You know that, right?"

Andrew's sweet, white smile in his dark face was plenty grateful.

"And the second thing—sort of the third thing too. Benny may not appreciate it, but I do. Crick, Benny… they didn't have enough people standing up for them growing up. I'm glad you stood up for her today."

Andrew's dark cheeks tinged a little bit red, and his expressive eyes went sideways. "Benny deserves someone standing up for her, sir. She's really pretty special."

And now Deacon blushed, because he figured his father said it to him, and it was his turn. "She is, and so are you. If you're going to wait for her"—and his blush got darker—"that's fine. Just"—and now it was his own hard experience and not his father talking—"just make sure she knows you're planning to be there. Crick didn't know… I kept trying to get him to see the world before he settled on me. It's part of how we ended up where we are, you know? Just… if she shows any inclination back? Tell her you're waiting. You've got enough honor in you to see it through."

Andrew looked up then and smiled. "Thank you, sir. I'll think about it."

Deacon nodded and talked through another bite of sandwich. "Good… you can run away now, Private Blood-loss, but if you see Benny, tell her I'm being a good boy and having some cookies with my sandwich, would you?"

Benny had figured out that, besides red meat, Deacon's other weakness was those soft shortbread cookies with the dollop of fudge in the middle that the bakery made every Tuesday. She made a point to buy them for him, and he was grateful enough to make a point of eating them. He'd pulled up a stool at the counter and was pulling one out of the plastic bakery box and dipping it in milk when she crept back in from her room.

"Pull up a stool, Shorty. Have a cookie with me."

"I'll get fat," she sniffed, and he turned around and grinned at her. Motherhood hadn't made her fat—she was still as skinny and rangy as Crick had been, if significantly shorter.

"Honey, if you can't grow upwards, the least you can do is grow outwards. Now come sit, have a cookie, and we're going to pretend for a minute that you're just a kid, okay?"

"I'm almost a grown-up," she said, smiling a little. She hopped up on the stool next to his and took a cookie. He offered her his glass, and she dipped the cookie and grunted appreciatively with her first bite.

"You're still a kid, Shorty. You and Crick, life tried to hurry you along, but you both were still way too young when you got hit with the worst shit, you know?"

"Not as young as you were, Deacon," Benny said softly, and Deacon smiled at her grimly. Yes, she'd heard everything he'd said to Lisa, and although she hadn't pressed him, he could tell she'd been curious.

He sighed. Well, if that painful episode with Crick and the phone call-by-proxy had taught him anything, it was that truth really did need to be reciprocated.

"I'll tell you what, Shorty. I'll tell you something painful and embarrassing about my childhood, and you return the favor." He took another bite of cookie and thought rather sadly that it wasn't as good when his stomach was all knotted up, but Benny was looking at him with that hopeful trust that she had developed since they'd become roommates at the beginning.

"That sounds like a deal, Deacon," she told him softly, and he took a deep breath.

"My mother drank herself to death when I was five," he started, and then, since he was being honest, he added the details that mattered. He talked about that day, wandering the house, afraid to go outside because she'd needed him in the past, and how scared he'd been when she hadn't moved or breathed. He talked about how they found him after dark, when Parish had finally come home. He'd been hiding out in the stables, under a horse blanket, listening to the sound of something breathing. *It wasn't so lonely out here, Daddy. I'm sorry I left Mama when she needed me.*

He shrugged when he was finished and hoped he'd managed to keep his face stoic enough not to upset her anymore than she was already. "So you see, Benny, I'm not great at being alone. I… it's probably a weakness.

Maybe even a good thing Crick left, so he can see what a mess I can be if I'm the only heartbeat in the house...."

She threw herself on him and sobbed, and he stood and moved to the couch, which was better for this conversation anyway, and besides, they'd both finished the milk, and neither of them was up for more cookies.

When she was done crying, she looked up at him and wiped her face on his shirt. "You do fine, Deacon," she said. "There's no crime in not wanting to be alone. It's dumbasses like Crick and me who think we're going to push the world away before it can fuck with us again."

Deacon smiled faintly. "Well, I'm glad you think so, Shorty. I've always thought the two of you were particularly brave. Now, do you have anything you want to tell me?"

Benny looked down. She kept her head on his chest and wiped her cheek again.

"Crick had just left for Iraq, and I was so scared," she murmured. "When he was in Georgia it was one thing, but Iraq... it just...."

"Made it real." Yeah. He knew.

"Yeah. And so that kid... there was a party out by Discovery Park, and he gave me something to drink...." She looked at him earnestly. "I knew what it was, Deacon. I wanted to get drunk."

"You were fourteen, Benny."

"It wasn't the first time I got drunk!" She was confessing—he could hear her voice. She wanted him to know all the worst things about herself, and he couldn't let her.

"Kids get drunk!" he told her sharply. "Doesn't make me love you any less, Shorty, now get on with it!"

"I... I barely remember, Deacon. I remember saying 'no', and him laughing and telling me I didn't mean it. I remember waking up—I just fell asleep on the ground. I wasn't wearing anything, and there was blood on my...." She blushed, and Deacon swore. He was doing his best to not get all frightening and caveman on her, but the story made him want blood. The last time he'd wanted to hit somebody this bad was when Crick had been ambushed in high school.

He took a deep breath, and then another.

"Why didn't you tell us, Shorty?" he finally asked softly.

"Would it have mattered?" she asked, and deep down, he could hear the insecurity there. Oh God—her and Crick, both of them waiting for eternity to come home and find their shit out on the lawn.

"About you coming here to live? No. You could have been the belle of the ball, sweetheart—hell, you could have done half the freshman class willingly, and I'd still love you like the short person you are." Her giggle was gratifying—even if it was clogged and thick—but he had to keep going. "But this… this is wrong, Benny. Do you remember this kid's name? How old was he?"

"Keith Alston," she sniffled at last, "and he'd just gotten back from college."

Scumbag! But Deacon didn't say it out loud. "See, Benny—kids like that—odds are good you're not the first kid he's gotten drunk, you know? So now we've got a choice, and it's not an easy one. Hell, I don't like it, either way it goes."

"Do I have to let him into the baby's life?" she asked, and he could tell it was one of the most difficult things she'd ever done.

"Now that, darlin', is not part of the choice in the least."

Benny nodded, safe in Deacon's arms, and he made plans to call Jon as soon as she got up. It was time to keep his family safe again.

"Deacon?" Benny said quietly as he was mulling over his tentative plan.

"Yeah, Shorty?"

"Why'd Andrew do that? Hit him like that? I've never seen him lose his temper, not even when Shooting Star knocked him down that one time and kicked off his fake leg." God, that horse was a rank whoring bitch!

"He loves you, Shorty. Same as me."

Benny was quiet for a moment, and when she spoke next, it was uncomfortably. "Do you think maybe it's the same as you loved Crick?"

Great gobs of gooseshit—spare him from young lovers.

"Could be. Would that bother you?"

She grunted. "I don't know if he's seen me at my best."

Deacon laughed, thinking of Crick on top of the water tower, dizzy and feverish, or Crick sobbing behind the principal's office, remorseful and still coming down off his first (and only) high. A whole montage of

Crick flashed before his eyes then, bloody and battered but not beaten, embarrassed but still game, happy and eager, smiling that goofy, crooked smile that meant he was about to come up with something truly outrageous that nobody had ever considered.

"You don't love people at their best, sweetheart. You just love them because you can't help it. You're too young to worry about this right now, and Andrew's too good a guy to make you." Crick flashed behind his eyes again, this time on the day Parish had died. Crick had looked so old and so wise as Deacon had sank his head onto his lap and put his trust in someone with his whole heart.

"If you love them and have faith in them, you'll see them at their best every day."

DP @Crick—How's the replacement training going?

Crick @DP—Like shit. I used to think I was a fuck-up, then I joined the army.

DP @Crick—You'll do fine, Crick. I have faith.

Crick @DP—I don't know why. You've had a front row seat to my greatest-fuck-ups of all time.

DP @Crick—I've also seen your finest moments. No contest— greatest moments win.

Crick @DP—If you're trying to make me choke up like an asshole, you just did.

DP @Crick—Don't blame me. You're the one who's wonderful.

Crick @DP—Jesus, Deacon, who did you watch grow up?

LISA was reading Deacon's letters again. She got her own letters from her own parents, and they were sweet and newsy and she read them to Crick faithfully, but as she said frequently, they weren't Deacon. Crick had to agree. As shy as Deacon was to strangers, his letters showed the real Deacon, dry humor, understated wisdom, sharp mind, and all.

Andrew was all for rigging his car to explode, but we talked him out of it. (For one thing, we didn't like his chances in the county jail—Levee

Oaks not so big with the cultural diversity, you know?) But I called Jon, and we came up with a plan. We gave the fucker a reasonable choice—he could relinquish all rights to Parry Angel, or we'd charge him with statutory rape. Now I know what you're thinking—you're thinking that a scumsucker like this isn't going to just date-rape one fourteen-year-old, he's going to keep doing it. But that's okay—we told him he had to come clean to a judge. I'm sure you see the big ol' fucking catch twenty-two, but dumbshit has yet to figure it out. He's too scared of losing daddy's money to come clean to his own lawyer, and I'm thinking the trial is going to be more fun than I've had in a while.

Of course, it's scheduled for the day you get released and leave for home. Here's hoping we can think of better things to do once you get here.

Lisa finished reading the letter out loud and frowned a little.

"What? You get what's going to happen, right?"

Lisa nodded. "Oh yeah. They have the same sort of laws in Seattle. It's not the victim who presses charges, it's the state. Pretty clever of Deacon, though—gets the bastard right out of the baby's life at the same time he gets a sex-offender mark on his file. Win-win."

"So why the long face?" Crick was busy stocking the ambulance. He had been going to show Second Lieutenant Stick-up-his-ass how to do it again, but Stick-up-his-ass was busy writing a report about how slack Crick was on military training regulations. Crick had told the Captain it was coming, and the Captain had looked at Crick and shaken his head.

Lieutenant, I don't know what your life as a civilian was like, but I'm damned proud to have served with you.

It was one of the nicest compliments Crick had ever received that didn't come from Deacon or Parish, and Crick would treasure it.

"I don't know… this thing between Andrew and Benny…."

Crick looked at her over his shoulder as he tallied the drug inventory. "What thing?"

Lisa looked back at him. "The thing… the thing that made Andrew deck the guy who trash-talked her. C'mon, Carrick, you should recognize 'the thing'!"

Crick thought about it carefully—Deacon, pulling him away from Brian's crazed mother, helping him pick up his stuff off his lawn, running interference when he picked up his sisters. "Yeah, okay, I recognize it," he said softly. "The Thing." Of course.

"So it doesn't worry you?"

Crick looked at his hands, scorched brown by the sun, and the tiny little store-room in the ambulance bay. He'd hated being an EMT. He hadn't thought about it until this last week, but he might have to be an EMT back at The Pulpit, just to help Deacon with the money a little. He could have been an art student this entire time, if only he'd been aware, just a little, that "The Thing" had been real and not just a terrible, fragile hope.

"The only thing that worries me is that Benny will make the same mistake I did," he told her.

"And what's that?"

"She'll shit all over it instead of believing it's true."

Crick @DP—Deacon?

DP @Crick—? ? Crick? ?

Crick @DP—Are we going to be okay when I get home? Are we going to know how to talk to each other?

DP @Crick—Not at first, I would imagine.

Crick @DP—I'm nervous, dammit. Don't go all shy and mysterious now.

DP @Crick—I'm a different person to you. I've let you down. I've fucked up. You'll probably be disappointed at first.

Crick @DP—SHUT THE FUCK UP.

DP @Crick I'm being serious here.

Crick @DP—So am I.

DP @Crick—I dread the moment when you look at me and decide if I'm a god or a man. Either way, you'll be disappointed.

Crick @DP—News for you: I had that moment. You're beautiful either way.

Crick @DP—Deacon? You still there?

DP @Crick—We'll be fine, Crick. Noworryss.

Crick @DP—What's wrong?

DP @Crick—Hands shaking. You wrecked me. Simple as that.

KEITH Alston might have been a good-looking kid, if Deacon hadn't been looking at him with the taint of what he did to Benny tarnishing that dimple-cheeked, pretty face.

"Yes, your honor. I'm here to confess to what I did. Anything that'll get me out of child support, right?"

The judge—the same one who had seen to Deacon's trial—raised his grizzled gray eyebrows and looked drolly at Jon. Jon smiled back with enough innocence to rehymenate an entire brothel.

"Son, are you sure you don't want a lawyer?"

Keith shook his head. "No, sir—I just want to wash my hands of this brat and get the hell out of here."

Judge Crandall narrowed his eyes, and Benny smiled sweetly from her spot on the plaintiff's bench with Parry Angel on her hip.

"Then by all means continue there, son."

And that's all it took to get the spoiled little rich kid to confess to statutory rape—after he'd signed away all his rights to baby Parish.

DP @Crick—You should have seen the look on the kid's face as the bailiff hauled him away!

Crick @DP—I'm glad Benny doesn't feel threatened by him anymore.

DP @Crick—Yeah, lots of celebrating here.

Crick @DP—Good.

DP @Crick—That's a little restrained.

Crick @DP—I'm worried about when Benny moves away, that's all.

DP @Crick—Way to piss on my parade—thanks. Thanks a lot.

Crick @DP—Well, it's not like I haven't hurt you enough by leaving. I just don't want it to happen again.

DP @Crick—Aren't you getting ready to leave soon?

Crick @DP—Tomorrow morning, actually.

DP @Crick—So let's be happy for right now. Can't we be happy for right now?

Crick @DP—Yeah, Deacon. We can be happy for right now. Not a problem.

Crick looked at the cell phone and swallowed the weird emptiness in his stomach. So close—he was so close to being home. What if Deacon took one look at him and didn't want to see him anymore? What if Crick was the one with the mystique, and Deacon had forgotten what a pain in the ass he could be?

DP @Crick—Screw that. I'll be happy when you're home.

Crick @DP—Are you sure I'm worth it?

DP @Crick—Absofuckinglutely.

THE next day, Crick threw his duffel over his shoulder, shook hands with his CO and all the other guys in his unit, and hopped in the ambulance because Lisa had asked permission to drive him to the airstrip in Kuwait so he could ship out. He was just about to get into the passenger seat when he groaned.

"Awww... fuck it all!"

"Whatsamatter, Punky? Forgot you signed up for another tour?" Lisa grinned at him cheekily from underneath her flak helmet. The road hadn't necessarily been safe in the last month or so.

"No—I forgot"—he looked furtively around, feeling like an asshole. "I left some of my shit in your lockbox," he said meaningfully, and Lisa's eyes widened. Their entire convoy was already gearing up and shipping out, and she still had his sketchbooks, not to mention some of Deacon's letters. Some of them he still had in his wallet or tucked into his flak helmet, but he couldn't keep them all there.

"Well shit, Punky—I'll have to send it to you. I've got your address. I'll ship them out as soon as I get back."

Crick's face relaxed into a smile. "Thanks, Popcorn—I couldn't have done this without you, you know?"

"I know!" she said cockily, hopping into the driver's seat. He followed on his side, pulling out his cell phone as he went.

Crick @DP—On the road, Deacon. See you soon. Love you lots. The butterflies and palm sweats have begun.

DP @Crick—Don't be nervous. I'll only eat you 'til you come.

It was the dirtiest thing Deacon had ever texted—what could he say? He got a little giddy on that last night. Crick was coming home.

Crick @DP—Dammit, Deacon, I'm gonna have a hard-on for a week if you do that again.

They texted a little as Crick pulled away, but Crick signed off so he could talk to Lisa, saying goodbye to her with conversation as they traveled.

DP @Crick—See you soon, Carrick James. Love you.

Crick @DP—Love you back.

THE family didn't know about the ambush on the convoy until the next day. The DOD called them at eight in the morning as they were shoveling oatmeal and scrambled eggs and talking about where they'd take Crick out for dinner when he got home.

Part IV

Keeping Promises

Chapter 18

A Long Trip and a Short One

CONFUSION. So much confusion.

If Crick was dead, Deacon was pretty sure his heart would simply stop, and that would be the end of it. If Crick was going to stay in the hospital in Germany, that was easy—Deacon, Benny, the baby—they all had their passports and travel visas in order for exactly that reason. But the dry voice on the phone that first morning had been adamant that hauling ass to Germany was a less-than-perfect idea.

Son, if he's not good enough to make it until he's stabilized and transported back to the States, all you're going to do over here is grieve in a strange place instead of a familiar one. We suggest your family sits tight, and we'll let you know when he's on his way to the Medical Center in Virginia.

Which left Deacon sitting on the kitchen floor, gasping, trying to come up with a plan. His vision was black, and he didn't think he could breathe, but... he had to, right? He had to come up with a plan. He had to pull money out of his ass to buy plane tickets, make a schedule, ask Andrew and Patrick if they could cover, make sure the baby was well enough to travel, and....

His vision was still black. Crick was hurt.... *"Lieutenant Francis and his driver were caught in the shelling outside of Kuwait this morning, son. Lieutenant Francis is in surgery and will be for quite some time."*

Oh God—his driver too. "Lisa?"

"We're sorry, son—Private Arnold didn't make it."

Deacon tried to catch his breath now. Crick was going to be devastated—his one friend over there, hell, his first actual friend-without-benefits ever—and she hadn't made it. And Crick could have been just like her.

Deacon rested his forehead on his knees, wishing he could just faint like a girl because consciousness was not doing him any fucking favors, when he felt little hands on his shoulders.

"Deek-deek...."

"Heya, Angel," he rasped and then looked up through the dimness in his vision. Benny, Andrew, and Patrick were all standing over him, waiting for the news.

"He's in surgery," Deacon managed. "When"—*when!*—"when he's stabilized and on his way to Virginia, they'll call us, and we can go meet him there."

Benny whimpered a little and flopped limply next to him. He wrapped his arm around her shoulders and held her as she quietly fell apart.

"Patrick, you said someone showed interest in Lucy Star's yearling?"

"Yes, sir." The older man looked suddenly ancient—Deacon was reminded that he'd been on the verge of retirement this year, but he'd decided to stay until Crick was home to help with things.

"See if you can make that sale—we're going to need the money. And while I'm gone, see if you can't pull out some of our sperm stock and knock her up again this season." They had been going to let her lie fallow this year to give her a break, but she was going to have to dig in deep like the rest of them. They'd need that horse to sell later.

"Yes sir," Patrick said quietly. He crouched down and ruffled Deacon's hair. "He'll be fine, Deacon. I have faith."

"It's more than I've got," Deacon said, staring at the peeling finish on the kitchen cabinet with empty eyes. "I'll have to borrow yours."

They packed and put tickets on standby at Sac International and then simply went about their day. What else was there to do? Deacon was distracted—Shooting Star bit his fingers hard enough to bruise and he barely remembered to cuff the old bitch, and he almost let Even out in the same pasture as one of their in-season mares—which wouldn't have been so bad, but she was a relative of Even's and they were planning to inseminate her with another sample.

When Deacon almost got kicked in the head by one of the skittish young yearlings, Andrew saddled up Lucy Star, walked over to Deacon with the reins, and said, "Go ride. Just go. Don't worry about us here. Just go. You've got your cell. We'll call you when there's news."

And that was how Deacon found himself out at Comet's grave and then at Promise Rock.

His body liked the ride. It liked moving with the horse—Lucy still had a smooth-as-lube gait, and Deacon's legs and stomach fell into that rhythm, the one that said as long as his body could move, his soul would be okay.

He thought he'd end up staring morosely at Comet's grave, but as it turned out, he just didn't have that much melodrama in him. It hurt too much to look there, at the greened-over impression in the soil. It was getting hot again, but the ground was wet enough that there were still yellow wildflowers all over the field. That damned horse had loved to eat those wildflowers, and Deacon and Crick had always loved this time of year at The Pulpit. Looking at death was going to make him suicidal, and he couldn't. He had to keep Benny and Parry Angel in mind because they needed him. He was their family.

He eased away from that place, then, and urged Lucy into an easy canter toward Promise Rock.

The place was full of ghosts—not all of them Crick's.

Parish had taken him there at least twice a week the summer after his mom died. That September, after Deacon started kindergarten and the press of bodies and personalities had sent him home in tears on a regular basis, Parish had told him to pick one kid, just one, and make that kid a friend. If Deacon could do that, Parish promised to take them both to Promise Rock every week until it got too cold to swim.

That's how Deacon had gotten Jon—easy-going, grinning Jon. Deacon had caught him sobbing in the bathroom that very week because his parents were going away again and they wouldn't be there when he told them about school, and Deacon invited him swimming, and that had been fate.

Jon had tried to kiss him at Promise Rock. Deacon hadn't minded. It had seemed so natural. Girls were great—girls gave him a hard-on, same as boys, but Jon already knew him, so that was easier. Jon had seemed more disappointed than Deacon when it stayed just a brush of uncertain lips and a fit of giggles, but since it meant that Deacon wasn't going to lose his friend, he was fine with things.

He and Amy had lost their virginity here. Her body had been so sweet—small, vital—her skin had been smooth, and her breasts had been soft, fleshy miracles in the palms of his hands. The inside of her had felt so smooth around his cock—sweet and satiny and precious, like fine fabric. Amy's body had been sweetness, softness, all joy. Almost too much joy, it seemed sometimes. Deacon felt awkward with that much comfort; it made him feel a little weak—silly, like a steel-toed boot in a perfume store.

And then there had been Crick.

Deacon had known. That first time Crick had visited the swimming hole with him and Jon, Deacon had known about Crick's crush. He'd known it and thought, *He's so pretty, and I love him already, but not yet.*

Crick had been too young, plain and simple. He'd been too young in high school—Deacon could see that, but, oh God, he had seemed so lost. The night of Brian Carter's funeral, they'd put him into his own room, and Deacon must have gotten up six times, walked to Crick's door, heard him crying, and put his hand on the knob.

The only thing that had stopped him was knowing that if he did that, Crick would have no choice in his future, none at all. That goofy smile, that fine mind—Deacon had believed Crick could do anything. He hadn't been shy and happy in the quiet; he'd been fearless. Why would he want to stay in this crappy town with someone who knew—even back then, when he was barely twenty—that in spite what of his test scores said about his future, his heart wanted the simplest of lives?

Deacon remembered the day his father died. He'd wanted to stay self-contained. He'd wanted to grieve like an adult, shoulder the weight of The Pulpit, and be the older brother Crick had always needed. And then Crick had approached him like an equal, like a friend, and Deacon had leaned on him, fell into him, and another link of love had wrapped itself in the chain around Crick's chest, whether he liked the weight or not.

Deacon had been so weak at Jon and Amy's wedding. Weak and foolish and not thinking straight. The next day had been….

And he couldn't do it. He couldn't say it was a mistake. He'd tried to give Crick everything—his freedom and love to make it perfect—and Crick had....

Crick, who had so many virtues Deacon admired, had suddenly been all about his one, most painful flaw.

Deacon looked at Promise Rock some more. Green-dappled shadows fluttered over the granite, the valley wind scoured the blooming flat of Levee Oaks, and he heard his own voice in the rushing quiet.

Please—I'm not here to fight, God. I'm not here to bargain. I'm just here to ask. I kept my promises, as much as I could. Crick's kept all of his. This place, it's our holy place, and we promised to be there for each other. Please… just please. Please just let him live. I've got nothing to give you. I can't give up The Pulpit, because it's not just mine anymore. I can't bargain with my life, because Crick's going to need me when he gets better. I can't promise not to kill myself if he goes because I'm the next best thing to a daddy, and Parish taught me better than that, so it would be a lie. So I've got nothing, God. I've just got "please." Please. Please.

He didn't know how long he stayed there, but he was thankful to Lucy Star for her patience. Eventually, though, he had to move. Lucy Star deserved a nice canter, and his body was moving with the horse again, and that was the best therapy the world had to offer.

He spotted a rattlesnake on his way back, and his sense of responsibility spoke up and insisted he'd been goofing off for too long. Benny found him in the garage, opening up the gun safe.

"Deacon!"

He looked up, startled, and saw that her face was white and she was shaking. "Benny? What's wrong?" And then both of them together said, "Has there been any news?"

Deacon blinked and closed the safe, keeping it from snicking shut with his ass before he turned to look at her. "There hasn't been any news—I saw a rattlesnake moving in from the west field. Can't let it set up shop, right?"

A considerable amount of tension flowed out of Benny, and she put her hand out to the doorframe to steady herself. Deacon made a connection that he didn't think he'd ever make.

"Benny?"

She swallowed. "Yeah?"

"You and Parry—you're mine. You're"—and now he swallowed. "You could be the only connection I have to Crick for a while. Parish raised me better than to leave people who need me, okay? That wouldn't…." He breathed deeply and went for honesty.

"I can't say it hasn't crossed my mind, but one thought of you sent it running on its way, okay? No matter what happens, I won't be letting you down."

Benny nodded vehemently, and then, because she was Benny and so much like her brother, she launched herself at Deacon with enough force to back him into the gun safe and leave a bruise on his hip that would be there for weeks.

"I just saw the gun and got so scared," she confessed, and he whispered into her hair (dyed an amazing color purple this month), "I know, baby. But I won't leave my girls, okay?"

"Okay," she nodded, but she was crying, and he held her for a long while after that. Finally she sniffled and wiped her face on his shirt and laughed and said, "But could you do me a favor?"

"What, Shorty?"

"Could you have Andrew go shoot the rattlesnake? The last time you did that you ended up shooting a horse—I don't think your luck with guns is any better than Crick's."

He couldn't help it. He broke into wet, snotty giggles, and so did she, and they clung together and giggled and cried some more until they heard the baby making noises to let them know she had woken up from her nap.

Benny wiped her face again and ran in to get the baby, and Deacon closed the gun safe very carefully and went to get Andrew. All things considered, Benny was probably right.

So they waited that day in some sort of terrible limbo. That night, when Deacon would usually be texting Crick, he called their DOD contact instead. The gruff, kind-voiced man had been replaced by a crisp, no-nonsense woman, and she told them that Second Lieutenant Francis had come through his first surgery and was waiting to stabilize before his second. "Call us tomorrow for an update," she finished, "or we'll call you if anything changes drastically."

"Oh good," Deacon snapped, feeling like his entire life had slipped into a surreal universe where air had turned to Jell-o. "So every time the phone rings, we get to think Crick is dead?"

The woman in Germany gave a surprised little snort and became a human being. "No, sir, I'm sorry—we'll call you if he's stabilized too. Please, don't assume the worst. The doctors say he's fighting pretty hard."

Deacon mumbled "thank you" and hung up. "Fighting hard?" he asked, even though Benny hadn't heard that part of the conversation. "He'd goddamned better be."

The phone rang even as he said it, and he snatched it up and said, "How is he?"

Jon said, "I was hoping you could tell me, you stupid asshole—how hard is it to pick up the goddamned phone?"

Deacon snorted and passed on the newest update, and Jon said, "And by the way, I stopped Patrick from selling the yearling."

"Why'd you do that? We're going to need the—"

"Plane tickets and hotel fare are on me, Deacon."

"Don't make me beat the shit out of you," Deacon growled. Wonderful. Another asshole who didn't think he had any pride.

"Backatcha, dumbshit. My family has six gazillion travel miles that they never use—you get them. My parents owe you for raising me, so shut up about it."

Deacon took a deep breath through his nose and prepared to say *No, thank you anyway,* when Jon said, "Don't tell me we're not family enough to do this for you, Deacon. It would break my heart."

Deacon let out that deep breath. "I wouldn't dream of it," he murmured, giving Jon the numbers and vendors so he could pay for their tickets. He didn't tell Jon that they would probably have to sell the yearling anyway, just to keep making payments and feed the family while they were gone. It meant too much to his friend to piss on his parade now.

And then there was more waiting. The next morning Crick was back in surgery, and they were off to do their thing. Benny came back from Amy's with a scarf that could have fit around the house, and Deacon suggested she make it a little wider the next time and maybe make a blanket for the baby. Benny blinked at him, looked at the four miles of knitted acrylic rope she'd produced, and said that might be a good idea for something to do on the plane as well.

That night, Crick was out of surgery and fighting for his life. Deacon and Benny didn't even pretend to go to bed. They sat on the couch and watched the DVDs of Crick's favorite shows one after another until they fell asleep, Deacon on his end and Benny on hers. They were in the middle of season four of *Gilmore Girls,* the one with the guy in it who reminded Deacon of Crick, except Crick's eyes were brown and his smile was a lot goofier.

The next day there was no change, and Deacon hung the phone up and put his fist through the wall of the laundry room, not even sure he'd done it until Benny came running in with the first aid kit. But she patched up his hand, and he patched up the wall and was sanding it smooth when the phone rang again.

It was the older, gruff guy, and he sounded really tired, but he told them that Crick was out of danger.

"We'll be shipping him to Virginia tomorrow morning—you'll be able to see him the next day."

Deacon sank to the floor then, still holding the drywall bucket, and said a silent "thank you" to God, who was apparently done beating the shit out of them and had decided to leave them to their own devices to screw things up.

Benny trotted in and saw him, and because she was Crick's sister, she thought the worst. "Crick… Oh my God… *Crick…*."

"Pack the baby's bag, Benny," Deacon said serenely. "We're going to Virginia."

They were about done in then. They had to sleep that night, and sleep early, if they were going to have the ranch ready to take the red-eye out of Sacramento the next night. Deacon lay in bed that night looking around. The walls were still painted olive green and purple, and the trim and the pillows and the finishing touches were all still Crick's. Yeah, they had two years on them now, but they hadn't been hard years—Deacon had probably slept on the couch more than he'd slept in his own bed.

Sometime since February, he'd bought a calendar with fuzzy kittens on it and pinned it in the spot he was saving for Crick's promised sketch. He'd been thinking Hunk of the Month, but….

He closed his eyes and thought of Crick's body and wondered about his own. In spite of his glib texts to Crick, he hadn't felt anything—desire, arousal, anything—for as long as he could remember. It was like his body had slipped under, into some world of its own, on sexual hold somehow. The only exception had been the drunken mistake with Becca, and he couldn't remember that, not that he wanted to much anyway.

What would it be like to share a bed again?

Imagining Crick breathing next to him was what sent him off to sleep.

The plane ride seemed over much too quickly, and Deacon only remembered the hotel room so he could get back to it. He and Benny were tear-assing down the hall of the hospital when they were abruptly stopped by the sound of a familiar—and unwelcome—voice.

"I don't care what he says," whined Melanie Coats. Her usually tangled hair was back in a smooth braid, and she'd recently purchased a blue polyester pantsuit. "My entire church put up for this plane ticket—I've got to see him."

"The patient doesn't want to see you," the doctor with the clipboard said sharply, looking at the two MPs next to him with expectant eyes.

"Well of all the ungrateful...." Melanie turned away and caught sight of Deacon and Benny watching her warily as she stalked away.

"It figures you'd be here," she sneered. "We'd hoped the Army would make a man out of him—but not with you hanging around to—"

Deacon stepped in and ducked his head, pitching his voice very, very low. "Your son was injured for his country, Melanie. If you don't want the social worker to show up at your house instead of mine, you'd better not say a word to damage his reputation here. That's his decision, and I'll die to honor it."

It was an empty threat—Deacon and Benny had told the social workers repeatedly that Crystal and Missy were in worse straits with their parents than they had been at The Pulpit, but no one had listened. Melanie didn't know that, though, and Deacon was fifteen yards at most from finally seeing Crick, and he put all of that frustration in his voice.

Crick's mom backed away, looked furtively around, and slunk off to her hotel room, Deacon assumed. He knew it wouldn't be over—Driving While Gay was bad enough, but a lot of people went to Melanie's church. He was sure his poor ranch would suffer some more bad business, but it didn't matter. There wasn't much he wouldn't do to spare Crick one minute of that woman's company, especially now.

The two MPs hadn't left the doctor's side, and they looked suspiciously at the three of them—even the baby—as Deacon approached and asked for Crick's room.

"Only family is allowed," they said sternly.

"I'm his sister," Benny said, "and this is my baby, and"—she looked at Deacon, and Deacon could see her eyes widen as it sank in. Deacon might have been Crick's one and only emergency contact on the list, but he wasn't—at least in the eyes of the military—family.

"This is my husb—"

"Bernice Angela Coats, you will not say that lie when your brother is just down the hall," Deacon snapped, and Benny turned unhappy eyes towards him.

"But Deacon...."

"Go see him," Deacon said roughly. "Let him know we haven't blown him off for a day at the beach, okay?"

Benny bit her lip and nodded, eyes bright, and pushed Parry Angel's stroller down the hall while the baby squealed happily into the echo.

"Look," he said to the doctor, ignoring the MPs, "I don't care what that woman said to you about who she is, but we're his family."

"Sir," the doctor said, pitched at a whine—he was a busy man with things to do, and Deacon had no doubt about it, but dammit, this was *Crick.*

"Don't 'sir' me, Doctor," Deacon snapped. "You listen to me. My father and I raised that boy. When he was nine, we took him in and taught him about horses and about family when his family taught him nothing but how to dodge a bottle. We celebrated his birthdays and his report cards and told him he was smart and had faith in him like nobody else in his life. I was there when he turned eleven and his parents forgot his birthday, and I was there when he was twelve and got busted doing bad shit behind the bleachers. I was there when his best friend died in the tenth grade, and I was *there*, goddammit, when that rank bitch dumped his shit on the lawn without so much as a 'good-fucking-bye' to him that same night. I was *there* when we scattered my father's ashes and he cried like I couldn't because it hurt so bad. I was *there* when he broke our hearts and took all that talent and signed up for the Army, and I am *here now*—not because my church sent me, but because I spent blood, sweat, and tears to see him well. *I'll* be the one changing his bandages. *I'll* be the one helping him to the bathroom. *I'll* be the one driving him to physical therapy, and if that doesn't qualify me to go in his room and see him right now then there is *nothing* on the planet that does."

The doctor had been backing away as Deacon spoke at first—and looking at the MPs like he expected them to do something. But Deacon wasn't threatening violence; he wasn't even angry. His expression was bare and naked, and his eyes were desperate. He stood there, his shyness and embarrassment gone, and nothing left but the raw need to see Carrick etched into every line of his face.

It was like the woman on the phone, Deacon realized. The man hitched a breath, and the bureaucracy fell away, and the humanity returned.

"I'll get you his care instructions—we'll be releasing him in about a week. Will you be escorting him home?"

"Damned straight," Deacon said, closing his eyes in relief.

"Well, before you leave, we're going to have a long talk about bandages and exercises and—"

"I was an EMT for almost three years—I know the drill. Give me the particulars then. I'll be good for it." But for now... right now....

"Then go ahead and follow the girl in."

Crick was lying back on the pillows when Deacon stepped in, but Benny was holding Parry Angel up on the railing so the baby could coo and drool on him.

His hair was still short, but not regulation short, and he had a bandage taped up on the lower part of his cheek and around his temple. They'd shaved some of that dark hair so the bandage would stick. His left arm was heavily bandaged, and his leg as well—Deacon thought he could see the lumps of bandages under his hospital gown too. There was some blood seeping through the gown, at any rate.

But his brown eyes were alert, and he smiled at the baby with a hint of awe.

"Look what you did, Benny—she's so big!"

"She's fat," Benny said indulgently, blowing a bubble on the baby's neck until she giggled. Parry's giggle was like flowers and sunshine, and it certainly did a number on the rather plain hospital room.

"That baby is perfect," Deacon said quietly, and Crick looked up so quickly he had to grimace when he strained something in his neck.

Deacon walked up to the hospital bed, and Benny moved without being asked. He took Crick's hand in his then, figuring, what the hell—it was just a hand. But their flesh touched, and his eyes closed and then squeezed tight shut, and when he opened them, his face was a little wet—but then, so was Crick's.

"Good to see you stopped slacking and finally got your ass home," Deacon muttered, and Crick nodded. Their eyes collided, locked, skidded over the words while saying deeper things.

"Well, you know. Real men miss the smell of horseshit." Crick tried a grin then, and it was… it was Crick's grin. It was crooked and game, if a little tired and a little hurt. Deacon saw him then—Deacon's Crick—in the injured man on the bed.

Deacon tried a quiet smile back, and Crick made a little sound in his throat. Then he sighed and hit the button that raised his bed. "Little sister, could you do me a favor?"

"Anything, Crick—for right now. When we get home, you get to clean the house and do all the shit I don't like to do. You're low man on the totem pole, buddy!" She said it sharply, but she made Crick laugh, and Crick looked at Deacon—and it was a sly Crick. The Crick who liked to skirt the law a little, and who stayed out of trouble by the skin of his teeth.

"Could you go get Deacon a soda? I've got to—" And he blushed, so Deacon knew he was telling the truth. "They took my catheter out about two hours ago, and it's time…. I was hoping Deacon could help me to the john."

Crick swung his legs over the bed, his two bare shins pale and hairy in the fluorescent light. Benny made a little "eww" sound and made a laughing escape. Deacon moved in like the professional he'd once been and slid his shoulder under Crick's good side to help him up.

Crick wrapped an arm around his shoulder, and Deacon turned his head to the side, closed his eyes, and felt his nose brush Crick's hair, his neck, his jawline.

"Just get me to the bathroom," Crick murmured, and Deacon made a sound that might have passed for a grunt but felt more like a whimper.

Crick leaned on him pretty heavily on the way there—this wasn't just a ruse—and when they got into the tiny little room, he parked his IV at the door, closed the door gently so he didn't squash the tube, then gave Deacon terse instructions.

"Here, help me turn around—I'm going to lean on you and grab my equipment."

"Do you want me to put a cheerio in the bowl so you can aim?" Deacon asked dryly, and Crick leaned into his arms and fumbled with his gown, choking on a laugh.

"You bastard—if I piss all over myself, I'm going to blame you."

"Here." Deacon reached to the front and pulled the gown to the side for him, and Crick did his thing gratefully.

"I understand taking my first dump's going to be a community event too," Crick muttered, and then he leaned forward and dropped the lid down on the seat. "Here—help me sit."

"I can just take you back...."

"Shut up," Crick said thickly, easing his torn body onto the seat and turning around. He reached his good arm around Deacon's waist and pulled Deacon between his spread thighs.

Deacon went willingly. His hands shook... oh God, his goddamned hands shook, but he buried them in Crick's short, thick hair anyway and pulled Crick's head to his middle. Crick fumbled with Deacon's over shirt and then pulled his T-shirt out of the waistband of his jeans and laid his cheek against the bare skin of Deacon's stomach. Deacon's whole body shuddered, trembled, and he shivered convulsively around Crick. He ran his hands over his good shoulder, the middle of his back, anywhere there wasn't bandaged skin to hurt. He bent his head and dropped kisses in Crick's hair, and Crick clung to him, held him so tightly his knees almost gave.

There were no words. Not a single thing to say, not a single "I'm sorry" or "I missed you"—it was all there in Deacon's shaking hands on Crick's face, in Crick's convulsive clutching of Deacon's body.

Deacon's eyes burned, and he closed them tight against tears, because he couldn't afford them, and then he remembered if he could cry in front of anyone, it would be Carrick. The tender skin of his stomach was already slick with Crick's tears.

"Christ you're skinny," Crick muttered against him, and Deacon choked back a laugh.

"And your shoulders doubled in size—good God, boy, are steroids Army-issue?"

"I think the shoulders come with growing up," Crick said, half abashed. His breath tickled Deacon's tummy, and Deacon found himself chuckling into Crick's hair.

"You do manage to do things the hard way," he said after a moment, and Crick laughed a little hysterically into his stomach.

"Yeah? All you had to do was stay home and mind the ranch— somewhere in there, I think you turned into me!"

Deacon laughed some more, a little droplet sputtering out from his lip with his breath. "That there's a compliment I don't think I deserve. God, Carrick... it's like I can feel my skin for the first time two years."

Crick's hands pushed under his shirt and rubbed the skin at the small of his back, and Deacon shuddered with electricity and something wild. It wasn't desire—not with Crick in the shape he was in—it was more like... like life. Like vitality and reality. Like the world had been a dim, distant, black-and-white, soundless, scentless, emotionless void for the last two years, and all of it was surging back in the blood under his skin, activated by the lightning of Crick's touch.

Crick heaved and shuddered and clutched him tighter, and Deacon almost prayed for his heart to stop, just thump and cease, right there in his chest, in his throat, because it was threatening to explode out of him, there in the tiny confines of the military hospital bathroom.

"Promise me something," Deacon rasped, and Crick gave a muffled "mmm" against him. "Promise me that if you ever leave me again, you'll shoot me in the head while I sleep before you go."

Crick looked up at him, his shiny, dark, red-rimmed eyes shocked and wide under spiky lashes. "Deacon...."

"Promise, okay?"

"I'll promise never to leave again," Crick said, shaken. Deacon could tell the violence of the words got to him, but he couldn't take them back.

"That'll do for now," he muttered, swallowing his fear. "That'll definitely work for right now."

They couldn't stay there forever—time didn't fold itself into an envelope and just get sent somewhere else while they held each other like lovers in a place that didn't allow for that sort of thing.

Benny came in to the hospital room at some point and cleared her throat delicately to be heard through the door. "Guys... guys, unless Crick's made of pee, it's probably time you came out, okay?"

Crick groaned—his body was probably sore and more than sore, and together they hauled him up and walked him slowly into the hospital room and set him down. He lay back down, obviously tired from his short trip, and Deacon pulled the covers over his skinny, vulnerable legs.

"You ready for your nap yet?" Deacon asked. Neither of them could meet the other's eyes or the waterworks would start again, and they both looked scrupulously away from Benny.

"Just about—but you gotta tell me a story first." Crick closed his eyes, and Deacon pulled up one of the visitor's chairs.

"Yeah? What, you want princesses and unicorns?"

Crick smiled a little. "With me in a frilly dress and you in shining armor on a fearless charger? Don't think so."

Deacon shrugged. "My armor's tarnished and I shot your horse—I think you can skip the dress. What do you want to hear?"

"Tell me about the horses," Crick said. "Tell me about home."

Deacon swallowed past the lump in his throat. Home was an iffy thing right now—home was a stack of bills he could barely pay, selling horses he'd rather not sell, and Even working the wonder-cock so much it was a shock that the horse didn't just topple over in exhaustion. Home was disapproving neighbors pulling out of contracts and angry clients spitting on him as they took their horses to someplace smaller and dirtier because they were afraid Deacon would give them "horse-aids." Home was an endless parade of horseshit because the last muckraker's mother left the crack house and dragged her kid away by the ear about two weeks after the Driving While Gay trial and Deacon didn't have the heart to try to find another one.

Home was a constant, panicky, breathless anxiety riding Deacon's chest and shoulders, a bitter, self-recriminating fear that he would let down all the people who depended on him to succeed and betray the memory of his father who had never, not once, betrayed Deacon's trust in him.

"The mustard flowers were out when we left," he said, remembering how they looked over Comet's grave. "And the rains went on for so long that the cherry blossoms are out too—you know that evening smell? Hay and wildflowers and water? There's some poppies out this year in some of the fields—they make it sweeter. We bred Sugar to Even again, as soon as she came in season. I'm not saying they'll make another Comet, but their temper is so sweet, I'm thinking we couldn't hate whoever they put out. The stream by Promise Rock is pretty deep; when the snow melts some more it'll be pretty cold. We haven't" —he glanced up and saw Benny looking at him with poignant eyes; she knew all he wasn't saying, but she didn't interrupt—"we haven't taken the baby yet. Last year we just set her in her car seat on the stream bank and let her look at the leaves. She'd nap or gurgle—Crick, they make the best noises when they're that small. This year, we'll have to get her a little life jacket and some floaty things. You can take her swimming, we'll call it physical therapy, right? She's fun, Crick. She can sit for hours with the same four toys, making noises, moving them around. You just wonder what she's thinking when she does it...."

"Benny was like that," Crick said dreamily, but his eyes were half-open and he was already mostly asleep.

"Yeah? Well Parry Angel must have gotten that from her.... She'll sit and play in the mud with a little plastic doll for hours and hours and...."

Deacon talked until Crick was asleep, and when he was done, he looked up and saw Benny sitting on the edge of Crick's bed and stroking his hand. The baby had fallen asleep with Crick, lulled by her Deek-deek's voice, and was snoring unselfconsciously in her green-and-pink-flowered stroller.

Benny turned her own tears towards Deacon and shook her head. "That was the nicest lie in the history of lying, Deacon. I don't know how you did it."

"It was all the truth," Deacon said with some dignity, and Benny shook her head and wiped her face on the shoulder of her lime-green T-shirt.

"Deacon, when he gets home he's going to see the truth—and he'll know that's not it."

"I'll make it the truth," Deacon told her with quiet ferocity. "I swear, Benny—I won't lose our home."

Benny nodded. "We'd still love you if you did, Deacon. Your armor's not tarnished at all, you know—that was a lie too."

"Shut up, Shorty. Let's get back to the hotel room. You guys can take a nap, and I'll get a book and come back. Look quick, is anybody out there?"

Benny hopped off the bed and looked through the observation glass to the room. "You're clear."

Deacon stood and leaned over the bed, kissing Crick softly on the temple without the bandage. "Love you, Carrick James—we'll be back later today, all right?"

Crick stirred and muttered, "Won't leave you, Deacon. Promise."

Deacon closed his eyes, and four months worth of guilt hit him on the head. He trusted that promise and hoped he hadn't just paid it back with lies.

Seven days later, Crick was ready to go, and Deacon needed to be home. Their third day in Virginia, Andrew had called in a panic—a lawyer had come by with a certified letter from the bank, asking for the all the payments on the ranch within thirty days or they'd lose it. Deacon had called Jon in the same panic, and Jon said yes, it was illegal, they couldn't do that, and then had hung up and called back and told them what had brought the notice on.

"Melanie and step-Bob are apparently big churchgoers," Jon said in disgust. "And they know the president of the bank personally. Look, Deacon—you put me in charge of your affairs, so I'm going to move your loan to another bank. Your credit is excellent, and you're being discriminated against, and it's illegal. You tell me how far to take this, and Amy and I will take it two hits further for revenge, okay?"

Deacon had clutched his cell phone to his ear and looked out of the bathroom at Benny and Parry Angel, both of them sitting on the floor while the baby watched her favorite Disney show, excited that something so familiar would be seen in such an exotic locale.

"I want to keep my home, Jon. I want to live the life I've always lived with the people I care about. Whatever we have to do to make that happen, whoever we have to sue, whatever I have to sign, I'm there."

"Good, Deacon. I'll be there the day you get home with Crick. I've got some shit that needs your signature, okay? You get home, settle him down to a nap-nap, and call me. If you want to keep The Pulpit, we need to kick this into gear."

Deacon shuddered and hung up. It was time to go visit Crick.

On the last day, as they approached Crick's room, Crick was sitting up in bed wearing Army-issue sweats and a white T-shirt. There was another man in the room—an officer, by the looks of him—and he and Crick were talking companionably, if a little bit formally.

Crick caught sight of them and said, "Sir, um, excuse my sister and the baby—they're trying to get in."

The CO turned and stepped back, smiling at Benny to make her more comfortable. Her eyes were saucer-big, and Deacon had to laugh. Crick, Benny—neither of them were particularly comfortable with authority.

"Hey there. You must be Deacon. Crick says you're taking him home?"

Deacon smiled and flushed and extended his hand in greeting. "I've got to get instructions," he said apologetically. "But yeah, once we've signed everything and I get instructions and meds, we're good to go." He looked up at Crick and gave a nod. "I'll be back in a bit. Drool over the baby; you've got a backlog to make up for."

Crick had improved nicely over the last week. His bandages were lighter now, and he could sit up and move and get to the bathroom by himself. (He'd been right though—his first bowel movement had been a public event, and not a pretty one. Benny had left the room in an embarrassed flounce, saying she had enough of that with Parry Angel, but she'd gotten an orderly to come help Deacon with the clean up. The orderly had been impressed that Deacon knew what he was doing, and after he left—with a big ol' bag of laundry—Crick said sourly that Deacon would do anything to see his ass again. Deacon had said, "I reckon so" with so much amiability that it made Crick smile a little and blush.)

At the moment, Benny could set the baby on his lap with no worries, and Crick got a good grip on her, bouncing her a little on his good leg. Deacon strode away briskly, looking to scare up Crick's doctor.

He was coming back about an hour later with what felt like half a ream of paper instructions, a bag of painkillers and antibiotics, and numbers written in sharpie of who to call in California for physical therapy. Crick still had shunts to be removed from his internal injuries and muscles that needed to be stretched and worked. Some of the skin on his arm and leg and his hip had been burned badly, and the bandages needed to be kept clean and dry, and all in all, just reading the instructions made Deacon feel queasy. It had been close, so damned close. Crick had made it through by the skin of his teeth—and a lot of lost muscle and damaged viscera as well. But what was left of him seemed to be sound, and Deacon could only be grateful that all of that and his crooked grin were coming home.

Crick's CO met him down the hall. Deacon had asked at the pharmacy and learned that the guy was leftover from Crick's boot camp days. Deacon thought it was damned decent of him to check in on an old recruit.

He nodded respectfully as they passed, and the man—thirty-ish and bland, with pale eyes—stopped him.

"The girl didn't come?" he asked, and Deacon blinked.

"Sir?"

"Crick—he told me before he shipped out that… what was it?" The man stopped a little to remember, and Deacon managed to catch on to the fact that Crick had given a cover story. "Right—something about how he could have had everything he wanted and he thought he was getting kicked to the curb instead. I was just wondering if the girl was still waiting for him, since she didn't make it to the hospital."

Deacon's estimation for the Captain went up a few more notches, even as he searched for as much truth as he could spare. "That situation is still waiting for him, sir," he said after a moment. "If I can keep the ranch, Crick will have anything he wants waiting for him there."

Captain Roberts nodded and frowned, and Deacon felt acutely uncomfortable as the man's pale eyes searched his face.

"Sir?" he asked at last, eager to get back to Crick. Their flight left in a couple of hours, and Deacon didn't want to have to hurry Crick's fragile, healing body through the gates.

"Why didn't he say anything?" the captain asked at last, faintly.

"Sir?" Deacon's heart about stopped in his throat.

"He was there, in my office, and I asked him if he'd been recruited drunk. All he had to do was say he was… you were…." Captain Roberts blushed. "Just one sentence, and I would have written him up his…."

"His what?" Deacon asked, flushing with anger now and not embarrassment. "What would you have written up?"

"His dishonorable discharge." The man had the grace to blush himself.

"Crick may have made a mess, sir, but he also made a promise. There's not a dishonorable bone in that boy's body."

Captain Roberts looked at him there, embarrassed and a little angry, but still looking him in the eye and standing up straight, and said, "I would imagine you'd know something about that."

Deacon ducked his head and looked away. "I have my days, sir."

"Well, I hope this is a good one. Take care of that boy—he impressed a lot of people while he was serving."

Deacon looked the man in the eye and shook his hand, saying, "He impressed me first."

Chapter 19

Coming Up Close

THE trip home sucked—what else could it do? The doctors had wanted to keep him an extra couple of days after all, but Crick had begged to go home, and Deacon had begged some more, and more convincingly, so his original release date held. To make the trip easier, Deacon had managed to score some first-class tickets from Atlanta to L.A., so Crick wasn't all squashed up like a pretzel, but the plane from L.A. to Sacramento was a commuter flight and didn't have first class seats. Crick was in agony by the time they got off that one, in spite of the pain pills Deacon made him swallow.

Deacon had been good about other stuff as well—getting a porter with the little electric cart to take Crick to the gate so he didn't have to hobble, cane in hand and every nerve ending on fire, or keeping Crick hydrated and finding him good seats in the airport while they waited. On the cramped commuter flight, Deacon sat with the baby on his lap the whole time so Crick could have the extra seat to stretch. He didn't say much, and often when he spoke, his cheeks colored and he looked away. Crick knew that his shyness—the terrible introversion that Deacon had managed to hide so well through most of his life and had never once allowed to color his relationship with Crick—had kicked in.

It hurt almost as much as the shredded skin, violated muscles and perforated entrails.

Deacon was shy with *him*. With Crick. One of the handful of human beings he had ever talked to with an open heart. It had taken Crick nearly ten years to figure out that Deacon was different with him and Jon and Amy and Parish than he was with the rest of the world.

It took him one plane flight to realize that if Crick had lost that place of honor for good, he'd lost everything.

But there wasn't much he could do about it on the plane, and Deacon looked so tired anyway. His face was just as pretty and composed as it had always been, but the bags under the eyes and the deeper grooves in the sides of his mouth were a testament to the fact that he was not nearly the easy-going man that Crick had planned to seduce on a spring day. When they were at LAX and Deacon left them sitting to go find the guy with the electric cart, Crick asked his sister why Deacon looked like death warmed over.

"There's something going on with the bank," she told him, feeding the baby crackers one at a time. (Any more than that and they ended up on the floor.) "He won't tell me, but he's been spending an hour or two at night with Jon on the phone, trying to figure it out. And we lost some more clients this week—I think he's been juggling finances too."

Crick looked at her, his entire body one big mass of aches, and tried to wrap his head around the kind of panic Deacon must be feeling.

"He can't lose The Pulpit," he said after a moment. "It would kill him."

Benny frowned at him, and he suddenly saw the mother and the adult who had sprung up in the last two years. "Deacon's stronger than you think. What would kill him is thinking he'd let us down. You tell him the weight of your happiness doesn't rest on The Pulpit, and he'll survive if it goes."

Crick frowned back, not in any mood for this argument. "How could he not know that?"

"I don't know, genius—how could you not know that he wanted you when he'd just slept with you? If you could go off and join the Army after that, he can think you only love him for the goddamned ranch." She stood up restlessly from the vinyl seat then, brushing her hands off on the pockets of the black hoodie she was wearing over a bright pink skirt. "This conversation is pissing me off. Me and Parry are gonna go to the bathroom—try not to join a cult or anything while we're gone."

Crick had stayed put until they boarded the plane, but Benny's words rang in his ear nonetheless.

For one thing, Deacon had told her what made Crick join the Army—and he really couldn't believe Deacon had opened up that much to anybody else. Apparently, Benny had made the short-list, and while it made Crick happy to know Deacon had someone else in his camp, Crick got the definite impression that Benny would throw him over for Deacon any day of the week, and that sort of hurt. But really, what made him ponder that moment for the entire hour and a half they were over California was the cold, hard truth.

Deacon had forgiven him—he could see it in every line of the man's body. There was no anger in him, no lingering resentment. The shyness was worse, much worse, but still, there wasn't any anger, and that was something. Crick just hadn't reckoned on the fact that Deacon wasn't the only one who had a right to be pissed.

This fact was made acutely painful when they arrived back at The Pulpit.

Jon was there at the airport to pick them up in his big-assed Mercedes, and as Crick leaned on his cane and Jon hopped out to get the bags, instead of the hug he was expecting, he got a restrained smile.

"Glad you made it back, Carrick."

"Glad to be back," Crick said awkwardly. He was wondering what he had done now.

When they got into the car, Jon made a couple of attempts to talk to Deacon about business, but Deacon put him off each time.

"We had a deal," he said. "You have my time after Crick's settled. His head's about ready to blow off his shoulders—let's not strain it any more than we have to, okay?"

Crick looked at him gratefully from the backseat, and Deacon managed a wink and another blush before Jon spoke again.

"Fine—you go ahead and put Crick first now—he'll appreciate it when you're trying to support six people in a one-room apartment with a job skill that went out of fashion fifty years ago!"

"I can EMT too," Deacon said with a smirk. "That should get us a two bedroom apartment the very least."

"I've got my GED," Benny chimed in proudly. "Hell—we might even get the one and a half bath and the good kind of peanut butter!"

"You're going to college, Benny," Deacon said, his good humor suddenly evaporated. "Jon and I have seen to it. Dammit, one person in this family is getting the fuck out of dodge and going somewhere besides Iraq!"

"Amen to that," Crick added in spite of the dim tunnel his vision had become. Leave it to Deacon to set Benny up when the rest of what he loved was apparently going under.

The bedroom looked pretty much exactly how Crick remembered it. Of course, the little cedar box with all his letters in it was new, and so was the calendar with the kittens, but the rest of it....

"Damn, Deacon—I swear the comforter still has creases from the bag!"

Deacon was settling him back on the pillows after another couple of pain pills and his antibiotics. "You still like it, right?"

Crick looked around the room and smiled. Oh yeah—it was the haven he'd meant it to be. "Absolutely!"

"Good. I don't think we can afford to do it up again."

"It's not too gay for you, is it?" Crick asked, realizing how very, very light-toed it seemed after two years of desert fatigues and stinky man-feet.

Deacon laughed in earnest—his first real laugh since Crick had arrived and stumbled into the house, intent on rest and quiet before he killed himself to escape the pain. "Wait 'til you see the girls' rooms. This place looks positively butch compared to Benny's!"

And with that, Deacon went to fetch Crick some lunch. Crick was asleep before he came back, but when he woke up several hours later, there was a cooling bowl of soup with some garlic bread on the end table by the bed.

He awoke vaguely when Deacon came in to change his bandages and the sheets underneath him—his shunts had been leaking overmuch, and Deacon deftly re-sheeted the bed without hardly moving him. A few hours later, Deacon woke him up for more pain pills and to shovel some soup down his throat (different soup—the other stuff had been taken away), and by the time Crick awoke, disoriented and needing to pee like no racehorse in history, it was well into dark.

He stumbled out of the bed and into the bathroom, and a voice from the other side of the bedroom said, "Crick? Is that you?"

Crick grunted and peed, his eyes crossing it felt so good, and then took stock of his fragile body. It hurt—no lie—but he was so glad to be pissing in his own house that he was glad he'd told Deacon to take him home now instead of waiting like the doctors had suggested a few days after Deacon got there.

"Sort of," he said belatedly to the question. "Jon? What're you doing in the study?"

"Waiting for a fax from the ACLU," came the sober, no-nonsense reply. Crick tried to wrap his head around that and opened the medicine cabinet for his pain meds. He was pretty sure it had been long enough—he was starting to know the all-encompassing ache that went with the loss of his chemical shield. The small, mostly-full bottle caught his attention, and he looked at it and frowned.

He took his own pills and staggered out of the bathroom, eager for his own bed again. "Jon?" he called, pretty sure he hadn't heard the fax machine beep.

"Yeah?"

"Did Deacon see a shrink while I was gone?"

"If only. Why?" Jon came out of the study as Crick positioned himself on the side of the bed where Deacon had put the absorbent pads in case his bandages wept through.

"There was a bottle of Valium in there, dated September two years ago."

Jon grunted. "How much was left?"

Crick would have shrugged, but that would have meant moving. "Most of it."

Jon let out a humorless laugh. "That figures. Go to sleep, Crick."

Crick's eyes were closing, but something about Jon's tone bothered him. "What was it for? He didn't mention anything in his letters…."

Jon muttered an oath. "Crick—no offense, because I'm really glad you're back, okay? I'm really glad you're okay, and I seriously missed you, right? But you're going to have to ask Deacon about this, because it's pissing me off all over again and I can't talk about it."

Ask Deacon—okay. "Yeah, because Deacon's so forthcoming about himself," Crick said dryly, and Jon's laugh was a little less bitter this time.

"You got me there."

"Where is he, anyway?"

He heard a yawning and a stretching and the general restless sound of Jon working the kinks out of his body and wished his own body worked that well. "Outside, doing horse ranch shit—feeding and mucking and giving carrots to all the orphaned horses of the world and telling Even he's the world's biggest stud and all the shit that makes the barn his favorite place and dealing with reality his least favorite place."

"He's ducking out on you?" That didn't sound like Deacon at all.

"God, I wish! No, ducking out on me would mean that for one lousy nanosecond he didn't try to take on every responsibility like it was life or death. Ducking out on me would be an improvement." Jon sighed and gave up and sat down next to Crick's legs. Crick felt the bed depress and wished that Deacon were there instead.

"He looks so tired," Crick muttered, not wanting to make Jon mad at him again but needing someone to talk to.

"Yeah," Jon sighed, apparently deciding that Crick's voice in the dark wasn't too irritating. "We had an easy year there—after the baby was born, you know, things went pretty smooth. And then everybody got sick... Christ, that was bad."

"I couldn't get them to tell me how long he was in the hospital that time," Crick told him plaintively, and Jon laughed—again, that curious, dry, humorless laugh that said he'd aged quite a bit in the last two years as well.

"About as long as you were."

Crick sucked in a breath. "I would have come back," he said seriously, feeling a hideous smack of retro-panic hit his chest. "I would have gone AWOL and come back."

"And spent the next few years in military prison. Which is one of the reasons we all contributed to the conspiracy of silence." Jon rubbed his hands through his hair—still long enough to be sexy—and blew out another breath. When he spoke again, his voice was almost dreamy with weariness and with worry.

"I wanted to write you—God, Crick, I wanted to write you twice a day and unload. I wanted to tell you what he looked like and how worried we were. I wanted you to know everything so bad—and what can I say? You ended up in Iraq because you... you just don't think sometimes. I actually wrote an entire letter to you once, right after Benny came here to live. I told you everything—stuff I don't even want to say out loud, you know? And there was the letter, on the table, with a stamp, ready to go out in the morning, and I woke up in a cold fucking sweat, because I dreamed that you got the damned thing, went AWOL, and then got hauled away and we had to live through that whole separation thing all over again." A short bark of bitterness in the semi-dark. The light from the study illuminated Jon's profile, and he was still as beautiful as a soap opera star, but now he looked more real. Worry had made him that way.

"I woke up the next morning and ripped the damned thing to shreds. Buddy, that's one letter you will *never* get." Jon's hand as he patted Crick's good knee was gentle. "And I've got all that in my chest right now. Seeing you hurt—man, it makes me remember all those times in high school when Deacon and I just worried about you. It makes me remember his letters to me when I was away at school, reassuring me that you were okay. You were my family too, and I love you, and I'm glad you're back. But you hurt him so bad…. I'm going to be pissed at you for a while, you know?"

Crick sighed. His chemical shield was up again, and he was tired, and his body felt so far away. "I love you too," he mumbled. "I'm pissed at myself too. But I miss Deacon… where's Deacon?" His eyes closed before Jon could answer the question.

Sometime in the night, he felt a kiss on his temple and breath stirring his hair. "Deacon?"

"Mmmm… be right to bed."

There was a reassuring warmth then, and Crick felt him, right there on his un-bandaged side. Deacon's chin nuzzled his shoulder, and his warm, rough hand spanned Crick's middle under his T-shirt. Crick grunted and turned his head so he could kiss Deacon's forehead, and then sleep slammed down on him, and the moment was gone.

There was movement in the morning—a fresh-smelling, showered Deacon was moving him off the peri-pad again and then stripping his bandages and giving him a quick sponge bath with warm water and some soap that smelled exclusively Deacon. There was antibiotic cream and a brisk, impersonal physician's sort of touch, and Crick barely managed to focus his vision.

"Deacon," he mumbled, sure this was urgent, "why is there Valium in our medicine cabinet?"

Deacon laughed a little, and in the sharp morning light streaming in from the window by the mirror, the lines at his eyes seemed deeper than Crick remembered them, even as his quick, tight grin asserted itself.

"Why—you want some for yourself? You're on a pretty spiffy cocktail already!"

Crick grunted, the cloudiness of the last sixteen hours clearing a little. "I didn't feel this stoned in the hospital. Do you think they made the take-home shit stronger?"

"I think flying 'bout knocked you senseless," Deacon told him back. "I told you, we could have come back for you and let you recoup there." His hard, capable hands were busy taping up a bandage over the shunt that came out between Crick's ribs, and Crick carefully put out a hand to cover them before they could move off again.

"I couldn't spend one more moment away from you," he said, knowing it was maudlin but not caring. "I don't ever want to have to take a leak to have to hug you again."

Deacon smiled then, and Crick's breath lurched in his throat. It was *his* smile.

"The last time I saw that smile, I made you strip naked in front of the camera," Crick said in awe, and Deacon blushed again.

"Yeah, that was fun," he muttered. He went to move his hands, but Crick wouldn't let him.

"You never, ever have to be embarrassed in front of me," he said, feeling stronger than he had in two weeks. "Please, Deacon—keep the smile for me, but, you know... lose the shyness."

Deacon rolled his eyes. "Always been there, Crick. You just didn't know to look. Now Amy's coming by around nine. The doc okayed some travel as long as she stays on the couch here, so you two get to veg around and watch Oprah or whatever. I'll be out and about—Benny's got my cell phone. I guess the social worker's supposed to be here around eleven...."

"Social worker?" Crick felt so lost. This was a different house than the one he'd left, even if their room was still the one he'd painted. His grip on Deacon's hands loosened, and they went busily about their tasks on Crick's body.

"Yeah, step-Bob and Melanie were busy talking while you were in Virginia. She's got to come by to make sure we're not dressed in bondage

equipment and having sex on the table when the baby's in there with us."
Deacon's sigh was long-suffering—he'd done this before.

"Deacon, did they really say that?"

Deacon shrugged. "She's not a bad lady, really—she just acts like
she's got a four-by-four up her ass. I don't think she was really all that
excited about taking Crystal and Missy away in March, and I'm pretty
sure she doesn't think I'm some sort of sexual deviant, but she's got to do
her job, you know?"

"No, I don't know," Crick muttered numbly. "How could anyone
think you were a sexual deviant, Deacon? I don't understand...."

Deacon's tight, busy grin got pretty wicked this time. "I don't know,
Carrick—I've had my hands all over your body for two days now when
you've been fast asleep, and I've liked it. Doesn't that give me some
pervert points right there?"

Crick's shoulders hitched a little, and he managed a laugh. His hand
came up, bandages and all, and he rubbed his fingers through the back of
Deacon's hair as the man grinned down at him, weight of the world on his
shoulders and all.

"You only get pervert points if I didn't like it," he said softly,
wondering if Deacon had dreamed of even a tenth of the things Crick had
in the last two years.

"You weren't conscious—didn't count." Deacon shrugged, that
wicked little grin not easing up in the least.

"You'll have to do it again when I'm awake," Crick told him, his
eyes as serious as he could make them.

Deacon stood, done with the bandages, and bent and kissed him
softly, careful for the new, shiny skin at his temple and cheek, which was
still red and tender.

"We'll have to wait until your body's up to that one, Crick. Right
now, it really does look like growing your hair out's going to be the first
thing you do when you get back."

"Dea—con," Crick whined. "Aren't you horny at *all?*"

Deacon's grin became positively diabolical. "You know, I have to
admit that when you were gone, not so much. I talked about it to make you
feel better, but honestly, it was like I was a neutered cat or something—
just wasn't on the menu. But now?" He reached down and brushed Crick's

lips with his thumb. "Now, yeah. I'm horny. Hurry up and get better, baby—that thing'll come."

And then he was striding out into the morning. Crick heard his sister in the next room and the baby's happy gurgle and felt like a seven-ton slug as his eyes closed and he fell right back asleep.

He awoke a couple of hours later, feeling so much better it was almost like he had a new body. A quick brush of the teeth and wash of the face and, with a lot of assistance from walls and doorframes, he was able to limp out to the front room. He came to a halt when he saw Amy there, sitting in a little upholstered wooden rocking chair that he'd never seen before. She had a tiny, perfectly round bump in the center of her stomach under her pretty peach maternity shirt.

"That's new," he said with a smile, sitting down tentatively on the worn plaid couch.

"So's me not getting a hug or something, Crick," Amy complained, and Crick turned his full wattage smile on her and pushed himself back up to do just that.

"I was afraid you were another member of the 'everybody hates Crick' club," he confessed as she reached up to hug him, and she grunted negative as she held on tight.

When he'd sat back down, she said, "Deacon's forgiven you completely, sweetheart—that's good enough for me."

Crick eyed his sister warily as she walked into the room with a bowl of spiced oatmeal for him. "Thank you—but did you hear that?"

"Deacon and Amy are nicer than I am," she sniffed, going to turn on the television. The baby, who had been busy toddling from one end of the room to the other, flopped her bottom in front of it and squealed.

"Oh yay!" Benny said dryly, "Spongebob!"

"Hush your mouth," Amy replied, taking up the knitting that she'd set down when Crick walked in. "It's the one with Squidward and the claw machine—I'm a fan."

"Oh geez… I actually remember this one from high school." In spite of the changes to his world and the two missing years in an alien desert, Crick was suddenly lost in the normalcy of it, of the women knitting and the baby bouncing excitedly on her bottom—all of it tied together with the familiar cartoon.

It was a nice moment—and it was completely killed by the stentorian knock on the door.

"I've got it," Benny said tightly, putting down her knitting. Crick squinted, trying to remember who this could possibly be.

He didn't count on a dead ringer for Nurse Ratchet from *One Flew Over the Cuckoo's Nest* in a polyester pantsuit.

"Mizz Abernathy, come on in," Benny said, her voice as neutral as she could make it. Crick watched the woman walk into the room and set her briefcase down on the kitchen table with a proprietary air and grimaced. Who was this stranger, and why did she look like she was weighing the house and finding it lacking?

"Would you like to come into the living room? It's sort of the walking wounded in here, you know." Benny was trying to crack a joke— and Crick was suddenly very, very wary of this person and more than a little bit angry.

"So I see," Ms. Abernathy said, and Benny gestured that she should sit down on the stuffed chair, kitty-corner to Crick on the couch. Her face softened a little when she saw Crick's scars and his bandages, and he extended his right hand in greeting.

"Forgive me if I don't get up," he said, trying to remember all the shit he learned about keeping his head.

"Understandable—so you're Benny's brother?"

"Yes ma'am. So you're the tight-ass who said Deacon was a sex deviant?" Fuck. So much for maturity.

"Crick!" Benny hissed, and he didn't care for the pinched, terrified look on her face one single bit.

"Well I'm sorry!" he snapped back. "You're walking around this woman on eggshells, and the baby is happy and fine, and you're happy and fine, and Deacon doesn't deserve to have her come in and make him feel like shit!"

"This woman" managed to regain her composure after a moment and said, "There was some concern about Mr. Winters having an inappropriate relationship with your sister, Mr. Francis. We understand that the two of you were engaged in sexual conduct when you were still in high school as well."

Crick looked at her and felt his face turn red. His blood was rushing so hard through his body that his wounds throbbed with it. "I. Wish." The growl was low and angry, and she flinched away from it.

"Well, you were living here with him when you were sixteen."

"Because my parents kicked me out when I came out of the closet!" And why did this particular event seem to have defined his life? Jesus, it seemed like two years in Iraq would give him some better stories to tell!

"I… I was under the impression you—and your sister—ran away," she said, seemingly disconcerted, and Crick's expression got darker.

"I went to a funeral and came home to my shit on the lawn. Deacon helped me pick it up, and Parish gave me the spare room to keep it in."

"At least you got your shit on the lawn!" Benny spat. "I told them I was pregnant and managed a set of pajamas and a black eye before Deacon came and got me." She looked at the social worker with understandable loathing. "And I told you all of this—and you ignored me. But I notice you're not ignoring Crick."

Ms. Abernathy had the grace to flush. "Your brother is very convincing."

Crick glared at her. "So is my sister. You just didn't want to listen. And all that crap you were saying about an inappropriate relationship—" He shuddered to actually consider this, but it explained a lot about Deacon's introversion, which seemed to have gotten even worse. "Um, did you actually say that crap to Deacon?"

"He denied it," she conceded, "but you weren't here to collaborate. If Bernice here hadn't been so adamant that he wasn't forcing himself on her…."

Oh God. Hearing her confirm it…. Thinking about Deacon accused of the worst sort of conduct while he was trying to keep his family together in the best sort of ways… Crick couldn't do it. He stood up on shaky legs.

"Who would say that?" he asked, near tears. "Who in the fuck would say that about Deacon?" He looked at Benny in outrage, and her face was flushed, but she looked wearily resolved, as though she'd heard this before.

"Who do you think, Crick? And it only got worse when we sent her away at the hospital—she and Bob haven't shut up about him, I guess."

Crick held on to the back of the couch, wanting his strength back so he could kick something. "Are you high? Are all of the people in this town high? This is Deacon Winters you're talking about! God damn... how could you think he'd do this?"

Ms. Abernathy was pale now but sticking to her guns. "Mr. Winters was not exactly forthcoming about his reasons to take the girl in. And he seemed guilty in previous visits—especially about you."

Crick pressed the heel of his hand to his eyes to keep from weeping like a baby. "He was mortified, you bitch!"

"Crick!" Amy hissed, and he shook her off.

"Fuck that. Nobody says that shit about Deacon. You listen to me— you go tell whoever you report to that Deacon Winters is the best man I've ever known. You go tell them that I was the world's horniest twenty-year-old virgin and I had to seduce *him*, and you go tell them that he took my sister in because she's my family and he's just that fucking decent. And then you tell them to leave us the hell alone, you hear me?"

"Now Mr. Francis...."

"That's Second Lieutenant Francis to you—I served my country for two years, and I've been decorated on the field twice, and I learned everything I know about honor and decency from the man you just called a baby-raper. You want to come back on this property one more time? You'd better have a fucking warrant!"

"Crick!" Benny protested, and even Amy was trying to stand up, and Crick gave up on holding back the tears and looked at the social worker with a wet face and his own loathing.

"I'm serious," he said thickly. "Nobody does this shit to Deacon. Nobody."

Ms. Abernathy stood up and straightened her skirt with unnecessary force. "Well, at least you've put our minds to rest about some things," she said shakily, and Crick just stared at her and shook his head.

"What do in the fuck do I have to sign to get you the fuck out of here?"

Chapter 20

Secret Gardens

DEACON'S hand had never really healed right the second time he broke it. He'd managed to dislocate his thumb about three times since the cast came off, always unexpectedly, and always with a great deal of pain.

At least he knew the drill.

He was working one of their few two-year olds—their money-makers, if they could show them and get them papered—when the skittish thing pulled back her head at the exact moment Deacon noticed the social worker's car pulled up in the drive.

His lungful of "*Fuck!*" probably didn't make the impression he was aiming for—not that the woman seemed to like him anyway.

Andrew hurried over and grabbed the halter, and Deacon leaned against the fence, trying to see through the spots in front of his eyes. "Awww, fuck," he panted. "I gotta go set this!"

"Yeah," Andrew told him sympathetically. "Just make sure you're by the crapper when you do."

Something about the particular type of pain of setting the thing back triggered Deacon's gag reflex like nothing else. It was humbling, but it was true—the first three times didn't lie.

So Deacon was not exactly in the best form when he shouldered his way through the mudroom and then through the kitchen. When he got there, Crick and Ms. Abernathy looked up at him, startled, and he gave them a green smile through the spots in front of his eyes.

"Good to see you, Ms. Abernathy... Crick, I see you've met. Um, would you both excuse me... and, um...." Pain was taking over his body, radiating from his tendon, enflaming his entire arm. "Whatever you hear from the bathroom, would you ignore it?"

"Oh Jesus," Benny said, coming from the living room. "Deacon, you didn't do it again?"

"Yeah, Shorty—really did. You want to help me out since you know the drill?"

He didn't wait for an answer, choosing to stumble for the bathroom instead. When he got there, he carefully aligned his thumb with the doorjamb and then threw his full weight against it, howling as it popped back into the joint. *Wait for it... wait for it....*

When Crick limped into the room with the ace bandage from the other bathroom, he was sitting on the side of the tub, losing his breakfast into the commode.

"Deacon?" Crick sounded really tired—and mildly amused, but unfortunately, Deacon's only response was another heave. He stayed there for a minute, his ass on the side of the bathtub and his shoulders trembling, before he looked up and tried a shaky smile.

"Believe it or not, I feel better already." It was true—if they kept the thumb wrapped up against his hand, it would be good in a couple of days.

"I'm not sure I believe it," Crick said softly. Deacon sat up and put the lid down on the seat so Crick could sit. He did, gratefully, and held out the ace bandage, and together, a little awkwardly, they managed to wrap his hand in a way that didn't disgrace either of them. When they were done, Crick refused to relinquish it, sitting instead with Deacon's bandaged hand between his, stroking Deacon's wrist softly with his good hand.

"Is she gone?" Deacon asked, mesmerized by those strong fingers on the inside of his wrist. He'd seen Crick signing some papers—he assumed that Benny's actual brother had better luck at the bureaucracy game than her gay brother-in-law.

"Yeah, you started barfing and that pretty much cleared her out. She was horrible, Deacon. I'm so sorry you had to deal with that sort of thing while I was gone." He looked so distressed! Deacon pulled up a smile from somewhere and tried to calm him down a little.

"It wasn't so bad—same shit you've put up with your whole life." He closed his eyes and just savored that touch on his arm. Ahh… God. He didn't even care that they were in a bathroom again, it just mattered that Crick was there, touching him.

"No, Deacon—that was worse," Crick said, but Deacon thought it probably wasn't.

"You signed stuff? So Parry can stay with us?"

"Yeah—I've got full custody of both of them now. Harder to take them away with the blood tie, I guess. Dumb-asses."

Deacon thought he'd be able to smile at this, but his throat worked, and he managed a nod instead.

"What?" Crick still knew him—his expressions and his noises and things.

"Nothing." Deacon shook his head, but Crick's grip on his arm got firmer, and Deacon sighed. "It was nice—even just on paper—to be that baby's daddy, that's all."

Crick looked away. "Can't help you with that one, Deacon," he said at last, and Deacon found he could manage a real smile after all.

"She'll be ours to raise for as long as Benny lets us. It'll be enough, right?"

Crick's expression was a lot older than Crick himself. "Deacon, man, you've got to start asking for more in life. I'm serious. It's like there's these whole unexplored places in your heart of things you want but won't give a voice to. I would *never* have known how bad you wanted kids, do you know that? If Benny hadn't shown up with one in the oven, it never would have occurred to me that you would have missed out on something that is so big, it's almost like your arm or your leg or something."

Deacon shrugged. "You would have figured it out—you're still pretty young. You get the right to be self-centered when you're young."

Crick's grimace was all twist and darkness. "Like you've ever known."

Deacon didn't have anything to say to that. He stood up then, because there was more shit to do, and brushed his teeth quickly while Crick watched him with troubled eyes. When he was done and had washed his face for good measure, he bent over, rested his good hand on Crick's good shoulder, and kissed his temple. "You've done your good deed for today, Carrick—you made our family safer than I ever could. How about you go take a nap in front of the television and let this old man go do his chores?"

"You're twenty-seven, Deacon." But he was smiling a little when he said it.

"Some good years left," Deacon grinned, starting on his way out the door. Crick's voice stopped him.

"Deacon?"

"Yeah?"

"Are you ever going to tell me what the Valium's for?"

"Not if I can help it," he said, and with a thump on the doorframe with his good hand, he was gone.

And ah, God... sweet, merciful God, it was so damned good to have him home.

Deacon tended to his bandages—fewer every day—and to his medicine, doing everything in his power to keep Crick healthy and pain free in the next week, and Crick seemed to be bouncing back like a rubber ball.

He was grateful for his first shower, even though it was sitting on the stool inside the bathtub, and Deacon was grateful for the chance to see him, all of him, whole and well and clean and getting healthier, under the spray.

"I'm going to have scars," he said mournfully, and Deacon couldn't gainsay it.

"You're going to walk on your own," Deacon said, passion in his words. "With some PT, you'll be able to use your hand—Crick, you can ride a horse again."

Crick looked down at himself under the sluice of warm water and antibiotic soap and grimaced still, even as Deacon soaped up his chest and his side, being very careful not to use enough force to draw blood as he scrubbed Crick's shunts and healing burns.

"I was pretty once," he said, and Deacon actually smiled.

"Never knew you were vain, Carrick. I still think you're pretty." Oh, how he did too. Crick's body was functional—the scars were meaningless. Crick was sitting there, working on getting better. His muscles were still connected; his graceful, rangy, long limbs still moved on command. His eyes could still see, and Deacon felt Crick's sensitive fingertips ranging

Deacon's chest, his stomach, and his shoulders every night as they let Crick heal and reacquainted each other with the touch of skin from another human being. Crick, sitting up and alert and able to move—well, damn, that was the most beautiful thing Deacon had ever seen.

Crick squinted at him through the warm water. "Deacon, how long have you loved me like this?"

Deacon knew he blushed, but he couldn't help it. He closed the shower curtain on Crick and made a business of sopping up the water on the floor.

"Does it matter?" he asked when Crick seemed to be waiting for an answer.

"Only because it's another thing I didn't know about you when I thought I was seducing you," Crick said. They were doing this at night. Crick had gotten enough strength to move slowly about the house and help with the housework, and Benny was grateful. He couldn't chase the baby—and certainly didn't trust himself alone with her just yet—but she was getting good at sitting on his sound side and listening to a story (but never a song). He sounded tired and young and a little sad, and Deacon thought wearily of all he had left to do out in the stable after he put Crick to bed. He wasn't sure he had the strength for more than being happy Crick was home.

"You say that like I have lots of secrets, Crick." The thought was ludicrous. "If you haven't figured it out yet, I'm a very simple guy." Deacon felt a sudden thrill of dread, enough to make him peek around the shower curtain. "You're not thinking of getting bored with me yet, are you?"

Crick grinned back at him, completely unashamed by his nakedness—or by his scars, at least now. "Never. I might get mad at you, frustrated, and absolutely convinced that you can't answer a question with anything other than a crooked answer, but never bored."

Deacon shook his head, embarrassed again. "You just like things dramatic," he muttered. "There's no reason to get all excited about the fact that I've loved you in one way or another since you walked up to The Pulpit when you were a kid."

Crick lost his grin and became suddenly as open and as vulnerable as that kid Deacon remembered. "And you said *I* wrecked *you*. God*dammit*, Deacon—you have *got* to give a guy a warning before you make my heart beat like that."

Deacon managed another grin as he turned off the water and offered a big, fresh towel to Crick as he hoisted himself to his feet. "Maybe you should just get used to taking a compliment, you think?"

He engulfed Crick in the towel then, like he was taking care of a really big child, and let Crick lean on him while he got him back to the bed. With some maneuvering—and a lot of groping, at least on Crick's part—Crick was clean, dressed, and in bed again, trying hard not to fall asleep.

"Are you coming to bed, Deacon?" he asked—and it was a legitimate question. Between the legal paperwork and the ranch work and the extra time spent tending to Crick, Deacon had gone to bed late and woken up early since Crick had returned.

"I've got some shit to do first. I'll get here eventually." He smiled again. It had been over a week since Crick had gotten back, but seeing his dark head on his pillow still filled him with a boiling joy.

But tonight, Crick was regarding him with a quiet, unsettling sort of intensity. "Deacon, you're going to have to talk to me sometime, you know? The world is just not this busy."

Deacon sighed and pulled up a chair next to the bed and sat down. "It actually is—at least right now. But what did you want to talk about?"

Crick shook his head against the pillows, his eyes closing in spite of his best efforts. "How about why you can't seem to gain any weight."

Deacon looked down at himself—in fact, he had been doing pretty well on that score. The last family meeting (where this was getting to be ritual) had him at one-seventy, which was a little thin but not by much. But that had been before they'd gotten the call from Germany about Crick—he seemed to have lost some more in the last few weeks.

"I guess I've been worried about you, dumbass. Maybe you don't get yourself halfway blown to kingdom come, and I'll start eating bacon, cheese, and shortbread cookies again."

"Being underweight is rough on your heart, Deacon," Crick said seriously. "You know—the same heart that Parish had?"

Ou-uch. But Deacon knew where it was coming from too. They would never get over that whole "please don't leave me" thing. Ever.

"My cholesterol's good," Deacon said mildly. "Look, Crick—we don't have guarantees here. We just don't. I'll keep myself as healthy as I can, but I'm not going to promise nothing bad's going to happen. Jesus, after the last two years, about all I *can* promise is that NorCal seems to be off the map for a plague of locusts."

Crick laughed a little, and his eyes closed completely. Deacon stood and kissed him—the shiny, scarred part of his face, because he loved it all—and then dropped a kiss on Crick's lips. Crick's mouth opened and let him in, and *oooh*... they hadn't done this yet. Crick's breath was minty, and his mouth was warm, and for a minute, just a minute, Deacon let himself fall into that kiss with closed eyes.

It reminded him of how long it had been since he'd been touched—truly touched—all over his body. It reminded him of how badly he'd missed Crick, and of those two weeks they'd had together, when Deacon had wanted him so bad it made the muscles in his stomach taut and his cock hard just to *look* at Crick, just to know that the boy was his.

Crick gasped, completely awake now, and reached his arms up to wind them around Deacon's neck, and Deacon wondered if he'd get a medal for pulling away.

"Ahhh... God, Carrick—I've *got* to go."

"Dea- con!" Crick whined, and Deacon took pity on him. He used his thumb to smooth over Crick's swollen mouth.

"How long 'til you get your shunts taken out?" he asked, although he knew almost to the hour.

"Three more days," Crick said sulkily, and Deacon grinned.

"Well, that'll give us a day to shoot for. I can't promise it'll rock your world—or even that we'll hit a homerun, but I'll pencil in some 'Crick time', okay?"

Crick glowered. "It's not nice to mention 'Crick time' and 'pencil' in the same sentence, you know."

Deacon laughed out loud and playfully peeked under the sheets. Sure enough, a larger-than-pencil-sized tent was popping up from Crick's white boxers, and Deacon ducked his head under and gave it a kiss, the cotton soft and tasting like laundry detergent under his mouth. He was gone then, laughing out the door before Crick could do more than whimper and groan.

He sobered the minute he got to the stables.

He, Andrew, and Patrick had been working as long and as hard as they possibly could, and he still had an hour and a half of stall-mucking to do. He tried to keep it down—he'd promised Andrew that he'd leave it for morning, but he couldn't do that. He'd promised Jon two hours of paperwork and lawsuit filing the next morning, which was when he'd usually be doing the muckraking, and Andrew and Patrick had a full roster of their own.

Benny found him hours later, standing in the corner of the last stall, leaning on the pitchfork and asleep on his feet.

"Dammit, Deacon," she swore, waking him up enough to make him drop the pitchfork and stumble, and she pulled her hooded sweatshirt tighter around her nightgown and picked her way across the stall carefully in her flip-flops. Deacon recovered the pitchfork, and she ripped it out of his hand.

"Benny—"

"Fuck off, Deacon. My brother came and got me because you put him to bed three hours ago and promised 'It'll only be a minute, Crick'. Look at you—you were sleeping on your feet, dammit!"

Deacon frowned. "Did you just tell me to fuck off?"

"I'm pissed!" she snarled. "Two years you've been pining away for my brother like a lost dog. Now that he's here, you can hardly spend ten minutes in the same room!"

Deacon flinched guiltily, and maybe it was the sleep still pumping sluggishly through his brain, but he let slip something he'd been trying to keep close to his chest. "Well it's not going to do Crick much good to be home if I lose it as soon as he gets here!"

Benny stopped for a minute and took a deep breath, setting the pitchfork against the side of the stall with undue care. It was spring, so Shooting Star had been left out in the pasture for the night, which was a good thing, considering her temper.

"Deacon, you know, as much as we love this place, it's not our home without you."

Deacon flushed—it was truly one of the nicest things anyone had said to him. "I promised your brother he'd always have a place to come home to," he said back, repaying the compliment with honesty. "I... I can't let him down."

Benny shook her head, looking too old for her age. "Well, why don't you ask me to help—"

"Because you do enough around here!" he told her sharply. "You are not a full-time employee—you're a girl, and a mother, and you get some down time!"

"What do you get, Deacon?" she asked at last, wearily.

"Your brother's safe," he said with a smile. And then he sighed. "I guess I'll finish this tomorrow."

"I'll finish it tomorrow," Andrew grumbled, coming into the stall wearing a pair of sleep pants and a T-shirt. His prosthetic foot was pale and bare next to his real, coffee-colored one, and Deacon didn't miss Benny's wide-eyed fascination with his feet.

"You've got a list of shit to do tomorrow," Deacon muttered. "I'm sorry I woke you up."

"I'm sorry too—go to bed." He stopped and noticed Benny's non-judgmental interest and said, "Was there something you wanted to know?"

Benny grinned at him. "They couldn't afford to make them match?"

Andrew grinned back—he really did have an amazing, dark-eyed smile. "Everyone's so busy not looking at it, I think they figured no one would notice."

"I noticed," she said impertinently, and he took a game step towards her to ruffle her hair.

"I'll be sure to let the doctor know the next time I go in for a fitting. Now both of you go inside and get some sleep—and Deacon?"

Deacon blinked up at him—he'd been nodding off a little, even in the face of their flirting. "Mmm?"

"I'm feeding in the morning. Sleep in."

And he couldn't think of a reason why he shouldn't. "That sounds like a plan."

It might have been, if Crick hadn't been awake and pissed when he was finally showered and ready for bed.

"I'm sorry," he muttered groggily, scared away from going to snuggle by Crick's glower.

"Deacon! It's past two in the morning—what were you doing?"

"Muckraking," he muttered shortly, grabbing his corner of the covers and curling into a little ball.

"Deacon," Crick said insistently—well, he'd had three hours of sleep, he could be insistent. "You're working yourself into the ground.

You have all these meetings with Jon you won't tell me about. We're all living off of peanut butter and Top Ramen—isn't it about time you told me how bad it really is?"

Deacon grunted. "The peanut butter and Top Ramen is Benny's idea—I told her we're not cutting into the food budget, but she seems to think that's gonna help."

"You didn't answer my question."

Deacon burrowed even tighter into his little cocoon. He could deal better with these questions with just a little bit of sleep. *Just a little, Crick—please? Just a couple of hours, and then I'll be honest when I'm on my way out to save our asses?*

"I don't want to," Deacon said bluntly. "I'm sorry I wasn't in sooner...."

"Since when does muckraking take so long?" Crick was digging in his heels—Deacon knew the sound.

"Since I fell asleep doing it," Deacon yawned, and Crick must have figured he wasn't kidding, because there was some careful shifting on the bed, and then a bandaged arm came over Deacon's arms and locked around his chest.

"Deacon, you keep trying to protect me, and I get that—but it's starting to feel like you're lying to me, and I hate it. I'm not a little kid. When I get my bandages off, I can even help and everything!" That last bit sounded petulant, but Deacon couldn't blame him. He was chafing at the bandages and chomping at the bit.

"When you're up to it, I'll tell you everything," Deacon promised, feeling magnanimous. "Right now, we both need our sleep."

"Well, neither of us are getting any until you're honest with me." Oh God, he was like a dog with a bone.

"About what?" Deacon snapped, finally out of patience.

"I don't know, Deacon—how was detox?"

Deacon snapped upright as though he had been shot, the bandages from Crick's arm catching on his chest as the arm slid down. "Godawful," he muttered, simply stunned into brutal frankness. "How'd you know?"

Crick's dark eyes gleamed at him unhappily in the darkness. "I put some shit together—like the Valium in the cabinet and the fact that Benny and Andrew refused to have beer in the house. And boy, didn't I feel stupid, too—I mean, what did you write? 'Let's just say any alcohol is too much'?"

"What did they tell you?" Deacon asked, feeling panic rising in his throat like bile. They didn't know that much, he thought dizzily. Benny knew he'd spent some time drunk—she knew he'd lost a lot of weight. She didn't know about him, naked in the bathtub in his own filth, begging Jon for a Valium so his body didn't give out. She didn't know about three days of the shakes, toned down with the V, and the fact that he'd barely been able to feed the damned horses for her first week living there.

"Benny told me you were a full-blown alcoholic—and that you were walking away from the liquor store empty-handed when she came to talk to you and you figured out she was pregnant." Crick still sounded angry at Deacon for withholding, and Deacon breathed a sigh of relief.

"Not one of my finer moments," he muttered. "Can I not live through it again tonight?"

"You still didn't tell me about detox," Crick muttered implacably, and Deacon pulled up his knees and scrubbed his face with his hands.

"It was a laugh riot, okay? Two weeks of happy-happy joy-joy fun the likes of which my body has never seen before and will, praise God, never see again. Please"—Deacon was surprised at how much his voice shook—"please, Carrick. Don't make me tell you that story. You used to think I was something, okay? You used to look at me like I was special. Don't make me tell you about being a shaking puddle of puke —I couldn't stand it if you looked at me like I was still that puddle. I can go sleep on the couch if you want... if you can't deal with me the way I am, the way I was, I can sleep on the couch and you don't have to worry about me coming to bed late, but....." Oh damn. *Pull it together, Deacon. You've got too much shit to do, and it's too late for that crap. Pull it. The fuck. Together.* "Just don't make me tell you about that, okay?"

He was shaking. His bare chest and shoulders were shaking as he hugged his knees, and Crick was pulling himself clumsily up.

"I said I'd go sleep on the couch," Deacon muttered, trying to swing his legs out of bed, and Crick's voice was like a whipcrack.

"Don't you dare get out of this bed, Deacon Winters." Crick's good arm looped over Deacon's shoulders, pulling Deacon stiffly into his chest. Deacon was reluctant to go, but Crick kissed him on the temple and murmured, "Please? Please, Deacon—don't go away mad. Just talk to me."

"Crick...." He was still shaking—he couldn't seem to stop. "I'm fine, okay? I just need a little bit of sleep."

"You're not fine," Crick muttered, lying down and pulling Deacon with him. "And you keep talking like I'm going to change my mind about you when I find out the worst—it feels like you don't trust me to know you, Deacon, and that hurts."

Ah, God. Crick felt good. He felt strong—strong enough maybe to take some of the weight off Deacon's shoulders. "Don't ever think I don't trust you," Deacon muttered. "I just don't want to hurt you." He was tired... so tired. And it felt good to lean on Crick for a minute. The shaking wasn't all the way gone, but it was easing up with every breath.

"You don't want to hurt me?"

"Mmm." He was falling asleep on Crick, hypnotized by his warmth and the sweet feel of his breath in Deacon's hair.

"Then once, just once, when I ask you how you are, admit that you're not okay."

Deacon groaned softly and turned against Crick's hard body. "But I am okay," he muttered. "Right now, I'm great."

And Crick must have taken pity on him, because that was the end of the conversation as Deacon remembered it.

Chapter 21

Therapy

CRICK sat in the passenger's seat of the pick-up, wondering why keeping Deacon good to his word made him feel like shit.

It was pretty fucking bad, Crick, what do you want me to say?

The stubborn asshole had told him about detox—sort of.

Patrick found me in the morning—I was sort of a mess. Jon brought me the Valium and helped me clean up the house. Look—can we not talk about this anymore?

Because it had been the end of another long night—this time, Crick had been the one to go out to the stables to find Deacon asleep on his feet, and this time, Deacon hadn't been able to come right back in and go to bed. He'd showered and kissed Crick and had gone into the study to sign the paperwork Jon had faxed him while he was out at the stables.

Crick had pretty much broached the most painful of subjects to get him to put the paperwork away and come home to his arms.

Crick thought bitterly that what he should have done was rip out a shunt or something, just to get Deacon to relax and spend some time with him—and he believed Deacon when he said he wasn't avoiding him too. It was hard not to believe him when he was treating a day taking Crick to the doctor like a day at the circus.

"So, you want to go get something real to eat on our way back?" he asked excitedly as they took the I-50 exit from I-5, and Crick grinned at him, completely unable to piss on his parade.

"Absolutely—steak, I'm dying here—and maybe we could go grocery shopping for Benny on the way back."

Deacon's eyes got big. "Yeah… I wonder where she gets those cookies with the fudge in the middle—those are awesome."

Crick couldn't help but laugh. That core of sweetness in the guy was absolutely untouchable. Getting to it might be a bit tricky, but the results were definitely worth it.

Deacon came with him in to see the doctor. He asked nicely, and since he'd been the one who'd been doing the bandage-changing, it made things easier. Crick sat there in his boxers, waiting for a clean bill of health, and was reassured when the paunchy, fifty-ish man with thinning hair looked at his shiny, pink scar tissue and nodded approvingly.

"Good—whoever's been taking care of your dressing is doing a bang-up job there, Lieutenant Francis. We can leave the bandages off, unless your regular clothes start to chafe—"

"They don't," Crick said with some relief. The doctor had pulled the shunts out, and all that was left of what had felt to be head-to-toe swaddling were two little white gauze pads, turning a little bit pinkish from the trauma of the removal. If it weren't for his arm and the ache in his hip, not having to deal with the bandages would have been almost like having his old body back.

His arm was hard to look at, though.

The skin was… twisted, was what it looked like. As though someone with red-hot hands had tried to give an Indian burn to a wax figurine. The muscles in his hand and arm felt as though they were on perma-flex, and his hand was pulled up into a hideous parody of a hand—more of a harpy's claw, really, and he wanted the bandages back just to hide the shape of the thing.

He didn't even want to think about using it on a set of reins yet.

The doctor didn't seem particularly upset about it, though, and neither did Deacon. The doctor took his hand in that dry, practical grip that physicians had and extended his fingers, asked him to squeeze, prodded at the webbing between his fingers, and pronounced it all good.

"Okay, Lieutenant, it's not as bad as it looks right now. Your musculature's still good—it was torn, but they did a not-bad job stitching it together. What you need is some physical therapy. What I'm going to do is set you up. In fact"—the man turned towards his computer console and typed for a minute—"in fact, I've got an appointment for you today. Jeff's on site today and he's got a space open in about forty-five minutes. Give you two a chance to get a soda or something and make your next appointment, and there you go. He'll spend some time massaging your muscles and showing you strengthening exercises, and you'll be seeing him at the out patient facility in Citrus Heights from now on, how's that?"

Deacon looked almost disappointed, and Crick winked at him. "Don't worry, Deacon—we can find other reasons to come to Sacramento, okay?"

Deacon flushed, which reminded Crick of something else he wanted to ask. "Hey, Deacon—can you give us a moment here?"

Deacon looked surprised, but because he was Deacon, he left Crick to his privacy. Crick was pretty relieved—if Deacon heard this next part of the conversation, he wouldn't stop blushing until Christmas, and then Crick would never get him naked.

"He did a good job nursing you," the doctor said as Deacon left. "Your brother, right?"

Crick grimaced. "So—you're my doctor, right?"

The doctor looked confused, but he nodded.

"So, you're not obligated to tell the Army anything about me, right?"

The doctor, still looking confused, nodded again. "As long as you're not a danger to yourself or others, what you say here is privileged information, son. Why—what's on your mind?"

Crick gave a sigh of relief. "Okay—here's the deal. That guy's *not* my brother, and I like to be on bottom. Unless you give me a clean bill of health for that kind of sex, I am *never* going to get laid—so am I good?"

Crick was unprepared for the guy's eyes to bug out, nor for the five-minute fit of coughing that followed, but eventually he did have a doctor's note that said Deacon could fuck him until he screamed for mercy (not in those exact words) and his delicate innards would in no way be damaged, harmed or traumatized. Given that little piece of paper, which he planned to produce at a strategic moment, he was in a decent frame of mind when he met his physical therapist.

His physical therapist, PA Jeff Beachum, was the gayest man Crick had ever met. He actually trilled when he talked and minced when he walked and eyed Deacon with such undisguised and fascinated lust that Deacon turned red and mumbled something about more soda before turning around and running away, leaving Crick in the small room with a bed, a sonogram heat massager, and Jeff, the only man on the planet who could make Crick look straight, giggling hard enough to wet his pants.

"Thanks a lot," Crick said, trying to appear stern. In reality, he was charmed and more than a little bit relieved. Besides Deacon, he was starting to feel like the only gay man on planet Earth—the Army and Levee Oaks would do that to a guy. "Who's going to defend me from you now?"

Jeff flashed him a happy grin. "Oh babydoll, if you so much as whimper, that smoldering ball of testosterone will be back from the soda machine in no time. Now sit down here, take off your shirt and hold your arm out, will ya?"

Crick did as he was told, and Physician's Assistant Beachum started doing the same things Crick's doctor had, except with a little more passion and verve. Crick found himself gritting his teeth and keeping his whimpers to himself.

"So," he rasped, "what gave him away? I didn't figure it out until I was grown, and he had to tell me."

Jeff laughed. "Okay—now spread your fingers. Wider. Wider, dammit, you'll never get yourself off if you can't wrap your hand around it, right?"

That last one surprised Crick, and he managed to half-uncramp the claw of his hand.

"See? Give a guy some motivation, and see what he can do? And to answer your question, it wasn't your boyfriend—I wouldn't have read him either. You're the one who has 'I'll stick my ass in the air any day of the week and twice on Sundays for this man' tattooed across your forehead."

"Thank God," Crick said with feeling—partly because Jeff let go of his hand, and partly because, "I thought my doctor texted the whole building!"

Jeff laughed some more—he seemed to do that a lot, but Crick couldn't complain. Deacon liked to laugh quietly, but sometimes a little bit of relief from that sort of intensity was nice too. "Why, what'd you say to Herbert? He doesn't shake easily, you know."

Crick repeated the conversation, and Jeff actually stopped torturing the tendons in his elbow long enough to put his hands between his knees and whoop happily. "Oh my God. *Tell* me I have permission to give him shit about that! Please. Please. Pretty, pretty, pretty, pretty please with a cherry on top?"

Crick grinned wide enough to make Jeff put his hand on his chest dramatically. "That would depend on whose cherry," he said with a smirk. When Jeff was done laughing at that, Crick told him, "Go ahead, tell him—knock yourself out—I don't see what the big deal is."

"The big deal? The big deal is that he's bombproof. He's a legend. The story is—and his son has come in to confirm it—that his son came out to Herbert when he was giving the kid the facts of life speech. Herbert was full into the song and dance about always using a condom—'it protects against disease, it protects against pregnancy, it's just generally a good idea'—when his kid goes, 'Dad, I don't have to worry about pregnancy—I'm gay'. And Herbert—without missing a beat, mind you—says, 'In that case, let me tell you about lubricant, because you're going to want to know'. Honey, if you managed to rattle Herbert, you're not just my kind of guy, you're a by-golly act-of-God."

Crick laughed a little and then sobered. "Yeah—I think Deacon would probably agree with you there."

Jeff made sympathetic noises before he raised Crick's arm over his head and almost made his vision black out. "Yeah? It must have been rough when you went away. Tell me about it, baby—I'm all ears."

By the time Crick's PT session was done, he couldn't remember when he'd laughed so much—or when his heart had been lighter. As Jeff had him put his shirt back on and let him sit down after a particularly grueling exercise, he said, "Wow, do they pay you double for the head shrink? I haven't talked so much in ages."

Jeff inclined his tousled, salon-cut dark head modestly. "All part of the service, my boy." He looked up, brown eyes twinkling. "Seriously—most guys need to talk when they get back. I like to think it makes up for the pain I put you through."

Crick nodded vigorously. There had been quite a bit of that, it was true. He tried flexing his hand some more, and it hurt, but it moved and he hadn't thought it would actually do that. Jeff nodded approvingly.

"Good—you keep doing that. In fact, if you really want to see some improvement, get your little old lady on and take up knitting or spinning. I know of cases where your kind of damage has made almost a full recovery. It took a couple of years—and there was still pain—but there wasn't anything those women couldn't do with their two good hands, you know? And one of them can knit one hell of a doily, too."

Crick rolled his eyes. "I don't know about doilies—and I reckon my sister could teach me to knit, she's been doing enough of it. What I'm really wondering about is stable mucking—can I do any of that?"

Jeff widened his eyes and gestured for Crick to proceed. "It's not every day someone's PT goal includes shoveling horseshit, Lieutenant— any particular reason that's on the list?"

"Deacon needs help. I would give about anything to let the guy get more than four hours of sleep a night," Crick said with a grimace, and Jeff pursed his lips and raised his eyebrows.

"That's almost the most precious thing I've ever heard. You know what would *really* help that guy?"

Crick held out his hands in a classic shrug. "Thrill me."

"Exactly. You get him laid, and the world will seem a *whole* lot less dire, trust me."

Crick smiled, although there was a wealth of things he *hadn't* told Jeff that weighted the expression down a little. "Well, the world will seem a whole lot less dire when he's not getting an ulcer because he thinks he's going to lose our home, either. We lost a lot of business, thanks to step-Bob and the bitch who spawned me." Yeah, they'd come up in conversation, along with "driving while gay."

It was Jeff's turn to look thoughtful. "Hmmm… you know, I just might be your fairy Jeff-father in all senses of the word, sweet thing—I might have an answer to some of your woes right there. You ever hear of Project RIDE?"

By the time Crick left the little PT room, Jeff on his heels filling out a business card with the details of Project RIDE, Crick had a little more optimism about the world. He also had Jeff's personal number and a promise to call.

"Now make sure and tell your scary brooding boyfriend that you're not my type," Jeff had trilled. "It's just that"—and he gave Crick a crooked smile, the kind that told Crick maybe the guy knew more about loneliness than he'd let on in forty-five minutes of physical and emotional therapy—"everybody needs a friend, right? Even your fairy Jeff-father."

For the first time since he'd come to in his hospital gurney in Germany, Crick let himself remember Lisa and the winsome smile she'd given as she'd flopped butt first in the shaded sand next to Crick. Jeff looked that way too, and Crick thought wistfully that a friend wouldn't be a bad thing to have, especially when his family was still grappling with his return.

"Absolutely," he said sincerely, holding out his hand and clasping Jeff's when he returned the gesture. "Deacon even lets me pick out slippers and plan slumber parties, if I ask nice."

Jeff grinned wickedly. "Can we do his makeup?"

Crick just shook his head, thinking about Deacon's reaction to that one. "Mmm... no."

That wicked grin cranked itself up a notch. "Ah, well—a boy can dream."

While they had lunch at Outback, Crick was all about Project RIDE—and Deacon started catching his excitement.

"You say they need a new stable? That's promising.... He gave you the number?" Deacon took a healthy bite of his prime rib, and Crick made careful note of how much he had left on his plate.

"Yeah. They use the horses as physical therapy, so they *have* to be sweet-tempered. Mostly they run off volunteers, but sometimes there's stuff they can pay us for—they get donor horses that need breaking, and we can charge for that. And they get government funding, so...." Crick's face fell. "Well, maybe that's not a plus."

Deacon laughed his quiet laugh, and Crick smiled at him, feeling a lump in his throat that no amount of soda could wash down. He felt it then, acutely: the difference between having a friend and being friends with your lover—no amount of easy conversation with Jeff was ever going to make up for one honest, quiet laugh from Deacon.

Deacon caught his regard and looked up. "What?"

Crick blushed and grinned and shook his head. "Thinking about loving someone and being in love and dumb shit."

And now it was Deacon's turn to blush. "You had one hell of a conversation with your physical therapist, didn't you?"

Crick looked away. "I'd forgotten, you know. How nice it was to have a friend."

Deacon reached across the table and grabbed his damaged hand, which was something they could do in Sacramento or Citrus Heights or even Roseville, but not in Levee Oaks. The fact that it was the warm touch of his flesh on Crick's abused skin didn't escape Crick either. To Deacon, it was Crick's hand, not a claw, not something to be avoided. It was just Crick's, and Deacon didn't care that it was flawed.

"I haven't really had a chance to tell you how sorry I am about Lisa."

Crick looked up at him suddenly and saw it there, all of it—no jealousy about Jeff, just simple understanding about his friend and his desire to give Crick support.

"I miss her. She kept me sane over there, you know? I keep…." He swallowed and looked down at his empty plate. Deacon had needed to cut his meat, and he'd done it so quietly and with so little fuss that Crick had hardly noticed. "I keep thinking I want to text her or something, to tell her how I'm doing. I had this idea fixed in my head, of her over there and me here, and me still being her friend. I just… I can't make that go away."

"You're going to miss her. It's going to be right there in your chest for a while—just let me know what you need to do to deal with it."

Crick blinked a little and then some more, trying to get a hold of himself. He was going to take a page from Deacon's book and do this in private with only Deacon as a witness. "Jeff's a start, I guess," he said at last, thinking it was true.

Deacon sighed and got a tighter grip on his hand. "You… Crick, you and Benny, you break my heart. You're fearless and you're social—you should have friends. You should be at parties. I used to fantasize about you, when you were lining up art schools and thinking about going away. You were having parties in a dorm room and saying outrageous shit, and you were surrounded by people, and all of them loved you."

He smiled that tight, fierce grin, and Crick's heart broke—it was Deacon's fantasy for Crick, but not for himself. And Deacon had never wanted to hold him back.

"You know how you keep saying that all you want is me and The Pulpit? All I want is for you to want more. You have all these plans for everybody but yourself. I like having friends, you're right. I want friends. But I don't want them more than I want my family. You and Benny and the baby and Jon and Amy and even Private Blood-loss. You're my family—I want you to have us all."

The tight, fierce grin grew open and dreamy, and Crick's heart flipped over in his chest a little, and his scarred, clawed monstrosity of a hand gave a convulsive clutch under Deacon's rough, perfect fingers.

"Okay," Deacon said through that sweet, trusting smile. "I'll dream that for you."

That night, Deacon left paperwork on the desk for once and let Andrew do the muckraking. He showered early, while Crick was still sitting up in bed, watching the television that had been set up on the dresser while he was gone. Deacon came out in his briefs, with his hair combed and freshly shaved, which he didn't have to do, and Crick looked at him with a hopeful curiosity.

"You look like you've got plans," he said, and Deacon's tight, fierce grin turned embarrassed.

"I… I could always go do…," he started, reaching for a T-shirt from the dresser.

"Deacon, so help me, if you go do bills tonight, I'm going to kick your scrawny ass halfway to Canada. Get in bed, will you?"

Deacon did, and Crick reached over to turn off the light.

"No," Deacon murmured. "I want to see you.…"

Crick turned it off anyway. "Please," he begged, hating himself for turning Deacon down in even the smallest of ways. "Let me imagine my body's perfect, just for tonight."

Deacon was close to him, close enough for Crick to smell his shaving cream and feel the clean moisture radiating from his skin. His eyes, that pretty green in the light, turned depthless in the dark, and his perfect mouth turned up at the corners right before Crick had to close his eyes.

"Your body *is* perfect, Carrick."

The taste of Deacon's breath on his face made his skin shiver and his cock instantly hard. The minute Deacon's mouth closed over his, Crick wrapped his leg—his scarred but sound leg—over Deacon's hips and groaned, pulling that bony, tough body flush against him, pushing his groin up against Deacon's and groaning some more to find that Deacon was just as hard as he was.

It was Deacon's turn to groan, and his tongue swept Crick's mouth, and he claimed Crick for his own, again and again. Crick could have been lost in that kiss forever, but Deacon pulled his mouth away to place shaky kisses down Crick's jawline.

Crick arched his back and exposed his neck, and still, still tried to press his bare chest closer to Deacon's. The slick of their skin together was heavenly, and Crick couldn't get enough. Deacon apparently felt the same way, because as he kissed his way to Crick's collarbone, tormenting with the slight rasp of teeth, he still stayed close, skin to skin, and the smooth gloss of shower-clean was rapidly made sticky with sweat.

Deacon's mouth lingered on Crick's chest. He suckled the sensitive nipples until Crick whimpered, afraid he was going to spill in his pants before the good stuff happened. Deacon moved on before he could do that and spent some extra time on Crick's tender, shiny scars. He kissed the new skin on Crick's shoulder, the ridges of shrapnel scars along his ribs, the twisted mess of skin on the left side of his stomach, each kiss a benediction, a claiming. *This is still you. I still love this. Don't worry, Crick; the whole of you is precious to me.*

Crick writhed under each kiss, thrusting his hips out against Deacon's stomach and then his chest as the man moved patiently down his body.

"I'm going to cream in my shorts if you don't move soon," he gasped. Deacon chuckled against his soft abdomen, and Crick threw his head back and groaned. He didn't notice that Deacon's hands were shaking until he fumbled Crick's shorts twice. Crick finally caught a clue and put his own hands—the scarred one and the whole one—over Deacon's and helped him strip off the boxers. There was already a damp spot on the front because Crick was leaking pre-come like a spigot, and the air hitting the head of Crick's cock was something of a surprise.

Crick sucked in air past his teeth at the cold, and then Deacon's tongue, rough as a cat's, made a playful swipe across his head, and Crick laughed gruffly because it felt *soooo* good. Deacon opened his mouth then, done with foreplay, and took him inside.

Crick grunted with surprise. It was so quick, and Deacon's mouth was so warm and so wet, and he moved his head once, twice....

Crick felt Deacon's chest muscles trembling against his thighs, and even though he had stars exploding behind his eyes, he realized that Deacon's movements were rough, trembling, barely restrained.

Oh God. Oh God—he's holding himself back. He... he's clumsy with wanting me....

The thought was a revelation, and it was enough to make Crick grunt, trying to resist, wanting to comfort him, wanting it to be good for him too, but Deacon was insistent. He shoved his mouth forward jerkily, and his teeth barely grazed the skin of Crick's cock, and Crick was deep, deep in his throat when he came.

"Gaaaawwwwwddddddddd," he gasped, tightening his hands in Deacon's wet hair, and Deacon curled up around him, grabbing his ass with rough, jerking fingers, wrapping his legs around Crick's calves, burying his head into Crick's groin and clutching Crick's naked, spasming body to him with trembling strength.

Crick eventually fell limply from Deacon's mouth, and he reached down and hauled Deacon up by the armpits with a little help from Deacon himself. When they were situated and Crick was wrapping Deacon tight and hauling his face into Crick's chest, Crick felt the clammy fabric of Deacon's briefs up against his thigh.

"God, Deacon... you...."

"Yeah," Deacon chuffed out a breath. "Hope you weren't expecting the world's greatest lover. He just came in his shorts."

Crick shivered, holding Deacon even tighter. "That is *so* fucking sexy," he muttered in awe.

"You're so easy," Deacon mumbled, and Crick could feel his embarrassment scorching the skin of Crick's chest.

"In your bed? I'm a sure thing."

Deacon chuckled lowly, and then, miracle of miracles, he fell asleep. Just like that. No bills, no stable mucking—just content, happy Deacon, cuddled up against Crick's chest like he'd always dreamed.

So it wasn't an entire night of sweaty, sensual passion, but Crick was thinking that it was a start—a good start, but a beginning just the same. He was thinking that with passion like that—the kind of passion that made a man just curl up and come from the wanting of his lover in his mouth—he and Deacon were on their way to a stellar year of make-up sex. He was thinking that he might not have needed the doctor to write him a note after all.

A week later, he was thinking that if Deacon didn't fuck him and do it proper, he was going to climb the fucking walls.

"My God, honey, your shoulders are tight enough to bounce a quarter off!" Jeff sounded appalled as they started working on Crick's PT, and Crick couldn't blame him.

Crick had applied himself assiduously in the past week—he'd had Benny teach him to knit so he could do something useful with his hand when he was resting, which was still more often than he'd like. He'd picked up more of the housework and had dedicated himself to mucking out four stalls a night, just to do his share.

Deacon was appreciative and supportive—and in return for Crick's hard work, he dedicated himself to getting to bed before twelve o'clock, so they could at least fondle each other and one of them (usually Crick) could come before they fell asleep, exhausted by their day.

But Crick still hadn't been pounded into the mattress like a railroad spike, and the stress was starting to tell.

"We've been busy this week," he prevaricated, not wanting to bore Jeff with the financial troubles again. He'd called him during the week, and Jeff had returned the favor, and Crick was starting to recognize the rhythm of talking to a friend.

"You've been stressing over money is more like it," Jeff said wisely, raising Crick's arm over his head and stretching it obscenely while Crick tried to be a man about the whole thing and not whimper.

"Deacon told me a little about the money—it's bad. Not as bad as I think he sees it, but it's bad."

And it was too. The Project RIDE money would help, if it came through—and they were crossing their fingers that it would—but still, they needed horses to break. It was what Deacon was best at and what nobody would give him a chance to do.

"Well, sweet thing, you know what's great at relieving stress? And it's free?"

"Sex," Crick said dryly, not needing a diagram.

"Damned straight. And you know what you've got to convince that tasty hunk of man to give you?"

Crick sighed. "He's still afraid of hurting me… ouch!"

Jeff laughed. "Which is why I'm your physical therapist and not the guy in your bed, I guess. You know, Crick—sometimes, you've just got to take matters into your own hands."

Crick passively allowed his arm to be twisted like a pretzel and then re-formed to something like a human limb again while he stared into space with a busy brain. He suddenly had an idea—and he was pretty sure it was better than the idea that landed him in Iraq in the first place.

Chapter 22

How To Save A Dying Pride

DEACON sure did like young Private Blood-loss. He was going to hate to let him go.

"Look, Andrew," he was saying, pacing back and forth in the little stable apartment that Andrew had been living in, "we love you here. I mean, flat out—I couldn't have done it without you this last year. You eat at my table, you play with the baby—there's not a whole hell of a lot I wouldn't do for you. But… and not this month, and probably not next month, but we're coming up on a time when…."

He looked away. Andrew was watching him with patient eyes, and Deacon found his pride was sitting up and roaring in his chest, because Andrew wasn't just a friend, and he wasn't just an employee. The guy was *family.* Saying this, having this conversation—well, it felt like he couldn't provide for his family, and that hurt.

"You're worried about paying me," Andrew said, and Deacon grimaced.

"Yeah. Don't worry about the apartment. You're welcome to stay as long as you want. We like you here. And you're *always* welcome to eat at our table—but in a couple of months, if things don't improve, you may want to go looking for another job."

Andrew snorted. "Yeah, because having a front row seat to you working yourself to death is gonna be soooooooo entertaining. No worries, Deacon. You just offered me room and board. I'll work for that until things get better."

Deacon looked around the little apartment to avoid gaping like a fish. The room next door was stuffed with tack and extra saddles and bags of grain—you could barely see the cot next to the wall. They'd done Andrew's up right, though. It had padded carpeting—a dusty blue—and they'd replaced the cot with Crick's old twin bed with the drawers underneath it, as well as his end table and lamp. They'd bought him new bedding, though—the old stuff was sort of stained. It was fairly obvious that Crick had always had the sex drive of a hamster on Spanish fly. Deacon had even bought him a small television and some nice blankets to hang the walls with—the place looked homier than most dorm rooms or first-year apartments, at any rate.

"You can't just...." Deacon swallowed past the lump of pride and embarrassment. "I mean... don't you have plans with your life?"

He managed to look at Andrew in time to catch the boy's rather sardonic smile. "I think you and I are a lot alike, Deacon—and there's not a whole lot of places in the world for men like us anymore. I like it here. If you don't mind, I'm going to call the place home for a while."

Deacon was pretty sure his embarrassment alone raised the temperature in the stall apartment about ten degrees. "I don't mind," he said, swallowing again. "In fact, I'm much appreciative."

Andrew grinned then. "Good—now go to bed. Man, Crick needs to be nailed into the wall more than any man in history."

It was true—Crick had been snarky and snarly for the past week, and Deacon knew he was a little disappointed about the sex. And so was Deacon for that matter. It just... damn. Deacon just wanted him too bad. And by the time they were done with the finessing part, the part that made sure Deacon wouldn't hurt him or be too rough with his healing body, well, one of them—usually Deacon—was falling asleep.

But still, being told to go nail your boyfriend was more than a little embarrassing.

"I've got bills to do tonight," Deacon sighed. It was the first of the month—time to decide who to pay and who to put off—not exactly Deacon's favorite chore.

Andrew sighed and shook his head. "Deacon, you know, I know you love this place, and I know your father put a lot into it. But this isn't the only place in the world—or, hell, even in the state—where you can make a horse ranch work. Maybe you should think about just picking up and moving while you can. I'd come with, you know?"

Deacon didn't realize he was just standing there, mouth-breathing, until he caught some dust in his throat. The idea was… it was….

He coughed out the dust and blinked and tried to think past the muzz in his head that came with too much thinking about the subject and too little sleep.

"You'll have to excuse me, Drew," he said at last. "I think you blew my little tiny mind."

Andrew chuckled and yawned and stretched, looking at Deacon pointedly. Deacon grinned and took the hint. Time to let the man sleep.

He took a shower when he got in the house to wake him up for a little bit and then sat down in front of the bills and started to strategize on how to pay one guy and put the other guy off. When that got old, he moved on to the lawsuit paperwork for Jon, which actually seemed to be working, since they'd managed to get a few clients to pay up what they owed and to shut their yaps about "horse AIDS" (fuckers!). He was almost done with that when he heard a noise from the bedroom.

"Ouch!"

Deacon was half out of his chair. "What's wrong, Crick—something snap? Something bleeding? You okay?"

"I'm fine, dammit—just using a muscle that hasn't been worked in a while. Hold…." Crick made a sound then, a sighing, sexy kind of sound, the kind of sound that made Deacon's dick ache and his palms sweat. "Mmmm… yeah, hold on a sec…."

He dropped his pen on the hardwood floor with a clatter and had a hell of a time picking it up. By the time he'd gotten himself situated, he was listening to Crick breathing on the other side of the wall and trying to remember his own name.

"Deacon?" Crick called, still breathless and wanting.

Deacon. Oh yeah. That was his name. "Ye—ah?" His voice cracked half an octave in the middle of the word, and he stood up slowly, wondering what was going to be waiting for him in their bed.

"C'mere a sec, wouldya?"

Deacon stood at the doorway, trying to remember his own name again.

Crick was lying on his back, his injured side artistically covered by sheets, but otherwise completely naked. His knees were bent, and his legs were spread a little, enough for Deacon to see that he'd oiled up his body from his rampant erection to his sagging, heavy testicles to the fairly large adult toy that was protruding from his dilated asshole.

Deacon couldn't move. He might have made a sound—something whip-spiffy, like "uhhhnghh...."

Crick gave him a crooked smile, the kind with the upper teeth gnawing gamely at his lower lip. "Deacon?"

And Deacon realized how hard this was for him—how exposed he felt, with his wounds covered in sheets and the most vulnerable parts of his body on display.

"Shut up," Deacon muttered, shucking his sleep-shorts, briefs, and T-shirt. "I'm getting naked."

"Yeah?" The hope was hard to hear.

"You wanted wine and flowers?" Deacon muttered, getting down to business with the plug. He tugged at it gently, feeling the resistance, enjoying the power as Crick groaned and his cock flexed, the length of it coming off his stomach and snapping back with a slap.

"No," came the strangled reply.

Deacon tugged again. "Getting impatient, were we?"

"Ye-esss...." Crick writhed as Deacon teased him, so Deacon got on his hands and knees and pinched Crick's sensitive nipple with one hand while he tormented Crick's lower body with the other.

"Couldn't think of another way to tell me?" Deacon asked wickedly, giving Crick's cock a good stroke just as a change of pace.

"I got a doctor's note," Crick whined, and Deacon went back to playing with the toy in the way it was intended to be played with. "I didn't have a chance to g-g-g-givvvv... God, Deacon, stop fucking with that thing and fuck *me*!"

Deacon laughed, low and evil, and moved down to suck Crick's cock into his mouth, in spite of the lube, and Crick bucked against him and whimpered some more. Deacon scooted around the bed and positioned himself between Crick's knees.

"You really want me there?" he asked, eager and giddy and ready to play. "I mean, that plug is pretty damned tight... it might even be bigger than me... you sure it doesn't just feel better there?"

"Gawwwdddd... Deacon!" Crick begged, and Deacon grabbed it and yanked, liking the slippery, heavy way it slid out of Crick's ass, liking the way Crick's entire body came off the bed, shuddering, and the way his cock jerked against Deacon's stomach, spattering come between them.

Crick groaned, and Deacon dropped the plug and pushed himself closer, setting himself right there at Crick's sloppy, softly dilated entrance, and captured Crick's mouth in a hungry, wanting kiss.

"So you're all done now," he teased, sliding forward enough for Crick to clench around his swollen cockhead, and Crick groaned. "I mean you pleasured yourself, and you came, and now, I just need to go beat off in the shower, right?"

"Fuck you, Deacon," Crick moaned, and Deacon laughed, that shiver of power zinging right up his spine. Oh God—all this time of being at Crick's mercy, of living his life in the sure knowledge that Crick held his beating heart right there in his hands, and finally, Deacon got a little back.

"I thought I was fucking you, Crick," he said, and then he teased just a little too much because *he* couldn't stand it anymore, and he slid his cock home inside Crick where he'd always wanted to be.

Crick came off the bed then too, growling with urgency, and Deacon pinned him down with a hungry, half-angry kiss and hard hands on his shoulders. Crick returned the kiss, and Deacon's hips started to piston— not smoothly, but rough and hungry and demanding. Crick's head fell back, and his eyes closed, and Deacon growled back, wanting... wanting... oh God, how he wanted this, wanted this moment, Crick's body, Crick's complete submission just to him.

He hit Crick's prostate, felt it slide under the ridge of his cockhead and Crick's head came off the bed and he sank his teeth into the tender joining of Deacon's neck and shoulder, and that about did him in.

"You done? You ready to be done?" he taunted, putting his hands on either side of Crick, and Crick fell back against the bed again, wrapped his arms around Deacon's ribs, and begged him some more.

"Oh God... Deacon, come. Please, please, please, please. I need to feel you... God, just fuck me and fuck me and... cuuuuuuuummmmm...."

That last word was on a long, drawn-out hiss as Crick's body spasmed again, and Deacon couldn't last another second. With a final, brutal thrust, he was flush against Crick's ass. His vision darkened, and his cock jerked inside Crick's body. He buried his face in Crick's neck and made a groan that was spawned pretty much from his taut, twitching groin. Crick echoed it, his arms coming up around Deacon's shoulders to anchor him, hold him, press their bodies together as they shivered in the aftermath of being one whole person instead of two damaged souls.

It took a while for Deacon to pull out—long after he should have been thinking about Crick's comfort—but Crick seemed reluctant for him to go. Deacon slid to the side, and Crick's arms came around his shoulders, and then he bent and pulled up the sheets to cover them both.

Deacon panted against Crick's chest, grateful for the sheet to hide them. He lived in fear of the day Parry Angel learned how to use a doorknob—she could already climb out of her crib.

"Did you really get a doctor's note?" he asked when he had his breath back, and Crick grunted.

"Yeah—I thought you'd be a stubborn asshole about not wanting to hurt me. Turns out I was right."

"So why didn't you produce the note?" Deacon asked, smiling. His eyes were closed, Crick was there, and all was right with the world.

Crick didn't answer, and Deacon looked up to see what he was thinking. Crick turned his brown eyes away, looking troubled.

"What? Why didn't you pull out the note and say 'Deacon, fuck me silly'?"

"Would you?" Crick asked softly.

Deacon grinned, trying for once to be the guy who lightened the mood. "I thought I just did."

"Yeah, but would you, if I'd asked? Deacon, you're awfully closed-up these days. I know you're trying to keep the worst of shit from me, but... it's like...." Crick sighed and moved his hand to push at the hair that had fallen into Deacon's eyes. "It's like you've gotten used to being all alone. Even with Benny and Jon, you're still alone. You... you're so focused on keeping The Pulpit, on being your father, you've forgotten to be Deacon. The only time I've seen you be open with anyone here is when you've got the baby on your lap."

"Yeah," Deacon muttered, turning away from that soothing hand. "The baby can't talk yet. Just wait. Eventually I'll run away from her too."

Crick's hand rubbed his shoulder, his upper arm, and Crick placed careful kisses from the tender center of his neck down the curve of his spine between his shoulder blades.

"Wouldn't it be a lot more fun to take us with you?" Crick said softly.

Deacon closed his eyes and allowed Crick to touch him with reverence. The skin under Crick's lips rippled, shuddered, and the sound Deacon made in the back of his throat sounded a little like pleading.

"I'd rather keep you right here, in your home," he said softly, and Crick wrapped his arms around Deacon's shoulders again and rested his cheek against Deacon's back.

"It's not home if you're not here," he said softly.

"I'll keep that in mind." Deacon snuggled back into Crick's embrace then, allowing himself to be comforted, allowing himself to relax. He closed his eyes for a moment and set his fairly reliable internal clock for a nap, and fell asleep in heaven, wrapped in Crick's arms.

A few hours later, he woke up reluctantly. Crick had rolled over to his other side, and they were doing the butt-to-butt snuggle, which made it fairly easy for Deacon to pull on his sleep shorts, clean up the sex-toy, and go back to what he'd been doing before Crick called his name.

Crick found him there a half an hour later as he stared haplessly at a pile of bills.

"Deacon," Crick huffed, pulling on his boxers with his good hand rubbing his eyes with the back of his left hand while yawning. "Sex isn't relaxing if you don't get to sleep afterwards—since when did bills take this long to pay?"

Deacon grinned at him all sleep-mussed and pretty because he was a damned sight better looking than the grim scenario on the desk in front of him. "Since we ran out of money to pay them. Here," he said, surprising himself by the impulse to let Crick in on the torture. "Want to see how I'm doing this?"

Crick blinked, leaning eagerly over his shoulder, and Deacon felt some serious guilt. Crick was about the same age he'd been when he'd had to take over The Pulpit—it wasn't like the guy couldn't handle the details.

"I've got two major piles—I've got bills I need to pay and bills I can put off to next month. The trick is getting all the bills I need to pay out on about two-thirds the money we're used to getting, and making sure I don't put off the same bill twice in a row, because that fucks up your credit."

Crick started sorting through both piles on the table, blinking when he saw the one for the mortgage. "Isn't this bigger than it used to be?"

Deacon sighed and rubbed his eyes. "Yeah—we had the old one through the local bank. Step-Bob and Melanie got home from Virginia and opened their big traps about you and me setting up sodomy central, and the local bank tried to make us pay the whole damned mortgage in one month."

"Oh my God!" Crick swore, and his hand—his left hand, which meant he'd been surprised out of self-consciousness—came down on Deacon's shoulder. "That was right when I got home. You were dealing with that when you brought me home? *Deacon*—you should have said something!"

"You were sleeping, Crick. What was I going to do, wake you up and say, 'By the way, the douche-bags who abused you are trying to spread the joy'?" Deacon chuckled a little, but Crick didn't return the laugh. "Anyway, Jon and I moved all our shit to a different bank, and their mortgage interest was higher, so, well, bigger mortgage."

Crick didn't respond—he was busy scanning the desk to try to get the lay of the land. Curiously, he reached for three unopened envelopes on the corner of the desk.

"Parry Angel's getting mail?" he asked semi-facetiously. "No—wait. This is a college account—I recognize the envelope. And one for Benny, too. And...." There was an angry silence as Crick tore into the third envelope.

"Deacon?" Crick said after a moment, his voice a dangerous level of quiet.

"What?" Deacon was trying to decide whether to pay the water bill or the trash bill and pretty much figuring they could haul their trash to the local landfill.

"This is my bank account."

Deacon looked up. "Yeah—it's got your college money, your muckraker money. It's where we put your military checks and your disability. We had to move banks—it helped, by the way, being your executor—but all the info's still the same. You remember. We set that up before you left."

"Deacon, there's six figures in this account."

Deacon blinked at him. He looked pissed off, and Deacon was beyond figuring out why. "Yeah, Crick—you're pretty set up...."

He was unprepared for Crick to rip the bank statement for The Pulpit right out of his hand as he held it. Hands shaking—both of them—Crick picked up the phone handset next to the desk with his good hand and awkwardly jabbed the twenty-four-hour banking number from the statement with his thumb, then followed the voice menu directions until he got a human being.

Deacon just looked at him, at a loss—he didn't know what Crick was thinking, or even why he was so angry, and he especially didn't know what he could possibly be doing with the two bank statements. And then Crick spoke, his voice terse and as pissed off as Deacon had ever heard him.

"Yeah—this is Carrick Francis—and I'd like to close out my account and have all the assets transferred to my executor's account."

Deacon gaped, his vision going red and his face going pale and cold as Crick gave over the information that would take all of Crick's dream money, all of his carefully hoarded college chances, all of the plans they'd made for his future, and dump them into the black whirling vortex of a money-pit that The Pulpit had become.

"Don't you dare!" he growled, as angry as Crick was, if not more so.

"Shut up, Deacon," Crick snapped.

"It's not going to make a damned bit of difference, you jackass!" Deacon shouted. "If we can't make the damned thing pay for itself, all it's going to do is put it off for another eight months!"

"Well then that's eight months to figure out how to keep our home!" Crick yelled back. "What in the fuck is your mother's maiden name?"

"Holmes! Oh, fuck—Crick don't!" as Crick spoke the first part of password politely into the phone. "Well I'm not going to tell you the rest of fucking password!"

"You don't have to, asshole." Crick shifted his attention to the person on the other end of the phone. "You're goddamned right I still want to do this, lady—don't you hang up on me now. Yeah, I'll punch it into the phone, just wait."

Crick shifted the phone again and squinted at the little letters next to the numbers on the keypad. "I-M-I-S-S-C-R-I-C-K-2," he muttered, and Deacon made a grab for the phone too late when he realized that Crick really did know the password.

"I knew you wouldn't change it—you told me what it was when I was in Iraq, and I thought you were kidding," Crick hissed, and Deacon turned around and threw his fist through the goddamned wall with a lungful of *"Fuck!"* as Crick finished the transaction.

Benny pounded into their room looking furious and scared, just as an angry, awkward silence fell over the echoes of Deacon's fist punching through the drywall.

"What in the fuck?" she asked, glaring at the both of them. "You two idiots are going to wake the baby. Dammit, what are you fighting about?"

"Deacon, let me see," Crick muttered, and Deacon held his bruised knuckles to his chest.

"It's nothing," Deacon grunted. "Just your brother throwing his goddamned future away...."

"Don't be a stubborn asshole," Crick snarled, grabbing his hand and dabbing at the blood with some tissue from the desk. Benny ducked out and came back in half a second with some gauze bandage and ointment. "I was throwing my money into our home."

"You were throwing money into my problem!" Deacon snapped, his pride lacerated and bleeding at his feet.

"I was trying to keep you from killing yourself before you hit thirty, dammit! I just got here. I'd like to see you more than ten minutes a goddamned day!"

"Where'd you get the money?" Benny asked, wrapping Deacon's hand like a pro.

"My college-slash-Army pay-slash-disability fund," Crick grated, pitching Deacon a sour look. "Do you have any idea how much money he was sitting on while he was killing himself to make ends meet?"

"It wasn't my money!" Deacon protested, too hurt to hide it.

"Cool!" Benny said practically. "Can I throw my college fund into the pot?"

Deacon and Crick both shouted "No!" at her, and she stepped away and glared at them.

"So Deacon, now you know what we'd do to protect you. And Crick? Tell me how that felt?"

"Bite me, little sister," Crick growled, and Benny blew a raspberry at him.

"Thank you, Shorty," Deacon said politely, and she threw her arms around him in a hug.

"His heart was in the right place, Deac—don't ever doubt it."

"I never have," he muttered before she let him go and pattered down the hall.

Silently, Deacon pushed past Crick and went to sit down. All his checks were written, just waiting until he had the money to cover them. Methodically, he began stuffing each envelope with the check and the receipt, and licking the envelope shut.

Crick watched him in the unnerving quiet, and after seeing what he was doing, began to help.

When they were done and each envelope had a stamp, Deacon stacked them neatly to put in the morning mail and turned around to go to bed. Crick followed him, turning off the light, and Deacon crawled into his side of the bed, grabbing the comforter in the early morning chill and wrapping his shoulders tight as a Christmas package on the edge of the bed.

He was unprepared for Crick to snuggle up behind him, almost exactly the way they'd fallen asleep earlier that night, wrapping his long, damaged arm around Deacon's shoulders and kissing his neck. In spite of himself, Deacon began to relax against him—God, he'd forgiven him for Iraq, right?

Crick lifted his head and put his lips against Deacon's ear and whispered, "Because of you, Deacon, I will *never* come home and find my shit on the lawn."

Deacon's body relaxed a little more. "Yeah," he conceded.

"Are you okay?"

"Sure."

Crick sighed in his ear again and held him tighter. "Every time you say that, it sounds more and more like a lie."

Deacon woke late the next morning and swore when he heard everybody out in the kitchen, including Crick. As quick as he could, he slid into yesterday's jeans and brushed his teeth, hitting the kitchen just in time to hear the front door close as Benny and Andrew left for their morning at Amy's. (Amy was getting pretty big these days—as soon as Crick was mobile, Benny had gone back to visiting at her house and helping her with her chores.)

"Dammit," he muttered. "I wanted to tell Benny to get shampoo when she went to Wal-Mart."

"She's got a cell phone, Deacon," Crick said from behind him, using both hands to sip coffee out of the mug he'd bought Parish for a long-ago Christmas.

Deacon looked outside the kitchen window, frowning. Someone had just made the turn into the driveway, and he didn't recognize the old brown Ford.

"Yeah, but I always forget during the day, which is why we've been using hand soap for a week." He risked a glance over his shoulder at Crick, not quite meeting his eyes. "You let me sleep in."

"You needed it." Crick put his coffee down deliberately and came to wrap his arms around Deacon's waist, and Deacon actually breathed a sigh of relief and fell into him. He couldn't be mad at Crick—it was like his entire body was hardwired against it. He wasn't sure if he'd ever be ready to apologize, but he wouldn't expect Crick to, either.

"I'm sorry," Crick said, and Deacon almost fell down.

"Why?" Deacon muttered, turning his head and searching Crick's brown eyes. God, he was pretty. Growing up and into his height and size hadn't changed his appealing, narrow-cheeked, big-eyed beauty, and Deacon had a minute to think muzzily that maybe it was just the way he saw Carrick and not what he actually looked like.

"I forget you have pride too.... You're usually so good at being unassuming, Deacon—I forget how proud you are of us, you know?"

Deacon was going to respond—he was truly on the verge of something intelligent about 'Fuck pride, I have you'—but a shriek from Benny drew his attention, and he swore, even as he went tear-assing out the front door without a shirt or his shoes.

Melanie was driving the strange car, and Step-Bob was right there, on Deacon's front lawn. He'd apparently knocked Andrew on his ass—from behind, they later learned, by kicking his prosthetic leg out from under him—and he was pitched in a tug-of-war with Benny for Parry Angel.

"You keep your hands off my baby, asshole!" Benny was screaming, and then Deacon was there.

Bob didn't see him, he was so intent on stealing the screaming little girl away from her mother. He sneered, "Ain't no faggot niggers gonna raise my blood, you little whore!" while giving Parry a particularly vicious yank.

The words were damned ugly, but Deacon didn't hear any more of them. His first punch stunned step-Bob enough to make him let go of the baby, and the second punch made the guy's knees weak enough that he would have fallen if Deacon hadn't grabbed him by the front of the shirt.

Deacon's third punch broke the guy's nose, and the blood spatter was fairly stupendous. That was when his vision went red, and he didn't remember much more until Crick, Andrew, and Patrick pulled him off.

Chapter 23

Not Okay

OH CHRIST—Deacon was going to kill the fucker.

His fists just kept hammering away at Bob's face, and he was shouting incoherently as he worked the douchebag over.

"Don't you *touch* my family, you fucker—*my* family—you leave *my* family the fuck alone...."

His face was twisted in rage, and his body, still too thin with stress, was a gnarled tree root made of iron. Crick gave Andrew a hand up and waited until his leg was situated, because he was going to need help pulling Deacon off.

And even with one man on each of Deacon's arms, hauling him away, he might have overpowered them and succeeded in committing murder. It was Patrick who thumped him on the back of the head, and that instinctive flinch, left over from childhood, seemed to break the terrible spell of fury that had possessed him.

With Crick and Andrew wrenching on his hands, Deacon let go of step-Bob's collar. The fucker dropped where he stood, and Deacon shook them off to turn for a second and stalk away, his bare feet padding mindlessly on the small-gravel driveway. The baby was still screaming, and Melanie was wailing in the front of the car, but without the violence of Deacon's attack on the asshole who had caused all the chaos, it felt like silence. Crick and the others watched Deacon in the sudden stillness, and when he turned back, he was Deacon again, and not the avenging angel that he had become for a moment.

"Patrick, call the cops," he said roughly, looking at step-Bob with so much hatred they were lucky the guy didn't burst into flames. Step-Bob groaned, and Melanie gave a muffled sob from the car, and Deacon spat on step-Bob's twitching meat sack before he turned to Benny and the baby.

"You all right?" he asked softly, and Benny nodded, holding Parry out for him to check over.

The baby calmed almost instantly in his arms, wrapping her chubby little arms around his neck and giving a little hiccup against his chest.

"Sorry, sweetheart," Deacon crooned. "Didn't mean to scare you like that. No big-bad-mean guy's gonna get you while Deacon's here, right? That just won't stand, will it Angel?"

"Deek-deek," she said sadly, and Deacon kissed her fuzzy little brown head as she whimpered against him. Crick came around behind him and put his hands on Deacon's shoulders, grateful when Deacon leaned back.

"You okay?" Oh God—it was such a reflexive question. Crick knew what the lie would be before Deacon even opened his mouth.

"Spiffy, Carrick. No worries, all right?"

"Cops are on their way!" Patrick called. He'd taken a few steps away with the cell phone. Crick glanced over at the man and had a sudden thought that he was old—old enough for retirement, old enough that this sort of shit wasn't a lot of fun anymore.

"Good," Deacon murmured. "Could you call Jon next? We're probably gonna need him too."

By the time the sheriff arrived, Bob had picked himself up off the ground in a bloodied daze and gotten back in the car. The Ford Whatsit peeled out past the sheriff's car as it turned on the drive, and with the exception of Patrick—who was off trying to round up the horse who'd escaped the ring when the fuss broke out—the sheriff found them all in the kitchen, tending to the wounded.

"Will you stop fussing, Benny!" Andrew took Crick's sister's hands rather tenderly in his own as she tried to put some ointment on his skinned elbow. "I'm fine."

"Really, Benny," Crick said dryly. "The guy lost a leg in the war— I'm thinking a few scrapes won't do him in. Deacon, stop being a baby— it's just hydrogen peroxide."

Deacon grunted. His knuckles had been soundly abused by step-Bob's false teeth, and Crick thought that since it was unlikely he'd go in for stitches, a couple of butterfly bandages would have to do.

The young man in uniform stood politely in the open doorway, waiting for them to acknowledge him. He was handsome in a practical sort of way, with brown hair cut short, brown eyes, and a square-chiseled, capable sort of face.

"Yeah, we see you," Deacon muttered. "You just missed them, but come on in anyway."

"I'm Officer Perkins," he said with quiet confidence. Crick let Deacon shake him off to wipe his bloody hands off on the kitchen towel and extend a hand in greeting to the officer. To the officer's credit, he didn't think twice about shaking it.

"Deacon Winters. You might want to check hospitals—I worked him over pretty good."

The officer raised his eyebrows. "Any particular reason?"

Deacon scowled. "That man trespassed on my property and put his hands on my family. Nobody puts their hands on my family. No-fucking-body, you hear me?"

Crick fought the inappropriate urge to chuckle, because seeing Deacon get all caveman was something special.

Officer Perkins raised his eyebrows and nodded, then got out his little notebook and started to ask some serious questions.

"Okay—whose child is it?"

Crick, Deacon, Benny, and Andrew all said, "Ours!" and the poor guy had to start all over again.

"I take it you're the mother, right?"

Benny nodded, her lips pursed. Parry Angel was sitting in the high chair, eating the last of her Deek-deek's favorite cookies to make up for the trauma, and Benny put her hand protectively on the baby's fuzzy brown head.

"And you would be...?"

"I'm Benny Coats."

"Like the guy who got his face beat in?"

"That would be the sperm donor who created me, yeah."

Officer Perkins's eyes widened. "And who's the baby's father?"

"A guy with a restraining order and a sex-offender ankle bracelet," Benny said flatly. "You want to know who's been raising her? You're looking at them, but Deacon's the one she loves best."

Officer Perkins looked at Deacon with his hands out in a "help me here" sort of gesture. "And you're related to the girls how?"

Deacon blushed hard enough that Crick could feel his body throwing off wet heat. "I'm Benny's brother's boyfriend."

Those brown eyes got even wider, and he looked at Crick, who had started to edge himself protectively between Deacon and the new threat.

"So how did Benny and the baby come to be living here instead of with your parents?"

Crick found himself growling, so it was Benny who put it into words first. "Because when my dumbass brother here was out getting blown up in Iraq, Deacon picked me up off the front lawn and took me in. Do you want to see my room? The social worker wanted to see it—and she wanted to see the baby's room and she wanted to see my medicine cabinet and to check if I was on birth control and that woman damned near wanted to do a pelvic exam. Now my dumbass 'father'"—she included air quotes—"got it into his tiny pea brain that my baby would be better off with him...."

Officer Perkins nodded his head and tried to take over the conversation again—he was the one writing the report, after all. "Okay—now did he say why?"

And it was Deacon who spoke. "I believe his exact words were that he didn't want no 'nigger faggot raising his blood'."

Perkins winced and looked at the three men. "And, um, which one of you was he talking about?"

Deacon and Andrew met eyes and smirked. "I don't actually know," Deacon said on a reluctant chuckle. "Drew, any ideas?"

Andrew's chuckle was a little less reluctant. "I don't know, sir—you are kind of tan."

Crick shook his head violently. "It's not funny," he said, feeling a surprising amount of anger after the fact. "What made him think he could come here and do this? I've got legal custody of Parry and Benny—he was trespassing and kidnapping. What would be going through his teeny-assed-pea-brain?"

Officer Perkins cleared his throat. "I can answer that," he said, nodding to Jon as he came in. "Is Mr. Coats a church-going man?"

"Christ yes," Crick responded.

"Well there's a tent revival going on in that vacant field out by Elverta. There was a guy out there yesterday going off about the evils of miscegenation and homosexuality and the usual—probably lit a fire under his ass and made him feel empowered."

"I'm surprised you all didn't have a chapter out there yourselves," Jon said dryly, situating himself by the counter near Deacon and Crick.

Deacon said, "Easy there, cowboy. Officer Perkins has been fairly decent to us."

"Yeah," Benny acknowledged irritably, "but we all remember the last one."

Officer Perkins had the grace to flush. "I'm sorry about that. You need to know we're not all like that. I really would like to be a friend here, all right?"

Jon nodded, considering him carefully. "Well that would all depend on whether or not you're going to arrest Deacon here for protecting his family."

Officer Perkins looked down at his notepad and shrugged. "I'm thinking that's a big 'no'. Although it will depend on how badly Mr. Coats was injured—did Mr. Winters use more force than necessary to stop the crime?"

"If the bastard got into the car by himself, I'd call that a big 'no' as well," Crick snapped, and Deacon put a restraining hand on his arm. Crick looked down and saw Deacon's knuckles, taped together with butterfly bandages and covered in gauze, and got mad all over again.

"I honestly don't remember," Deacon said, and there was something odd about his voice, something remote and alien, that reminded Crick of the day his father died or the moment Crick told him about the Army. "I've… that's weird. He just… he needed to let go of the baby, that's all."

Suddenly Deacon was the center of attention, the place he least liked to be. "I've got to…." He swallowed and flushed again. "Are we done, Officer?" he asked, and Crick could see the effort it took for him to focus on the question.

"Yes, sir. I think we are."

Deacon nodded and shook his hand again. "This here's Jon Leavens—he's a friend of the family, and he helps us with legal stuff. If you need to arrest me, give us a call so Jon can arrange bail."

"You're awfully casual about that," Perkins said dryly, and Deacon shrugged.

"At least this time I'll probably be awake when you all pound down my door." And with that, he started padding—barefoot and still bare-chested—for the mudroom, making to go outside that way.

"Deacon, where are you going?" Crick asked as Deacon put his hand on the knob to go outside.

"I've got to go shift the hay," he said tersely, and Andrew rolled his eyes.

"Well, that was something we were going to do today," he muttered as the door slammed, and Crick leaned back against the counter and pinched the bridge of his nose.

"It's hot. He'll get tired of that in an hour," he muttered. It was true—they were having a heat wave early into June, and it was probably going to hit one hundred and five that day. They could afford to give him some space to work off his stress—he sounded like he needed it—but... God. Crick hated that tone of voice. He hated hearing the complete separation between Deacon's emotions and his reason. He really hated the fact that nothing short of an emotional meltdown could break through that alien ice wall that Deacon had just slammed up between himself and the world.

Officer Perkins watched him go with raised eyebrows. "That is either the most laid-back man or the most tightly wound man I have ever met."

"Why?" Jon asked, dumping out Crick's tepid coffee and stealing the mug for his own. "What'd Crick do now?"

"Saved the ranch," Benny grunted. "But it was the way he did it that sucked."

"The ranch is in trouble?" the young sheriff asked, looking hopefully at the coffee, and Jon poured him some—probably out of a sense of guilt for saying something nasty, Crick figured.

"From the same fuckers you're supposed to be out arresting," Jon told him dryly, handing a plain brown mug to the guy. "They keep spreading bullshit about 'horse AIDS' to the town, and people won't let Deacon break their horses. Which is a shame—it's the thing he was born to do."

Perkins nodded thanks for the coffee and took an appreciative sip. "Don't worry. There's a whole other carload of people in uniform checking the hospitals and the address you gave us over the phone. But your buddy there—he sure does take your family seriously," he said to Crick, and Crick shook his head.

"It's his family—we... we just sort of gather around him, like satellites. He... he just burns that bright, you know?" Crick blushed, and Jon sent him a crooked smile.

"Pretty much," Jon agreed. "So, Crick, how'd you save the ranch?"

Crick grunted. "Joined our bank accounts. Do you have any idea how much money was in my college fund?"

Jon nodded. "Yes I do, dumbshit—do you have any idea how much it meant to him that you could still go?"

Crick shook his head, feeling the rightness of this even as he said it. "I don't get to go away to college. Not after what I did to him. I don't want to go, not anymore. If Deacon's life is here, so's mine. I can draw anywhere. Deacon can only make his living on a horse ranch."

Jon shook his head and put a hand on Crick's shoulder. "I might forgive you yet, jerk-off."

Crick accepted the sentiment—and the hand—and Officer Perkins interrupted his train of worry about what was going through Deacon's head by saying, "What do you draw?"

Crick laughed a little. "Anything I want."

"But mostly Deacon," Benny inserted dryly, and Crick blushed.

"I miss that sketchbook," he confessed.

"Where is it?" Benny asked, and Crick fought the temptation to put his face in his hands and groan.

"Probably at Lisa's parents'... oh, God. I should go talk to them. They're up in Seattle... now that I'm almost fully functional again, I owe them a visit, don't I?" He did—he must. He wasn't sure if it was written in the soldier's handbook or something, but he'd been the last person to see their daughter alive, and he'd been her best friend and confidant for over a year. They'd want to talk to him. He knew that if he'd never come home, he would have wanted Lisa to come talk to Deacon.

"I don't know, Crick," Benny said soberly. "I think that's between you and your heart, you know?"

"Who's Lisa?" Officer Perkins asked, and the entire family looked at him at the same time.

"She was my ambulance driver in Iraq," Crick said, feeling it all over again. "What are you still doing here?"

The guy blushed. "I...." He laughed self-consciously and made to leave. "I'm sorry. I... I just...I moved here about a month ago. You're like the nicest family I've met here...."

Jon started to giggle, just like he used to in high school, and Benny caught it next. Andrew rubbed his eyes, and Crick just stared at him, shaking his head. "*That* is the weirdest thing I've heard all day, and that's saying something. Jesus, buddy, maybe come see us when we're not fighting off rabid relatives or something, you think?"

Poor Officer Perkins was backing out of the door, blushing almost as badly as Deacon had, and Jon laughingly called him back. "Don't worry, that's just Crick. Tell you what—you come Sunday night for dinner and bring some flowers for my wife who's more pregnant than sweet right now, and you can get to know us, how's that?"

The guy blinked and looked hopeful and skeptical at the same time. "Do you even live here?" he asked Jon.

"He's wanted to his whole life," Crick said dryly. "Lucky me, I got the gay chromosome."

Jon shrugged. "Yeah, being het's a curse. Have you met my wife? When she's not pissed off about being twelve months pregnant, she's über-hot."

"I'll have to ask Deacon about that," Crick said smugly. "I wouldn't know."

Jon laughed sincerely and slugged Crick in the good shoulder. "Okay. Okay, I give. I did miss you, and I think I've just totally forgiven you." He looked over at their poor blushing cop friend. "You're still welcome to dinner—but we might need to know your name."

"Shane," the guy said, still blushing. "Shane Perkins. And I'd love to come to Sunday dinner. Man, the people in this town will die of thirst before they admit they have enough water to share, you know what I mean?"

Crick suddenly forgot his banter with Jon and looked at their new friend grimly. "Buddy, we know exactly what you mean. I'm going to go out and talk to Deacon. I know we should give him his space, but I can't stand that he's out there working through this alone."

And brother, was he working.

His back was shiny with sweat, and the muscles in his arms, neck, back, and chest rippled with effort as he grabbed a bale off the back of the truck with the hay hooks and threw it up against the stable wall under the protective overhang designed to shelter it. Crick was pretty sure his calves and thighs would be flexing under his jeans too, and he tried not to think of how sexy it was to watch Deacon's body move—there were other things to work on right now. The haystack was almost surgically neat, and Crick had to admire the efficiency with which Deacon moved. It was a chore he'd been doing since he was big enough to hoist a hay-bale without hurting himself.

He was talking to himself as he worked, and from the sound of it, he was cursing out step-Bob but good. "Dumb-fucking-son-of-a-bitch… fucking kill you, asshole… come here on my property, touch my family. Fucking stay the fuck away from my family if you want to keep your fucking balls. Dumb-fucking-son-of-a-bitch…."

Crick took one look at that furious energy and thought that maybe he'd be better off waiting to speak until Deacon didn't have potentially deadly weapons in his hands. He made to turn around and leave when Deacon surprised him by coming up out of his own head long enough to call out.

"I'm sorry, Crick—was there something you wanted to talk about?"

"Just checking on you," Crick told him, somewhat reassured when Deacon's tight, fierce little smile came out to play.

"I'm working shit out."

"I figured. It's getting hot—you may want to put this off until evening."

Deacon shrugged. "There'll be other shit to do then."

"Yeah," Crick conceded, and then, because he'd been thinking about it in the kitchen, he said, "Hey, Deacon—you think there's any way I can take trip to Seattle in the near future? I need to make a visit to Lisa's folks. It's only right."

He was unprepared for the effect of the request. Deacon actually *dropped* the hay hooks—didn't hook them in a bale and let go, *dropped* them—and the leather gloves on top of them, and then his back and neck, which were facing Crick, began to shake with tension.

"Leave me?"

"Just for a couple of days," Crick soothed. "I'd ask you to come with me, but you're so busy here... I don't want to take you away from...."

"Leave me?" And Crick's heart started to pound in his chest—it was that voice again. That lost, alien voice, the one that came from the throat of a small boy locked in a big house with only the echo of his own heart for company.

"No," Crick backpedaled. "Won't leave you. Swear. You can come with me... or I just won't go...."

"*You're goddamned right you won't go!*" Deacon roared, whirling at Crick with desperate speed. In a second, in a heartbeat, Crick was pressed against the back wall of the stable with Deacon's sweating, heaving, bare skin flush with his own.

"You won't leave me!" Deacon ordered, and Crick nodded furiously.

"I won't leave you." Oh God—he smelled like last night's sex and sweat and rage, and he looked like he'd taste like salt.

"Not ever again... you won't fucking leave me. You promised!"

"I promised," Crick said, mesmerized by the furious intensity of Deacon's green eyes. He was almost insane with the idea of Crick leaving—terrified, angry, hurt—all of the things Crick thought he'd been feeling for two years but hadn't shown.

"You won't leave me," Deacon hissed, pulling Crick's head down in a crushing kiss, invading his mouth with a punishing tongue and smashing Crick's body against the wall so possessively that Crick wondered if his skin wouldn't just open up and take Deacon inside. He tasted like... Deacon, but bitter. There was no sweetness in his mouth, no gentleness in his breath or his kiss, and he mashed Crick's lips hard enough to hurt.

Crick tore his mouth away long enough to say, "I won't leave you, I swear, not ever again," before Deacon took his mouth again in another blazingly angry kiss. Their bodies went nearly instantly erect, both of them, and Crick ground himself against Deacon's hipbone as his cock swelled so fast, so hard, it literally hurt.

Deacon jerked his own hips against Crick's thigh and hissed angrily in his ear, "You won't leave me, you won't, you won't fucking leave my side... dammit, Carrick, you promised...."

"I promised," Crick grunted. "I promised... Deacon, the tack room...."

Deacon kept kissing him, biting his neck and then his chest hard enough to leave marks. His hands moved Crick's shoulders sideways, and Crick went with him, stumbling slightly as Deacon pushed him backwards through the open door of the stables. Andrew's bedroom was right inside, and the spare room, the one filled with tack and a small space of bed, was right next to that one. That was where Deacon pushed him, one stumbling step, one angry, fierce kiss or suck or even bruising bite at a time.

Crick opened the door to the tack room and practically fell into the stifling, dusty dark, and Deacon slammed the door shut behind them and slammed the latch home. Crick dropped his pants and went to kiss Deacon again. Deacon ripped away long enough tear Crick's T-shirt off and then to whirl him around and bend him over the bed, leaving his ass in the air.

"Stay there," he growled, and Crick did. He heard Deacon dig in his pockets, and then the jeans hit the ground. Deacon's thumbs, oily with something that smelled like cherries, spread his ass cheeks and pressed smoothly into his anus, then stretched it roughly, making it ready, and Crick buried his head in the dusty mattress, right next to a bag of horse feed, and groaned.

"God, Deacon…."

"I said stay there!"

"Ain't moving," Crick moaned, and those thumbs worked him, hard and rough and fast, and his hips jerked. He moved his hand down to grab hold of his cock, which ached mightily, and Deacon grabbed his hand and shoved it back next to his head.

"Said stay there," Deacon muttered, positioning his cock at Crick's back door.

"Yes sir," Crick whined, and he was completely submissive. The military had taught him how to take orders, had taught him it was a matter of life and death, and right now, he knew Deacon's life depended on knowing Crick was going to be there for him for as long as he needed him.

Deacon was oiled too, but whatever he was using for lube was grainy and not as slick as it might be, and it burned as Deacon thrust the head of his cock in Crick's ass. Crick groaned, liking the edge of pain, liking the roughness, because *God* did Deacon need him, and that was enough to turn a saint on. Deacon popped inside, only his thick shaft there, stretching him, thrusting into him until Deacon's rough, curly brown pubic hair was ground up against Crick's ass and their testicles smacked together with the force of their joining.

Crick buried his face in the dusty mattress and howled with the angry joy of it.

Deacon pulled back and thrust again, still chanting, "Don't leave me, don't leave me, you'll never fucking leave me again, you hear?" and Crick found himself begging the same way.

"Fuck me, Deacon, please, just pound me, oh God, please, grab me... grab my... oh God, yes!" Because Deacon, who was merciful and wise, reached around and grabbed his cock with his slippery hand and gave it a hard stroke, and another, and another, and Crick's words turned to gibbering, and Deacon's words turned to rough pants. Crick gave another howl as his come spattered up against his stomach and another as Deacon's cockhead brushed his little bundle of nerves, and then another as he did it again.

Deacon grabbed Crick's hair, which was long enough to get a grip on now, and dragged Crick's head back to hiss in his ear. *"Don't fucking leave me."* Crick groaned in response as Deacon's hips kept pounding him into the mattress. "I mean it, goddammit."

"I won't leave you," Crick moaned softly, his body used and full and still quivering as Deacon fucked him into Jell-o. "I love you, Deacon. I'll never leave you again."

Deacon jammed his hips forward one more time and came, roaring, biting Crick's shoulder hard and grunting against the sweaty, slick skin of Crick's back as his hips jerked again and again and again.

"You're goddamned right you won't," Deacon panted against him into the sudden stillness of their bodies.

They stayed there for a while, Deacon shivering in sexual aftershocks, Crick recovering from the sudden sensual assault. Deacon clasped his wrists around Crick's middle and held Crick so tight he could barely breathe. Crick put his good hand over the hands at his waist and let all his weight rest on his bad shoulder. Deacon's hands were shaking—not just trembling, shaking—and the sweat between Crick's back and Deacon's cheek was thicker and hotter than it should have been.

"Deacon," Crick asked into the silence. "Deacon, are you okay?"

Deacon's voice was really his voice now. It wasn't the lost five-year old, it wasn't the fierce sexual dominant—it was Deacon. Crick's Deacon. And Deacon was in pain.

"Not so much, Crick," he choked, and Crick nodded. He straightened, and Deacon fell out of his body. Then he turned and sat his bare ass on that little spot of bed and wrapped his arms around Deacon's waist. Deacon hid his face against his own shoulder for a moment, and Crick reached his good hand up to the back of Deacon's head and pushed him down. Deacon followed that urging and sank to his knees naked in the dusty straw, buried his face in Crick's middle, and sobbed.

Chapter 24

Naked Words, Naked Hearts

OF COURSE, the tricky part was sneaking past the entire family to get to the shower. They were both covered in sweat and dust and hay, and they smelled like hot, sweaty, dusty sex in the hay, and you couldn't hide the fact that you'd been crying for an hour using nothing more than a rumpled T-shirt and your lover's sweating hands on your face.

In the end, they dressed as well as they could, stuck their heads out of the stable to make sure they didn't shock Patrick into a coronary, and walked into the house, hoping the cop was gone. He was, and Jon and Benny were sitting in the lovely, air-conditioned cool, eating pie that they had apparently bought while Deacon and Crick were otherwise occupied.

Because they were family, they both looked up, saw Deacon's face as he slunk toward the bathroom, and didn't say a blessed thing. Behind him, he heard Jon call Crick's name, but he didn't stay to hear what was asked or how Crick responded. By the time Crick got to the bathroom, Deacon was already in the shower, looking with gratitude at the new bottle of shampoo Benny had put on the ledge.

"Mmm," Crick muttered, grabbing for the bottle before he could. And then Crick tended to him, as simple as that. Washed his hair, washed his body clean, rubbed his warm, soapy hands over Deacon's chest, his back, his neck.

"What'd Jon want?" Deacon muttered, content this once to lean back in Crick's arms and be tended to.

"Wanted to tell me they've got Bob in custody, but we probably shouldn't press charges or you'll be in for assault."

Deacon grunted. Well, damn—the shitbag would get to walk. "Anything else?"

"Wanted to know how you were." Crick's hands soaped his chest, and Deacon almost whimpered, they felt so good on his skin.

"And?"

"I told him you were not okay."

Deacon wondered if he could live with the thought that he hadn't been able to stand it, that he'd crumbled like rotten mortar.

"What'd he say to that?"

"*Thank God.*"

Deacon let out a puff of air that might have been a laugh, the water spattering off his face and into the air in front of him. Crick's arms came around his shoulders, and Deacon was being rocked softly as his body was made clean.

When the water ran cold, they dried off, and Deacon was in the middle of putting on briefs when Crick said, "Stop at underwear. Andrew and Patrick have it for the day. I declare today 'Deacon's day off'."

"Yeah, oh mighty maker-of-laws—what are we going to do on 'Deacon's day off'?"

"My plan is to hang out in bed for a while and talk and sleep in. If we get *really*—and I mean *really*—ambitious, I'm thinking a trip to the swimming hole, with or without family. But right now, get in bed. I want to hold you when you're not all sweaty and covered in man-sex."

They talked. And then Crick left and came back with sandwiches, and they talked some more. Deacon fell asleep, which surprised him as much as he thought it surprised Crick, and when he woke up, Crick was still there, head pillowed on the shiny skin of his outstretched upper arm, watching him with calm, dark eyes. Deacon blinked and smiled.

"You didn't leave," he murmured.

"I promised. I'll keep it, Deacon, I swear."

A month later, Deacon stood at the prow of the blocky white ferry as it maneuvered smoothly around the San Juan Islands. The day was crystal July blue, and the waters of Puget Sound were a chill indigo.

In the end, he and Crick had decided to go see Lisa's parents together. Deacon was no longer ragingly psychotic about a four day trip, but, well, the entire family—Benny, Jon, Amy, Patrick, Andrew and Crick—had all taken it upon themselves to send him on vacation before Amy had the baby.

"We want you here in thirty years, asshole!" had been Jon's final word on the subject, and Deacon found that he didn't have much fight left in him when it came to being separated from Crick.

So here they were, and Deacon couldn't make himself be sorry. Crick was getting coffee from the concession inside the ferry. He'd been working on his hand, and the fact that he could carry the little Styrofoam cup was a source of not-so-quiet pride.

Deacon's heart wasn't completely healed yet—and maybe it would be scarred his whole life, but then, Crick had been living with a scarred heart too, and they'd managed to survive the consequences of that. As it was, whenever the fragile thing started to bleed too much, Deacon would wrap their words from that day around it like clean gauze, and it would keep pumping and healing and keeping him healthy for a future with the guy who had broken it in the first place.

"Deacon?"

"Yeah?"

"What made you stop drinking? You never told me. Benny said you were walking away from the liquor store in the first place. You never told me why."

"That letter you sent. The one where you asked me to write you something real." Deacon paused and swallowed, eyeing Crick warily from his position on his stomach with his head pillowed in his crossed arms. *"The only real thing I had was that after I went to the liquor store, I'd get to be home with a bottle. I couldn't write you that. I had to make 'something real' something better."*

Crick reached out with his scarred left hand and stroked Deacon's hair out of his eyes. "You always seem so strong, Deacon. I swear, today was the first time I've seen you really cry since your father died."

Deacon reached out and captured his hand, stroking it gently. "That's because you didn't see me about five minutes after you left me in Georgia."

"GERMANY," Crick said into a lazy quiet.

Deacon's eyes jerked open—he'd almost been asleep, his head pillowed on Crick's stomach, their hands laced together over Deacon's chest.

"Tibet," he said randomly.

"No, idiot—I meant I want to talk about what happened in Germany."

Deacon scowled unhappily. "Yeah—'Tibet' wasn't the right answer the last time we had this conversation either."

Crick flopped his scarred hand in a passable imitation of a smack on the top of Deacon's head. "Puhhleeeeze, Deacon? I tried to tell this story to Lisa, but she was so mad at me for cheating on you that she wouldn't hear it. You're the only person on the planet who will think this is as funny as I do!"

"Lisa didn't even know you when you were in Germany," Deacon muttered, and from his position on the pillow, Crick nodded.

"I'm telling you—just once I want a friend who isn't crushing on you, Deacon. She had it bad."

"Jeff isn't...."

"The hell he isn't. Jon, Amy, Lisa, Jeff—hell, Officer Perkins was crushing on you."

"Officer Perkins is straight!"

"The hell he is. Believe me, Deacon—I've seen that look in people's eyes. A lot. Lisa took one look at my sketchbook and fell in love."

Deacon pushed himself up to look at Crick with a puzzled frown. "You have got to be making that up."

Crick shook his head. "What can I say, baby—you're a catch. Now can I finish my story?"

"The one where you get laid by a complete stranger in Berlin? Yeah, Crick—you go ahead."

Crick did, of course, completely oblivious to Deacon's sarcasm, and he'd been right—Deacon was laughing by the end.

"He took one look at you and said, 'Yeah, he's lonely, I can see that'? Damn, Crick—that's almost as sad as 'I love you, Crick' when I was blind drunk with Becca!"

"We'll get to that later," Crick threatened, *"but yeah. And then I spent half the night showing him your pictures and reading him your letters."* He shook his head. *"He told me to close my eyes and say your name when he kissed me—and I did."*

Deacon turned to his stomach and scooted up the bed, propping himself up on his elbows as he looked into Crick's apologetic face. *"Close your eyes and say my name,"* he whispered.

And Crick did.

About a half an hour later, after they'd put their underwear back on and caught their breath, Crick said, *"Oh yeah. And I topped."*

Deacon choked out a laugh. *"And why in the* hell *would I want to know that?"*

Crick's blush was a slow burn down his neck and across his stomach. It stopped at the mottled scarring, but otherwise it was a constant on his faintly brown-tinged skin. *"I...."* He swallowed and smirked at himself and looked away. *"I had this... you know. This weird romantic notion, I guess, that my ass would always be yours."*

Deacon started a low chuckle that broke into a loud guffaw and continued to work its way into a belly laugh. When he was done, he wiped his eyes and looked unrepentantly into Crick's offended scowl.

"Carrick James, that's awfully damned sweet if you, but I've got to tell you that if I've got to claim one of your body parts, that's not the one I'm after."

"Okay," Crick said, rolling his eyes. *"I give. Which part of my body is more interesting than my ass?"*

Deacon rewarded his obtuseness with a smack to the head. *"Your heart, you fuckin' moron. Man, I get about fifteen minutes a day max out of your ass—it's your heart I want twenty-four-seven. Jesus, Crick—stop thinking in your pants!"*

Crick turned a shining grin to him then and attacked him with a happy, playful kiss, and they didn't talk for another fifteen minutes at the very least.

CRICK *leaned forward to wipe the milk mustache off Deacon's upper lip with his thumb. Deacon put his glass of milk down on the end table, balanced his sandwich plate on his lap, and waited patiently for him to be done. Crick took the opportunity to rub his finger up the re-formed bridge of Deacon's nose.*

"It's bad enough that you grew three new chest hairs while I was gone—you had to go and do this."

Deacon scowled and put his plate on the end table next to the milk, his desire for the barbecue sandwich gone. "Says the guy who got himself blown halfway to Kuwait."

"Yeah, but I put myself in harm's way. You haven't told me how you did this yet."

Deacon flushed, knowing that this might be the worst part of the rip-the-heart-open show-and-tell game they'd been playing. "Same way I did Becca Anderson. I don't fucking remember."

Crick was honestly surprised. "Deacon!"

Deacon really wished he hadn't eaten so much of that sandwich. "I'm a blackout drunk, Crick. I don't just drink to feel better—I drink until the world ends. I woke up one morning, and there was a trail of blood from the doorframe to the bed and all down my shirt, and in a puddle on my pillow. My nose hurt like hell, but I could still breathe, so I assume I set it myself on the way to bed."

"Deacon—that sort of drinking... for as long as you say you did it— how bad was detox?"

Okay. Okay. Look the monster in the face and say its name, and it won't have the power to harm you anymore—wasn't that how the story went?

"Patrick found me naked in the bathtub, covered in puke. If Jon hadn't gotten here with the Valium prescription, I probably would have died."

Crick had long ago finished his sandwich, and suddenly Deacon was being embraced long and hard.

"I'm gonna kill Becca Anderson," he choked, his face wet on Deacon's chest. "I'm gonna fucking walk into that bar and rip that fucking cu—"

Deacon pulled back and grabbed his chin. "You stop that right now, Carrick. I smelled the gin before I dumped it down my gullet. I could have pulled back if I'd been strong enough...."

"No." Crick shook his head. "No. I will never believe that was your fault. A man walks into a bar and orders a soda, then he's got a good goddamned reason, and if you can't respect that, you're no better than the puke he leaves on your shoes."

Deacon shook his head. "You can't do that—you can't absolve me of the whole damned thing, Crick—that's not right...."

"You're right—it wasn't—but it wasn't you who did the wrong. Okay—you forgive me for Germany, and I'm grateful and I'm overwhelmed, and I'll love you forever for it. But you listen to me—I'll say it a thousand times a day, but we've got better things to do with our time. You have done nothing to forgive in the matter of that woman, you understand me? She spiked your drink, and that's the end of it, okay?"

Crick was still in tears over it, so Deacon soothed him like he used to when Crick was a boy. He fell asleep leaning against the pillows with Crick cuddled against his chest.

A few minutes after Deacon woke up from his nap, as they were playing with their laced hands in the sunlight coming in through the window, Crick said, "Bob."

Deacon said, "George."

Crick said, "You keep trying to make that schtick funny and it's not. I'm being totally fucking serious here. You could have killed him."

A puzzled shrug. "And that would have been bad because...."

"Because you would have ended up in prison, asshole! Next time, just... I don't know. Just walk away."

Deacon thought about it long and hard. "No promises," he said at last. "I can promise to try, for you. But he hurt everyone I love—and he's dumb and he's mean. I can promise not to look for trouble again."

Crick looked away for a minute and brought Deacon's knuckles to his lips for a soft kiss. "You have to forgive him."

Deacon jerked his hand away. "The fuck I do! I was there, Crick, remember? Parish and I used to ice your bruises on the weekends because no one was there for you on the weekdays. Do you know we called social services? And you got beat harder and those people did shit, so we stopped. I swear, if I'd known that all it would take to get you kicked out was for you to out yourself, I would have kissed you on the front lawn before I turned eighteen, just to get you out of their lives. Forgive him? Forgive him? I picked your sister up off the porch with a baby in her belly and a black fucking eye. *That man has been dicking with my* family...."

He was ranting. He was raging... *and Crick looked at him and smiled faintly until he subsided.*

"Deacon—what made you forgive me?"

Deacon stopped. "The day the levee broke," he said after a moment, and Crick raised his eyebrows. Another thing Deacon never talked about. Deacon shrugged and pulled his knees up under his arms.

"There I was... I'd just shot your horse.... God, Crick. I still have nightmares about shooting your horse... you don't want to...." He couldn't finish that thought, because it was too awful, because Comet wasn't Comet in the dreams. Comet was never a horse when the dream ended, and Crick was always dead, mutilated and bloody at his feet in the pouring rain. "Anyway, I... I don't know how long I spent, digging a grave like an asshole. Jon told me I was missing for two hours, so probably for an hour and a half or so. And I was screaming at the horse for leaving me, and then I was screaming at you for leaving me, and then God broke the fucking levee, right in front of me, and I was screaming at God. And that water... Jesus, Crick. It came right up to my chest—my feet almost left the fucking ground, and I was thinking 'Is that all? Is that all you got? You took Crick away from me and that's all you fucking got?' and the water receded and I was so crazy—I thought I won something, you know?"

Crick was looking at him wide-eyed, and he blushed.

"I didn't say it made sense. But I thought, 'That's it. I beat God.' And then God sucked me right into Comet's grave when the water left, and I barely made it out. And I realized that it's not whether you beat God—it's what you have when the fight's over. I wanted you. I wanted you alive so bad... and just like that, the fight was over, and what I had was The Pulpit... and you. I wasn't going to be mad at you if I still had you. Just wasn't."

Crick was quiet so long Deacon started to regret he told the story. Maybe too many words really were bad. Maybe he had the right idea, keeping them all close to his heart.

"Deacon—God, Deacon. You amaze me." Crick was looking at him all wide-eyed again, with that same fuzzy glow in his face that he used to have when he had been in grade school and Deacon was a god and not just a very shy boy with a very wonderful circle of family.

"I was certifiably insane—not amazing. Crazy."

Crick shook his head and reclaimed Deacon's hand. "Come here." He was bigger, so he pulled until Deacon sprawled gracelessly over his wide chest, looking at him with surprise and a certain amount of embarrassment.

"What were we talking about again?"

"We were talking about how you're going to walk away from step-Bob, because if you can face God down in the middle of a fucking flood and be glad because you still had me, then you can ignore a bit of human trash for the same reason."

"He hurt you." Deacon heard the stubbornness and didn't care.

"Not as much as I hurt you," Crick said softly. "And you forgave me."

Big sigh. Looking into those brown eyes, that goofy, crooked smile, that narrow, appealing face, Deacon's brain just shorted out. No room for animosity or a lifelong grudge—Crick was smiling at him, just him, and Deacon's anger was far, far away.

"If I promise not to kill him on purpose, can we just be done with this?" Fine. Fine, fine, fine. No more fantasies about beating the guy's face in. He was done.

"Not a problem. Can you kiss me again?"

Deacon smiled from his perch on Crick's vast chest. "Yeah, not a problem either." And it wasn't.

"What are you thinking?" Crick asked him now, balancing coffee and keeping the satchel at his hip carefully away from potential disaster. Deacon looked up from that mesmerizing, cold water, took his coffee from Crick's game hand, and turned his face up to the summer sun.

"I'm thinking that this is about the prettiest place I've ever seen," Deacon said seriously. "I'm thinking that I could live here, like Lisa's parents, on one of those islands. We could stock up our shit and bring the horses and only see the rest of the world once a month, and life would be pretty fucking okay."

Crick looked out at the blue sky and the indigo sea. They'd gotten a good hotel room—one that overlooked the Sound in Seattle—and they'd woken up that morning, looked out, and seen whales out in the distance. Deacon had stared at them as avidly as a child until he caught Crick staring at him instead of the whales.

"What?"

"I forget sometimes what a kid you are."

Deacon blushed. "I'm still older than you."

"Yeah, but not by much."

"You'd miss home," Crick said with affection, and Deacon turned to him, trying to articulate the thing that had been brewing in his chest since they stepped off the plane.

"I'd be home. Don't you see, Crick? Just because we've always made our lives in The Pulpit doesn't mean we have to keep trying there when it's not working."

"Deacon!" Crick was honestly shocked. His hair, long enough now to whip in his eyes in the fierce, cold wind, flew about his face as he stood absolutely still on the prow of the moving boat.

But Deacon couldn't stop. "See, here's the thing. With the money you put in the bank account, we've got some space. We could sell the land, keep the horses, pick up shop and just fucking move. Probably not here, but you know, there's land in Gilroy or Salinas—places where nobody has ever heard of us, nobody gives a crap about who we are or what we were like as kids. It would just be us and the horses and the ocean, about forty-five minutes away."

Crick finally moved. He wrapped his game arm around Deacon's shoulders and steadied his long body against the railing, and pulled Deacon in to kiss him on the temple. Doing a thing in public like that, for the two of them, was almost like they'd sprouted wings and flew in the wind gust of the ship like the eagles they'd seen playing above them.

"Your daddy's ashes are scattered on that land, Deacon. Don't tell me that doesn't mean something to you."

"It's a holy place because of what's in our hearts, Crick. We can make another place for our family to worship where the worship doesn't cost us our blood."

There was quiet then, nothing but the roar of the wind and the grounding hum of the ferry's engine.

"Are we really going to lose it otherwise?" Crick asked, and his shoulders slumped with the words, giving Deacon some of his weight. "I don't want to leave our home, Deacon. I can see how this has gotten to you. I know you hate the lawsuits and the appearing in court and the paperwork. And I always swore I'd do anything to get the hell out of Levee Oaks. But The Pulpit is like a whole different place, and I don't want to go."

"Do you think I do?" Deacon retorted bitterly. "But there's going to come a time, if we keep losing money, where we can't break even. Where we won't be able to afford to buy anything close to what we're going to have to leave. Wouldn't it be nice, if we have to leave our home, to not have to start over from scratch?"

Crick's breath was reassuringly warm in Deacon's ear. "Well then… how about we wait until that time happens, okay? When it comes a month where, if we keep losing we won't break even, we'll have a family vote then, and decide."

"Family vote?"

"Yeah—Benny, Jon, Amy, Andrew, Patrick—family. The weight of this isn't all you, Deacon. We'll take up the slack."

Deacon swallowed, feeling light and powerful—he was a god with a ten pound barbell if his family was there to help him with this.

"All right then. Family."

At that moment, the intercom belted out "Anacortes," and that was their stop. Time for Crick to go face up to his own demons now that Deacon's were all put to rest.

The Arnolds lived in a crooked three-story house that was built organically into a hill. The thick green growth of ferns and redwoods that surrounded it—and the fact that the house itself was painted a weathered blue—made it look like something out of a fairy tale, and Crick laughed softly as they walked up the steps.

"I called her 'Popcorn'—but I maybe I should have called her 'Pixie', you think?"

Deacon smiled reassuringly and then blushed in spite of himself. To Deacon, this journey alone seemed incredibly brave, and he said so.

Crick stopped dead on the landing and turned to him. They didn't touch, but Crick's eyes were warm as he said, "I don't think I could do this without you. Have I thanked you yet for coming with me?"

"No need," Deacon muttered, shoving at Crick's hip to get him to move.

It was Crick who knocked at the door, and when the sweet-faced, middle-aged woman with jeans, a sweatshirt, and a silver-blonde ponytail opened the door, it was Crick who started to introduce them.

As it turned out, he didn't need to.

Her face, which had set into grief-lines and sadness, lit up as soon as she laid eyes on Deacon.

"I know you!" she said with a genuine if tearful laugh, opening the door and gesturing for them to enter. "You're Crick's Deacon—and that would make you Crick. Oh my God! I'm so glad you two came."

Deacon turned a rather special shade of red. "Thank you, ma'am," he muttered, and they were ushered in.

"My husband will be so sorry to have missed you," Mrs. Arnold told them as she seated them in the living room. It looked like a comfortable room in spite of the doilies on the furniture and the ornate area rug on the hardwood floor. The floor had scratches on it from the old dog by the fireplace, and the area rug was clean but not without spots. There was even some dust on the drapes and above the mantelpiece, and since both men were well acquainted with dust and less acquainted with rooms that had been decorated by what seemed to be a family of pixies, the dust helped put them at ease as well.

"We can come back tomorrow," Crick offered, although they had planned to go sightseeing the next day, and Deacon felt a little bit guilty at the relief that came when Mrs. Arnold shook her head.

"No, I'm sorry—he's taking our youngest to visit colleges in California. She's thinking of going to Cal Arts Valencia or USC. He wanted to show her around a little."

Deacon caught Crick's eye, and they both smiled a little crookedly. It was good to know someone was going on to live their "if only"s.

Crick sighed then, looked the woman in the eyes, and spoke the truth. "I'm so very sorry about Lisa, ma'am. She was about the best friend I've ever had—it… I miss her every day."

The woman's eyes grew bright, and she reached across from her seat and patted Crick's knee. "So do I, sweetie. But I'm so glad she had you over there. You know she wrote me, didn't you?"

Crick shrugged. Lisa asked if she could tell her mother about him— he didn't think it was that big a deal. "Yes ma'am. We read our letters to each other. Helped pass the time."

Deacon couldn't keep the strangled noise from escaping, and to his surprise, Mrs. Arnold clapped her hands together and regarded him fondly. "He really is as adorable as she said he was.... She thought you were a very lucky young man, did you know that, Carrick?"

Crick shot Deacon a very dry look, but Deacon was too immersed in his own mortification to return it with much aplomb.

"She told me a couple of times. Yes ma'am."

"And you did such a good job on his pictures—here," she said, rising. "I'll go get your sketchbooks. You'll be wanting them back."

The rest of the afternoon was... sweet. It was the only way Deacon could think of it later. Neither of the men was much used to mothering, but Lisa's mother managed to cram an awful lot of it into a few hours. They got an earful about how Lisa had wanted to earn her own money for college and how the Army seemed like the way. They got to read her letters home and see her pictures growing up and even her old room. It was as pixie-fied as the rest of the house, with pastel colors and little-girl frills, and Crick told Deacon privately that he didn't wonder that the poor woman had ended up with the biggest fairy in the U.S. military—a crack that got Crick a solid thwack on the back of the head when Lisa's mother wasn't looking.

By the time they left the house to take the bus to the last ferry, Crick had cried a little, and so had Mrs. Arnold, and all of them had mourned a rather extraordinary young woman.

And Deacon was prouder of his lover than he had ever been in his life.

"She really was an awesome kid, Crick," Deacon said as they boarded the ferry. "And she loved you like a brother...."

"Sister," Crick sniffled. "She said I was the big sister she never had."

Deacon laughed and smacked him on the back of the head again. "You were both certifiable." And then he grabbed Crick's hand. "And I'm so glad you had each other, man. I really wish she'd been able to come home, but I'm so glad you had her while you were there."

And Crick, with his one-track stubbornness, managed to turn even that to his advantage. "Did you see their house, Deacon? That was her grandmother's house. She loved it—she grew up there. I want our house to be like that. I want Parry Angel to bring her kids to our house and all her friends to come to dinner. Tell me we can make that happen—please?"

"Man, we'll do what we can, okay? We'll put it to the family and do what we can."

And it was the best that he could give.

Chapter 25

Keeping Promise Rock

IN THE end, it was a near thing.

They proposed the plan to the family as soon as Jon brought them home from the airport. Jon wanted in immediately. "We'll move with you," he proclaimed grandly from the kitchen table, and Deacon said that was awfully swell of him to commit to, since his poor wife was stuck at home with her feet up while she gestated. Jon pulled out his cell phone, punched in the number, and said, "Amy, if Deacon ups and moves The Pulpit to Gilroy or Bumfuck Egypt, you want to go with him, right?"

He held the phone to Deacon's ear in time to hear Amy's "Hell yes—why did you even need to ask?"

And that was the start of the very first family meeting.

They did it once a month, on the first, as Deacon added up the bills and figured how much the ranch had lost that month. The entire family gathered in the kitchen, Deacon put the facts and figures on a big pad of paper and showed them the property available on the market for the assets they had.

Amy showed up at the second meeting with a new member of the family. Miss Lila Lisa Levins was small, wrinkled, and greeted with enthusiasm by everybody—including Parry Angel, who was convinced that 'bee-bee' was her very own personal doll and got to come home with her.

Miss Lila Lisa wasn't the only new family member to start showing up at the meetings. Jeff showed up at the second, after he'd been a regular at the family dinner table—and not just on family night either—for a couple of months. Officer Shane showed up at family dinner as well—although he and Jeff took pains to sit far away from each other. The entire family agreed that once Shane outed himself by looking at Jeff in disgust and saying, "I won't bite you, I like my guys more butch," he seemed entirely less awkward and creepy, and family dinner relaxed considerably.

And still, it came down to a cold, clear night on the first of February when Deacon couldn't make himself vote.

"We're so close either way," he said to the circle of expectant faces. "We're so close to making money and not losing it… but damn. We're so close to not having anything to spend on a future if we decide to leave. Guys… I can't do it. This is my…." He couldn't look at them. Couldn't even look at Crick, who would understand more than anyone.

"I'm this close to voting we move, just because that's what I think is best for all of you, and because I want to stay so bad."

And with that, he turned around and walked barefoot out of the kitchen to brood in the wet cold.

It had been milder this year—in fact, it had been too mild. People were predicting a drought, especially after the heat wave of the summer before, and Deacon stood out there for a good half an hour, bouncing on his numb toes. He had gained weight back—enough to keep the family from nagging him, but not enough to keep his shirt from flapping around his lean stomach in the foggy breeze. A particularly ambitious gust of wind had just flown up his shirt and made him think about picking his bare feet out to the stables when Shane pulled into the driveway so quickly he almost skidded off the drive and into the muddy dirt by the workout ring.

The stern, introverted young officer didn't even wait for the engine of his beat-up black GTO to die, which was good because sometimes that took a while, before he was squelching across the land far too quickly for safety in the slick mud. He went down once but bounced up on wet and muddy knees and was pounding up the porch before Deacon realized that a slight, muscular young man was following him at a more sedate pace.

"Don't vote! Deacon—don't vote! You can't vote yet—I've got news! Dammit, did they vote yet?"

Deacon had to smile at the guy. Usually Shane was just silent. Sometimes he'd break the silence by bursting out with something outrageous but sensible or awkward or simply odd—but he was never effusive and never, ever this excited.

"I don't know yet," he replied, feeling his tension build up in his stomach. "I'm not... I took myself out of the vote."

Shane nodded excitedly and then interrupted him by screaming, *"Don't vote! Guys, don't vote yet!"* into the house, and Deacon's eyes bugged out, even as the young man caught up to them, climbing up the front porch diffidently with his hand extended.

"He's very excited," the guy said in slightly accented English. "I'm Mikhail Bayul—I'm...." His delicate, Slavic features flushed in the dim light of the porch. He was wearing a fleece-lined denim jacket and a knit hat over his curly blond hair, but his hand was still a little cold as Deacon took it.

"Shane's boyfriend?" Deacon supplied, wondering how three such socially inept people could actually end up in company together.

"Yes. Shane's boyfriend. We have some...." They both looked behind Deacon because Shane had rushed into the house, and the screen door slammed behind him with a big, fat smack. Mikhail laughed sweetly, his gray eyes looking adoringly to where two hundred and ten pounds of graceless goodwill had just disappeared. "We have some news. Shane has talked of nothing but your family for months. I dance the fair circuit— Renaissance Faires—all over the country—you know what I mean?"

Deacon nodded, surprised a little. Benny had actually convinced Andrew to take her and Parry to one in Fair Oaks that June. She'd come back chatty and excited, with some clothes that Deacon was fairly sure could only be worn at other Renaissance Faires, and generally with a glimpse into an entire world of merchants and dreamers that Deacon had sort of admired.

Mikhail smiled, apparently relieved that he wouldn't have to explain. "There are horses—jousting horses—at the fairs. We get to know people, the regular attendees, you know?"

Deacon nodded, hearing Shane's bass rumble in the kitchen, probably explaining the same thing with less grace and more weirdness.

"Anyway, those horses are special. They're trained for sweetness and strength—they have to be. They have big men in armor on their backs, and lots of noise and clanking and play-fighting. They need to be broken very carefully, and the stable that tends them is going out of business. We need another horse breaker who uses weapons."

Deacon blinked, and Mikhail swore. "My English is usually better, I swear," he muttered. "I'm nervous," he said at last, bluntly. "This is as close as he's ever let me to anyone he considers family. He doesn't really like most of his other one. You're important."

And there it was, the terrible blush, and it seemed to catch, because Mikhail was blushing too. "We're not good with people, are we?" he asked, and Deacon shook his head no.

"So you meant the lances and stuff they use on the back of the horses—that takes a special sort of breaking. You say the stable that breaks them is going out of business?"

"The owners of the business are older—it's hard on the body. They're ready to retire. Shane—he stepped up for you. They're ready to have you show them your technique, and then they'll give you their clients if they're all agreeable."

Oh Christ—it was a dream job, dropped in his lap because Deacon and Benny had been willing to give a guy the benefit of the doubt and the guy had fallen in love with their kitchen table.

Deacon's hope couldn't be contained in his chest—it spread to his face in a goofy grin that Crick might have recognized, but no one else. "'Scuse me," he muttered to the bemused Mikhail, and then he pushed past him and sprinted into the house.

"Don't vote!" he said breathlessly. "Shane's right... don't vote!"

Crick caught him bodily with his strong right arm, practically picking him up around the middle and setting him to rights on his feet. "Calm down, Deacon—of course we voted to stay here and keep hoping. Now we just get to say we told you so!"

Deacon grinned from the bottom of his toes. "It's a dream job, Crick."

Crick nodded, his eyes gleaming. "Yeah, Shane told us. See. I told you—ask for more in life. Sometimes it delivers."

Deacon sobered. "What have you gotten lately?"

"Same thing you got, Deacon—us and home."

It was more than enough.

THAT April, they had a picnic at Promise Rock.

Crick made Deacon dress up—a nice western shirt, new boots, a little bolo at his neck, and Crick wore the same. Benny bought a new sundress in sage green, and Amy too, and if the dresses seemed to match, well, Deacon thought they'd just shopped together. He was pretty sure the fact that Parry Angel and Lila matched in a complementing lavender was on purpose—but it was damned cute, so he smiled at Lila in her little car seat and carefully helped Parry dangle her chubby little feet in the shallows, shrieking with her when it was too cold.

He didn't catch the rather wry look of conspiracy between his nearest and dearest—but then, it wouldn't have been much of a conspiracy if he had.

Benny's little sisters couldn't make it. They were living with their grandmother now, and she didn't approve of Crick and Deacon, so that was that, and it did make the day a little less bright. But Amy's parents were there and Patrick brought his sister, and that was wonderful. Shane brought Mikhail, and Jeff brought... no one. Deacon had remarked quietly, in a private moment, that Jeff's eyes were as sad as Crick's had been in Iraq, and Crick had been surprised to realize he was right. Whatever reason Jeff had for not bringing someone, it was private and painful, and Deacon resolved again to keep an eye on their favorite PT genius.

But today was all about celebrations. Andrew set up the sound system across the creek from the truck, and they'd set up a refreshment table under the oak tree, and Jon showed up wearing a....

"What in the hell are you doing in a suit?" Deacon asked, flummoxed. Jon wore jeans to court unless he was working for Deacon for free.

Jon smirked. "You really think this is just a family picnic, don't you?"

Deacon shrugged. "Okay—we're signing some papers. That's why we decided to have the picnic, right? To celebrate the papers?"

"Oh, and that's it? That's all she wrote?"

"It's your anniversary," Deacon said in disgust. "I gave Amy the chocolates, what else is there?"

Jon shook his head and raised an eyebrow at Crick, who was standing over his shoulder. "He's gonna kill us all—we should get started so he gets all choked up and manly before he gets the chance."

Crick nodded, trying hard to contain his glee. "Yeah. It's your barbecue, hoss—you've got the legal documents."

Jon nodded, flipping his movie-star hair out of his eyes and gesturing at the small gathering of good friends and beloved family to gather around. Amy came running to his side with a legal folder and some pens, which she laid out on the refreshment table, and Jon began to speak.

"All right folks, it's time to proceed. We ready, sweetheart?"

"When you are, baby!" Amy chimed. She had Lila on her hip and little rocks on all the papers to keep them from fluttering away in the April breeze.

"Good to go then. Okay, folks—you all know why we're here. We're going to make a few things official today, and you all are the people we want to be witnesses, you all know that, right?"

Everybody nodded, and Jon went on, ignoring Deacon's grunt, because dammit, the guy was just being damned dramatic.

"So there are two documents over there—"

"Two?" Deacon interrupted, and Jon threw him a droll look.

"Shut up, Deacon. Crick said it's my barbecue, let me cook." There was some laughter, but mostly, Deacon got the feeling that everyone else knew something he didn't, and that made him damned uncomfortable.

"So," Jon continued, "one of those documents you all know about. It's the document that makes Crick an equal partner in The Pulpit, and since that's a big deal, and since this hunk of drought-ridden rock is finally in the black after some fucked-up years, I think that alone is some celebration, right folks?"

Deacon grinned at the cheer that came from their little circle. Parry Angel, who was happy in Andrew's arms as he stood by Benny, gave a happy little squeal for the excuse to clap her hands.

"And the other one... Benny, you want to talk about this one?"

Benny smiled and stepped into the center of the circle. Her hair was bright butter yellow this month, and it looked good with the dress. So did the maturity that seemed to sit naturally on her now that she was nearly eighteen.

"Okay, you all know that the one thing Deacon wasn't giving up—even when things looked hella crappy for us—was my college fund, and you all know I'm going off in the fall and that my guys are taking care of my baby for me while I'm gone." She teared up a little—as she might. It had been a hard damned decision for her, and she and Deacon had sat up for a lot of nights hashing it over. What it had come down to in the end was that she wanted a good life for her baby—and a mama Parry could be proud of.

"So, the thing is, Deacon keeps having to explain to people who he is to my little girl, which isn't fair, because"—sniffle—"no one's been a better father to her than my brother's boyfriend, right?" Everyone chuckled except Deacon, who blushed. "So what we're signing today is a custody agreement. It gives Deacon rights to my baby—because I know that he'll never abuse it because, you know, it'd be like watching an eagle turn into a pile of buffalo crap while it was in the air. Deacon just doesn't hurt people, and he deserves the best. So the best is my baby, and until she's old enough to piss off her parents like everybody's kid, he has the right to visit her, the right to weigh in on her future, and just generally the legal right to be in her life. And you're all signing it, so the whole world will know that nobody can tell him he's not really a part of my baby's life. And Deacon stop blushing—how could you not be real to her…."

Benny started to cry in earnest then, and Deacon held out his arms and let her cry on him. She got his pretty tan dress shirt all goopy with mascara, but he didn't care, because he was a little bit choked up himself.

"Thanks, Shorty—that's a real nice surprise," he said softly, and the sly look she gave him through her tears and her make-up was enough to make him blink.

"That's just your wedding present, Deacon—that's not really the surprise."

Deacon rolled his eyes, but nobody else did. "This isn't a wedding, it's a picnic—but if Jon doesn't shut up, we're all going to starve to death."

Jon cleared his throat. "Actually, Deacon, what we're doing here is a legal reformation of your immediate family, with witnesses, in front of the people who love you, with vows, entertainment, and refreshment."

"You don't look like a preacher," Deacon said drolly, and as Jon stuck out his tongue, Crick took his arm and said, "He doesn't have to be, Deacon. He's just our master of ceremonies. But think about it— everything he said, that's a wedding, isn't it?"

Deacon blinked, feeling thick. "This is a wedding?" The family nodded back at him, and he frowned. "Holy shit—you're serious."

Crick's half-smile was half-sly and all vulnerable. He took a deep breath and pitched his voice so everyone could hear him. "Okay, so here's the thing. Three years ago, Deacon and I...." Crick blushed really hard, so hard Deacon could smell his aftershave, could see the sweat popping on Crick's forehead in spite of the mild day in the middle of the wildflower fields in the shade. Crick turned toward him, and now they were in the center of the circle of their friends, hands clasped, and Deacon had the sudden, very real awareness that, yes indeed, this was a wedding.

Theirs.

"Okay," Crick said after a cleansing breath, "before I tell that story—or part of that story—I've got something that needs to be signed too." Crick looked at Amy, who nodded.

"That's me—document princess," she said dryly, and he grinned at her, and everybody laughed.

"Thanks, sweetheart."

"Any time, brother-mine." And nobody laughed at that, not even her parents.

"It's a present for Deacon," Crick continued, "because he's always afraid he'd let us down, so I put together all the ways I see him, and sketched them all together, and I hope you all sign the back of it, because you're the people who love him, and I'm pretty sure you'll see him that way too." Crick looked over at the table like he was checking some things. "Well, maybe some of those sketches are just how I see him, but you get the picture."

There was another chuckle, and Deacon turned his head to look, but Crick grasped his chin to pull him back to the center of the circle.

"I want to see it!" Deacon complained. He'd been overjoyed that Crick had started drawing again, and now he knew what he'd been working on.

"Later, Deacon...."

"Well it looks pretty damned big!"

"Well, we needed something to cover the fuzzy kitten calendars you keep buying. Now shut up and let me finish!" Crick scowled at him, and Deacon subsided, and then he blushed, and then he teared up all over again, in front of friends, family, God, and everybody.

"Three years ago," Crick began again, "Deacon offered me everything in the world I ever wanted, and...." He stopped, and something shook his shoulders that wasn't a laugh but couldn't be described as much else. "And I was a total dumbshit, and I didn't understand what he was offering, and I ended up in the middle of the fucking desert keeping some jackass from shooting a snake with an M-16. And Deacon waited for me to get *that* out of my system, and he was here for me when I got back. And everybody here, even the new guys, they know that it wasn't that simple, but it's the only words I've got. I just wanted everybody here, when I asked Deacon to offer me everything again—except school, Deacon. That ship has sailed. Anyway, ask me, here in front of God and everyone, if I want the world. Ask me if I want you, and your home, and your enormous, indestructible damned heart. Ask me."

Crick closed his eyes, looking so very nervous, so very frightened. Deacon wanted to reassure him, wanted to say something, wanted to touch his face and tell him it was all okay, that they didn't have to do this, that they knew what was in their hearts and no one else had to. Then Crick opened his eyes and smiled. It was that goofy, gamine, little-kid grin, the one that had captured Deacon's attention a zillion years ago, the one that had broken his heart and remade it a zillion times since.

"Go ahead, Deacon," Crick murmured, that grin in place on his suddenly adult face. "Ask me."

And oh God, it was his turn to speak. His whole body blushed, and he was mortified and embarrassed, even in front of these people who loved him, but still, he managed a few words.

"I love you, Carrick," he rasped, suddenly as nervous as he'd ever been. "Please stay." And then he held his breath for an answer, knowing he should never ever ever take something like that as a given.

"Of course I'll stay," Carrick muttered, his eyes shiny, his grimace through his tears something Deacon would remember pretty much until his heart stopped. "What kind of asshole would turn something like that down?"

Deacon didn't have to answer that one because Crick's mouth came down, and they kissed sweetly, like first-time lovers, like lifetime partners keeping a promise forever and ever and ever.

Everyone gathered at Promise Rock, people who loved them and knew how hard-fought their joy really was, cheered.

Later, when the picnic had wound down and the hugs had subsided (although Benny still broke into happy tears every so many minutes), Deacon got a good look at the sketch.

It was… him. Deacon working horses, Deacon holding the baby, Deacon sleeping. One of the smaller sketches had been drawn from the picture Benny sent the day the levee broke. One of the larger ones showed Deacon nose to nose with a horse who looked suspiciously like Comet. The center sketch, the one that all the others surrounded, showed Deacon as a young man, godlike to Crick, his arms over his knees, his eyes thoughtfully bent on the world beyond the penciled green canopy of Promise Rock.

"You like?" Crick asked quietly, and Deacon nodded, searching for words for a minute.

"I'm still not a god," he said apologetically.

Crick stood behind him and pulled his shoulders back against that wide, strong chest. "Better than a god," Crick murmured. "You're the reason to have faith."

There was a lull in the chatter then, and for a moment, fraught with breeze and sweetness, it was just the two of them again, at home on Promise Rock.

AMY LANE teaches high school English, mothers four children, and writes the occasional book. When she's not begging students to sit-the-hell-down or taxiing kids to soccer/dance/karate—oh my! she can be found catching emergency naps, grocery shopping, or hiding in the bathroom, trying to read without interruption. She will never be found cooking, cleaning, or doing domestic chores, but she has been known to knit up an emergency hat/blanket/pair of socks for any occasion whatsoever or sometimes for no reason at all. She writes in the shower, while commuting, while her classes are doing bookwork, or while she's wandering the neighborhood at night pretending to exercise and has learned from necessity to type like the wind. She lives in a spider-infested and crumbling house in a shoddy suburb and counts on her beloved mate, Mack, to keep her tethered to reality—which he does while keeping her cell phone charged as a bonus. She's been married for twenty plus years and still believes in Twu Wuv, with a capital Twu and a capital Wuv, and she doesn't see any reason at all for that to change.

Visit Amy's web site at http://www.greenshill.com. You can e-mail her at amylane@greenshill.com.

Also by AMY LANE

If I Must

AMY LANE

http://www.dreamspinnerpress.com

More Stories of Enduring Love

from DREAMSPINNER PRESS

CPSIA information can be obtained at www.ICGtesting.com
Printed in the USA
BVOW11s1352221213

339795BV00007B/254/P